AIRBORNE RANGER
C 75

Sam was on the radio getting a commo check when he saw the first movement. As he sat paralyzed, eyes glued to the trail, an NVA soldier walked through. The second one in sight was a huge Chinese soldier wearing a green beret. Then five more NVA came into view. Every eye in Team 3-1 was wide. "Estimated enemy: thirteen, visual confirmation," Sam whispered in the phone. "Do you copy? Over."

"Affirmative," replied X-ray.

Before Sam could finish his report, the NVA were very close. Heart racing, Sam set the handset down and picked up the claymore detonator, the clacker, then waited for the NVA point man to get within the kill range of the first claymore. Then he squeezed the clacker. . . .

CHARLIE
RANGERS

John L. Rotundo &
Don Ericson

IVY BOOKS • NEW YORK

Ivy Books
Published by Ballantine Books
Copyright © 1989 by John L. Rotundo and Don Ericson

Library of Congress Catalog Card Number: 88-91240

ISBN 0-8041-0288-0

Manufactured in the United States of America

First Edition: February 1989
Eleventh Printing: October 1993

To the thirty-five hundred or so Rangers, LRPs, SEALS, and Marine Force Recon, who served their country in Vietnam, volunteering for our kind of operations. Their numbers were small, their deeds spoke for themselves.

And to my wife Louisa, who through good times and bad, before, during, and after my war stories, was always there for me.

—JOHN L. ROTUNDO

This book is dedicated to my comrade John Rotundo, whose friendship will ever remain special. And to the Rangers who made the ultimate sacrifice.

But most of all to Susan, my wife, my friend, and our typist, for her countless hours of typing and her patience in listening till the wee hours of the morning to repetitious, boring war stories. She was patient and never questioned me about my experiences in Vietnam because she knew I wasn't ready to share them with anyone.

—DON ERICSON

What about the emotion you feel when you kill someone who was trying to kill you, and you stand there, looking down at the guy, thinking, "I'm alive and he's nothing," and you feel *great* . . .

—KENT ANDERSON

Table of Contents

Acknowledgments

JOHN L. ROTUNDO

To Anne Marie Bucceri, a personal friend, for keeping my letters down through the years which helped me place names and dates to make this book possible.

To Vera Rotundo, my mother, for saving all my letters from Vietnam, and for her support, both during and after my tour of duty.

And a special acknowledgment to co-author, Don Ericson, whose friendship or rather brotherhood has meant and will mean more to me than most people can ever realize.

DON ERICSON

We gratefully acknowledge the support and encouragement of Owen Lock, Editor-in-Chief, Del Rey Books. It's been a long two years. Your hand-holding is deeply appreciated and will be eternally remembered.

To Sam Agner, who restored many forgotten memories, I thank you. You were, and always will be, like a brother to me. The times we spent together in Charlie Rangers in Vietnam can never be relived, but they will never be forgotten.

To John Leppleman, whose recollection of the attempt to capture General Giap was much appreciated, and further clarified the mission of Charlie Company. John also compiled the list of Charlie Rangers found in the Appendix.

PROLOGUE

MEMORIAL DAY WEEKEND, 1986/ WASHINGTON, D.C.

We drove our rental car down Constitution Avenue looking for a parking space as close to the wall as possible. A car was just pulling out, so John L. waited for it to clear, then pulled into the vacant spot.

As we crossed the street and neared the wall, an eerie feeling came over us: stenciled on the wall were 58,000 names, some of which would forever hold a place in our hearts.

Before long we came across a volunteer wearing a yellow baseball cap and carrying a book which listed all the names on the wall.

"I'm looking for Thorne, Kevin Thorne," John L. told the volunteer.

She opened her book immediately. "I've got a Kevin G. Thorne," she said, "February twenty-seventh, 1971."

John L. looked at Don for a moment, then said, "It was the twenty-eighth; maybe they record the day of death as it was back here in the World." He looked back at the volunteer. "That's him. Where do we find him?"

The volunteer's fingers followed the name and said, "Four west, line ten. Follow me and I'll show you." We walked past the sea of people to the fourth panel left of center. "Count down ten lines from the top and he should be listed on that line." A rush of emotion swept over us as our eyes scanned the line. Sure enough, at the extreme right of the panel was the name.

"Hi, Thorney," John L. whispered, mostly to himself.

Don turned to the volunteer again and said, "Now we'd like to find William Murphy and a soldier named Rucker."

The volunteer thumbed through her book. "I found William Murphy, but I can't find Rucker. I need his first name or the exact date of death," she said.

Don couldn't remember Rucker's first name or the exact date of death, so the volunteer began to show us where Murphy was located. We walked along the wall anxiously looking for Murph. Don's heart was pounding when he saw *William Murphy* etched in granite. He stared morosely, memories of Murph flooding his heart.

John L. took out his camera and lifted it overhead to get as close to the names as possible before taking the picture. He had always had the impression that the names were all within easy viewing distance, but being this close to the center took him by surprise how high from the ground it was.

We spent the next hour touring the wall, looking at pictures left by loved ones, and the letters written by family and friends to those names listed on the wall.

Our next stop was the statue of the three grunts. We were struck by the lifelike look of the eyes on the statue. There was quite a bit of conversation around the statue, people posing with one another.

To the west of the wall were benches, and that area seemed a meeting place for ex-GIs. Here also, a lot of conversation was going on as people met one another for the first time in fifteen or twenty years. It was quite unlike the atmosphere one found in front of the wall, where the only sounds heard were hushed whispers and occasional crying as somebody found the name of a loved one or a departed friend.

Hoping to see a familiar face from the past, we sat on the benches watching the hundreds of people pass by. Don noted that almost every other person walking by was dressed in camouflage fatigues, uniforms worn in Vietnam only by the elite forces. At the wall, that's about all anyone wore.

As is normal for combat veterans, we looked for the patch on the shoulder that would tell of the wearer's unit. We looked for jump wings, and the combat infantryman's badge (CIB) that signified the wearer has seen combat. But by and large, we saw neither. Most of those we saw wore large patches reading *Vietnam Veteran and Proud of It*, or *I Spent My Time in Hell*.

It became a joke between us, especially when we caught sight of a group of four wearing pistol belts and black berets which added a bit of "Rambo" to their outfits.

"What did you do in the war, Daddy?" John L. asked Don.

"I was with the 97th Dempsey Dumpster Division, Airmobile," Don replied.

"Did you see action, Daddy?" John L. asked.

"I don't want to talk about it, son. It was Hell."

We laughed.

It was late afternoon that Sunday when Don spotted someone in camouflage fatigues bearing what, from a distance, looked like the red and black scroll of the Rangers. Don was patronizing a "Dempsey Dumpster Commando," so he asked John L. to check the newcomer out.

"Which company were you with?" John L. asked.

"Echo, 75th."

"No shit! I was with Charlie Rangers," John L. said excitedly. "Hey, Don, come here, we got a keeper," John L. yelled.

The three talked for a few minutes, then a fourth appeared, wearing a dark blue suit and a black beret.

"I'm Mike Kentes, Echo, 75th," he said as he struck out his hand. We quickly found out that Mike was the president of the Ranger/LRRP Association, and after a brief conversation, Mike and the two of us left for an evening of drinking, dining, and camaraderie.

Mike explained about the Ranger/LRRP Association and what it was trying to accomplish. In fact, there was to be a reunion in November, with all the companies represented, and Mike invited us to attend with any other Rangers we could contact.

VETERANS DAY WEEKEND, 1986/
WASHINGTON, D.C.

As the plane was approaching Washington's National
Airport we were high on the anticipation of seeing Agner,
J.C., Wells, Fats, and whoever else might show up for
our first gathering in seventeen or so years. We were also
high from our share of cocktails on the plane. Don
reached into his carry-on bag and presented John L. with
a black baseball cap with an Airborne Ranger scroll on
it. As the plane taxied to the terminal, it seemed we sat
for hours before the doors opened. We were anxious to
make a second assault on the Vietnam Memorial, this
time in force. As we walked up the ramp into the terminal we spotted Agner, Wells, and J.C. waiting for the
Illinois contingent of Charlie Rangers. While we were
shaking hands, Don and Agner embraced and everyone
agreed that it was a reunion long overdue.

The only one missing was Fats, whose plane was due
in a half hour. The five of us made our way to the cocktail
lounge and proceeded to pound down a few, telling war
stories and getting reacquainted. At the appropriate time,
John L. and J.C. made their way to the terminal to greet
Fats. When we were all together, we somehow made our
way to the Sheraton National Hotel, where the reunion
was to be held. After checking in we went downstairs to
the lounge to meet other Rangers.

The next afternoon we were again relaxing in the
lounge when Don noticed someone standing to the side.

"Can I help you?" he asked.

"I'm Owen Lock, Editor-in-Chief of Del Rey Books,
my company published *Charlie Mike*." We all started
laughing. When we stopped, Owen asked, "What's the
matter?"

"Come here, asshole, I want to talk to you," Don
replied, obviously feeling the effects of the alcohol. As
Owen joined them, Don said, "*Charlie Mike* was a novel,
fiction, and most of it was bullshit! Scott was a butter
bar, a two-mission commando. Each of us here has fifty
times the bush experience Scott had."

Owen began probing the group about what exactly was

wrong with the book. "Good reading, but not true to life," was one reply. The comments went on and on about what was wrong with it.

"Why don't you write a book?" Owen asked Don.

"I don't know the first thing about writing a book."

"That's okay," John L. chimed in, "Scott didn't know the first thing about combat." As the group laughed, Owen persisted, telling Don just to write the story the way it was.

"Give me a break, no one would believe it. In fact, I can hardly believe it myself. It was life in the fast lane and we're all very fortunate to be here today," Don said.

"But that's what I want to hear," Owen replied.

"You want to hear about cutting off ears and shooting a gook in the head and watching his brains come out the other side?" Every time Don mentioned another gory possibility, someone else would jump in with his own, even grosser, story.

Finally Owen looked Don in the eye and said, "I didn't think that LRRPs were noted for shooting their mouths off and not delivering. Why don't you write a book about the way it really was with Charlie Company?" As he was about to leave, Don shook his hand and told him he'd think about it.

The next day we took the other members of Charlie Company to pay our respects to Thorne, Murphy, and Rucker. Later all six of us walked to the statue, where Don recruited a young lady to take a group photo and the others had her take pictures with their cameras for their own memories. As she took the pictures, a crowd gathered behind her also taking photos of the six Airborne Rangers wearing black baseball caps or boonie hats bearing the Airborne Ranger scroll. A feeling of pride ran through us. By the time the woman had taken a picture for each of us who asked, the crowd around the statue had grown to almost a hundred. Then some of the strangers asked if they could have their pictures taken with us. In fact, one oriental wanted his picture taken with us. We joked among ourselves about holding a knife to his ear, but we were really caught up in the attention that we were getting; we loved every minute of it. Finally, it seemed, we were being thanked for what we went through some seventeen years ago.

After we returned to Illinois, we decided to take Owen Lock up on his dare. The fact that both of us had served in the same company and the same platoon would make the overall story easy to tell. The hard thing was that, for the most part, we'd been on different teams, pulling only a few missions together.

So in writing this book the reader should be advised that missions referring to Team 3-1 were part of Don's past, and missions referring to Team 3-3 or Team 3-5 were part of John L.'s. Stories regarding the rear were pretty much the same for both. Our military experience prior to Vietnam was not unusual, so we have spared the reader two versions of it: Don's will have to do.

What follows is the story of the two nineteen-year-old kids, armed with M-16s, claymore mines, and a radio. Two kids who had the power to play God. This is not an attempt to glorify war, nor is it an attempt on our parts to cop out on any setbacks in our lives by "blaming it on 'Nam." It is the story of the unit we served with in Vietnam, a unit of highly skilled and professional volunteers who served with Charlie Company, 75th Infantry, Airborne Rangers. Or as we called ourselves, Charlie Rangers.

When we originally agreed to put this book together, we wanted to tell it all, the way it really was. We have made as honest an attempt as possible. However, as the manuscript is about to be published, we have learned a lot about laws that will not permit us to do exactly that. For that reason, in four places names have been changed or deleted. Our First Amendment apparently guarantees the right of free speech, but not necessarily the right to write the unvarnished truth.

Don Ericson & John Rotundo

CHAPTER 1

MILITARY HISTORY/BASIC TRAINING
Don Ericson

As the train pulled out of the Woodstock station, I was starting to wonder if I had done the right thing. I had volunteered for the draft in February 1968. It was against my father's wishes. We'd had several one-sided conversations on the subject, and I had always lost. I guess he feared that I might do something stupid like die or get wounded in our television war. A war that was glorified by John Wayne in *The Green Berets*. I went to see it twice. The first time I saw it, it stirred my imagination; the second time, I knew that I wanted to be part of it.

I was an apprentice carpenter and enjoyed building things at the time that I decided to volunteer for the draft. I received my draft notice and informed my boss. His first comment was, "Do you want to get out of it?"

Before I could answer, I thought to myself, Can this guy really get me out of the draft? With a puzzled look on my face, I said, "No, I might as well get it over with."

He persisted. "I can get you a deferment because you're in apprentice school."

Again I declined; my mind was made up and my master plan of deception of volunteering for the draft would continue. In retrospect, I had it made. I was just out of high school, had an excellent job, a '67 Corvette, and a couple of good-looking girlfriends. However, something was missing from my life. Life was too easy; there was no challenge. Maybe 'Nam was the answer.

As I came back to reality, the train was pulling into Dearborn Station in Chicago. I walked to the induction center, which was a few blocks away; there I would take my physical and the oath to my country.

The physical examination was a riot. Here, myself and fifty other warm bodies stripped to our shorts for our examinations.

A short, dark-haired older fellow introduced himself and started explaining the standard operating procedures (SOP). "Gentlemen," he said, "you will proceed down the taped yellow line on the floor to stations one through fifteen. Give your paperwork to the gentleman at that particular station," and so on and so on.

Each station was a real treat. I went from one to another having my ears, eyes, and nose checked, having blood taken, urinating into a bottle, et cetera. The last station was the best. Fifty guys standing on a yellow line with our BVDs around our ankles.

"All right, gentlemen, bend at the waist, grab your cheeks, and spread 'em," came the order. Naturally one guy grabbed the cheeks on his face for a laugh. The doctor—I assumed that he was a doctor—wearing what looked like a dirty butcher's smock, went from asshole to asshole inspecting each and every one. What a disgusting job.

As we finished dressing, names were called and we were divided into two groups. The first was made up of just the people who were taking physicals; the second was my group, the ones who were being inducted immediately. Then, more names were called off, poor bastards who'd just been drafted into the marines.

From there, my group was taken to swear the allegiance to the flag and country. Then we were informed we'd take basic training at Fort Campbell, Kentucky. I'm in for two years, I thought, I hope it gets better.

After about two hours of filling out countless forms and

sitting around, an NCO (noncommissioned officer) escorted our group of thirty to a waiting bus, which went directly to O'Hare Airport (a quick trip, because by then it was about eleven o'clock in the evening and there was no traffic).

When we arrived at O'Hare the bus drove us directly to the plane that was to take us to Kentucky. It was a C-47; in fact, it was to be the first large plane I had ever been on and God, it was a World War II relic. The plane ride was short, a couple of hours at most, but extremely rough. I was relieved when my feet touched the "terra firma" of Kentucky.

Our group was then led into a hangar to await truck transportation. As we sat, I noticed two soldiers walking through the hangar wearing green berets. They were impressive. That, I thought, was what the ideal "macho fighting soldier" should look like.

The truck finally arrived and we were on our way to who knew what. I kept thinking I'd probably get a drill sergeant like Sergeant Carter on *Gomer Pyle, USMC*. Then the trucks pulled up in front of a long two-story building with a group of men in front of it.

Apparently, these are the drill sergeants, I thought.

All of a sudden the screaming started. "Get out of those trucks, you sorry sons of bitches. Your mama ain't here now and you are all mine." As we jumped, stumbled, tripped, and fell off the trucks, we were told to stand on another line.

As soon as I stood on the line with my gym bag in hand, a drill sergeant came over and knocked the bag out of my hand. "What are you smiling at, you dick-lick?" he screamed in my ear.

"Nothing," was my reply.

"You say 'Nothing, Sergeant,' " he shouted back at me.

Now, I was born with a permanent smile on my face. To this day I can see humor in just about anything. That smile was to get me in a lot of trouble in the future.

"Give me ten push-ups, shit brain," he hollered. I got down and did the push-ups and returned to my feet. By then he was giving the others in the group a similar tongue-lashing.

The smile was still on my face when a muscular black drill sergeant appeared in front of me. On his chest was a combat infantry badge (CIB), a set of jump wings, and his right shoulder bore a patch that was probably from 'Nam. He put his face close to mine and he stared right through me. In a whisper he said, "Don't be an asshole, fuckhead, wipe that shit-eating grin off your face or I'll knock it off." The smile disappeared, at least for the time being. He was the most intimidating person I'd ever met. He got his point across without screaming. He was also the meanest looking person I'd ever encountered.

We were taken to the quartermasters and issued fatigue shirts, pants, socks, underwear, T-shirts, khaki shirts, khaki pants, dress greens, low-quarter shoes, two pair of boots, ties, belts, hats, and a dress overcoat. The overcoat itself had to weigh thirty pounds, and looked like a formless lump of material.

On to the barber shop. It only took thirty seconds to dehair each of us. It was amazing how alike everyone looked when bald.

The next stop was the infirmary, for shots. Everyone received vaccinations for smallpox, diphtheria, tetanus, and various other diseases. During the next few weeks I saw reactions to the smallpox vaccination, in particular, ranging from no reaction to golf-ball-sized lumps oozing pus.

After the shots, we were formed up in half-assed formation and ran back to the barracks. The drill sergeant was trying to call a running cadence to a bunch of bald street punks who didn't know their left from their right. All while we were trying to balance a forty-five-pound duffel bag on our shoulders. Four or five of the new recruits had already fallen behind and were literally being kicked in the ass by the drill sergeant who brought up the rear. The whole time I kept smiling, thinking those poor bastards were really going to have a tough time. As the last stragglers were arriving in front of the barracks, we were formed up again. Our group was told it would be First Platoon, Echo Company, First Training Brigade.

"From this day forth, you will answer everything with, Echo One. Is that clear?" the drill sergeant shouted.

"Echo One, sir," we replied.

Our reply became louder and louder every time he shouted back at us.

"My name is Sergeant Bozman. I will be your mother for the next eight weeks. You people will dread the day you met me. Since you pussies got your shots today, you get to rest today. This is not to say that you will smoke, joke, and shoot the shit; you will unpack and square your shit away, the army way. Is that clear?"

"Echo One, Sergeant," came our reply.

"Fall out, dummies, and pick a bunk," he shouted.

Unfamiliar with the command "fall out," everyone just stood. "Get out of here, assholes," Sergeant Bozman yelled in disgust.

When the dust settled I was standing next to a bunk bed set up with a guy I had seen at the induction center in Chicago. "Hi, I'm Don Ericson."

"Tom Pemberton," he replied. He was from Chicago and was about twenty-five years old. I could tell that he had street smarts. He had been drafted and already hated the bullshit.

Through all the talking around us, I heard the door open, then Drill Sergeant Bozman yelled, "Atten-hut." In walked a second lieutenant whose face was covered with pimples. Not just zits, but white pimples; his face looked like a pizza.

"Stand at attention by the side of your bunks. This is a full shakedown inspection of all your belongings. Don't move," said the second lieutenant, trying to bring a deep voice up from his puny body. He sounded more like a soprano. My smile got wider. Pemberton was chuckling softly.

The first recruit searched produced a pack of Zig-Zag papers for rolling cigarettes, a four-inch switchblade, and a few white pills he said were aspirins. The inspection went on with varying results until the last recruit was done. "This is on the house," the second lieutenant said. "The next time you're caught with these things, you'll receive an Article Fifteen." An Article Fifteen (fifteenth article of the Uniform Code of Military Justice) was the army's way of disciplining troops, by taking away their pay or reducing their rank without resort to a court-martial.

The next day was devoted solely to the army's idiot tests and filling out more forms. As we were running back to the barracks, I noticed the same guys falling out of formation as before. They were some pretty tired individuals—overweight, uncoordinated, and just sorry people. God help this country if they were to fight on its behalf. I did keep my thoughts to myself.

That day I was called out of formation to take another test. I reported to the clerk in charge and was told to report to room 20. When I entered the room, an E-6 staff sergeant explained why only I was there. I had scored extremely high on a certain test and the army was obliged to ask if I wanted to take another test for the Special Forces. At that moment all I could think of was John Wayne in *The Green Berets*. I agreed to take the test. Again, I scored extremely high. The staff sergeant instructed me on all the requirements needed to join the Special Forces.

"First you must volunteer for the Airborne," he said. "Is there any problem with that?"

"No, no problem," I replied.

"You must make a three-year commitment to the army. Right now you have only a two-year commitment. Are you ready to enlist for another year?"

I could still see John Wayne in the back of my mind and those two Green Berets in the hangar. It didn't take me long to make up my mind. Before I knew it I was signing more forms. I opted for the engineers, because they worked with demolitions; blew up bridges and all that.

I rejoined my platoon, then in the middle of PT (physical training). I found my squad and moved up next to Tom. "Tom," I said, "I just joined up for another year."

"You asshole," he screamed at the top of his lungs. Every eye in the platoon was on us, including Drill Sergeant Bozman's.

"Get down, you two dummies, and give me ten," he shouted.

We did our ten and got up. It was now my turn for the obstacle course and I was off. When Tom caught up with me, he gave me a dirty look and whispered, "I can't leave you alone for a minute, can I?"

Tom and I sat together in the mess hall that evening and I tried to explain my feelings, and my desire for excitement. All he could say was, "It's your life, but you could find yourself dead."

I dreaded the idea of being a truck driver or a cook for two years. I had to be part of our television war.

Basic training was a breeze. The army seemed to have geared the training and classroom work to the mentality of an average eighth-grader. By the time basic training was over, my physical abilities had dropped substantially. A perfect score on a PT test was three hundred. I got two hundred and ninety on my first test and the last one I took I dropped to just passing. I kept pace with the rest of the platoon; why kill myself? The bottom line was, I was becoming just another number in the great green machine.

Graduation from Basic was my first taste of military parades. Our company marched in front of the commanding officer's reviewing stand mostly in step. Once in a while you could see a soldier doing the little military skip to get in step with the rest. When the pomp and circumstance was over, we received our orders.

I was to report to Fort Leonard Wood in Missouri for Advanced Individual Training (AIT). Tom was to stay at Fort Campbell and be a truck driver, cook, or something like that. He was happy, he wouldn't have to go to 'Nam, and that was fine with him.

AIT FORT LEONARD WOOD

I boarded a Continental Trailways bus and settled in for the long ride. I had my transistor radio to my ear as the bus ambled along. I laughed to myself because "On the Road Again" by Canned Heat was playing. From then on, every time I heard that song I would think of that nasty bus ride, sitting next to that stinking bus bathroom.

The bus arrived at Fort Leonard Wood at about ten o'clock in the evening. There again were our drill instructors to meet their "new meat" trainees. This time the trainees were in a neatly lined formation. Again, like at Fort Campbell, the drill instructors would tour the ranks hoping to find the weak link, trainees or certain soldiers who looked vulnerable to their abuse. As the cadre (another name for drill instructors) toured the ranks they put flashlights in people's faces at random. Wouldn't you know it, I got a light shined in my eyes. "What ya smiling at, dipshit?" he asked.

"Nothing, Drill Sergeant."

"Wrong answer, dipshit, I'm a drill *instructor*. Give me ten push-ups," he shouted.

After my ten push-ups, I was face to face with a drill instructor who looked like Porky Pig but outweighed Porky by a hundred pounds. Why the army didn't throw him out for obesity is beyond me. By then I had the bozos figured out and stared right back at them. The smile was gone as my stare burned right through him. He saw I wasn't about to be intimidated and left for the next sucker.

As I was standing at attention, I heard the drill instructor verbally attacking another trainee. "I'll rip your eye ball out and skull-fuck you, trainee." "I'll rip your head off and shit in your neck, trainee," the instructor screeched. It was all I could do to control my laughter. These were classic lines. Every time I thought that I had heard them all, along came another; I wondered who made them up.

Engineer AIT was a piece of cake. We were instructed in the construction of permanent bridges, floating bridges, rope tying, and briefly touched on demolitions. We had classes daily on basic infantry formations, cover and concealment, and a whole gaggle of night courses. For target detection we would march out to the range and watch an instructor light a cigarette or shine a flashlight in the distance. Since it was winter in Missouri by then, we froze. That was one of the most miserable times I had ever spent.

On Saturdays, for harassment, our platoon was formed up and we marched or ran around the whole post just to be out of the company area. It was probably the commanding officer's way of keeping us busy and out of the local town, Waynesville, and away from the local whores. When they were off Saturdays and Sundays, the trainees would hustle off to the local PX (post exchange, like a 7 Eleven) and consume as much 3.2 beer as they could. Most would end up throwing up outside and stumble back to the barracks. It took massive quantities of the weak beer even to get a buzz.

One evening a tall white hillbilly came in full of liquid bravado and tried to take on a big black dude. The black guy beat him to a pulp. After a week in the hospital, the white guy returned.

One point I noticed was that even in basic training, the blacks stayed in their own groups and the whites in theirs. It was a two-class army, a two-class system. Growing up in a small midwestern town, I was never exposed to blacks. My attitude was, if I was left alone I didn't care what color anybody's skin was.

There were two guys desperately trying to get out of the army. One constantly kept pissing in his bed. The soldier on the bottom bunk must have had to beat the shit out of him more than once. The drill instructor came in one day and told him to pack his gear. That was the last we saw of him. The other trainee went AWOL (absent without leave).

During AIT, I made friends with a trainee named Dave Miller, who was thirty years old. He had been in the army before and decided to reenlist. For that reason, his wife had divorced him. Dave didn't care; on many occasions he said that it was no great loss. Dave took a lot of abuse from the drill instructors because of his age. He was in an army of nineteen-year-olds and the cadre had a ball at his expense. "Do this, old man. Do that, old man." Dave was tough. "Fuck 'em," he'd say.

AIT was finally over and again we paraded in front of the commanding officers. About half of the platoon went to 'Nam and the other half went to Germany. I envied the guys going to 'Nam, but told myself my turn would come.

Out of the whole company only Dave and I were going to Fort Benning, Georgia, and jump school.

We were given seven days' leave after finishing AIT. As a joke I had wanted to buy master sergeant stripes and a fistful of medals and sew them on my dress greens to impress my friends back on the block, but I figured that my nineteen-year-old face would give me away. I arrived home only to get a lot of grief about enlisting for another year. My family couldn't understand the desire to serve with the best, to have the best training possible. I never considered the fact that I might die. The television war couldn't be that bad. The naïveté of youth . . .

JUMP SCHOOL

When I left Midway Airport in Chicago the temperature was twenty degrees and I would be landing in Columbus, Georgia, where the temperature was sixty degrees. Far different from the temperature I was exposed to in Missouri.

I arrived at Fort Benning at eleven o'clock Sunday morning and reported to the clerk. I was assigned to Class 49, Barracks 32. I found my way to the barracks and set up my gear. Dave was already there and had his shit squared away. "How's it look?" I asked.

"Not bad, so far."

Dave helped me set up. By then the barracks was almost full. The door opened and in walked an instructor with the shiniest Cochran jump boots that I had ever seen. (According to an unwritten military law only Airborne personnel can wear jump boots. According to a written military law only Airborne personnel can wear bloused (Class A military, green uniform) boots with their dress uniform. An honor exclusive to the Airborne.)

The instructor was an impressive individual. Lean and mean, no fat on his body. "Gentlemen," he said in a normal voice, "school starts tomorrow. Get your shit together and lock your duffel bags to your bunks. The PX is up the street.''

I looked at Dave and said, "You mean they're not going to call us trainees? Maybe we'll be treated like human beings.''

Dave shrugged his shoulders and said, "Let's get a beer, I'll buy.''

We pounded down a few beers and left to return to the barracks. On the way back I couldn't help but wonder why the cadre hadn't been screaming and carrying on like fools. My only conclusion could be that because jump school was voluntary, they didn't have to motivate you; if you failed, you failed yourself. That is what I was looking for in the army—the challenge of pushing myself to the limit. The question was, Just how good are you?

Morning arrived early: 0530. "Get out of bed, you assholes,'' the cadre screamed. As I lay there I thought to myself, These pricks *are* going to hassle us just like the rest of them.

Fifteen minutes later we were on the road, running. This isn't so bad, I thought to myself; a nice slow easy run. Everyone was keeping up with no problem. After the run we had breakfast, and after breakfast the whole training company ran about a half mile to the parade field, where we were ushered into a long set of bleachers. Once we were settled, the commander of the school gave a short speech on the school, the lineage of the Airborne, and what was expected of us.

"The first week will be physical training, the second week you will be taught how to fall properly without getting hurt. Let me emphasize, gentlemen, that you will run everywhere. If you are instructed to do push-ups, you will drop and you will say 'One Airborne, two Airborne, and so on and so on.' And you will always give one extra push-up for the Airborne Ranger in the Sky,'' he explained.

I had heard the term "Airborne Ranger'' before, but had never given it a thought. Everywhere we ran, almost every song was sung to cadence; the song sung most frequently was "I wanna be an Airborne Ranger, I wanna live the life of danger.'' The term would come to mean more to me in the future.

After the commander finished, we were given a demonstration of HALO (high-altitude low-opening) jumpers. As we looked up, tiny black specks were falling toward us at an incredible speed until the white puff of parachute canopy opened and they landed in front of us. The commander commented, "Oh, by the way, if your chute fails to open, the fastest speed you can attain freefalling is one hundred and five miles an hour." A groan rose from the bleachers. He then said, "You will learn the fastest two-handed game in the world, that being throwing your reserve chute out manually. If your reserve should fail to open, you'll never have to worry about anything again!"

After the first week of physical conditioning, the running was getting easier. I was always a pretty good runner, with plenty of stamina but no speed, but the Marines in our platoon were *tough*. As the Army "students" ran in formation, the Marines ran *around* the formation barking like dogs. The Army always had a dislike for Marines, so the instructors were always dropping them for their barking. After the Marines were dropped for their pushups they would rise and yell, "Airborne Recon," "recon" being Force Recon, an elite Marine unit.

Time passed very quickly. We were busy learning to exit a mock-up of a door of an airplane. Busy learning how to land with right, left, forward, and the dreaded rear-landing fall. The rear landing was the worst, as you couldn't see behind you. There were five key landing points: the point of impact was the balls of the feet, then the calf, then the thigh while rolling to the side, followed by the fourth point which was the buttocks. The final contact point was the side and back muscles. At the last second before impact you pulled down on the risers (the section of the parachute that attaches the harness to the main chute) and pulled your hands tightly to your chest. Upon contact with the ground you rolled in the direction in which the parachute was blowing. We were taught to never land standing up, to always execute a PLF (parachute landing fall), but whenever no one was watching and the wind wasn't blowing, I always stood.

We learned the PLF from a rope device attached to a

thirty-four-foot tower. The first time was the scariest: after attaching the roped harness (an actual harness without the chute) you stood in the door position assumed while exiting a real aircraft, hands on either side of the doorjamb, staring straight ahead, knees bent. After receiving permission to jump, we yelled "Airborne" at the top of our lungs. I leapt off the tower, hands firmly grasping the reserve chute and my chin to my chest. I was surprised that the impact of my chin hitting my chest didn't break my neck. As I jumped I could feel myself falling, supported by air. All of a sudden the fall took up the slack of the rope and my body was jerked back skyward. When the weight of my body finally put tension back on the rope, I was now sliding down the rope heading for earth. Since the rope had a swivel on the end you never knew what direction or PLF you would be executing. Shit, I thought to myself, I'm going backwards. The dreaded rear PLF, the ground was now screaming toward me. I tucked my head, pulled in the risers, and got up smiling, proud of myself. I had executed a letter-perfect rear PLF.

"Okay, asshole," the instructor screeched, "what did you do wrong?"

"Nothing, Sergeant" I screamed.

"Did you count, dummy?" was his reply.

"No, Sergeant!"

"Did you check your canopy, dummy?" he screamed even louder.

"No, Sergeant," I said rather meekly.

"Drop for ten, dummy, and then do it again," he snarled.

I never forgot to count and check the canopy again. One thousand, one thousand one, one thousand two, and look up to see the canopy. I really don't know how I could have forgotten that; scared maybe?

Training was over and it was time for the real thing. The entire company ran to the bleachers by the airfield where we were to "chute up" for the big one. After we chuted up, checked and rechecked one another, the instructors checked us out. The wait was torture: the chute and the harness were heavy, and the straps cut deep into my crotch; it was almost impossible to stand erect. My back was breaking, but with the straps tight, I felt sure the son of a bitch wouldn't fall off. Even so, my mind started to play tricks on me, and I imagined the headline: "Dummy student dies when parachute falls off."

After chuting up we sat in the bleachers waiting our turns while chanting like we were at a pep rally. "Airborne, Airborne, Airborne," was the chant led by one of the instructors—brainwashing, but it worked. No one had time to think about being scared of the impending jump. "Airborne, Airborne, Airborne," over and over. Then it was our turn. My iron bird was a flying boxcar, a C-119, so old that looked like its last mission had been an air-drop to support Sherman's march.

As we entered the plane I can honestly say that I wasn't scared. While the plane taxied down the runway I scanned the faces of my classmates. As I watched, the apprehension in their eyes slowly turned to terror. I began wondering if I looked as scared. The plane was shuddering down the runway, gaining speed, and finally jumped off the ground. We were gaining altitude and the air was getting colder. Then the plane began bobbing and weaving. As I happened to glance back, a soldier threw up on the floor. I quickly looked away.

The jumpmaster held up six fingers, meaning six minutes. "Oh shit." It seemed just seconds had passed when the next hand signal was given: *Stand up*. Everyone was up, panic was now in everyone's eyes. *Hook-up* was the next signal given. *Click*. I attached my static line with great care. It snapped on firmly but I still checked it very carefully. *Check equipment* was the next command. I checked out the soldier in front of me and was checked out by the soldier behind. Then we turned completely around and were double-checked. Mostly we looked for misrouted static lines. The static line's only function was to use the jumper's weight against the steel cable attached inside the plane when you jumped. But if the static line was routed under your arm, when you jumped it would break the arm. Our running song kept playing in my head. "Stand up, hook up, shuffle to the door, jump right out, and yell for more!"

Stand in the door was the next command. Thank God, I wasn't first. Looking out the door of the plane twelve hundred feet in the air, that poor guy had the best view in the house. But the anticipation was killing me.

The jumpmaster's eyes were glued to the red light, as were everyone else's. All of a sudden the pilot hit the drop zone and activated the green light signaling go. The jumpmaster tapped the soldier in the door, and he was gone. Even over the roar of the engines and the rushing wind from the open door, the word "*Go*" drowned my senses. "*Go! Go! Go!*" I screamed, trying to drown out my fear. The soldier in front of me jumped. Then it was my turn. I jumped, closing my eyes. I was in perfect position, being hit by the prop blast and being hurtled earthward in a ball. I was out. Out in the "wild blue yonder," falling completely out of control. The prop blast threw me like a piece of paper in a tornado. Then I felt a huge jerk on my shoulders and body, the chute opened; "Thank God," I said to myself. I had forgotten to count, but didn't give a damn. What a feeling! What a view! God, it was indescribable.

I was enjoying the view too much to practice pulling on the risers to steer the chute to the right or left. Screw 'em, I thought. It was *my* ride down. I'd gone through too much running and PT; this was my reward. I looked around. The sky was full of chutes. They looked like dandelion seeds adrift in a summer breeze. I watched a soldier trying to get off another soldier's chute. The chute of the soldier on the bottom was stealing the air from the chute on top. Then the soldier on top was sliding down the silk of the chute below. He made it. It could have collapsed his chute if it took too much air, but he got off in time and the air refilled his chute. He was lucky.

The ground was coming up fast but I was coming down straight. My toes hit the ground and it was like landing on a marshmallow. I did a right PLF and got up. The first thing I did was to look down to see if my pants were wet. Nope, I was dry. God, that descent was great. And I had landed far enough away from the instructors to light up a cigarette and savor the moment. After enjoying the smoke, I rolled up the chute in the proper manner and double-timed from the drop zone to the awaiting trucks.

After I checked in my chute and crawled into the truck that was to take us back, I saw Dave and gave him a thumbs-up "Airborne!" Everyone on the truck had a different story, but we all had a good laugh on the poor bastard who'd thrown up in the C-119.

The rest of my mandatory jumps were just as much fun. From then on, the army would pay me fifty-five dollars a month jump pay. I was entitled to wear the silver wings and the garrison resembling a McDonald's hat with a glider patch on it, another privilege exclusive to the Airborne soldier.

Our company of students stood at attention in dress greens on the road; our pride was evident. The company commander congratulated the company, once more instructing us to uphold the strong Airborne tradition of pride and honor in the silver wings we wore on our chests.

Then we all stood up and yelled, "Airborne." That was the end of my training at Fort Benning. Jump school had been what I had expected of basic training. The teaching of teamwork and stress on physical training were what I had been looking for. But, had basic training been as demanding, half the recruits would have been sent home.

SPECIAL FORCES

As the bus Dave and I were riding pulled into Fort Bragg, our new home, our new-found pride was being smashed. Everywhere we looked were Airborne personnel. Fort Bragg was the home of the 82nd Airborne Division, the Special Forces, and the XVIII Airborne Corps. So much for our funny-looking "cunt" caps and silver wings. Now I would have to come back to reality and once again become a student.

The bus came to a halt in front of a three-story *brick* building. I could barely believe my eyes; ever since I'd joined the army, I had lived in World War II wooden barracks. The orderly room at Fort Leonard Wood was even heated by wood-burning stove.

We were instructed to form up behind the bus by an NCO (noncommissioned officer) who then called off our names and assigned us to buildings. With three other students, I was assigned to a second-floor room in the brick barracks. Dave was going into light-weapons training, so he was housed in the building behind mine. Four men to a room was something foreign to me, it wasn't the army I was used to, by any means. I hauled up my gear and introduced myself to my roommates, Hollister, Carpenter, and Lucian. They were all just as green to the army as I was.

Lucian and I became fairly good friends, but Carpenter and Hollister had different personalities and they stayed pretty much to themselves.

The order came down that a formation would be in fifteen minutes. The formation was taking shape when one of the doors opened and out walked one of the sharpest, meanest looking first sergeants I'd seen to date. The starch in his fatigues was rock-hard, the shine on his boots could have fired up a laser, and his beret was cocked just so. His chest bore the patches of a seasoned veteran, jumpmaster wings, CIB, and his name and US Army embroidered, not stamped on like the trainees in front of him.

"Atten-*Hut*!" he said in a deep voice.

On cue, out walked a captain in starched fatigues. "At ease, men," he said. The captain welcomed us to Fort Bragg and the Special Forces Training Center. For a half hour he explained what was expected of us. The dos and don'ts, training schedules, et cetera, et cetera. Then we were trucked over to the quartermaster and issued our TA-50 (field gear). After returning to the barracks and putting away our gear, we had formation in which we were assigned platoons. Our first class was to be at 1300 hours, right after lunch. Before lunch, however, we would have a "police call" (military slang for cleaning up cigarette butts, trash, et cetera). It would be the first of many.

After lunch was more orientation to Special Forces.

Training would be in two phases followed by a final FTX (field training exercise).

Phase 1, classroom training at Fort Bragg, was almost the same training as Engineer AIT but more intensified: rope knots, rigging, bridges, and finally demolition. We were taught how to construct homemade bombs, and where and how to place shaped charges. The classes were excellent.

All during Phase 1, the students pulled police call after police call, not just in the company area but around parade fields, roads, and even around the PX. I was really getting sick of that nonsense. The police calls were bullshit and the lifers (career soldiers) were just having fun with us. I never realized exactly what the score was until one day we were on police call by the road and two guys laughing hysterically drove up in a car. "Hurry up and graduate," they yelled, "so we don't have to do that anymore." I saw they were wearing green berets with the red background of the 7th Special Forces group right down the road.

At that time, my chances of going to 'Nam were almost nonexistent. Fort Bragg was already overloaded with Special-Forces-qualified people. The Special Forces soldier, my ideal, had become nothing more than a professional cigarette-butt "picker upper." It's not to say that Special Forces weren't any good; they were just not used to their full potential. They were skilled, highly professional soldiers. Their training was the best the army had to offer but the handwriting was on the wall. And I'd be damned if I was going to sit out the war at Bragg.

For Phase 2 we lived in tents at Camp McCall outside Bragg. Camp McCall had been used during World War II, but by the time I was there only the roads and concrete slabs bore evidence of any previous use.

The classes were good, the compass course excellent. Survival training began with our learning to cook a chicken under a number-ten can (twice the size of a coffee can) with a flash fire. We whittled a stick down to the size of a pencil, stuck one end in the ground and the other into the chicken breast, covered it with the can, and then covered the can with a generous amount of pine needles. Once they burnt down the chicken was supposed to be done. Mine was still raw inside. I threw it away.

The next part of the survival class was how to kill a live rabbit. We were all sitting in a circle around the instructor, who was holding a fluffy, pretty white rabbit. The instructor scanned the audience for a squeamish individual to slit the rabbit's throat. His eyes met mine; I was grinning again.

"Come here, troop."

I got up and walked over to him and took the rabbit in my left hand by the scruff of the neck. Hoping I would whittle "Bugs" down to inedible scraps, the instructor gave me a knife. With a flick of the wrist I snapped its neck. He was dead. I handed the knife and limp rabbit back to the instructor, this time with a real smirk on my face.

"Sit down, asshole," he said.

I had ruined his fun. But I'd grown up hunting with my father, and had often killed a wounded pheasant or rabbit by hand rather than eat buckshot from the extra shotgun shell.

For the next demonstration, an instructor slit the throat of a goat. I still remember the slit throat's opening and closing. Seeing that firsthand, I wondered if I would ever have the nerve to slit a human's throat to perform a tracheotomy. It looked so simple to put a tube in that opening. After a while the goat gagged and dropped.

The instructor improvised a smokehouse out of ponchos and we hung strips of goat meat on branches inside. When the jerky was done we tried it; not bad, but I wouldn't order it in a restaurant. Another police call.

My favorite classes were map reading and navigation by compass. Plotting azimuths (going from point "A" to point "B") was easy and interesting. Day navigation with a map was easy using a compass, because you could utilize terrain features to determine where you were going. Night navigation was another matter. I would always be bumping into heavy brush or walking into swamps in the dark.

I don't know what finally pushed me to get out of Special Forces. Maybe it was the lifers' bullshit, maybe it was the police calls, maybe it was because I would be

stuck at Bragg for another two years. Whatever, I knew
I had to make a decision. If I graduated and was assigned
to a Special Forces group at Bragg, I would have to sit
there or reenlist to get to 'Nam. *Hurry up and graduate*
kept ringing in my ears.

I was granted permission to see the training commander of Camp McCall. I knocked on the door and a
voice said "Enter."

"Private Ericson reporting," I said.

"What's the problem, troop?" The captain was in his
early thirties. Steel gray eyes stared right through me.

"I want to 1049 (military request for transfer) out of
here, sir."

His stare grew colder. "You can't do that, troop. You're
still in training. Why do you want out?"

"Because I'll be stuck at Bragg for my entire enlist-
ment."

"How do you know that?" he snarled back at me.

I wanted to say that I didn't want to be a lifer or put
up with police calls for two years, but I didn't, because
he was more than likely a lifer himself. "Because there
are too many of us," was my reply.

"It's out of the question."

"Sir, I'd like to terminate myself, then."

"And if I won't let you?" he replied.

"Then I'll flunk out," I said. I had him; I'd figured
every angle.

"You fucking quitter. You asshole leg."

A "leg" or a "straight leg" is a non-Airborne soldier;
being called one is the biggest insult you can bestow on
a paratrooper. After a verbal assault on my parentage, he
gave up. After signing the necessary paperwork I was
told I'd have to pull "asshole duty" at Camp McCall
until orders assigned me to my next unit. God, I prayed
more than once it would be Vietnam. I gave my final
salute, I noticed that there was no CIB (combat infantryman's badge) on the training commander's fatigue shirt.
Maybe that fatigue shirt was at the cleaners.

While pulling "asshole duty," I thought about my decision. Right or wrong it was done. Special Forces was
the first thing I ever quit in my life. I had a nagging
feeling in my stomach because I was called a quitter.

That captain probably wanted out of McCall as badly as I did.

I finally received orders for Vietnam, and was given a thirty-day leave before reporting to Fort Lewis, Washington, the jumping-off spot for Vietnam.

As I sit here writing, almost twenty years later, I can still say that duty in Vietnam was to be the greatest experience of my life.

CHAPTER 2

SEPTEMBER 1969/CAM RANH BAY
Don Ericson

The thirty-day leave was up, so my parents drove me to O'Hare Airport, from where I was to fly to Fort Lewis, Washington. The good-byes were painful for my family and me. Not much at all was said.

I boarded the plane. Twenty others were on it; about one hundred people short of capacity. After an hour in the air a stewardess came over to me and asked if I wanted a little conversation.

We talked about everything and anything for the next hour and a half. There weren't many passengers, so she had little to do until it was time to serve the next meal. She asked if I was to be stationed at Fort Lewis, and I replied, ''No, I am on my way to Vietnam.'' She wanted to show me around Washington while I was there, but I explained that I had to report to Fort Lewis immediately. She looked sad and commented that Seattle had beautiful sights.

As I was departing the plane she handed me a piece of paper with her name and address on it. She lived and flew out of Chicago. I said I wouldn't be back for at least a year. She said, "Well, you never know." As I turned to go, she kissed me on the cheek for luck.

It was raining as I hailed a taxi for Fort Lewis; not a hard rain, just enough to keep everything soaked. I reported in and was instructed to sleep in any available barracks to our rear. The sergeant took a copy of my orders and that was that.

Most of my time at Fort Lewis was spent on out-of-country processing, which meant filling in several pounds of paperwork. Shot records were checked. Formations were held and names read off for flight manifests. My name finally came up; after three days and two nights at Fort Lewis, I'd be leaving at 0500 the next day.

The last night at Fort Lewis, I went to the post theater and stared at the screen completely oblivious to what was playing. My thoughts were on the future . . .

Our 0500 formation was held and names were read off. As we boarded the bus, we gave our names again so we could be physically checked off. It was a short ride to the awaiting Flying Tigers commercial jet. There we were checked off yet again as we got off the bus. The army had to be able to account for everyone.

It was a long flight: eighteen hours, ten-thousand-plus miles of sitting. I had a seat alongside a leg second lieutenant who was as old as I was. We made a little small talk but had nothing in common. I tried to sleep but couldn't; the excitement of seeing America's television war firsthand was almost unbearable. Eventually the captain announced that we would be landing in Yakota, Japan, to refuel. We were to wait in the US Air Force terminal during the two-hour layover.

I was walking around the terminal when I heard a group of soldiers laughing hysterically; I wandered over to find them watching a television playing a rerun of *The Lone Ranger* dubbed into Japanese. Tonto's Japanese was hysterical, and even Silver looked as though he didn't understand when the Lone Ranger spoke.

Our two hours in Japan passed quickly. Then we were headed for beautiful Southeast Asia. The rest of the trip was uneventful. Before I knew it the captain was on the intercom again saying, "Fasten your seat belts." I could now feel the descent of the airplane. For hours I had seen only water from the window, then as the wheels touched the ground all I could see were different shades of green. A silence fell over the passengers. I wondered what percentage of the planeload of "green troops" would come back in one piece or come back alive. I wondered whether my fellow passengers were having the same grisly thoughts.

When we touched down, I had no idea what *time* of day or even *what* day it was. I had too many other things on my mind. The plane had now taxied to its final resting place and the door swung open. We were filing out when I got my first whiff of 'Nam. The air conditioning on board had only been off for a few minutes and already the oppressive heat and odor was filling the cabin of the plane.

It was a heat that covered you like a heavy blanket. The odor was a nauseating combination of aviation fuel and an aroma that I couldn't identify. Both, however, accented each other.

We followed the leader to the main terminal; I was amazed at the size of the base. The runways seemed to go as far as I could see. Quonset-type hangars with sandbags halfway up their sides were the garages for the huge military war planes. There were people moving everywhere with their own secret missions of daily life. It looked like "Any Military Base, USA."

We arrived at the terminal only to stick out like sore thumbs; we were extremely "clean and green." A group of soldiers off to the side were all laughing and pointing in our direction.

"Hey, Cherry, what took you so long to get here?" one yelled.

"Hey, New Meat," came another comment.

They were going home; their year was up and they were waiting for their "Freedom Bird" back to the World.

As we walked through the terminal there were Vietnamese military and civilians, everywhere, all talking their singsong language at once. Once outside we were ushered into military buses and taken to the 544th Replacement Center.

There to greet us was a huge "welcome" sign and

another sign under it stating that the "Alert Condition" was now "white." I hoped that was good. No one else seemed to be excited about it. The compound appeared to be secure enough.

Cam Ranh Bay looked like any "pretty, Stateside" post. There were two-story barracks with metal roofs lined up in neat military rows, twenty-four wooden-foot guard towers with huge searchlights scattered here and there, and sandbag bunkers by each barracks.

Can Ranh Bay is where I was introduced to my first "piss tube." A piss tube consisted of a hollow metal pipe or a container for shipping rockets or artillery rounds that was pressed into service as a urinal. The tube was embedded a few feet down into the sand to allow for drainage of the liquid. Some of the higher-class tubes had three sides for privacy. It was a novel solution to the age-old problem of sanitation. Later in my tour of duty I would see some of these overworked tubes filled to over-flowing capacity, especially around the enlisted men's saloon. That was when the bare wall of a building was more convenient.

We were told at our formation that there would be two formations a day, one in the morning and the second at noon, at which personnel would be assigned permanent units and departure times.

KP (kitchen police) was nonexistent; the Vietnamese were paid to pull KP. That didn't hurt my feelings at all. I was also introduced to REMFs (rear-echelon mother-fuckers) or the "Saigon Commandos." These were the soldiers who stayed in the rear; the ones who were clerks, truck drivers, or troops who were mainly noncomba-tants. Somebody had to do it, I guess.

I spent most of my time in the EM (enlisted men's) club just wasting time. My name was called at the next formation. I would immediately leave for the air termi-nal. I was assigned to the 173rd Airborne Brigade.

Our short plane ride from Cam Ranh Bay ended in a place called Phu Cat. Phu Cat was about one-twentieth the size of Cam Ranh Bay. A building thirty-by-forty feet was the terminal. I did notice that in Phu Cat I was see-ing more and more of the war, helicopters flying every-where I looked. There were infantrymen wandering all

over, covered with dirt, still carrying their rucksacks and
M-16 rifles; something almost never seen in Cam Ranh
Bay. The war was getting closer.

After regrouping in the terminal, we were instructed
by an NCO to get in the back of a waiting truck for our
next designation; Phu Tai, the 173rd processing area.
During the ride I felt really helpless. Here I was in an
open truck without anything, not even a stick, to defend
myself. I was in a combat zone, Vietnamese people everywhere staring right through us. They weren't smiling
or waving to their American liberators. They were looking at us with utter disgust and disdain. Even as I write
this, looking back at my photo album I can still see the
absolute horror of their poverty. It was not the North
Vietnamese Army they feared; it was the thought of being uprooted again and again because of the war. They
had nothing; even their houses were constructed of cardboard. The Vietnamese that I had just seen for the first
time were primitive. It made me realize that America was
truly a blessed country. Everyone laughed at President
Johnson's "Great Society" but it was true. No matter
how you saw it or what you read of poverty, you would
never understand it unless you saw it firsthand.

After arriving at Phu Tai, we went through the brigade
in-processing in a couple of hours. The most important
part of processing was finance—I sent all my money directly home with the exception of twenty-five dollars a
month. Twenty-five dollars went a long way when beer
was fifteen cents a can and a pack of cigarettes was
twenty cents.

Processing now out of the way, we had an uneventful
truck ride to Cha Rang Valley. Cha Rang Valley was the
173rd's in-country training school. The school was basically for orientation to Vietnam. We were instructed to
bathe daily to prevent jungle rot and ringworm. Jungle
rot came from dampness; the dampest places on your
body are your crotch, between your toes, and under your
arms. Ringworm was a parasite in the dirt that made its
way to your body. The entire time that I was in Vietnam
I never wore socks or underwear.

We were instructed on the local customs and were told

not to call the Vietnamese gooks or dinks. However, we always did.

In true Airborne tradition, we had PT daily and ran everywhere. The nights were taken up with visits to the legs' compound, where we listened to a Korean band butcher some of our favorite American songs. Hell, it was something to do.

While at Cha Rang Valley I stayed mostly to myself until I met John L. Rotundo, a tall, medium-built kid who came from Ohio. We sat through class after class, mostly yawning and laughing quite a bit at the other new troops. His warped sense of humor matched mine, so we got along well. Little did I know that years later we would be reunited and writing this book.

I knew once training was over John L. would go his way and I would go mine. I'd never gotten really close to anyone during my previous training in the military; I had a friend here and there, but I always knew that when training was over I would be by myself again. As green as I was to the military, and to Vietnam, I never dreamt I'd be forming a bond, a closeness, a brotherhood that would last to this very day.

After one particularly boring class on the PRC-25 (military field radio) our class was introduced to a rather short bull of a man wearing camouflage fatigues. He had my full attention just because of his appearance and the "C 75th Airborne Ranger" scroll on his left arm. The whole class stared. He was one of the "elite" breed we sang about. I looked at John L. and we both smiled. I knew what I wanted to do. The recruiter's name was Culeford and he was looking for volunteers for Charlie Company Rangers. He said Charlie Company worked in six-man hunter-killer teams sent into the jungle via helicopters, ten to fifteen miles behind enemy lines. The rangers wore camouflage fatigues and covered their exposed skin with camouflage paint. He explained that even though they traveled with only five other team members, the Rangers' chances of surviving in Vietnam were far greater due to their training, camouflage, and noise discipline. Line companies fighting in Vietnam announced themselves by the noise made by a hundred or so men. But each movement of a Ranger team member was carefully thought out to *avoid* noise. Leaving out nothing, Culeford carefully explained the pros and cons of Ranger life. At the end of his speech he asked for a show of hands. Only two hands rose and one was mine. When the class was over, I gave Culeford my name.

He was a friendly fellow who shook my hand without letting his stripes get in the way. "Do you think that you're good enough? Do you think you have what it takes?" he asked.

With no hestitation I replied, "Yes." Looking back I must have looked pretty pitiful in my brand-new jungle fatigues, new jungle boots, and my "Gomer Pyle" baseball hat.

He accepted me after a short conversation, and I was instructed to report for whatever assignment the 173rd sent down. (My orders were to report to the 173rd Engineers at Bong Son.)

Culeford said orders for Charlie Company would arrive in about two weeks, shook my hand, and bid me farewell.

John L. and I went to our designated assignments after a few good-bye beers.

SEPTEMBER 1969/CAM RANH BAY
John L. Rotundo

The Continental Airlines 707 was on its final approach as the pilot put on the No Smoking sign. Those of us who were smoking drew on our last nervous puffs before putting our cigarettes out in the small ashtrays in the armrests and waited for the plane to touch down.

It had been a long flight from Seattle, eithteen hours to be exact. As the aircraft came to a halt, talking within the plane ceased and the stewardess began preparing for our arrival. Then the front door opened and an individual came aboard and announced our arrival to Cam Ranh Bay, Republic of Vietnam, and instructed us to take a seat in the waiting buses, which would take us to in-processing.

As I deplaned, the extreme heat was oppressive and already I could smell the burning shit. Welcome to Vietnam, I thought.

The next three days were spent filling out forms, forms, and more forms: "In the event I become lightly wounded or not so seriously ill, I (DO) (DO NOT) want the army to notify my next of kin," et cetera.

Every day formations were held and names were read off assigning individuals to units. Those whose names weren't called pulled police calls and stood formations endlessly while others shipped out to their new homes.

The afternoon of the third day I finally heard my name. A handful of us were led to pick up our duffel bags and were told to stand by. I was assigned to HHC 4/503rd, 173rd Airborne Brigade (Separate). That meant I was being assigned to an Airborne unit. Back in July, when I took a "short" to get to Vietnam, one of the guarantees was that I was to be assigned to an Airborne unit; the 173rd was the only one there in September of 1969. This army is all right!

We departed Cam Ranh Bay later that afternoon for Phu Cat Air Force Base, which would be our first stop. At Phu Cat we were met by a liaison from the 173rd who announced that it was too late for transportation to Phu Tai, the 173rd's rear area. We were left to hang around the terminal for the evening. We made the most of our situation by sleeping on chairs or crashing on the floor, wherever we could find space. The next morning a bus picked us up for the ride to Phu Tai and another day of in-processing before we were taken to Cha Rang Valley and the 173rd's jungle school.

Once again we were lectured on the customs of the Vietnamese people, their history, culture, and so on. The conversation of the instructors then turned to the history of the 173rd Airborne Brigade, which had been formed on the island of Okinawa in 1963 as a unit trained for jungle warfare in Southeast Asia. It was the army's only separate Airborne brigade.

In May of 1965, the 173rd deployed to Vietnam, making it the first army ground combat unit committed to the war in South Vietnam. Its "official" nickname was the "Sky Soldiers," but everybody affectionately referred to it as "the Herd," and in battle after battle with the Vietcong or NVA (North Vietnamese Army regulars) the 173rd had distinguished itself every time. So much in fact that the cadre went on to tell us about the documents taken from prisoners of war ordering them to avoid contact with the 173rd when possible and indicating that a lot of the enemy's movements were rerouted to avoid contact. In 1967 the 173rd made the only airborne assault of the war, and that meant that those of us being assigned to the Herd would continue on jump status, so we would continue to receive the extra $55 a month as an active paratrooper in addition to the $60 a month everyone in Vietnam received for hazard duty: combat pay. As a PFC, I would be getting $275 a month. With three hots and a cot thrown in for free, I could send home $200 a month; after a year in Vietnam, I would return home and have over $2000 in the bank. Not too shabby.

Other instructors came on stage and discussed the kinds of booby trap as well as the varieties of snake found in Vietnam. As the first day was drawing to a close I was milling around with a few other guys when a Spec-4 "volunteered" us for the burn detail. I thought he was kidding about the job, but he took us to the shitter, a basic outhouse, and made sure nobody was inside. The four of us then opened up the door in the rear of it, extracted the two full fifty-five-gallon drums from underneath, pulled them about fifty meters, and, after thoroughly dousing them with kerosene, lit it with some toilet paper. It didn't take very long to figure out which way the wind was blowing; in a flash the four of us were standing upwind as black smoke billowed across the compound.

Orientation continued the next day and we were told of the Herd's current mission. It was called pacification, which meant we weren't humping the bush looking for Charlie but were in the process of turning the war over to the Army of the Republic of Vietnam (ARVNs). During the lecture, I was sitting with another cherry I had just met.

"Hi, I'm Don Ericson," he said with an infectious grin.

"John Rotundo," I replied.

He seemed to be able to laugh at just about anything and that grin was on his face all the time. We immediately became friends as we now sat together waiting for the next speaker to take the stage.

An imposing figure strolled to the stage, dressed in his camouflage fatigues and built like a bull. His deep-set eyes seemed to dart around the room as he began his speech.

"Good morning, gentlemen. I'm Sergeant Culeford from Charlie Company Rangers."

Don and I listened intently as Culeford went into his talk about the Rangers, from the unit's creation in February 1969 from an assortment of previous "long-range patrol" units, LRPs (pronounced lurps), to the present. Each infantry division in Vietnam had its own Ranger company, as did the Herd, even though it was only a brigade. But the division companies were LRRP companies, the second R in the designation indicating that they did long-range *reconnaissance* patrol missions. That they were inserted in their AO (area of operation) and observed for any signs of Charlie (VC or NVA) and reported his movements, all the while remaining undected. I had read about LRRPs back at Fort Bragg, but this was the first time I'd seen one. We listened to Culeford as he continued. "The mission of Charlie Company Rangers varies in two ways. First of all we do not work under a division or a brigade. We are under orders from the First Field Force, which means our operations are not just limited to a division- or brigade-size AO; the entire II Corps is our AO, and we can operate in any area within the corps' boundaries."

He paused and looked around the room before he continued. "The second variation of Charlie Rangers is that we don't work in a LRRP mission. Ours is a LRP or long-range patrol with not much emphasis on reconnaissance except that we gather intelligence from what we get off the bodies of the VC or NVA we kill. Our six-man teams are designated as hunter-killers, and their primary mission is to make contact by ambushing any target of opportunity the team leader feels capable of.''

Culeford had everyone's undivided attention. ''American units have a bad habit of making a lot of noise when they are in the woods and that makes them prone to snipers, booby traps, and especially ambushes, because Charlie knows where they are at and which way they are going. However, a team of Rangers out there who know how to remain undected can set up its own ambush right under Charlie's nose and catch him half-stepping [being lax] because he thinks he's safe. Once contact is made, the team is extracted because the noise of combat has compromised its position; the team vacates the area. Of course, if a team bites off more than it can chew, we'll send in a reaction force of another Ranger team or even a line company. In addition we're supported by helicopter gunships, artillery, and even the Air Force if the need is there.''

Culeford went on to emphasize the discipline, training, and physical conditioning involved in making an effective Ranger team, where six individuals had to operate as one. He explained that Ranger duty is not without its hazards, as within the previous month two teams had been virtually wiped out with a team leader killed and the rest wounded. But even with that sobering information, the kill ratio for Charlie Rangers since February was an incredible fifty-five to one (not bad odds). He was not trying to paint a rosy picture; he was telling us that if we wanted to volunteer, there was a high level of exposure to contact but also a very good chance of coming home in one piece. Ranger duty was not for everyone but for those who desired to be with the best. He invited them to step forward and sign up.

I thought to myself, Hell, I had volunteered for the army right out of high school with a guarantee of going Airborne. After jump school I was assigned to the 82nd Airborne Division at Fort Bragg, North Carolina, which really sucked! Twice I had put in a 1049 (request for transfer) for Vietnam and both times it had been denied. It was when I dropped my nine months already in the service and took a ''short'' (short time reenlistment) that

I was successful in getting there. How many chances would I ever get to see war firsthand?

I looked at Don. "Want to go?"

He was grinning at me. "Why not?"

Culeford put down our names, rank, serial number, and MOS (military occupational speciality); he was sizing us up while he asked questions, apparently watching our reactions.

"Why do you want to be a Ranger? Do you have what it takes to be a Ranger? Do you smoke dope?"

After I finished with him and returned to my seat, I couldn't help but wonder if I had done the right thing or if I had just signed my own death certificate. Fuck it, I thought to myself, there's a war on and all my life I've wanted to actually see a war. Now, here I am in Vietnam. I don't want to be just an observer. It looked as if I was finally going to get my chance.

Our stay at Cha Rang Valley was drawing to an end. I received orders assigning me to LZ (landing zone) North English to be with Headquarters Company of the 4th Battalion, and Don was to report to the 173rd Engineers at LZ English.

After a week's stay at the jungle school we were ready to depart for our new homes. Don and I said our good-byes to one another, promising to keep in touch as we were waiting for our orders for the Rangers, but for one reason or another we never did.

I got myself ready, and along with my equipment and others, mounted the deuce and a half that would take us to LZ North English for my new temporary assignment as a REMF (rear-echelon motherfucker).

CHAPTER 3

OCTOBER 1969/BONG SON
Don Ericson

It was a short sixty-mile flight to Bong Son. It was midmorning as I entered the company area of the engineers. It looked as if it were deserted. Everyone must be out in the field, I thought. I checked in with the clerk and was assigned to a half-wooden half-tent barracks. The barracks was also deserted, so I picked out what seemed to be an unoccupied cot and put my gear into a wooden footlocker at the end of the cot, then walked outside to check out the area.

Bong Son was my first real look at Vietnam. LZ English was situated on a hilltop right outside the town of Bong Son. It was surrounded by some of the most beautiful countryside I'd ever seen. There were huge mountains with rivers and streams at their base, and the ground vegetation was every imaginable shade of green. The bright-red clay earth added an accent that only highlighted the deep green of the countryside. From high atop our hill, I could see the Vietnamese farmers scurrying about on their tasks.

As I was making my way back to the barracks, the troops began to come back in. A whole convoy of two-

and-a-half-ton trucks loaded with engineers was kicking up huge red dust swells, which covered everything in their path with a fine red powder. It almost looked as if everyone were wearing red uniforms.

I was introduced to my platoon sergeant, a fellow twenty-three years old, six foot five, and weighing a good two hundred and thirty pounds. He seemed friendly enough. As the rest of the veterans of 'Nam (veteran only because they arrived before you did) filtered into the barracks, I was beginning to be called all sorts of delightful names like "Cherry" (meaning green) or FNG (fucking new guy).

The days dragged on and on. My duties consisted mostly of filling sandbags and other bullshit like that. I could handle it because I knew I would be leaving soon. I pity the poor PFCs who spent their whole time in 'Nam with the engineers.

I did make one acquaintance at Bong Son; his name was Red. He told me of the ins and outs and the do's and don'ts of LZ English. "Always stay high," Red would say. "It's the only way to get through this shit. Never go into town at night; the VC own it. Just do what you are told and you'll be fine."

The army is truly amazing; here I was in a "war," a "combat zone," and I was polishing my boots. Not a spit shine by any means, but a brush shine. I had on clean fatigues every day and all I had to do was play the game and keep the lifers happy.

About a month had passed; my orders for Charlie Company eventually came down and I would be leaving soon, but the last few days with the engineers were extremely exciting. Our platoon was trucked out to a bridge three miles out where we filled sandbags for eight hours. I happened to glance up only to catch a glimpse of Red talking to a mama-san and saw him giving her some MPC (military scrip). I thought nothing of it and went back to filling the sandbags. It was common practice for GIs to buy Cokes or beer from the locals at inflated prices. A dollar for a Coke was not uncommon, even in 1969.

On the way back to LZ English I saw the fruits of Red's purchase. He pulled out the biggest joint I had ever seen. Now dope was everywhere in 'Nam—the officers and the senior NCOs just pretended that it didn't exist—and I watched as Red lit up the joint in the back of the truck. Every eye on him; you could almost see the other troops drooling for their chance at the huge cigarette. This cigarette I would find out later was known as the "Bong Son Bomber."

I was sitting next to Red in the truck but he passed the joint around the other way. I watched intently as each troop inhaled deeply, holding the smoke in to get the maximum effect. It was the first time that I was to try anything like that and I didn't want to look like I didn't know what I was doing. By the time the cigarette got to me, it was down to about three inches. I took the joint between my fingers, carefully pinched the now hot cigarette, and brought it up to my mouth. I inhaled deeply and held the smoke in and passed it back to Red. I held in the smoke as long as I could and exhaled slowly to look as if I knew what I was doing. The joint made it halfway around the truck again before it was too short and too hot to hold on to. I could feel its effects creeping up on me. By the time the truck arrived back at LZ English I was stoned. When the truck stopped, I tried to raise my leg over the side of the truck and watched my boot float over the side. I had no sensation of my foot's being attached to my body. I could feel a sense of helplessness. That was the last time I'd be that vulnerable, I told myself. Not in a combat zone.

Another memorable incident of my time at LZ English was when we were hit by rockets. I was walking out of the mess hall after lunch and something *woosh*ed by right over my head. For that brief instant I looked up and saw nothing. Then I heard explosions on the other side of the compound. All of the guards opened up immediately on the mountains across the valley a half-mile away with .50 caliber machine guns. I'm sure that they were firing at the trees. I guess the guards hoped they would get lucky. LZ English lost a major and a staff sergeant that day. Only six rockets fell; it could have been a lot worse.

The last night in Bong Son was a horror story for three lonely GIs. It seems the three GIs slipped out through the wire at night to pay a call on some of the friendlier women in the town of Bong Son. They were reported missing the next morning and a patrol was sent out to find them. The patrol found two mutilated GIs minus ears and penises. The third GI was never found, but I bet the VC had their fun with him.

I left the next morning and took the fifty-mile flight to An Khe, the rear area of Charlie Company 75th Airborne Rangers, where I was to attend Ranger school.

OCTOBER 1969/BONG SON
John L. Rotundo

My military occupation speciality (MOS) was as a radio operator, so I was assigned to Headquarters Company, where I monitored the battalion's radio network for six hours a day and hid the remaining eighteen. It was really just a ''getting over'' assignment; LZ North English was a huge compound and relatively safe. I was drawing sixty dollars a month combat pay, and the only combat I had seen was against the flies, mosquitos, and an occasional rat.

The Herd took good care of us, especially in the food department. We ate steak, roast beef, roast pork, turkey, burgers, all kinds of potatoes, and for dessert we had our choice of pies. I was beginning to wonder if perhaps the war had ended and somebody forgot to mention it to the Herd.

After my radio watch was over I was off, and I mean *really* off. Nobody hassled me with details, KP, or guard duty. There was an enlisted men's club on LZ North English, so after we worked we'd go down and chug a few beers to get our minds off the war.

As it was the first part of October, the monsoons were upon us. For the first week I was at LZ North English, it rained continuously for three days. On the fourth, the rain let up and it was like a beautiful spring day back home.

After a week, when I hadn't heard anything from the Rangers, I began to wonder if they weren't in the market for a radio operator, but perhaps just looking for Eleven-Bushes (11-B the standard infantry MOS).

The second week at LZ North English we started working eight-hour shifts on with twenty-four hours off. War is hell.

One evening after work, one of the guys I had been with at Fort Bragg came into my hootch and asked me to come with him. We walked to another hootch a couple of hundred meters away, and as we entered the hootch I could smell a distinct odor in the air. The hootch was dark except for the light from a couple of burning candles and four other soldiers were sitting on the floor in a circle. We exchanged greetings as I sat down. In the background a tape player was playing the long version of "In-A-Gadda-Da-Vida." We sat and rapped for a little while, then one of the guys pulled out a rather large cigarette with its end twisted up. He lit up and inhaled deeply, and passed it to his left. And so on.

This must be the killer weed—marijuana! I thought to myself as the joint reached the guy sitting next to me. As it was handed to me I hesitated for a second, not knowing exactly what to do. Everyone was smiling at me, very peaceful looks on their faces.

"Go on, man, take a hit and get nice," one of them said.

"There it is!" chimed in another.

I took the joint between my fingers and slowly raised it to my lips. Inhaling deeply, I took a hit, kept the smoke in, and passed to my left. Nothing happened.

We sat there and continued rapping, and passed another joint around. I still had the can of beer I had brought in with me, and took a few sips as well as another drag on the joint as it came around again.

Suddenly I felt very silly as I was watching the floorboards of the hootch; they looked odd. I got the giggles and so did everybody else. We sat and laughed for what seemed like an hour when I felt I had the urge. I got up and walked out of the hootch searching for the nearest piss tube. As I was walking in the dark the music of Janice Joplin was playing in another hootch but it did not sound right, and when I somehow found the piss tube even the simple act of urination seemed to take place in slow motion.

I began to worry; I could imagine myself walking over to the berm, standing on top of it, and skydiving off into the field below, killing myself like those others back in the World I had heard of, thinking they could fly.

Somehow I made it to my hootch and proceeded to crash as hard as I've ever crashed before. I awoke the next morning feeling very guilty. After all, being a head was not like me. I still longed to be a participant in the war, but all I'd done so far was live the good life, work eight hours a day, and eat, get drunk, and sleep. Now I could add getting high to my list of REMFing.

We had formation that morning, and word was the Herd was looking for volunteers for infantry school. Upon completion of the course, the volunteers would be assigned to one of the Herd's line companies operating in the field.

"There it is!" I said to myself. I raised my hand to volunteer along with a half-dozen others. Well, at least I wasn't the only one who felt the war was passing me.

On October 19, the deuce-and-a-half dropped us off at the Herd's infantry school at Cha Rang Valley. After we put our gear away we went for a swim until chow time. After chow we put on our rucksacks, complete with a fifty-pound sandbag, and went across the road to climb a hill. It wasn't the biggest hill I had ever seen, but it sure was one of the steepest. When we got to the top we then came down the other side. As we hit the bottom we were looking at the steps going back up the hill. There were seventy to be exact. Our instructor thought it would be good training for us to go up and down the steps with our rucksacks on. When we finished we went back to our tents utterly exhausted and crashed soundly.

The next morning at 0530 we were up and at the helipad doing PT. After a half hour of stretching our muscles we went for a little trot around the countryside. This was nothing like jump school where you ran on a level track. Instead we would run up one hill and down another, singing and chanting loudly when we passed the legs, who were still sleeping. We cut through a field and found ourselves back on the road, and took the road back to our area.

During the couple of weeks in the rear, I had really gotten out of shape. To make matters worse, I no longer smoked my usual Marlboros; when the SP (sundry package) came, the white guys would grab all the Marlboros and Winstons while the blacks would grab the Kools and the Salems. If you weren't quick you ended up with the Camels, Lucky Strikes, or, if you had no luck at all, the Pall Malls. That's when I began smoking Camels and found out one of their great advantages. When someone ran out of smokes and wanted to borrow one of mine, I'd offer him a Camel. Invariably they would decline my generous offer, which meant more smokes for me. Now those Camels were kicking my ass something fierce, but I had to keep driving on.

During the day we learned about weapons, map reading, how to "walk" artillery fire onto an objective, and patrolling methods. As I had gone to Fort Knox as a radio operator, most of this infantry procedure was new to me. I crammed as much information about the M-16 as I could. One point the instructors made over and over again was that if you kept it clean it wouldn't jam and you could depend on it. They taught us about the M-60 machine gun, M-79 grenade launcher, command-detonated claymore mines, and, finally, grenades—both the M-26 we learned about in basic training and the M-33 baseball type that had tiny ball bearings inside that were supposed to make it extremely deadly.

After two weeks we were deemed official grunts and sent back to our units to await orders to the field. I had lost about eight pounds at the school and felt I was in as good shape as I had ever been. And I was finally going to do what I had always wanted to do.

NOVEMBER 1969—RANGER SCHOOL/ AN KHE
Don Ericson

I arrived in An Khe just a little apprehensive. What have I gotten myself into this time, I thought. Anything had to be better than the engineers and filling sandbags. As I approached the company TOC (tactical operations center) I noticed the red and black Airborne Ranger scroll on a sign outside the door. Below the scroll was the First Field Force patch. Under that were the words "The Professionals."

I reported to the clerk and was instructed to go to the first metal barracks to the side of the TOC. The building was mostly empty: forty double bunks were occupied by only a handful of soldiers. The place was clean; it had cement floors, a metal roof, and wooden walls. Far nicer than the red dust of LZ English. The unit even had its own barber.

I carried my duffel bag down toward the other soldiers and was greeted by a blond-haired guy.

He jumped up and said, "Hi, my name is Smokey Wells."

I introduced myself and we proceeded to make small talk. Smokey was about my size but had approximately twenty pounds on me. He was from Ohio but his accent sounded like he was from the hills of Tennessee. Smokey was going through the school also and he told me that school would start tomorrow.

Smokey introduced me to the others sitting around. Roger Anderson, Lyle Roguski, Sam Agner, and Chip Paxton; there were a few others in the class but these were the ones I'd remember best. Lunchtime came around and we headed to the mess hall, which was by the school. It was just as clean as the rest of the place. Wood, metal, and concrete. It even had wooden trellises inside with fake ivy interwoven in. The food was just as good as the place looked. The civilian KPs were also another welcomed sight.

After we ate we walked outside and stood and watched the "Student Rangers" across the road rappeling off a

forty-foot wooden tower. It looked like fun. We proceeded back to the barracks.

Our training started at 0500 the next morning and we
had our tails run off. We ran three miles that first morning, just a warm-up for what was to come. After breakfast the classes began. Over the next two weeks we would
undergo intense physical training, as well as study advanced radio procedure to include coded messages, advanced first aid to include giving morphine and serum
albumin, map reading and night navigation, six-man team
tactics, ambushes, area of responsibility of each member
of the team. Every member of the team would be taught
every other member's job so that if the team sustained
casualties any man could take over any position. The
stress in the training was on teamwork; one man working
alone could jeopardize the other five.

We were being trained to fight North Vietnamese,
Vietcong style. Two could play that game, and we were
beating them at it. The body count of Charlie Rangers
showed it. For every one soldier we lost they lost fifty-
five. Not bad.

We were introduced to new weapons that found their
way to Vietnam by who-knows-what means. The 9mm
Swedish K was a stamped-out weapon with a folding
stock, a wooden pistol grip, and a perforated housing for
cooling purposes around its short nine-inch barrel. Due
to its short length and light weight it was a perfect point-
man weapon. But in my opinion it had very little range
and killing power. The American grease gun was just as
bad: the WWII-era .45 caliber machine gun could stop
an elephant in its tracks at close range but was basically
useless at any distance. The .45 caliber Thompson machine gun was also at our disposal but had the same char-
acteristics of the grease gun, and was very heavy. We
also had some twelve-gauge, pump shotguns floating
around the company, but they were rarely used because
of the dense vegetation in our usual AOs. A few twelve-
gauge shotguns were cut down (stocks and barrels), and
used as secondary weapons; their short length, about two
feet, made them easy to fasten to the back of the rucksack. In a close contact, the killing pattern of a sawed-
off shotgun would have been awesome. We had heard that

the modifications were against the Geneva Convention but I don't think that anyone cared. The last unconventional weapon that we were introduced to was the LAW (light antitank weapon). The LAW was a fiberglass, collapsible rocket launcher that was used once then thrown away. I can't imagine a Ranger team taking a LAW to the field, because the vegetation was too dense to fire it effectively, but we were exposed to it.

The training was excellent, and I was beginning to think I was becoming a training junkie. After going through Special Forces school at Bragg, the Ranger school classes were easy.

Classes continued on med-evac (medical evacuation by helicopter), how to get a wounded member of the team out of the jungle. A med-evac helicopter hovered above our outdoor classroom and we were given a demonstration of the jungle penetrator, a contraption designed for emergency pickup of wounded when no landing zones were available or the soldier needed immediate medical attention. Our helicopter pilots must have had brass balls trying to get someone out in these least desirable conditions. They constantly flew into contacts to pull men out, risking their own lives to hostile fire. They have to be credited for saving thousands of lives. However, during my tour, I remember only one time the jungle penetrator was used in Third Platoon, when a team was ambushed by a reinforced squad of NVA. The team had just finished breakfast and started moving out when the NVA initiated contact. During initial blast from the NVA, one soldier was struck in the chest with two AK-47 rounds. The team returned fire and broke contact with the help of helicopter gunships. The jungle penetrator was used to extract the wounded man, and I visited with him in the hospital a few days later. He looked as well as could be expected. Bottom line: he was alive because of the jungle penetrator.

Classes continued at a very fast pace. We ran every morning and every afternoon and had classes between. Rappeling from the wooden tower was my favorite. Rappeling was taught for quick infiltration where a chopper couldn't touch down. We were instructed on tying a Swiss seat with a ten-foot length of rope that was part of every

Ranger's basic load in the field. The rope was tied something like the outline of a diaper. Attached to the rope was a D ring which looked more like an oval. The D ring was hinged on one parallel side and was spring-loaded to snap back into the closed position. A longer rope, the stationary rope attached to the tower or chopper, was put through the spring-loaded hinge into the D ring and wrapped around once. Rappeling backward off the tower was fun. Rappeling forward or face-down, whether it was the first time or the fourteenth, was hairy. The trick to rappeling is to put pressure on the running end, or the end of the rope that's trailing to the ground, only once before you hit the ground. Speed is of the essence in an infil. The shorter time you are in the air the less time you'll be a target. I had it down pat going backward; forward was another story. Watching the ground screaming up at you while you're falling is something else.

Finally Ranger school was just about over except for a few tests and a massive timed run. Everyone graduated in our class and was assigned to platoons of Charlie Company. Myself, Agner, Roguski, and Paxton were going to Third Platoon. Wells and Anderson were going to Fourth Platoon. The only one who graduated with us and later changed platoons was Roguski. He asked to go to the communications platoon after a couple of months. I don't think he liked the six-man LRP concept, preferring to sit on a hill and pull radio relay (X ray).

After fourteen months in the service and constant schooling I was at last going to put my training to use. I was on my way to Phan Thiet and to see just how good I thought I was.

CHAPTER 4

DECEMBER 1969/PHAN THIET
Don Ericson

On my way to Phan Thiet, to Charlie Company, I had time to think. And worry. I had completed Ranger school, but as with any schooling or training nothing prepares you for the actual experience, the terror of going up against a faceless enemy. In this case, an enemy whose height and weight averaged about four foot eleven inches and around one hundred pounds. Yet an enemy who will try to take your life by whatever means necessary. Combat would be the hardest lesson yet. I was twenty years old and the only game I had ever hunted were pheasant or rabbit; now I would be hunting man. I couldn't have had better schools or better training. I was a professional killer by all standards, yet I still had my doubts; this was the NVA's backyard and their game. How can you beat your opponent when they've been weaned on war? How could my fourteen months of training compare? Maybe I was just plain scared.

That probably was the main reason I had volunteered for the Special Forces Recondo School even before finishing Ranger School. Every LRP company, including the Marines, could have a total of two Rangers or RECON men attend Recondo School for each three week training class. I was told I would be contacted with orders when there was a slot open.

Phan Thiet was a quiet fishing village on the South China Sea, totally devoid of any beauty. Its sandy soil was mixed with a reddish clay. I saw no trees in Phan Thiet. The Vietnamese gathered salt in Phan Thiet. When the tide came in, they would flood huge rectangular areas divided by dikes. When the tide went out and the water evaporated they retained the salt. Simple, but it worked.

I arrived in Phan Thiet and reported to the TOC. Sergeant Cheek, the Third Platoon sergeant, was there to greet me. He was a little on the heavy side and stood about five foot ten. As he shook my hand he welcomed me to Third Platoon and the Rangers. He was a friendly fellow with no Stateside military bullshit. He always called me "Irkson" to irritate me. He passed on a few rules: No KP, we didn't have to blouse our boots, and didn't have to wear a hat. However, we still had to salute officers. I could live with those rules. He informed me that I would be on Team 3-1 and headed me in the direction of the barracks.

I went to the tent that I was assigned to and had begun to unpack my belongings when Murphy came in. He was eighteen years old, at the most, with a huge grin on his face.

"You the FNG?" he asked.

I turned and raised the left side of my upper lip and grunted, "Yeah, that's me." He looked me up and down because I was a cherry, the new kid on the block, but seemed to accept me right away. I took the brunt of his cherry jokes in stride and there were a lot of them. Soon the remainder of the team filed in.

"You still got that shit-eating grin on your face, I see, Eric," said Sam Agner whom I'd gone through Ranger school with. "Good to see ya."

"I'm Mike Price, welcome, cherry." Price was the team leader.

Chic Loerra, a Latino from Chicago, grabbed my hand and while shaking it almost off said, "How ya doin', man?"

"Nice to see you again, Eric," said Chip Paxton, whom I'd also attended Ranger school with.

That was Team 3-1. The rest of the day was spent just getting acquainted with them.

The next day Murphy introduced me to a friend, a strange guy who didn't accept anyone right off the bat. I can still see him standing at the other end of the tent with an ear on a necklace around his neck, staring right through me with a scowl on his face. He walked up to me and said, "See what this is, cherry?" He snickered as he stuck the ear in my face.

I looked, raised my right eyebrow, and said, "Yeah, so what!" Because I wouldn't show any disgust, he didn't know how to react. Murphy was rolling on the floor with laughter.

The guy finally came around with a smile, and grunted. "You'll do." There was one Ranger who never forgot an old joke. One day when we were flying back to Pleiku after being exfilled, he slipped an ear to a teammate, who put it between his teeth then turned to face the door gunner, who was oblivious to what was going on. Finally the gunner looked his way, did a double take and pulled back his tinted shield. As soon as he realized what was dangling from the LRP's mouth, the gunner vomited out the door. We thought it was hysterical.

Later that afternoon, I was sitting on my cot getting my rucksack packed when I noticed the beads of sweat dripping off my face and onto the brand-new pack. It had to be one hundred and ten degrees even in the shade of the huge tent. The heat was absorbed by the olive-drab tent. The sides were rolled up but the lack of a breeze made it feel as though I was in an oven. I had only my fatigue pants on, no underwear, no shirt, and no socks, but was sweating like a pig. The last item to go in the rucksack was the claymore mine. Before I put the claymore in the pack I looked at it closely. I was awed by its power. The claymore mine was one of the "neater" inventions of the war. It was lightweight, maybe three pounds, with folding legs that would adjust to about four or five inches in height. The mine was about six by twelve inches, powered by an explosive material called C-4. It was shaped like a shallow crescent, the better to spread the over seven hundred double-O buckshot. The clay-more was a perfect tool for a Ranger ambush. I had seen them demonstrated at a distance, but that afternoon was the first time I had ever held one in my hand. The clay-more had raised letters molded on the fiberglass shell that read, FRONT TOWARD ENEMY. I imagined some peabrain GI had set a mine up backward and detonated it. What a surprise. As I put the claymore in my pack I checked and rechecked my load. Eight dehydrated meals, six one-quart canteens, sixteen extra magazines of M-16 rounds, one hundred rounds for the M-60 machine gun, and my poncho liner. Next I checked my web gear (a pistol belt with suspenders). On it were six M-26 fragmentation grenades, two canisters of CS gas, one field dressing, a lensatic compass, and a willy peter (a white phosphorus grenade). I also carried a Gerber Mark II dagger. As I was finishing up, Murphy came over and said, "How ya doin, cherry?"

"Check it out," I said. Murphy picked up the ruck and shook it up and down a few times. It clicked loudly as the adjustable strap clips banged loudly on the alu-minum frame of the rucksack.

"Tape 'em up," he said, "I don't even want to hear you fart in the woods.

I taped them up and hefted the rucksack on my back. Murphy said, "Jump up and down." I jumped up and down a few times and heard only silence, not a single click. He nodded his approval, but just as he left I was lucky enough to squeak out the meatiest fart I could. Perfect timing. I started laughing, as did the others in the tent who had been watching. Murphy couldn't help but laugh with the rest of us.

I couldn't believe the weight of the rucksack. Fifty pounds at least and the canteens weren't even full. I was ready, though, and I'd be going out the day after tomor-row. I pulled the quick release on the rucksack and one shoulder strap immediately let go and all the weight shifted to my other shoulder. I gently slipped the ruck-sack off and guided it to the ground. What a relief to my back; I felt tons lighter. I shoved the rucksack under my cot and asked Sam Agner if he wanted to go to our little twelve-by-twelve bar in the middle of tent city.

As Sam and I entered the saloon it was almost like a wild-west atmosphere. Rangers who had just come in from the field, still wearing camouflage makeup and smelling like yesterday's garbage, were eyeballing us as if to say who the hell are you coming in here. Undaunted we strode up to the bar and ordered two ten-cent beers. They arrived lukewarm.

Sam and I sat talking about our training with the Rangers and what we expected of the yet unknown missions. Sam had spent his first tour in Vietnam with the 101st Airborne, and got his baptism in the A Shau Valley. I had heard the US took heavy casualties every time we entered it. It was good to know I would be going out to the field on the same team as Sam. My thoughts were seesawing drastically: I wanted to be part of the television war; God, what have I done, these sons of bitches are going to try and kill me. Something inside of me was still looking for adventure, looking for that "living on the edge" feeling, that unexplainable excitation of challenge.

Sam and I had sat there for a couple of more beers when we decided to critique our team leader.

Price was a "pretty boy" who had been there only a few (maybe one) months before we arrived. Third Platoon was way under strength when our class arrived, so most of us were replacements for the Third. Price was the kind of guy who just didn't show emotion. We were skeptical about trusting him as a team leader. We retired early that night.

The morning of my first mission was tense. Not only for Sam, Paxton, and myself—the FNGs—but also, I'm sure, for Price, Murphy, and Chico, the old-timers. They had been out before and they more or less knew what to expect. We (at least I) didn't. In Ranger school we had gone through countless rehearsals, but this was for real.

We were on the chopper pad by 0600 and ready. I was scared but still had huge confidence in myself. Team 3-1 was now on the chopper, and I was sitting on the floor at the edge of the door with my feet dangling outside. At first I felt honored to have this position while the team leader and the RTO sat in the middle of the chopper. Great view; I could see everything from 1500 feet. As we were leaving the city and the surrounding villages I could see the huge lines in the jungle. The closer to the jungle we came, the more distinct the lines became. As we got closer, we could see that they were the results of defoliant runs that had been made with Agent Orange. Five hundred feet wide and as far as you could see from fifteen hundred feet in the air. It was if an artist had painted gray stripes on a green canvas and crisscrossed them from end to end. From the chopper they looked like superhighways; on the ground they were five-hundred-foot-wide absolute dead zones, devoid of plant life.

As we got farther out, it dawned on me that it wasn't an honor having my seat. Shit, I'd be the first one shot if we hit a hot LZ. I inched my butt backward but it was no use. I consoled myself by saying, Whatever hits us probably will kill everyone and not just me. For the rest of my tour in Vietnam I would "ride the door" even as a team leader; the excitement of the ride and the final infiltration were worth it. The wind whipping at you at speeds of ninety to one hundred and twenty miles per hour and the sight of your friends in their chopper one hundred and fifty feet away and fifteen hundred feet in the air are incredible.

On and off during the flight, I had been watching the door gunner nervously fondling his M-60 machine gun. He was now trying to get Price's attention to give him the one-minute signal. That accomplished, Murphy sitting next to me chambered a round in his M-16, and I followed suit. Murphy watched me but said nothing. He was all business, no screwing around now.

The helicopter was making a hard right turn and rapidly descending; the door gunner swiveled his machine gun up and was scanning the LZ. When I looked at Murph, he was smiling; grinning was more like it. I didn't know if my newness made him chuckle or if he just loved the excitement. No question now; he loved the excitement. The chopper touched down, and we were off and headed for the woods.

When we moved through the bush, I often glanced up toward Murph. He moved like a cat; if he broke a twig when he moved it was rare. On point, his eyes never strayed from his intended destination. He moved the team at an incredibly slow pace so as not to miss anything.

Murphy's biggest lesson for me was to never, ever walk trails. Wherever we went, we broke bush; noisier than walking trails, but we'd never walk into an ambush or a base camp. I like to think that Murphy taught me a lot about the woods.

As I sat crouching down next to the largest tree I could find I couldn't believe how quiet the jungle was. Maybe it was just the absence of the helicopter's roar. The heat of the jungle was having an effect and I was already half soaked with sweat. My eyes slowly scanned the jungle, moving everywhere, but my head was stationary. Every move in the jungle was slow and deliberate. Every action was planned ahead; noise, lack of noise, actually, was our ally. My senses would never be any sharper. Every leaf that fell from a tree or that moved in the wind caught my attention as if someone were waving a flag. Every crunch of a leaf or the snap of a twig under a boot sounded like a clap of thunder. To avoid betraying our presence in an area we never wore aftershave or used deodorant on the missions; the only other odor in the jungle was the smell of rotting vegetation. It always amazed me when we could actually smell the enemy. Maybe it had something to do with the NVA's diet of fish and rice. I'm sure they could have smelled us also if they had been looking for us. Our "ace in the hole" was that they almost never knew we were around.

As I glanced over at Price, he was giving the rest of the team the signal to move out. I would be walking fifth position, slack man, for rear security. Sam was walking sixth, rear security. Walking rear security was one of the hardest positions to walk in the six-man procession. Rear security walked backward more often than forward. The slack man always covered rear security when he turned to walk forward. The six-man Ranger teams moved at an extremely slow pace, every team member except the point man covering three hundred and sixty degrees as they moved. With only six men in the jungle any unnoticed detail of enemy presence would surely prove fatal.

Under Price's direction Murphy moved us up mountain after mountain. Mountains that were straight up and down, so steep you'd take one step forward and if you didn't keep your balance, and leaned back too far, the weight of the rucksack would have you sliding back down. That was my initiation to "humping the boonies." No training anywhere could ever get your legs in shape for it.

The mission ran smoothly, no problems. We never even saw a trail.

One of the scariest parts of the mission was my first night in the woods. We made our night halt right before dark and set up our tiny perimeter. Each team member would take a one-hour guard duty until daylight. It didn't make any difference to me; I was so keyed up I didn't think that I could sleep anyway. After I had finished eating, I lay down and dropped off immediately. I must have been worn out from humping those damned mountains.

I awoke two hours later when Sam shook me for my turn at guard duty. It was so dark I couldn't see my hand in front of my face. If there was a moon out, the triple canopy jungle was blocking it. I rationalized that if I couldn't see the gooks, they couldn't see me. As my eyes strained against the darkness, I imagined all sorts of things: What if the NVA could move without making any noise? I countered with, No one could move at night in pitch black without making noise. I won, I knew I was safe. I probably could have had my eyes closed because my ears were fine-tuned to any noise that might occur. I could have heard a pin drop.

Eventually I glanced down at the luminous dial on my watch and noticed that I had already gone five minutes into the next guard duty. I woke Murphy up by gently prodding his back. My shift was done.

Again I was back to mind games. As I covered my head with my poncho-liner blanket, I figured I was safe. When I was a little boy and I was afraid of the dark, I thought that if I covered my head the "Boogieman" wouldn't get me. Talk about false security. There I was a grown man and the trick still worked. I went fast to sleep.

The next morning we were off again, humping the mountains and ridgelines through some of the most rugged terrain I had ever seen. That afternoon we took a break at the top of a mountain and it started to mist. I looked at the valley below and could actually see the rain moving through the valley; it was gorgeous. Within twenty minutes we were soaked to the skin. The rest of the mission was much the same as the first day. The operation was everything I thought it would be. Complete silence in every aspect: if you had to cough, you coughed in a towel, worn around your neck, that we called a drive-on rag; if you had something to say, you whispered; if you heard something, more than likely so did the rest of the team; if someone saw something, more than likely another member saw it also. It was as if all eyes, ears, and noses were in sync with each other. The Ranger-team concept of finding the enemy was extremely good and perfectly suited for the Vietnam war. It took me only one mission to realize I had indeed found my niche in the Rangers; life was a challenge again.

The only anxious moment of the mission was the exfil, when the team was being extracted from the field. A single B-40 rocket round and we'd all be history, six-man team, four-man chopper crew. All went well this time out.

Our team wouldn't go out for another four days. The pressure was too great to risk putting teams in the field too frequently; every minute the men were in the field, every sense and every nerve was stretched or functioning to the maximum.

When we arrived back at our tent in Phan Thiet, Murph gave me a compliment by saying, "Not bad." I guessed I had passed the test. I took a shower and scraped the greasepaint off my face. I returned to the tent and lay on my cot completely drained. I lit a cigarette and lay back. I was already worrying about the many missions I'd have to pull. As I snuffed out my cigarette in the sand that was the floor of our tent, someone put on a cassette of Blood, Sweat, and Tears. The last song I heard was "God Bless the Child" as I drifted off into a deep sleep.

The next morning when I awoke, every joint in my body was hurting. After breakfast when I arrived back at the tent five new guys were standing in front of it. They had been assigned to Third Platoon. God, they looked pathetic. Did I really look that bad when I arrived just a short time ago? In the middle of the cherries stood a fellow who was about six foot two and looked like a stick man. His name was Richard Rath. He and I would become the best of friends.

Over the next few weeks we talked about everything.

He was from Ohio; his father died when he was small and he was raised by his mother. It was obvious he had led a sheltered life and thirsted for adventure. I told him that he had certainly found the right unit for adventure. Rath was straight-arrow at that time and would become in my opinion, the best hunter in the company. He had unbelievable patience and stamina. Probably his most important asset in a unit like Charlie Company was that he pursued the company's hunter-killer missions with great zeal. He was an excellent marksman; and by the time he left 'Nam he probably had a personal body count of twenty or so, all head shots. Best of all, Rath was going to be on 3-1 because Paxton was being shifted to team 3-3.

After a few missions with Price I realized that he never got excited about an infil and never got excited about where the NVA might be. He never showed any emotion. Sam and I talked about how Price was running the show. We talked about how we would run missions: We wouldn't hump the straight-up mountains or run parallel just off the ridgelines. We'd go right to the "blue lines" (creeks, streams, anything with water) where the NVA were. Everyone needed water to live and they were no different. We went on six missions with Price as the team leader and made zero contacts. That record has to say something about his tactics in the woods. After that Price received orders assigning him to the rear for the time being.

Sam was to be the new team leader and that couldn't have made me happier.

We were going out: we had breakfast and went back to the tent and cammied up. Sergeant Cheek came in and hollered, "Be at the helipad in twenty minutes."

It was 0600 and we were ready. We hefted our ruck-sacks, heavy suckers, and headed for the chopper. The pilots were already making preflight checks, door gunner and crew chief bullshitting on the side. We arrived and sat down on the perforated steel-plate helipad. No sooner had we sat down than the pilot started the turbines. Naturally. The rucks now weighed sixty pounds, and any break with the weight off our backs was a blessing.

We were barely loaded in the chopper when the damn bird leapt forward and the village of Phan Thiet sped by.

As the chopper was nearing the LZ, we all chambered a round in our weapons. Our eyes were scanning the woodline as the Huey was at treetop level.

Then the front of the chopper was arching back, we were below treetop level, and the butterflies were fluttering in my stomach. It was an extremely hard landing; the chopper bounced, and then bounced again. We were off in seconds. As I ran forward to the woodline, I stumbled and fell and the goddamn ruck, as heavy as it was rode up my back and pushed my face into the brush and dirt. Sam turned and looked, shaking his head, and was probably thinking to himself, You asshole.

Unscratched but truly embarrassed, I took my position in our tiny three-hundred-and-sixty-degree perimeter. I thought to myself, Why the fuck should I be embarrassed, I'm sure that all of these guys have made their fair share of mistakes. Sure, I was scared but they probably were scared, too. I was off the chopper and relieved. As far as I was concerned, the helicopter infil was the deadliest part of our mission. For those brief few seconds when the helicopter is coming in, you are most vulnerable. You're like a sitting duck in a multimillion-dollar machine. One RPG or a B-40 rocket could snuff you in seconds.

Rath made commo check and we were off through the woods. We snaked up the hills and valleys, crossed streams and creeks, until finally we were paralleling a huge mountain with an eighteen-inch trail running its length. It was under a perfect cover of triple-canopy jungle. Completely invisible from the air. It would have been impossible to see on Sam's visual reconnaissance (VR) the day before. The triple canopy prevented a lot of low brush from growing because it blocked the sunlight, so the ground beneath a triple-canopy forest was a perfect area for a high-speed trail.

I was crouched next to Sam as he discussed an ambush site with the assistant team leader and the rest of the team watched the perimeter. They agreed that it was too open and it had no cover, but before another word was spoken, Chico was blasting away with his M-16. Sam and I dove for the same spot on the ground and collided. We must have looked like two of the Three Stooges as we hit the ground. The team was now firing blind three hundred and sixty degrees to protect our tiny perimeter. Firing stopped. Sam signaled Chico to his position and said, "What happened?"

Chico responded in his Chicago Latino accent, "I saw seven, but I didn't chute cuz I thought they were ARVNs."

"Oh fuck! A body count of seven would have been great," I said under my breath.

Chico was really embarrassed and went back to his position. We called in the contact and an exfil; our mission had been compromised.

When we were back at camp, I was calming down while I pounded down a few beers and shot the bull with Murphy and Giossi. I was a juicer, but that night Murph said, "Come over here and try some of this."

I thought to myself about the first time I had tried marijuana with Red. "What the hell, it can't kill me."

The joint laid me right out; I don't think that I came down from that for two days. I was out, paralyzed. Only later did I find out that the joint had been laced with opium. The drugs went hand and glove with the times. "Purple Haze" by Jimi Hendrix was played constantly, not only by the heads but by the juicers; it seemed to go with the lifestyle and the killing. The music itself was like a drug.

In January, 1970, after about ten missions with Charlie Company, orders for recondo school came down, and I was to leave for Nha Trang via An Khe in a few days. Just another school, but I was looking forward to further training that just might save my life.

NOVEMBER 1969/BONG SON
John L. Rotundo

We arrived back at LZ North English on the second of November and were told to wait for our orders, as they should be coming "any day now." Oddly enough, just over a week later they arrived. I was going to First Pla-

toon of Dog Company, 4th Battalion, located about
twelve miles north of LZ North English in the An Doa
Valley.

On November 12 I said good-bye to my friends at LZ
North English, as I and two others from the school
boarded the Huey for the ride to our new home. Within
twenty minutes we were touching down at the helipad
just outside First Platoon's perimeter. Two grunts came
out to fetch the mail, rations, and us. We helped them
carry the mail and the rations back inside the concertina
wire. As we put the cases down, we were met by an
individual clothed in a white bedsheet. He pounded his
right fist to his chest as we neared and exclaimed, "Hail
Killecrates," and walked away. Before we could figure
out the greeting, the lieutenant came out of his hootch,
introduced himself, and welcomed the three new
"spoons" (cooks) to his platoon.

"Beg your pardon, sir, but I'm not a spoon. I was an
RTO (radiotelephone operator)," I said.

"Well, all the better," was his reply, and we were
divided among the platoon's various squads.

It didn't take long for the word to spread throughout
the perimeter that the platoon had a new cherry to hump
the radio on patrols. We spent the rest of the day meeting
other members of the platoon, learning the platoon's perimeter, individual fields of fire, escape and evasion
routes, as well as a general rundown of what we did.

Our job was to protect the village that was near our
perimeter, and by having a position as highly visible as
we were, it was seen as a deterrent to dissuade the local
VC from making house calls to steal rice or collect taxes.
We patrolled during the day and set up ambushes at
night, hoping to catch the VC entering or leaving the
village. We also pulled med-caps during which the platoon medic would take care of the villagers who were
sick or hurt.

On every med-cap a little girl from the village showed up
to complain about her stomach. She was about seven and a
real beauty. Each time Doc went through the motions of
giving her an exam and then gave her a little blue pill. Her
eyes always opened wide as she swallowed. The pill had a
sugar coating, and it was a real treat for the little girl.

There were three squads in the platoon and we alternated going on patrol and pulling "Hawks," night ambushes. The platoon had twenty-two people and each squad had six people assigned. The remaining four were the lieutenant, his RTO, and two others. When we were not on patrol we got up at 0600 and had a breakfast of C rations or LRPs. (A freeze-dried food pouch that was extremely lightweight. It got its name from the people who were supposed to travel with it—long range patrollers.) We experimented with different concoctions of Cs and LRPs. Once Doc made me a meal combining beef hash, beans and franks, beef with spiced sauce, and chili sauce. It doesn't sound very appetizing, but it hit the spot at the time. After eating breakfast we pulled a couple of hours' watch on the bunker. When our watch ended we would sleep, write letters, read, or dig a cat-hole latrine. It beat having to burn shit. At night, if we were in, we ate supper and then climbed up on the bunker for guard duty.

When out on patrol, the squad worked an area a couple of hundred meters from the perimeter hoping to catch some Charlies, but no dice. Since the perimeter was surrounded by rice paddies, we had to walk the dikes to keep our feet from becoming thoroughly soaked. On the way back, we never took the same dike that we had taken out. Even though ours was a friendly, "pacified" village, Bin Dinh Province had a history of being very sympathetic to the VC, so we never took chances. We departed the perimeter as the sun was going down, moved a couple hundred meters, set up and listened until it became dark, then moved a couple of hundred meters to our actual destination for the evening's ambush, making sure that everybody was in position, and putting out the claymores. All we could do then was sit and wait, no smoking or talking, just the the hourly sit-reps (situation reports) to the platoon to let them know we were all right. Our patrols and ambushes weren't bringing any results, and I wondered if maybe Charlie had gone home until it dawned on me that this was his home.

One afternoon we were on patrol when I heard explosions in the next valley. We stopped to look as the Air Force was working out with their Phantoms. When I heard their 20mm Vulcan cannons, I thought they sounded like an elephant fart. *Bbbbbrrrrraaaaattttttt*. The Phantoms were camouflage-green and -tan and were unbelievable to watch. They streaked in at their targets with amazing agility, dropped their loads, and then they'd be gone with a roar. I could imagine just the sight of a Phantom scaring Charlie to death.

A few nights later we were back at the perimeter when the word was passed that Stinger would be working out in the valley just to the west of us. Stinger was a converted Air Force C-119, flying boxcar, and although it was too far away to hear the miniguns work out, the continuous streams of red sweeping back and forth were something to behold. Every fifth round was a tracer, and Stinger could spew anywhere from 2,000 to 6,000 rounds a minute in a devastating line of death.

By late November it was getting cold enough in the valley to see your breath, and because it was still the rainy season, life could get a bit miserable. Every once in a while I thought of the guys back at LZ North English, stuffing themselves at dinner, them climbing into a soft bed to sleep. Yet I was still glad I had decided to leave it behind. Even though I was freezing my tail off at night, being a grunt was what I wanted to do.

For Thanksgiving Day a chopper brought us turkey, dressing, rolls, and cranberry sauce. They even brought us beer and soda rations. The food had cooled a bit by the time we got to it, but it was the thought that counted, and in spite of its not being hot, it wasn't bad. Since I had lost my taste for beer, I traded my beer ration for extra soda.

Thanksgiving afternoon we had an operation, and I went with the first squad up a hill while the rest of the platoon swept the area to flush out any gooks. About twenty minutes after we were in place the machine gunner blew his cookies all over the hill, not once but twice. Then upon returning, we had to string concertina wire. Since coming down from the hill my stomach had felt a bit queasy, and I was getting a headache, so when we finished I went to see Doc, who suggested I get some sleep. Of twenty-two men in the platoon, ten got sick that night. Happy Thanksgiving.

The next morning we were to be a blocking force while another platoon swept VC in our direction. As we were moving out to get into position, I was walking rear security, looking for any movement to our rear, when we came across a small stream. To cross it we had to use a shaky bridge made of old logs and boards. The entire platoon crossed as I kept my eyes to our rear covering their movement. After the platoon was across, it was my turn. I moved out, putting my right foot on the bridge as I stepped down with my left foot . . . with a *crack*, the board snapped in two, one piece falling into the water and the other flying up and catching me in the mouth. The impact knocked me back a step, but except for seeing stars for a few minutes, and the fact that my lips swelled to twice their normal size, I was all right.

We moved to our blocking position and waited, but the sweeping platoon could not make contact, so later in the day we moved back to the platoon perimeter. Following our standard procedure, we took a different way back, returning to the stream two hundred meters above where we had crossed before. This time we were to cross by way of a single log. I was still walking rear security when the platoon crossed the log. Then it was my turn and the platoon was covering my crossing. As I crossed, I looked down at the water rushing below me and thought to myself, What if I fell in . . . I wonder how deep it is? Two seconds later I reached out for a limb and lost my footing, swung under the log like a monkey, and *splash*! Waterborne!

The current was strong and I was making good time downstream, but the weight of my equipment kept pulling me under. Between gasps for air, I spotted a large tree limb, grabbed it, and swung myself around enough to get out of the current. From that position I could take off the my equipment and throw it on the bank. However, my helmet and rifle were on their way downstream somewhere. The platoon formed around me as two men tied ropes to trees then joined me in the water. One of them was a new guy in the platoon named O'Dougheraty. He was not new to Vietnam, for he was on his second tour with the Herd. I had watched him on ambushes and patrols. Although he was close to six feet tall and quite muscular, he moved silently through the woods. With the rope tied to a tree and the other end tied around their waists my buddies continued going under the water looking for my rifle and helmet. After about an hour O'Dougheraty came up with my helmet, but there was no sign of my rifle. The three of us were soaked, so another squad relieved us as we went back to the perimeter to dry off.

I caught quite a bit of ribbing about my excursion in the water, and the only thing that saved me any more embarrassment was that not only had my girlfriend sent me a four-foot artificial Christmas tree, complete with trimmings, but also that I was "adopted" by my church back home which got me a few good write-ups in the weekly bulletin. One of the parishioners was a grade-school teacher and her class sent me orders to play Santa Claus with four gigantic goody boxes stuffed with food and magazines. In the middle of the An Doa Valley sat a Christmas tree with boxes and boxes of goodies under it, just waiting for Christmas Day to roll around.

Everything was beginning to work out and I really felt that I had been accepted by the platoon. I was handling myself pretty well on patrols and ambushes, moving with the best of them, and generally had my shit together when on December 12 the lieutenant walked over to my hootch and told me to pack my gear. I was wanted in the rear for something but he couldn't tell for what, so when the resupply chopper came in I hopped on it for the short ride to LZ North English.

When I reported to the orderly room, I was told that my orders for the Rangers had finally come through. I'd thought that was a great idea, back in September when I had volunteered, but that had been three months ago, and I had a home with the Herd now.

"Top, just tell them I changed my mind," I said to the first sergeant.

"It's not that easy," Top said. "You've got to go to An Khe and personally tell them."

So on December 16 I found myself in the orderly room of Charlie Rangers at An Khe. With me was another PFC from the Herd, a guy named Norton, who, like me, had volunteered for the Rangers when he came into the country. Like me he had found a home in the Herd, and was told to go to An Khe and personally tell the Rangers he had no desire to serve with them.

The first sergeant called us into his office and we both told him we no longer wanted to be Rangers. He looked at us both, shrugged his shoulders, and said "Okay, no hard feelings."

Norton and I looked at each other for a moment, then back to the first sergeant.

"We'll cut orders and send you back," was all the first sergeant said.

Not knowing whether to believe him or not, Norton and I looked at each other again. As we left the orderly room we expected to get assigned to all the rotten details but we didn't. In fact the Rangers treated us just like one of their own. We had to clean weapons and pulled guard duty two hours a day, but for the most part the Rangers left us alone. We *knew* something was wrong; the army doesn't treat people that way.

We stayed in barracks with real bunks and ate in the mess hall with the only Rangers at An Khe at the time: the first sergeant, a couple of clerks, the instructors at the Ranger school, and the ten or so students who were going through the course.

As the clerk in the orderly room said we'd be back with the Herd in "a week or less," we decided to make the most of it. Norton was originally from California, stood about five foot eight, had a slender frame, and he didn't talk much. He let his actions speak for themselves.

During the day we'd go to the PX after we had finished whatever detail we had. One detail we didn't have to worry about was burning shit since they had the local Vietnamese do it. In the evening we'd watch a movie or just shoot the breeze with each other or with those going through the two-week Ranger course.

One of those going through the school was a fellow named Alister Scott who everyone called Scotty. Scotty was a British citizen who was as close to a professional soldier that you'll ever find. He had been in the British Army and seen duty in the Cyprus flare-up. After getting out of the British Army he came to the US and enlisted in the Marine Corps. He pulled a tour in 'Nam with the

Marines and got out. I guess civilian life didn't appeal to Scotty, because he enlisted in the Army and was going through the Ranger school in An Khe.

Scotty was a friendly individual who had no trouble drawing a crowd when he talked about his experiences. He never bragged about himself. Rather, he'd put things in their proper perspective. Scotty was six feet tall, with close-cropped red hair, and was very, very muscular.

When Scotty talked about a contact, his voice could rise just a little bit as his eyes would widen and he'd put his face close to the person he was talking to. When describing how a dead gook got killed, his favorite expression was, "I guess you could say he left his cake out in the rain, huh, pal?" his face six inches from the listener. But Scotty wasn't a bullshitter. He definitely had his shit together, and would prove it over the course of the next year.

As 1969 drew to a close, Norton and I were still awaiting orders sending us back to the Herd but nothing had come down.

As the current Ranger class was finishing up, Norton and I talked to one another about staying on. The Rangers had treated us well during the two weeks we stayed and seemed to avoid the normal Army harassment. And we had watched men train for two weeks and it got into our blood.

We proceeded to the orderly room and went to Top's office.

"Top, we changed our minds, we want to stay."

Top looked as us and said, "I thought you both had a home with the Herd?"

"That was bullshit, Top, we really want to stay."

"Well, if that's what you really want, I'll cut the orders. The next class doesn't start for over a week and I'd suggest you try and get into shape. Now get out of here." He waved us away.

Now all we had to do was to wait for the next class to start.

CHAPTER 5

JANUARY–FEBRUARY 1970—
RANGER SCHOOL/AN KHE

John L. Rotundo

The first day of Ranger school was memorable. Up at 0530, and in the next forty-five minutes we did just about every exercise you can name, plus some others that I think Culeford made up for us. After breakfast we again assembled at the training area. In the middle of the training area a platform rose forty feet above the ground. On one side of it was a skid from a chopper while the other was a wooden wall.

As Culeford worked into his orientation, his voice grew louder until he was nearly screaming at us.

"You're all a bunch of pussies!" he repeated. "You'll never become Rangers because you don't have what what it takes." We candidates stood at parade rest as he continued his verbal attack.

"It takes total dedication and discipline to be able to think and act as one. Most of you don't, and I mean *don't*, have what it takes. You think just because you're Airborne and can jump out of a plane that you can take anything, but you ain't seen nothing yet." He paused for a minute and stared at us, then continued. "For the few of you that do make it out of here can then, and only then, call yourselves Rangers!''

With his last words concussion grenades, smoke grenades, artillery simulators, and M-16s unexpectedly opened up near the platform. Two Rangers dressed in camouflage fatigues, faces cammied up, carrying rucksacks, flew over the top of the platform, rappeling down face-first while firing M-16s and yelling at the top of their lungs.

We stood watching in awe as the adrenaline in our bodies began pumping.

The fifteen-day school was designed to teach us how to read a map, patrolling methods, and procedures of a six-man Ranger team, including hand signals and other methods of silently communicating with each other. We would also learn methods of insertion and the method of extraction, how to make a Swiss seat and a German seat with our ropes, as well as the different types of ambush, how to read a trail, and, of course, PT. Besides early morning runs, we double-timed everywhere while we were in the training area. It was like being back in jump school.

There was a large rock painted yellow a hundred meters from where we trained, and whenever someone screwed up in training he had to ''Hit the Rock.'' That meant double-timing (was there any other way?) to the rock, assuming the push-up position with feet elevated on the rock, and knocking out ten push-ups. Actually it was eleven, because as you were doing them you had to count out loud; after number ten you did ''One for Airborne Ranger in the Sky,'' and double-timed back.

On Tuesday, the second day of training, we fell out with weapons, web gear, and a sandbag-weighted rucksack, and ran a mile. When we finished the run, we dropped our rucksacks and moved forty meters away, then low-crawled to retrieve them.

''Keep your asses *down*!'' Culeford shouted.

Of course, if you weren't low enough to please him, you had to ''Hit the Rock'' then low-crawl all over again. After the crawl, we did push-ups in mud puddles, and ended the day learning how to walk and crawl silently in water. Everything about a Ranger mission depended upon silence, and we couldn't maintain silence by splashing in water; we were taught to slowly pick up one foot from the water and slowly and carefully put it back in, one step at a time. Not only did it not make noise, but it cut down the rippling of the water. The same went for crawling in the water, slowly and deliberately, each movement designed to slow progress through the water silently and without disturbing it enough to draw attention. One of the most important things I noticed was that Culeford and the other cadre went in for those water exercises with us.

The next two days were spent in the classroom, where our map-reading skills were honed.

"Remember," Culeford would say, "a Ranger never gets lost, temporarily misoriented maybe, but never lost."

In the classroom we worked on understanding maps and on the identification of terrain features. The instructors stressed the importance of always knowing where you were on a map. A very simple method was by using back azimuth. There are three hundred and sixty degrees in a circle and a compass is divided into these degrees. By identifying two prominent terrain features a person would sight his compass in on one of these features. A glance at the compass would give him a reading in degrees. If the reading was over 180 degrees, you would subtract 180 degrees. You then sighted in on the other terrain feature and shot an azimuth on that. If the reading was under 180 degrees you would add 180 degrees to that figure. Once you had those figures, you oriented the map on the ground, making sure north was in fact north. From your first reading you drew a line from your first sighting back toward where you thought you were. You then did the same thing with your second sighting. Where the lines intersected was where you were. That was the simple part; the hard part was identifying the correct terrain features, and that's where the map reading really became important.

The training really paid off when we had to navigate a night compass course, that is, to find marked signs in the woods at night going up and down hills. All without getting lost. A few of us did get "temporarily misoriented," but we all made it.

The next day we learned how to rappel and it became one of our favorite activities at the school. Of course, the first time we tried, we were scared, but once we got the hang of it, it was fairly easy and a lot of fun. We would be required to carry a rope on our missions, and one of the reasons was because it might be necessary to conduct an insertion by rappeling in. We learned how to make a German seat, a configuration of the rope going around the legs and waist. Tied properly you had a double loop in your belt area. A snap-link was inserted and you were ready to try rappeling. The rope you would rappel from was put through your snap-link. If you were right-handed, you took more rope from your left side and put it under the snap-link and through a second time. This would help slow your descent. The rope would be anchored on one end with the other being dropped to the ground. As I'm right-handed, my left hand would control the rope and my right hand would become my braking hand. Wearing a glove on your braking hand was a necessity to prevent rope burns.

Once in position you leaned your body backward, right hand gripping the rope tighter around your back. On command you jumped backward and let up a little on the grip from your braking hand. Your rate of descent would be controlled by the pressure you applied with your braking hand. The first time you try it from the platform you're lucky to clear the platform, because you brake right away. Falling backward from forty feet in the air has a tendency to scare you.

As we dangled in the air the instructors coached us to let up on the brake and let ourselves fall a bit more before braking again, till we were on the ground. Since we screwed up the first time we all had to Hit the Rock, and double-time back before we could try again. The second time we all did better, but it wasn't till our fourth or fifth time that we all got comfortable and began looking like we knew what we were doing.

As we perfected our rappeling techniques, the instructors had us try rappeling face-first. It's hairy in the beginning but the secret is to let your body lean far enough forward when leaping and to avoid braking with your hands too quickly or too hard. The first time the ground rushes up to your face, the natural reflex is to stop, so you brake too hard and too quickly. When that happens your legs flip up and you end up suspended upside down. But after three or four tries we began to gain confidence. So much so that after a few more tries we began racing each other down the wall . . . face first.

After lunch we went back to the platform with our gear, including rucksacks, and practiced rappeling again along with climbing a rope ladder up one side of the platform and down the other. All those push-ups were paying off.

The next week we were taught the methods of patrolling in a six-man Ranger team. The team would walk in a file, one man behind the other. The *point man* usually carried an M-16 or a CAR-15. The CAR-15 was a modified M-16 with a retractable stock and a shorter barrel. Many people who went to the woods found the CAR-15 had a tendency to jam when firing, so they were usually left to the officers and REMFs. The *slack man* was number two in line. His job was almost that of another point man, as he had to be able to notice anything the point man missed. The team leader normally walked third because he could control the team best by being in the middle. The fourth man was the radiotelephone operator (RTO) and was never more than a few meters from the team leader. Just in case. The fifth man in line was the one who carried the thump gun, a basic M-79 40mm grenade launcher with the front sight removed and the barrel and stock sawed down to around 22 inches total length. Modifying the M-79 in this manner might decrease its effective range, but most of our contacts were within fifty meters of our positions, so maximum effective range didn't matter. Whoever carried the thump gun humped it tied to his rucksack, as it was not his primary weapon (the M-16 was), but the man still had to carry the ammo.

We also sawed the barrel off the M-60 machine guns just behind the front sight, so that the man carrying it wasn't always being caught up in vines, which could make noise as he was trying to get loose. Also, when fired with the front sight and flash suppressor removed, the M-60 put out one hell of a flash, not to mention the bark. With the flash created by the gun and the noise generated by its modification, the gooks didn't stick around long enough to find out who was shooting at them, because normally only a company-size unit would carry anything that big to the woods.

Throughout this part of the training we learned how to walk artillery and how to direct gunships. Artillery was hairy since there was always a chance of a "short round" landing on your own position, so we were instructed never to put ourselves between the guns and the target. Besides, when you're in contact it's tough to call artillery that close to your position without getting some of that shit falling on you. Helicopter gunships were by far the preferred method of direct support, because you could work them almost at your feet and still get out unscratched.

Different types of ambushes were addressed next. There were three basic types. A U-shaped, so named because it's designed to lure the enemy into the closed end where both their flanks will catch fire as well as fire coming from the front. This wasn't practical to a six-man operation, and was seen only by line companies for the most part. Usually on the receiving end.

The L-shaped ambush was named because it was shaped like the letter L. It would be set when ambushing a trail that made a ninety-degree turn, with Rangers on both the horizontal and vertical part of the imaginary letter.

The last of the basic ambushes was the linear, or line ambush. All that was called for here was setting the people up in a line of fire, facing the kill zone.

"No matter what type of ambush you set up in, remember you've got to have cover and concealment," Culeford said many times.

Cover meant something to protect you from incoming rounds, like a tree or some large rocks. Concealment meant you were effectively hidden from the enemy, either in high grass or other vegetation. You could be concealed and pull off your ambush, but without adequate cover you were leaving yourself open to incoming fire. You could have excellent cover, but the cover might block the vision that was needed to spring an effective ambush.

Culeford went on to tell us that our mission was to kill

gooks but not at the expense of getting one of our own killed in the process. A dead gook just wasn't worth the loss of a Ranger.

During the first week the instructors only talked about silence in the woods, but by the second week, we went out in a wooded area and tried it. It's tough to see a dry leaf on the ground and keep yourself from crunching it. We learned how to walk slowly and very quietly behind one another, planting one foot down, listening, and then raising the other. Low branches were moved by the point man's free hand and passed to the slack man, who in turn passed it back. That eliminated the chance of a branch's flying back and slapping someone, thereby making unnecessary noise. Sitting down was a deliberate movement, as you couldn't just park your butt anywhere. You had to look for a spot and ease yourself into position. Coughing or sneezing was done by putting the mouth into the crook of your arm to suppress the noise. If the team leader wanted someone's attention he got it by quietly snapping his fingers so that nobody outside a ten-foot area could hear it. Back in the classroom we learned the ins and outs of the actual mission.

The day before the mission, the team leader, sometimes the assistant team leader, and the lieutenant who would direct the UH-1D Hueys (called "slicks") from the back seat of an O-1 Bird Dog observation plane, would do a visual reconnaissance (VR) of the area the teams were going to be inserted in. The slick would fly over and pass the area so as not to give any indication to anybody on the ground that it was to be visited the next day. During the VR, maps were checked to mark any predominating features and any trails or streams were noted. Insertion and proposed extraction LZs were also marked at this time. After returning from the VR, the team leader would meet with the entire team to show them the area of operation (AO), primary LZ, proposed route of march, and any trails or streams that had been noted.

The normal mission was four days' length; it was felt that any longer and the troops' concentration wouldn't be sharp enough; fatigue and sloppiness might lead to compromise. If no contact was made after four days, the team was extracted. Since Charlie Rangers' mission was to make contact, most team leaders naturally looked for an area in which gooks would normally be found, then set up an ambush and blew them away.

During the briefing, the team leader would address the team on any special equipment that might be required, such as an M-60 machine gun or electronic sensors that would signal movement after the team departed. Sometimes the team carried a "sausage roll," three or four pounds of C-4 plastic explosive rolled up tightly in a burlap bag, then wrapped even tighter with det cord to make sure it stayed compressed. A blasting cap was also carried with the end crimped to make a slow-burning fuse. The length of the fuse determined the impact time. The sausage rolls were, in effect, shaped charges used to blow down small trees to make an LZ if needed.

Next item on the team leaders' briefing was the basic equipment that each member was to carry. Twenty magazines per person (minimum for the M-16s), at least one claymore mine, four fragmentation grenades, smoke and CS grenades, enough food and water to last at least four days, poncho liner, rope, and a first aid pouch. In addition the team leader carried a strobe light, signal mirror, a pen flare, and a signal panel, along with a vial of morphine.

The pace of training never slackened. By Wednesday of the second week we were practicing the immediate-action drill: the point man spots the enemy coming toward him but it's too close to set up a hasty ambush, so the point man opens fire on "rock-'n'-roll" (full automatic) while the rest of the team hits the deck, facing forward and slightly outward. After the point man expends his magazines he retreats to the rear of the team. As soon as the point man passes the slack man, the slack man empties his magazine in the same direction that the point man was shooting. This continues until the entire team has fired a magazine, then the team leader calls for a rally point somewhere to the rear, the team breaks contact, and hauls ass to the rally point. This is an excellent drill and obviously is designed to confuse the enemy, as he is still receiving fire while the team is making its getaway. After we practiced the drill for the umpteenth time, we did it with live ammo, and as much of a cluster fuck as this sounds, none of us shot each other.

On the last morning of school, we had to run the two-mile course with all our equipment (about seventy pounds) in twenty-four minutes or be dropped from the course. It was just after 0530 when we started, and even though we had been running everywhere for two weeks, I'm here to tell you this can kick your ass. I kept up with the group for the first half mile or so but began falling back till I was the last one.

Culeford was in a jeep behind us and kept pulling up next to me asking if I wanted to quit. I didn't say a word to him but in my mind I was thinking, Fuck you, asshole, I ain't quitting. It was then I remembered a book about the 101st Airborne in World War II. It was titled *Currahhe* and the author described how he made it through jump school and all the running they did by just putting one foot in front of the other while letting his mind wander to get it off the pain in his feet. That's exactly what I began doing, just putting one foot in front of the other while letting my mind drift off. And where did it go off to? Basic training at Fort Knox and the cadence we sang as we were running PT:

> I want to be an Airborne Ranger
> I want to live a life of danger
> I want to go to Vietnam
> I want to kill the Viet cong . . .

As I was thinking of this, I picked up pace, so much so that after a mile and a half I caught up with a sergeant who was in the class with us. As I caught him and began to pass, he picked up his pace. On and on we jockeyed for position, neither one saying a word but both of us knowing what was going through the other's mind. It became personal. My eyes were fixed on the ground in front of me and my stomach began to tighten as I reached down to wherever it is you reach down, and pushed myself more.

The sergeant was built about like me, and the more I poured it on the more I hurt. My gratification was in knowing the other guy was hurting as much as I was, and that we had come too far to give up now. He would start to pass me, and I would push myself not only to catch him but to pass him, and every time I succeeded he would come back, catch me, and pass me. We forgot about the overall purpose of the run; it became a gut-wrenching ego trip for the two of us.

Suddenly, out of nowhere it seemed, the finish line loomed. I'd be damned if he was going to beat me, so with a final burst of energy I kicked out. He obviously felt the same way because we kept pace with one another the last hundred meters or so as we crossed the finish line at the same time. One of the cadre called out "Nineteen minutes."

As we slowed to a trot I noticed that not all of the class was waiting for us. I turned around in time to see two men cross the finish line. Somewhere along the way we had passed them, but I had been too caught up in our personal battle to even notice. Trying to catch our breath, we stood and stared at one another, neither saying a word but each knowing what he had done to the other. We were two individuals pushing one another, two individuals thinking and acting as one, two individuals becoming Rangers. We made it!

While I was waiting transportation to Phan Thiet to join the rest of the company, one of the cooks asked me if I wanted some company while in Phan Thiet. Then he walked behind the mess hall. When he returned he was carrying Rat, your basic mutt, a mixed breed with the nose of a German shepherd and the curled tail that one found on all Vietnamese dogs. I had played a bit with Rat while at An Khe but never dreamed that she would be my companion. I remembered the day that the cook introduced her to me. It seemed when she was born she resembled a rat so much that's how she got her name. Now I was going to be looking out for her.

That evening while drinking a few beers with the other new Rangers, I spotted a familiar-looking character. It was my old buddy, Don, the guy that I had met at Cha Rang Valley during the Herd's jungle school. Don had been with the Rangers since November and was already

on his way to recondo school, which was conducted by
the Special Forces in Nha Trang.

We sat around talking with one another, catching up
on each other's activities for the past months. As darkness neared we moved to the outdoor theater and rolled
with laughter watching Zero Mostel and Gene Wilder in
The Producers. To this day, whenever the movie is
shown, I remember the two of us watching it, each with
a beer in his hand and enjoying every minute of it.

Saturday morning Rat and I went to the airfield to take
the Caribou down to Phan Thiet, but there was too much
weight already on board, so Rat, myself, and a few others would have to wait till the next day for a flight. We
went back to the Ranger compound and played the waiting game once again.

That night I heard some disturbing news. First of all,
my old home, LZ North English, had been mortared a
few nights earlier. One of the guys I hung around with
in the commo platoon was killed by the mortar attack
along with some others, including the 4th Battalion's XO.
I also heard that they had found the M-16 that I had lost
when I fell into the stream in November. Unfortunately
they found it on a POW.

The next morning Rat, myself, and the others who had
been bumped boarded the Caribou and flew to Phan
Thiet. After four months in-country, I was finally going
to see war firsthand.

As we were airborne, a song I used to hear all the time
at LZ North English kept going through my head. It was
by Blood, Sweat, and Tears. "And when I die . . . and
when I'm dead, dead, and gone . . . there'll be one child
born in this world to carry on . . . to carry on . . ."

JANUARY–FEBRUARY 1970—RECONDO SCHOOL / NHA TRANG
Don Ericson

After about a month with Charlie Company, I requested to attend recondo school. Orders were slow coming down but they did finally arrive. I left Phan Thiet a little apprehensive, but confident that I could put up with any bullshit, mental or physical, that the 5th Special Forces could throw at me.

The 5th Special Forces ran the recondo school in Nha Trang, a beautiful city with georgeous beaches on the South China Sea. I checked with the clerk in charge and he assigned me to a wood-and-metal-roofed building (good quarters by the standards that I was used to) and told me to wait for further instructions from one of the cadre.

Recondo school consisted of three weeks of training. The first week, phase one: techniques, map reading, first aid, and communications. The first aid class required each student to draw blood with a syringe. I drew blood from a fellow student fairly easily by tapping his vein first. Thank God, his vein came right up. The fellow chosen to draw my blood was less fortunate, however. He inserted the needle in the general direction and started angling around. Luckily I have a strong stomach, because it took him twenty seconds of probing to find the vein. Our instructor figured that if we could take blood then we could also find the vein to give serum albumin, a blood supplement carried by team leaders.

Every day started with PT, then classes followed; then lunch, followed by more classes. The classes were easy because they were an extension of what we had covered in Ranger school. The physical conditioning, however, running with full equipment, was making raw meat out of my back. At the end of phase one we had to take a fifty-yard swimming test. I had it made, for I was always a strong swimmer and the water felt great.

After the first week of classes, the instructors weeded out the poorly motivated students. Recondo school had an attrition rate of about sixty percent.

When phase two started, things were less hectic. After physical training and rope climbing, the choppers were next. I had learned to rappel in Ranger school, but that had been from a thirty-foot tower, not out of a chopper. The chopper was hovering one hundred feet above ground and the instructor tapped me on the shoulder. "Ready?"

"Ready," I said hesitantly. Standing on the skid of the helicopter was easy, because I was still leaning on the tension of the rope fastened to the floor of the helicopter. But all kinds of disasters ran through my head: What if I hadn't wrapped my rappeling rope around the D ring right? What if the rope harness around my waist came loose? Shit. Too many things to think of. I wish the goddamn chopper wasn't so loud, so I could think. I took a deep breath and jumped. I only pulled the slack once before the ground came up. It was perfect. I was proud of myself. What a confidence builder!

Next was the rope ladder. That was tougher. Forty pounds on my back; at least we were going down. The ladder climbing out was the hardest—just finding the rungs. Once you cleared the helicopter skids it wasn't so bad. My rucksack was trying to pull me backward and my feet were pushing the ladder away. Arms aching and eyes glued to the next downward step, I kept going. The ground was finally coming up and I stepped off the ladder with a big grin plastered all over my face.

The class consisted of US Army personnel, Thais, ARVNs, and Koreans. I made good friends with the Thais and the Koreans but stayed away from the ARVNs. I had already started to dislike most of them, because I really didn't think that I could trust them after having been around them in Phan Thiet. One Korean soldier and I talked incessantly about how much we hated Vietnam, and we spent a lot of time picking out the "yo-yos" in our class. We exchanged our unit patches and became good friends.

During the second week of intensified physical training, one of the students in another building freaked out. It had been a particularly tough day; up at 0430, full gear, forty-pound rucksacks, full fatigues, and jungle boots. We ran four miles on the road to the beach. Besides being too heavy, the straps of the rucksack rub your back as you walk; when you run, they gouge huge furrows into your back. The sides of my lower back were raw and bleeding. On this particular day everyone was beat and miserable. The student who freaked out was having horrible nightmares. He grabbed his weapon and started spraying the area. That no one was hit still amazes me. He was taken away and never seen again.

The next step in phase two was Hon Tre Island, a half-hour's voyage off Nha Trang. Hon Tre is a rugged rock with steep hills and I think that I hiked over every one of those bastards. The island was our outdoor class for patrolling, adjusting artillery fire and air controlling, survival, escape, and evasion.

One more week of recondo school and I was anxious to have it end. Many times in the first two weeks, I asked myself why I was going through more army schools. The answer always came out the same: "I want to stay alive."

The last week would be the final test in the classroom. A cadre-supervised patrol and mission. I was chosen to be a team leader and we went on a VR. As the chopper flew over our area of operation, I watched for all the blue lines (rivers and streams), picked primary and secondary LZs, then left. When the chopper touched down, we went to the classroom for team briefing. My instructor agreed on the LZs. The team was briefed on point, radiotelephone operator, assistant team leader, and all the remaining responsibilities of the team. After briefing, we joked about killing gooks, got our flight time, and left.

At 0430 my team was up and getting ready. Everything was checked and rechecked. I was getting butterflies as I scoured the map for possible trail-watching sites. The times that I had already spent with Charlie Company had taught me well. I hadn't been a team leader before, but I quickly picked up on procedure.

As I waited, I thought about my first missions with Team 3-1. Then at 0530, the instructor poked his head in and shouted, "Be at the deuce and a half in fifteen minutes." I jumped to my feet and yelled, "Saddle up." And we were off.

As the deuce and a half rolled up to the chopper pad, a million things raced through my head. I had never before been on a mission with these people; I hoped that they knew what they were doing. I hoped that they knew how to react under fire. I kept telling myself that they had the same training as I did, so they knew the drill.

We climbed aboard the chopper and took off. The camouflage makeup on my face itched more than usual, but the feel of the cool air on my legs, which were hanging out of the chopper, was calming me down. Below, the South China Sea was beautiful. If I hadn't been in camouflage fatigues, wearing makeup, and carrying sixty pounds of ammo, claymores, LRP rations, three grenades, and my M-16, I would have thought I was just on vacation. Vietnam was a beautiful country.

The chopper was already starting its descent and any serenity that I'd felt that short time was gone; the butterflies instantly flew back, but those butterflies would keep me sharp and alert. The pilot gave me the signal, one finger: one minute. I turned to my team as I locked and loaded my CAR-15. The rest of the team did the same. So did the instructor, who said nothing. I suspected that he had butterflies just like the rest of us.

A combat assault by helicopter is an extremely frightening experience because you have no idea what's waiting for you. I had picked an LZ with no obvious trails nearby, but in a triple-canopy jungle trails could be everywhere or anywhere. The unknown factor.

The chopper touched down and we were off in seconds, setting up a perimeter just inside the woodline. We sat in silence just listening, waiting for sounds, any sounds. Everybody was responding to their responsibilities: flank security, rear security, RTO next to me, the instructor on the left. I motioned the RTO ten feet to my right to make contact with the bird dog. The RTO smiled and confirmed radio contact. We sat listening for about ten minutes, then I motioned a direction and we moved out. The team responded perfectly, maintaining a good interval, everyone in his place.

We had moved out one hundred meters when all hell broke loose to the south of our position, in the next AO. My team was the first inserted that day and then two more teams were put in just as a safety. The second team landed in a hot AO: as the chopper came in, a .51 caliber machine gun opened up. My RTO was monitoring the

radio when the chopper was hit. Our instructor immediately took over our team and began monitoring the radio
himself. We were in a defensive perimeter when he came
over and told me what had happened. The chopper was
coming in to a quiet LZ when Charlie sprang his trap.
The chopper went down, killing the pilot and the copilot
and injuring three team members. A reaction force was
called in, and the area where the chopper went down was
secured. The injured and dead had been removed. The
classroom was over in the field. The instructor moved us
another two hundred meters and our orders were to sit
tight and avoid contact.

As it was getting dark, we set up a night halt. One at
a time we set out the claymore security, mixed our LRP
rations, and ate. It was a long night, two-hour guard
watches. I didn't sleep at all.

Morning finally came and our mission was terminated.
We were told to move to the nearest LZ, which was fifty
meters to our west. The move was uneventful and the LZ
was substantial.

We arrived back to camp safely. Debriefing was short
and sweet; we passed with flying colors, but the mood
around the school was somber.

Finishing up school was nothing, and we all slid
through. Unlike Stateside duty, students and cadre are
brothers in a combat zone because their lives depend on
it.

Graduation day was a complete zero. Later I was sitting in the NCO club with most of the other students
celebrating school's end. We were relaxing and watching
television when casualty reports came in. Major contact
had occurred in Phan Thiet, which caught my attention
immediately; I listened intently. Twenty-six NVA killed
and one Charlie Company 75th Airborne Ranger. An
eerie feeling crossed through my body and I somehow
knew that it was someone from 3-1, but I sat silently,
not really knowing.

School was over and I was glad to leave; getting back
to the woods with my team humping the mountains was
more exciting. There could be no dropping out in the
woods the way some of the turkeys did in recondo school;

you kept up or the team had to wait for you. If the team
had to wait, you were damn sure to hear about it later.

I waited for my flight for what seemed like hours at
the terminal in Nha Trang, but, in reality, just minutes
passed before we loaded into a Caribou. The Caribou
was an amazing plane; it could hold thirty-five passengers and could land on a five-dollar MPC. As we boarded
the plane, I noticed that my tigers were soaked. I usually
don't sweat much, but that day the temperature had to be
a hundred and ten. It was very annoying because my
South Korean friend had just traded me his Korean tiger-
stripe cammies for my US government fatigues. I was
dripping sweat.

As the plane taxied for takeoff, I laid my head back
and began thinking of the team hit in Phan Thiet. Then
the Caribou's engines roared. The plane seemed to leap
from the ground, banked hard to the right, over the South
China Sea. It had to have been one of the most beautiful
spots on earth: brilliant green-blue water surrounded by
some of the most astonishing green-hued hills and valleys. My thoughts drifted back to school and the people
killed on our training mission who would never see that
beauty again.

As the plane banked steeply, I could see Camp Rad-
cliffe and the home of the Rangers. I felt apprehensive,
not so much about going back to the bush but of finally
finding out which team was hit and who had been killed.

The plane touched down at An Khe without incident
and I headed back to our company area. The driver,
whom I didn't know, said nothing. I initiated the conversation by saying, "What's new?"

"Nothing much."

I could feel myself hesitating to ask about what had
been on my mind for days, but finally I blurted out,
"Who bought it?"

He turned and said, "Murphy."

My team; somehow I just knew it all the time. "Who
else?"

"That's it."

To this day I have guilt feelings. I probably couldn't
have done anything to change the outcome that day if I

had been there, but I wished that I could have had the chance to try.

I stayed in An Khe for a few days and then was on my way back to Phan Thiet.

CHAPTER 6

FEBRUARY–MARCH 1970/PHAN THIET
Don Ericson

It was early morning when I arrived in Phan Thiet; when I entered our quarters Agner and Rath were there. We were sitting exchanging all the niceties when I asked what had happened to Murphy? Since we were the best of friends, Sam didn't hesitate to explain.

The day had started as a usual mission day, up at 0430, breakfast till 0530, helipad at 0600, and they were off. It was a relatively short ride out, twenty minutes at most. The team was sitting in the chopper, legs hanging out, the wind whipping at their pant legs and cooling the sweat-soaked fatigues. At that altitude and speed, the air was cool and very refreshing. The sweat, however, was from anticipation and apprehension about what you'll find in the bush. Or who'll find you.

The team was infilled with no problems. Standard procedure: beat feet to the woodline; sit and listen; commo check, Lima Charlie (loud and clear). Murphy was point man as usual. As Sam got the team up and moving, they headed for their primary target: a hard-packed trail that Sam had seen on the VR the day before. The trail paralleled a small stream before disappearing into triple-canopy forest and then reappeared several hundred meters to the south. Up close, the trail was much larger than it had seemed from the chopper. *Much* larger: a four-foot-wide high-speed trail. Bingo! Sam couldn't have asked for a better target. Murphy was grinning with anticipation. Due to the terrain—sharp-rising hills with short sharp valleys—it was tough for Sam to pick a perfect ambush site: whatever cover the team had, whoever was out there had the same. Of course, our team was playing the enemy's game in his backyard and he didn't know the team was there—or so the team hoped.

One thing the six-man Ranger team needed was a good line of sight up and down the trails, so that the team wouldn't unknowingly ambush the point element of a much larger enemy unit like a company or, God forbid, a battalion. I was almost positive that our team could have taken out a platoon (forty men or so) with ease. 3–1 always initiated contact with claymores, and we got fantastic results by daisy-chaining claymores together with fuse detonation cord. Det cord burns at a rate of one thousand feet per second and looks like a plastic clothesline. We always crimped a blasting cap to the end of the det cord, but it really wasn't necessary because the fuse burned so fast that it was like a continuous explosion. One blasting cap was used to ignite the first claymore and the remaining daisy-chained claymores all blew in unison. The Rangers used it on our night positions for security purposes, and the legs and the REMFs used them to guard perimeters and base camps. Very effective, defensively, on gooks in the wire, the claymore had one drawback: it has a back-blast of twenty-five meters. Seven claymores daisy-chained together in a kill zone fifty feet across, all going off together, are almost as shattering to the rear as in the kill zone to the front but without the double-O buckshot. For our team, a good kill was sitting and watching the trail less than thirty feet away; we wanted to see who and how many were out there.

Sam found an ambush site, but it was surrounded by big boulders, not the best for visual confirmation but good for a kill zone and a defensive position. The claymores were out, the flank and rear securities were in position, the stage was set.

Sam was on the radio getting a commo check when he saw the first movement. As he sat paralyzed, eyes glued to the trail, the first NVA walked through. The second one through was a huge Chinese soldier wearing a green beret. Then five more NVA walked through. Every eye in 3–1 was wide. Estimated enemy: thirteen, visual confirmation, Sam whispered in the phone. Do you copy? Over. Affirmative was the reply by X-ray. Before Sam could finish, they were coming back the other way. The NVA seemed to know they were very close to Americans. Sam put the handset down and picked up the claymore detonator, the clacker. Sam's heart raced as he waited for the NVA point man to reach the kill range of the first claymore. Then he squeezed the clacker. Trees, rocks, dirt, bushes, and flesh were falling everywhere. The cloying smell of gunpowder and sulfur hung in the humid air of the jungle. The smoke, like a heavy fog, made it impossible to see, but reflexes took over and the team started pumping rounds into the kill zone, each man automatically firing two magazines into his area of responsibility.

Dead silence. No moaning from the kill zone (efficient). No movement up or down the trail. No friendly KIAs (killed in action), no WIAs (wounded in action). Perfect. As soon as the firing stopped the RTO was telling X-ray 3–1 was in contact and the Cobras were requested. X-ray confirmed and asked for initial body count. Sam replied, "Eight. What's the estimated time of arrival on the Cobras?" X-ray: "2–0 mikes (two minutes) out."

Still no movement in the kill zone, no movement up or down the trail. "Sam, I'm going out," Murphy whispered.

"No," Sam said, "wait until the Cobras work it over."

Murphy smiled and said, "C'mon." Sam gave in and they started crawling out to the kill zone to see what carnage the team had wrought. In the kill zone, five confirmed dead bodies lay in strange, contorted heaps, blood, flesh, and brains everywhere. And in the middle was the prize: the Chinese soldier's body with its green beret blown off; the American aluminum-frame rucksack, just like ours, still on his back but full of holes.

The bodies were still smoking from the blast. Sam and Murphy both smiled through their camouflage faces at each other; it was a good kill.

Murphy stood up to get a better look at the kill zone, and Sam yelled, "Get down, asshole." Murphy had made his last fatal mistake—he broke the 11th commandment: never stand up in a kill zone. An AK-47 went off twenty feet down the trail, ripping Murphy right up the middle. He fell. Sam returned fire, and silenced the AK, but another AK opened up and he retreated with dirt and bullets flying everywhere. The remainder of the team returned fire as Sam scurried for cover. Once back with the team, he grabbed the radio and asked, "Where the hell are the fucking Cobras?"

"Inbound," X-ray replied.

The next voice to come on the phone was the 0-1 Bird Dog in communication with the Cobras. "3-1, this is Bird Dog, over."

"Bird Dog, this is 3-1, we are in deep shit."

"Roger that, see the smoke and the bodies, pop smoke, your location, over."

"Smoke out."

"Roger that, got goofy grape," replied Bird Dog.

"Fire for effect ten meters three hundred and sixty degrees my location."

"Roger that, 3-1. Keep your heads down."

The Cobras were one of the masterpieces of the Vietnam war. Their electric Gatling guns could put a bullet in every square inch of a football field in a matter of seconds. When they opened up with their miniguns, time stood still while the sky rained lead death. Not to be overlooked were their 40mm cannons and the fifty-two rockets in their pods.

As the Cobras were working out, they received small-arms fire, which was quickly terminated. Sam thought that if the NVA were staying around firing at the Cobras, what the hell had the team hit? The more he thought about it, the more he thought about calling for more help. If the NVA were shooting at the Cobras, they were there to stay. Sam got on the phone to 0-1 and relayed the situation report: one friendly KIA, five NVA KIA. Reaction force requested. The reaction force was approved. "2–0 mikes out."

The Cobras left and everything became deafeningly quiet. The team was scared and everyone felt guilty that they couldn't get to Murphy's body. They didn't know who was still out there. The reaction force was on its way and 1–0 mike out. When the smoke was identified and the reaction force was down, an American captain had the wisdom to let a Kit Carson scout walk point! When the Vietnamese scout walked into Sam's kill zone the team members' hearts were pounding. Unknowingly the scout walked up within about thirty meters with everyone ready to blow him away; then the scout's slack man, an American with blond hair, walked into view, and the team sighed with relief. It was over, help had arrived, soon they would exfill. As the column filed past Sam's team, the captain shook Sam's hand, but Sam screeched, "You dumb motherfucker, why would you let a fucking gook walk point after a mission like this?" Red-faced, the captain realized his mistake, turned, and walked away.

Total body count: Team 3–1 had killed five NVA in ambush, Cobras had taken care of another twenty-one gooks, and Team 3–1 lost one Ranger.

Listening to Sam and Rath recall that day brought tears to my eyes. We sat in silence, remembering the times we had shared with Murphy. We all miss Murphy.

As an outcome of that mission came the following commendation:

HEADQUARTERS 173D AIRBORNE BRIGADE
                                                    dkp

GENERAL ORDER   20 MARCH 1970
NUMBER 589

AWARD OF THE ARMY COMMENDATION MEDAL FOR HEROISM
TC 439. The Following AWARD is announced:

AGNER SAMUEL S. JR. 267-82-2488
SERGEANT UNITED STATES ARMY,

Company C (Ranger) 75th Infantry 173rd Airborne brigade

Awarded: Army Commendation Award with "V" device

Theater: Republic of Vietnam

Date of Service: 16 February 1970

Authority: By direction of the Secretary of the Army under the provisions of AR 672–5–1 and US/RV Message 16695, AVA–S, 1 July 1966

Reason: For heroism in connection with military operations against a hostile force in the Republic of Vietnam. Sergeant Agner distinguished himself by valorous actions on 16 February 1970 as a team leader of a Ranger reconnaissance team engaged in operations northeast of Phan Thiet. On this day, Sergeant Agner spotted five enemy soldiers approaching the team's location. The team engaged in a fight and suppressed the enemy with superior fire power. Immediately the team was engaged by unknown enemy elements to their front and left flank. Quickly, Sergeant Agner directed the fire on these areas and called for effective air support. Seemingly, the enemy had been silenced, so Sergeant Agner elected to move into the now opened contact area to retrieve enemy equipment and documents, accompanied by two comrades. Upon approaching this area the three men were fired upon from three enemy positions. Sergeant Agner dove to cover for his man and directing team's fire on enemy positions.* When he himself crawled back to the perimeter, he continued to call in air support and direct fire, enabling them to make a successful break from the enemy. Sergeant Agner's valorous actions and dedication to the welfare of the team enabled the team to suppress an enemy of greater physical strength with a minimum of casualties. Sergeant Agner's actions were in keeping with the highest traditions of the military service and re-

*The original of the citation is garbled at this point.

flect great credit upon himself, his unit and the
United States Army.

T. M. Partin
Major, AGC
Adjutant General.

We were all proud of Sam.

FEBRUARY–MARCH 1970/PHAN THIET
John L. Rotundo

As we got off the Caribou we were met by the driver
from Charlie Rangers, who took us to our new home, a
series of platoon tents with sandbag walls. We were taken
to the orderly room to meet the CO (commanding officer)
and get the rundown of the company's operations. Because Charlie Rangers worked for the Corps, the commander was a major as opposed to a captain, as one
would generally find in a company-size unit. The XO
(executive officer) was a captain instead of a lieutenant,
but aside from those changes the rest of the company was
regular army issue.
As we stood at attention the major introduced himself
to us. "Good morning, men. I'm Bill Holt and I want to
welcome you to Charlie Rangers." His introduction of
himself as Bill caught us all by surprise as we now listened to him as he gave us the rundown of the operations
being conducted and the fact that the company was now
split. The first and fourth platoons were working out of
Dalat, while the second and third platoons were in Phan
Thiet. He went on to explain how the company was struc-
tured: he was the CO, Captain Colvin was the operations
officer. The company's XO was Captain Tolliver, who
was back at An Khe along with the first sergeant. The
company consisted of four patrolling platoons and the
commo platoon, which provided the communication for
the teams in the field. With the support personnel at An

Khe, the company numbered almost two hundred people, the largest of the Ranger companies in Vietnam. Each platoon had a lieutenant as platoon leader, a platoon sergeant (normally an E-7), and the teams. The teams' numbers were assigned by platoon, for instance, First Platoon's teams were numbered 1-1, 1-2, 1-3, et cetera. Second Platoon's teams were numbered as 2-1, 2-2, 2-3, et cetera. As he concluded his orientation we were given platoon assignments, and once again I was assigned to a commo platoon, rather than the Second Platoon, which I had been told I was going to.

I pleaded my case to him that I did in fact have a commo MOS, but that I had also gone to the Herd's 11-Bush school to earn an infantry MOS. I explained that I had been working in an infantry company when my orders for the Rangers came down and that I really didn't care to spend the rest of my tour sitting on my rear end listening to a radio and filling out log books.

The major lent me a sympathetic ear and told me that because the company was split, there was a shortage of skilled commo people. However he did promise me an assignment to one of the field platoons once the company was together again. It seemed to me that I was destined to sit out the war while thousands of grunts were trying to get my kind of job and get out of the field.

As we left the orderly room to find our respective platoons I noticed something different about the Rangers I was meeting from the guys in the Herd. The Rangers didn't wear peace medallions around their necks or give each other the peace sign; they wore a WAR medallion around their necks. Some even went as far as to wear necklaces of ears from dead VC or NVA, taking them off when they went to the mess hall or to the club. When they met one another, instead of flashing the two-fingered peace sign, they would flash three fingers, making a W, and say "war" to one another.

These guys were different, all right, and I could only hope I would make the grade in their eyes. After all, I was to be an REMF again, but I quickly learned that even an REMF Ranger was a good Ranger because everyone in the company looked out for one another. The fact that I was in commo platoon must have helped my standing since the commo platoon went on X-rays (radio-relay duty) and the X-ray was the team's only link with their support. No wonder everybody made me feel at home here.

I spent the better part of my first week meeting the other guys and relearning how to put up a two-niner-two antenna. The evenings were spent sitting by a campfire with the other guys while getting mildly shit-faced, or going down to the 192nd Assault Helicopter Company and drinking with the pilots and the crews. The 192nd was a top-notch outfit and would pull any trick to help out the teams in the field. Stories were told time and time again how those guys would cut off the tops of trees with their main rotor to get a team out, or come into a hot LZ to pick up a team in heavy contact. A special bond had developed between the two companies. The slick platoon's call sign was Lonesome Polecats and the gunships were known as the Tiger Sharks. On the top of the gunship's hut their motto was written in very large red letters: TIGER SHARKS ON TOP . . . YOU CALL, WE MAUL. We partied that first week as all the teams from the Second and Third Platoons were in, and I met a lot of people from the other platoons as well as a couple of Marines who worked coordinating naval gunfire from cruisers and destroyers off shore. Of course Scotty was always with the Marines, drinking their beer and drawing a crowd.

The following week the teams were going into the field again and I would be going out with the X-ray. I packed my rucksack the night before and made sure I had enough of everything I would need. As Scotty would tell us, "Better to have and not need than need and not have, huh, pal?" I packed extra food and magazines for my M-16. After all, I wasn't going to do any humping, just sitting, listening to the radio.

As the slick neared the LZ at the top of this mountain, the door gunners opened up with their 60s to clear out anyone who might be in the woods. When the slick touched down, we got out along with the security team that would be with us for the next four days. We put up the two-niner-two antenna while the security team put out claymores and checked the area for signs of recent activity. We immediately made contact with the TOC (tactical operations center), and not long after that the other teams began insertion. The radio came alive with their RTOs establishing contact with the X-ray.

"X-ray, X-ray, this is 3-2, 3-2, commo check over," the voice would whisper.

"3-2, this is X-ray, I have you Lima Charlie [loud and clear]. How me, over?"

This went on as each team, upon insertion, made sure it had contact with us before Charlie Miking (continuing mission).

The four days out here would be a vacation of sorts for the security team, whose members would use this time to write letters home or catch up on their reading. I didn't know what to expect, so I sat next to the radio and waited for a team to call in a contact so I could relay the information. Once in a while a team would call in for a commo check before the team leader was about to take his team into a valley, or a team would call in that it had found a trail and was going to set up an ambush. The RTO would furnish me the coded coordinates and I would relay the information to the TOC.

Nothing happened the first day, so as the sun was going down the RTOs called in night halt positions. Again I relayed the information and looked around the valley below me. Down there were teams from the Second and Third Platoon, each six men against who-knows-what odds, all settling down from a day humping the woods looking to make contact and, as of now, finding nothing.

Every hour the teams called in situation reports as the man on guard duty woke his replacement and the replacement made sure he had commo with us. I passed the radio watch over to another to get a few hours' sleep. I was awakened a few hours later as once again it was my turn to monitor the radio. Occasionally a call came in because one of the guys just wanted to hear a reassuring voice at the other end of the horn. We whispered jokes to one another just to keep the man alert; a day of humping could really wear a man out and a man on guard can't even think about falling asleep. In the Ranger school we were instructed that a man on guard who felt he was about to nod off should wake the team leader, who was to help him stay awake. But most of the guys didn't want to wake the team leader or another team member, so they used the X-ray RTOs to help keep them awake till the cobwebs had cleared.

The X-ray tour proved uneventful as none of the teams made contact, and on the fourth day they were pulled, the X-ray being last.

When we returned to the compound at Phan Thiet, we put away our commo equipment in the conexes (steel storage containers), took showers, put on clean fatigues, then were just left alone. That wasn't the army I was used to; nobody was hassling us to do some trivial detail just to keep us busy. A lot of the guys walked down to the shore and went swimming or just lay on the beach. I took Rat down to the beach one day and carried her out in the water with me. In perfect John Wayne fashion I told her to sink or swim and threw her in. After she hit the water she surfaced and began paddling to shore. I was very proud of her and for once she was clean—until we walked back to the tent city and she started rolling in the sand. Oh, well.

Since I was in the commo platoon, I occasionally pulled guard duty at night, but that was the extent of my night duty except for an occasional radio watch. The rest of the time was spent with the other Rangers doing whatever we wanted. In the evenings after chow we sat around the campfire with a beer and talked. One evening in particular the conversation got around to cameras. I had seen some of the cameras the guys took to the field and wondered about them. The preferred camera was the Penn EE which took extremely sharp pictures, and was incredibly quiet while the picture was taken. Since one of the mottos in the company was "Silencium Mortom" or silent death, and everything about the team in the field was geared to silence, it was by far the best camera for our purposes.

The next evening I decided to try some gin since it had been a while since I had tasted it. In fact, North English was the last time I had had any. I started in the late afternoon and by nightfall I was totally out of it. I couldn't even find the platoon's tent that evening, but crashed in the sand somewhere, waking up in the morning with sand in my mouth and a hangover to beat all.

Major Holt picked that morning to tell me my request

to be assigned to a field platoon had been granted. The most recent Ranger school class had an RTO in it, so that freed me up. I was assigned to the Third Platoon and would be going out with team 3–4 the next time out. My head felt like it was swollen to twice its normal size and everything was fuzzy, but I decided this wasn't a dream and I moved my gear to the Third Platoon's tent.

The team leader of 3–4 was a fellow named "Papasan" Williams, so called because, at 36 or 37 years old, he was much older than the rest of us. A sergeant E-5, he had been in the army, left, then had come back in. Papasan was short and had very narrow eyes that were set deep in his head. The ATL (assistant team leader) was "Butch" Jenkins, a black E-5. He and I had attended the Herd's 11-Bush school together in October of 1969. The point man was Hobo, a black from somewhere on the East Coast. With his constant smile and infectious laughter, Hobo had no problems making friends. Hobo was an immense help to me those first missions, for it was he who taught me how to wear my equipment so it would be as comfortable as possible, and all the other tricks of the trade that I used as long as I pulled missions.

I was assigned to carry the team's thump gun and that meant carrying its 40mm rounds. The M-79 was carried tied to my rucksack and would be used if we made contact in an area where it could be used safely. The day before I first went out, Hobo took me to the range to practice firing the thumper. Since we cut the stock off, the M-79 couldn't be braced with the right shoulder; the grip was held with the right hand, and the hand guard with the left.

There was a small hill downrange and Hobo had me pumping out rounds to hit it. My first round went low and exploded about twenty meters short of the hill, then I put a round about seventy meters beyond the hill. I kept shooting too long or too short. For whatever reason, I couldn't hit the damn hill. In basic training I had qualified as expert with the M-14; in fact, I was second-best shot in the company. While with the Herd, we'd found an unexploded M-79 round set up as a booby trap and brought it back to the platoon's perimeter; we set it on a paddy dike and I was given one chance to hit it with my

M-16. I sighted in, took up the slack in the trigger, and
bang—boom! So I knew I could still fire a weapon ac-
curately. Nevertheless, I was thoroughly frustrated. After
I fired twenty or so rounds with the thumper, Hobo said,
"If anything, you'd scare the shit out of the gooks." He
let me stop practicing. When we got back to the tent,
Hobo asked me for my gloves. I took them out of my
duffel bag and handed them to him. He used a pair of
scissors to cut the fingers off both gloves.

"This," he said, "will allow you to keep the feel of
the M-16 but the rest of the glove will absorb the heat
from the hand guard when it gets hot after firing a couple
of magazines."

Next he had me open the LRP rations that I would be
taking out to the field. All the time I'd eaten LRP rations
I'd never given much thought to the noise the package
made when opening. The noise discipline we were taught
about in the school was being applied. Hobo was like a
mother hen, making sure everything was in its correct
place and wasn't going to make noise. Dogtags were worn
on the tongue of our boots with the laces holding them
in place.

The next morning I let Hobo apply my camouflage
makeup since he obviously had done it so many times
before. We only did our hands and faces. We always left
our sleeves down while humping in the woods because
prickly plants and vines would tear up the skin. First we
put on a good base of bug juice (mosquito repellent) to
keep the mosquitos away. It also helped the cammy stick
slide across your face. After we cammied up we put on
our web gear and made last-minute adjustments, tight-
ening here and there. Then we'd lay on our backs, sliding
our arms through the straps of our rucksacks before
standing up. God, it was incredibly heavy. We were ready
to head for the helipad.

A deuce and a half took the teams to the helipad and
dropped us off. We dropped our rucksacks and just hung
around the slicks waiting for the crew. I lit a cigarette
and tried to look as calm as the rest of the team, but I
was scared. In a short time I and five others would be
out looking for Charlie. And if we found him we were
going to kill him and his friends; if he spotted us first,

he was going to try and kill us. My stomach began to tighten as I pondered my fate. All of a sudden LZ North English didn't seem like such a bad place after all. My thoughts wandered to my mom and dad, and I wondered what they were doing just then. I was already on my third cigarette when the crew showed up in their flight gear and the door gunner and the crew chief made their pre-flight checks. The pilot and the copilot sat in their seats and began their own preflight checks, and I puffed even harder on my cigarette, trying to draw courage from the tobacco. The crew chief went to the rear of the chopper and took off the strap that connects the main rotor to the tail rotor when the ship is parked. As he finished, the turbine began to whine, and in a minute the main rotor began turning slowly. It picked up speed until it was just a blur. Meanwhile the door gunner stood by with a fire extinguisher looking for signs of a fire as the slick hovered a few feet off the ground.

"Saddle up," Papa-san yelled, and we again leaned back into our rucksacks, then walked hunched over to the waiting slick. Since I was carrying the thumper, I would walk fifth in line. That meant I would sit in the door with Roberts, the rear security man, while Jenkins, the ATL, and Hobo sat in the other door. Papa-san and the RTO sat on the floor inside the slick. Once we were all in place, the chopper's engine was given more power, and we lifted off. I had a sinking feeling in my stomach as I watched the ground get smaller while we gained altitude. We flew at fifteen hundred feet and waited our turn as the other teams were being inserted. Papa-san grabbed my shoulder and asked how I felt.

"Fine," I lied.

There were so many things to remember, and all of them were going through my head at one time: how to walk through the woods without making a sound, how to suppress a cough, remember not to slap at mosquitos, don't let branches fly behind you—put them back in place by hand so as not to make any noise, the immediate-action drill, how to work gunships and artillery. Why didn't I stay at North English where I was safe?

"Lock and load." Papa-san yelled, "we're going in." The slick dropped altitude and began low-leveling to our

LZ. I pulled a magazine from my ammo pouch and fumbled with it, trying to make it fit into my M-16. Once it was in, I pulled back the charging handle and let the bolt slam a round home.

I looked at the trees flying by below me as we were only a few feet above them, and watched as the door gunner locked his belt of 7.62 rounds into his M-60 and raised it up into firing position.

Suddenly the slick began to slow down, and its nose rose up. Right in front of us I could see the LZ. It wasn't much, just space enough for us to land. I transferred the M-16 to my left hand and grabbed the frame of the slick with my right hand, placed my right foot on the skid, then swung my body around so both feet were on the skids as we cleared the trees. The slick was about to touch down.

The slick rocked as I looked through the cabin to see Hobo and Jenkins jump off and Papa-san and the RTO crawling to the now open door. Just like in jump school, I let my training and instincts take over, as I jumped with Roberts, the rear security man. As I hit the ground, the rest of the team, minus Roberts and myself, were running to the woodline to our front.

The slick roared as it rose, and in an instant it was gone, leaving us as we entered the woodline and moved in about fifty meters, then stopped, sat down, and listened. An eerie silence filled the area that just seconds before had been filled with sound. We sat for ten minutes listening for sounds of movement while the RTO made contact with the X-ray to be sure we had commo before moving out.

Silently we picked ourselves up and began to move out in single file with Hobo on point, Jenkins right behind him walking slack. Papa-san was walking third with the RTO right behind him, with myself and Roberts rounding out our order of march. Hobo moved very slowly, looking to his right and then to his left, each of his steps deliberate. The vines were incredibly thick and I was amazed at how quiet the team was. Sure, we had practiced silent movement at the school, but this was real life, we were doing it, and it worked!

After we had moved for about forty-five minutes, Papa-

san clicked his fingers very quietly to get Hobo's attention, then made a hand motion to signal a halt and a
break. We spread out, forming a small perimeter, with
each of us assigned an area to watch and listen. I lay
down, took off my rucksack, and rolled over on my stomach, facing out like the rest of the team.

Papa-san pulled a map from his thigh pocket and took
it out of the cellophane container as he and Jenkins quietly discussed moving toward a stream and looking for a
trail near it. I was still too excited by the infil to be tired,
so when Papa-san motioned us up I had my rucksack on
and was ready to go. Once again we moved at an excruciatingly slow pace. My thump gun caught on every damn
wait-a-minute vine and pricker we came close to. Each
time I had to stop, reach behind me, and grab hold of
the vine, making sure I didn't let it go, then replace it in
the position it had come from.

We moved for an hour before Papa-san called for another break. This one I welcomed, as the midmorning
sun was now giving way to the blistering afternoon sun
and I was starting to feel the rucksack. Once again we
formed a defensive perimeter, and Papa-san motioned to
his mouth to show that it was time to eat. According to
procedure, only one of us would eat at a time while the
others kept their vigil. I pulled out a chicken-and-rice
LRP, added some water from my canteen and waited for
the freeze-dried food to absorb the moisture so I could
eat it. It didn't take long to devour—or rather inhale—
our LRP rations as we had to eat quickly so the rest of
the team could eat.

After I ate, I took out my first cigarette since being
infilled. God, it felt good and I felt some of the morning's tension leave me. When everyone was finished, we
buried our LRP bags and made our way to the stream
shown on the map. After another hour Hobo stopped the
team and we all got down. Ahead we heard water flowing
over the rocks in the stream. Papa-san and Hobo dropped
their rucksacks and low-crawled to check it out. Five
minutes later they returned and we rose to follow them.
We were going to follow the stream. There were no trails
on either side, so Papa-san felt it would be relatively safe
to walk in it. We followed the stream for about fifty me-

ters but found absolutely nothing, so it was back to the bushes for us. Walking the streambed was hairy for a while, not knowing whether an RPD (Soviet machine gun) would open up on us while we were exposed, but it did feel good not having to back up to pry myself loose from wait-a-minute vines.

We moved away from the stream about fifty meters and took another break, as the afternoon sun was starting to drain us. Papa-san took out his map and began plotting our position. Our next course would be to our night-halt position, so again we leaned back and put on our rucksacks and followed Hobo through the woods.

We hadn't come across any trails or signs of activity, so after another break we headed for the first night-halt position. It was on a slight rise, and a few trees provided some cover. Sometime around 1600 we set out the claymores and alternated chow because night would descend awfully fast in the woods. We would sleep in a circle with our feet in the middle. That way, in case anyone heard anything during the night he could alert the rest of the team without having to move. For chow I watched Roberts break out a piece of C-4 to heat his water. The blue heat tabs the Army distributed to heat water seemed to take forever, but a piece of burning C-4 had water boiling for the LRPs, coffee, or cocoa in no time. I pulled out one of my LRPs, and, after heating the water, poured it into the freeze-dried mass in the plastic bag. It was there that I learned to remember to bring hot sauce on every mission! No matter how unbearable some of those rations may have tasted, they all became palatable with liberal doses of hot sauce. Of course some of them didn't need hot sauce, like spaghetti with meat sauce. That was good even cold if you were lucky enough to grab one when they opened up the cases before the mission. But I never went out to the field again without the hot sauce.

Each man pulled an hour's watch then passed the radio handset to the next watch and tried to sleep until awakened for his next watch five hours later. After my first turn, I crawled under my poncho liner and fell right away into dreamland. I was too exhausted from the day's humping to stay awake and contemplate our destiny.

The next morning the entire team awakened around

0600 and we heated up water for cocoa or coffee, as well as for our breakfast LRPs. After we ate we brought in the claymores and buried the LRP ration bags, being careful to put leaves or twigs over the hole so as not to alert anyone that we had spent the night in the area.

As soon as the RTO changed batteries in his radio and established contact with X-ray, Papa-san whispered, "Saddle up."

Once again we put on our rucksacks and followed Hobo into the woods. I felt pretty good that morning. I had survived my first day in the woods and hadn't screwed up once; three more days and I'd have something to tell my grandchildren about. Just then I was only thinking about not making any noise as the team glided into the bush. I was still amazed at how quiet we were, and thought about Culeford at the school lecturing us about noise discipline's importance to LRP missions.

We spent the rest of the second day and all of the third breaking bush, but never came across anything that even remotely hinted of the enemy. So on the morning of the fourth day we made our way to the exfil LZ. As other teams were being picked up before us, there was a short wait. Then Papa-san had the handset to his ear and he whispered to Hobo to pop smoke (throw out a smoke grenade to mark our position). Somewhere in the distance, we could hear the *whump*ing that unmistakably marked a "Huey" as Hobo took out a yellow smoke grenade from his web gear, pulled the pin, and threw it into the field that was our LZ. I watched Papa-san as he rogered the color of the smoke to the 0–1 that would guide the Huey in. In a minute the slick was inbound. When the bird began to flare (bring its nose up), we ran to it then climbed over one another to get in. Once the door gunner counted six of us, the pilot lifted off and we were on our way home.

I didn't know how to feel at that moment. On one hand I was glad to be going back, but another part of me felt cheated because we hadn't made contact. Hobo told me not to worry, the contacts would come, and besides, none of the other teams had made contact either. When we arrived back at our tents, we showered then sat around talking with the other teams while Papa-san and the other team leaders were at the TOC getting debriefed by Major Holt and Captain Colvin, the operations officer.

In four days we would go out again, and I was looking forward to that until Papa-san came back and told me I would be humping the radio on the next mission. I must have been carrying a sign on my back that said RTO. Hell, at least I'd be going to the field again, and not just sitting on my ass.

February ended, and on the first of March, 1970, we were going to the field again. Once more Hobo helped me pack my ruck. After most of the gear was packed, he put the radio in the rucksack so it rode high on my back, where it would be less uncomfortable, an important consideration as I was carrying the same load as the other guys in addition to the radio and four fresh batteries.

We were going to be working pretty far north of Phan Thiet, so the teams were ferried to a fire base about half-way out. From there we would be inserted into our respective AOs. We had just set down on the fire base and were milling around when one of the other teams yelled out that another team that had just been inserted was in contact. I had turned up the volume on my radio handset to monitor the action, when I heard the team in contact call for a reaction force. Normally the reaction force would have come from the teams not going to the field, but since we were already close to the contact area, the 0–1 in the Bird Dog decided to use the two teams at the fire base. Except for the two of us carrying radios, all the members dropped their rucksacks. Within five minutes two slicks landed and we were racing toward the contact area. As I monitored the team in contact on my radio, once again the adrenaline was flowing. They were holding their own, and it would be just minutes before our two teams were helping.

Around and around we circled but we never dropped altitude, and after fifteen minutes we found ourselves back at the fire base. Somebody had sent the gunships back to Phan Thiet and the 0–1 didn't want to infil us without air support, so we were sent back. In the meantime the team broke contact and was pulled, suffering no casualties. We were waiting at the fire base for the slicks to return to insert us, when X-ray came on the net and reported that *it* was in contact.

Once again we mounted up, this time everybody brought their rucksacks, and were en route to help out. As we neared the X-ray site, the door gunner opened up to clear the area of any dinks who might be hiding. I looked out as we came closer to the LZ and was amazed. The mountain that had been picked for the X-ray went almost straight up! How the dinks got up there I'll never know, but I didn't really care. With the two reaction-force teams as well as the team sent in with the X-ray, we had a small platoon force at the top of the mountain. We fanned out and checked the area for signs of the dinks, but found nothing, so we set up by the X-ray. We spent the night providing security to X-ray. That night fog rolled in and we tried to stay comfortable at the top of the mountain with just poncho liners for warmth.

The next day the fog continued and grounded the choppers until 1400. Then the slicks brought in another team to provide security and we boarded the empty chopper. It was close to 1630 when we were finally inserted. I hadn't pulled but one other mission, yet I knew an insertion so late in the day wasn't good. We always tried to be inserted in the early morning to give us a chance to check the area out for signs of the dinks; and an infil so late would leave us an hour of daylight at the most. That meant we would have no time to check out our area and we might even pull our night halt at the fringes of an NVA base camp. Since one team had hit a hot LZ and the X-ray had been fired on, we knew the AOs had dinks in them.

After our infil we only had time to work our way into the bush for a hundred meters before Papa-san decided that location was as good as any. I had checked with X-ray for commo as soon as we hit the LZ, but checked again. X-ray had me Lima Charlie so we put out our claymores and ate rather quickly. We couldn't heat water as darkness was just about on us, so it was cold LRPs for us that evening.

The next morning we awoke from a very light sleep and went through the usual routine, burying the LRP bags and policing up after ourselves. As we moved out, I no-

ticed Hobo was moving slower than I had seen him move
the previous mission, and he kept sniffing the air. When
we had our first break I asked him if he had smelled
something.

"Not yet, man, but ya know you can really smell them
out here."

I gave him a puzzled look as he continued in his whisper.

"They smell just like *nuoc mam*, just like the shit they
put on their fish that you smell all the time in Phan
Thiet."

I remembered the smell, of course, but I had thought
the VC or NVA would realize that the sauce would really
stand out in the bush. But I guess it didn't smell that
much to them. Again I had something to file away in my
memory.

We humped the next two days but heard, saw, and
smelled nothing, so on the morning of the fourth day we
made our way to the LZ, a field of very dry elephant
grass, a few small trees, and one large tree in the middle.

We formed a perimeter around the LZ as Hobo and
Jenkins went to work on the smaller trees with their ma-
chetes. Then Hobo strapped two claymores facing away
from us to the big tree to let the back blast do the cutting.
When the 0-1 radioed us to stand by, Hobo yelled, "Fire
in the hole," and depressed the clackers on the claymores. The big tree went down in record time but the
explosion set fire to the dry elephant grass surrounding
it. The fire spread quickly, coming at us as if it knew
who had initiated the fiasco.

"Let's *di-di* out of here," Hobo shouted as the six of
us ran for a small stream about a hundred meters away.

As we were running, I advised the 0-1 that we would
be using an alternate LZ. We didn't worry about the noise
now as the claymore had announced to anybody in ear-
shot that we were in the area. There was a small island
in the middle of the stream. Trees surrounded it but there
was an opening that was large enough for a slick. We
hoped. Word was there was nothing the pilots of the
192nd wouldn't do or couldn't do to support us Rangers.

Papa-san took the handset and directed the slick closer
to our location. When it was in sight, we popped smoke

and the pilot identified the correct color. We waited on the banks of the stream as the slick hovered for a moment above the trees then came straight down, his main rotor cutting off the branches of some of the smaller trees. Once he touched down, we ran, or rather splashed, to the waiting slick and boarded it. When we were all aboard, the pilot increased his power and rose straight up out of the LZ, turned around, and low-leveled out of the area. Then the door gunner turned to give us the thumbs-up sign, which we promptly returned. The pilot turned around and shot us a big grin just to let us know he was in control the whole time.

The legend of the Lonesome Polecats would live on, at least in my mind.

We headed back to camp for four days of relaxation.

Four days later we would be going out again, but that time we would try something new. The entire platoon was going to be inserted and each team would work out of the platoon's patrol base, fanning out to hump into their own AOs. The whole plan didn't sound too feasible to me, but what did I know? I was just a PFC with two missions under my belt. The company had grown in the short time I'd been there, and we were adding teams to each platoon. I was now going to be part of Team 3-3. The team leader was a very well built E-6 named Jim Niebert who was on his second tour in Vietnam, his first having been with the Herd. Niebert's reputation was that of a man who would go to any lengths to get a kill. He was hungry, so hungry he preferred to walk point so he wouldn't miss anything. The ATL was another E-6 named Josh. Josh was a huge, incredibly strong black who had a heart of gold. He was very quiet and kept to himself while in the rear. Josh was the one who had laid down a merciless base of fire with the 60 when Murphy was killed. Third in line was Chip Paxton, who would hump the radio. Walking fourth was a fellow named Boone. Boone was a real trip to watch. Nothing ever seemed to upset him. The only thing that ever got Boone excited was the fifth man on the team, Wally Geehold, who looked like he belonged in the rear as a clerk. Bespectacled and of average height and weight, something about

Geehold just irritated Boone. I rounded out the team and would walk rear security.

Niebert briefed the team on the new mission, and after bitching and moaning we got ready for the next day's infil. I was glad not to have to carry the radio or the thumper, so happily I went about packing my rucksack and making sure I didn't forget anything.

The next morning we were at the chopper pad with the rest of the platoon, and at the appropriate time we boarded our slick and headed to the LZ. The teams landed one after the other, and once we were all together we moved as a platoon-size force to what would be the platoon's patrol base. From there the teams moved out in different directions, one team at a time, till they were far enough away from one another not to have to worry about ambushing one another.

We were going to be out eight days in this one, so it would put us into a different mind-set.

On the first day we found nothing, so we pulled our night halt with nothing to report.

The next day we found a trail that looked like it hadn't been used in quite some time, so Niebert decided to follow it as it wound itself up a hill. I was doing my part keeping my eyes and ears tuned to our rear, and only occasionally checking out the rest of the team, when one by one they were diving off the trail. As soon as Geehold dove I followed right behind him, and in the process I could see the cause of the commotion . . . Elephants! Coming down the trail from the top of the hill we were climbing up. So much for what I had learned about elephants always staying on the low land. As these titans lumbered past us I watched as Geehold opened his thumper and chambered a shotgun round in it. I looked as Boone leveled his M-16 at Geehold's head.

"Go ahead, Geehold, I dare you."

Boone's eyes were twice their normal size as he was saying this and I couldn't tell if he was serious or not. Niebert clearly thought the whole sequence of events was hysterical. A close-knit group these Rangers are, I thought as Geehold removed the shotgun round from his thumper. Luckily the elephants had other ideas on their minds that day, so I'll never know how much damage an

M-79 shotgun round would do to an elephant hide. Of course, we got off the trail and began breaking bush, looking for something that would give us a clue to gook activity. But again we came up empty.

None of the other teams made contact except Sharkey's, which had a similar encounter with the elephants, except that the elephants were coming up the hill where his team was setting up its night halt. Their Kit Carson scout, Hai, threw a log at the elephants hoping they would be frightened off, but they kept coming.

"Elephants no scare," Hai said as he looked to Sharkey.

"No shit," Sharkey replied as the team vacated the area and gave it back to the elephants.

After eight days in the field with no contacts, we were exfilled and returned to the compound for rest and relaxation.

FEBRUARY—MARCH 1970/PHAN THIET
Don Ericson

Charlie Company had been working in a different area of Phan Thiet for two weeks and was getting minimal results. So the brass came up with another wet dream. At a specially called Third Platoon meeting held outside our tents after evening chow, Lieutenant "O.D." O'Donnell would unveil the master plan. We were all milling around when O.D. finally showed up. He always reminded me of Baby Huey; he was six foot two, weighed in at around two-fifty or two-sixty pounds. His cheeks were puffed out and his stomach hung over his belt a couple of inches. His military haircut didn't help his appearance at all. But he didn't harass us with Stateside lifer nonsense, so he was all right in my book.

"Listen up, men," he said, "we're going on another platoon maneuver." We all looked at each other with puzzled looks on our faces. He went on to say Third

Platoon would set up a base camp and run cloverleaf patrols out of the base. Three teams would run reconnaissance and ambush patrols daily; one team would protect the base while the others were out. All teams would rotate patrols so every team would get a break. Each team would return before dark every day.

A voice came from the rear, "How long will we be out there?"

"Ten days," O.D. replied. The platoon moaned. Ten days of playing line doggie, ten days to tell the gooks— no, I mean ten days to *advertise* to the gooks—where we were. After the complaints subsided, O.D. explained what he expected us to carry. Extra this, extra that, even entrenching tools. We would be digging in. Every man would carry an extra claymore mine for the defensive perimeter. Sergeant Cheek was just as angry as the rest of us. Cheek would always remain at the base to coordinate in case teams made contact. O.D. finished by saying, "You have one day to prepare."

Team 3–1 got together after the meeting to discuss the farce. "I don't even have an entrenching tool," I told Sam. He didn't either. Rath was chuckling, shaking his head in disbelief. "It's definitely going to be different," I added.

Third Platoon and what seemed like two tons of equipment were being loaded onto six Hueys for our great assault on an unsuspecting mountain. Six D-handle spades were also being loaded. Someone finally figured out that the unit was a hunter-killer, a target-of-opportunity operation that didn't need entrenching tools and so had never been issued them. There were a lot of disgruntled looks as the choppers were taking off.

The chopper ride was thirty minutes long, and boring. The pilots were playing games with each other; one would zoom up and then fall back, another would take its place, and so on. It was fun for us as we would see the other teams and give them the international one-finger salute. As the choppers neared the LZ, the pilots returned to formation flying. Team 3–1 would secure the LZ to protect the remaining five choppers that were coming in. The LZ was nestled in a saddle between two hills.

The jungle floor was two hundred meters below the saddle and the hill rose another one hundred meters. I questioned the logic of putting our platoon base on a hill that had a sister no more than a thousand meters away, tip to tip, but I kept the question to myself. Place an NVA mortar on the sister hill and we'd be sitting ducks.

The teams all got down without incident and reached the top of the hill within minutes. The terrain on the way up was manicured like a park in the States: Tall trees with very few branches and very little undergrowth, beautiful green grass and leaves scattered here and there. All we needed was a girl on a blanket, a basket of fried chicken, and a six-pack of beer and we could have had a picnic. The ants were already there.

The perimeter would encompass the entire top of the hill, about seventy-five meters across. One team set up at a time while the others provided security. Claymores went out, areas of responsibility were set. Each man's position had a clear field of fire over the rim of the hill. Our team was the last to set up, so we heard the other teams grumbling about the rocky ground as they tried to dig in. Great, I thought as my eyes were scanning the woods, we're making enough noise to raise the dead. *Clink*, another shovel hit a rock and the sound reverberated through the jungle. It was insane; no wonder line companies took so many casualties. I couldn't wait to get back to the patrols deep in the jungle and the security of Team 3-1. There, at least, we had control of the noise discipline. Here we were sitting ducks.

By the time Team 3-1 lifted the last shovelful of dirt, darkness was minutes away. The perimeter was set, every one was dug in, claymores were set out, and we could eat. While we ate, darkness fell, completely black. Our team was to go out in the morning after first light. As far as I was concerned, morning couldn't have come fast enough. It was a long night. I must have been awake at least three times an hour searching the darkness with my eyes and ears.

When my turn for guard duty came, a disgusted Rath handed me the Starlight scope. I had never seen a Starlight scope before and thought it might be interesting to use. The scope was supposed to magnify light from the moon and stars to make it possible to see otherwise invisible targets; at least that was my guess; no one ever explained its operation to me. I raised it to my eyes and understood Rath's attitude. Here was a piece of equipment that the army probably paid twenty thousand dollars for, and I couldn't see anything through it: just green fuzz; trees and bushes were barely discernible. Maybe if someone moved out there it would be easier to spot. I set it down next to me and said to myself, "Some fat military supplier sure got fatter on this thing." Nevertheless, I got so involved with the damned thing, I didn't realize my guard duty was over until Sam was shaking me. As I handed him the scope, I said, "Don't waste your time."

Sam picked it up, then looked through it only to set it back down. "You've got to be kidding."

I stayed up with Sam during his guard duty because I was just too keyed up. We agreed the operation was ridiculous: Third Platoon had excellent individual Ranger teams, but was not meant to act as a force unit.

The sun was just breaking the horizon when 3–1 finished eating its gourmet breakfast; mine was a beef-and-rice LRP ration with about a third of a bottle of Louisiana hot sauce. The hot sauce killed the taste of the beef and rice. I had used a chunk of C-4 to heat coffee in the C-ration can that I never went to the field without. I brewed more coffee in that one can than Mrs. Olson ever dreamed of brewing, but after four months' service it was getting a little ragged; I had contemplated getting another, but that one had fond memories.

As Sam and I discussed line of travel for the morning patrol, we realized that it was the first time we had had no visual reconnaissance of the area, no way of seeing the area of operation from another perspective. After Sam motioned the team over and gave a short briefing, we waited fifteen minutes. Then Sam gave the word, "Let's go kick some ass."

In the parklike terrain, "breaking bush" (being point) was too easy; we were extremely vulnerable, in the open with no cover. A squad of NVA alerted by our noise the night before could have been waiting in ambush and mowed us down. When I came to Vietnam I always hoped for the best but fully expected the worst could happen. With that attitude I had always covered my ass. As we went farther from our tiny base camp the jungle was getting thicker and the wait-a-minute vines were hanging on everything. As point man, I motioned for Sam to set the team down, and he and I rethought the line of travel. Sam pointed out an old trail running north and south on the map, so we changed directions and in twenty meters were out of the thickets and into some penetrable terrain. We moved about one hundred meters and the terrain stayed the same. As I pushed ahead, my eyes were everywhere, scanning the bush left, right, ahead, in the trees and on the ground. Suddenly, as I was looking at the ground, I saw color moving out of the corner of my eyes. I halted the team and motioned right. Every eye on the team—and every M-16—was on the ground. That's when I saw it on my right about five feet away: the largest snake I had ever seen. Approximately sixteen inches around, it moved for at least two minutes and we never saw its head or its tail. I had never been afraid of snakes until then. It had to be a python. We gave it full clearance as we skirted its domain, every eye watching as it went by.

When I reached the trail, Sam and I were disappointed; it must have been an old logging-truck road. Two grooves had been carved into the earth by a cart or a truck, probably the latter, because a cart would have left a separate trail of water-buffalo tracks down the middle. We sat watching the trail for the better part of the afternoon. Sam reasoned that if the gooks knew a platoon was sitting on top of the hill they might use the old trail for quick access to the top. We waited. We waited for three more hours, the sun's heat pouring down on us. Finally Sam and I looked at each other; the trail was a loser. Sam got on the horn, reported, and said, "3-1 is starting to head back."

"Roger, 3-1, negative contacts. All teams come in," Cheek replied. At least 3-1 wasn't the only team not to make contact. In Charlie Company making first contact was a status symbol: teams that frequently made first contact thought they were the best headhunters. And a dead AO was no excuse; you either found the gooks or you got second billing. Peer pressure really made you look for the enemy.

As we made our way back to the base, all I could think about was spending another night in the woods with twenty other guys. I assumed that all our patrolling would have alerted the gooks to our presence.

The moment we entered the base I collapsed in my foxhole and fell asleep. Staying up the night before and beating the bush for twelve hours had taken their toll.

I awoke to find Sam shaking me, telling me to eat. I opened my eyes and saw that I was still on the damned hilltop. I reached into my rucksack for the first LRP ration I could feel: chicken-and-rice. I was too tired to heat water, so I added cold water and began to inhale the results. LRP rations weren't too bad, but they looked like someone had thrown up in a baggy. Food was food, though. I ate.

After dinner, the team leaders had a meeting with Sergeant Cheek. Sam came back from the meeting with a disgusted look on his face. We had been assigned to guard the base the next day.

The night seemed to fly by. When I opened my eyes, the sky was already becoming light. I tried to move my body but only my eyes obeyed. I glanced down. My legs were still there. I tried to push my body out of the hole, then to sit up. My back felt like it was broken. I must have slept in the fetal position all night. I crawled out of the hole on all fours and swore I'd never sleep in another. I was still on all fours when I looked toward Rath's position. He was eating LRPs and chuckling at me. "Fuck you," I whispered.

By the time I had finished dusting off the quarter-inch layer of dirt that covered me, the last of the teams were leaving. It was 0600 and there was blue sky above us. After coffee and breakfast, I sat near my foxhole and started writing home. I tried to write my parents weekly but had missed a few letters here and there. I never really told them anything I did, as I didn't want them to worry. Most of the letters ran: "How are you? I am fine. How's the weather? Miss you." Just enough to let them know that I was still alive. My parents' letters were full of the neighborhood events and my mother never missed sending me a box of Cheez-its every week. And every letter from home had a piece of Dentyne in it: she noted that she was worried about my teeth and not my breath.

I had just finished closing the envelope when Sam and Rath came over and sat down with their feet resting on my bed (my foxhole). "Do you do that at home?" I asked.

Without another word they both bore down with their boots on the pathetic poncho-liner blanket at the bottom of the hole. By then my poncho liner was covered by an inch of fine dirt, and they both were giggling. "Thanks," I said as I jerked the blanket up. Dirt flew everywhere, covering both victims. It was my turn to giggle. After the dust settled I threw the blanket to the side and the three of us sat with our feet in the hole just staring at the bottom. "This is really boring," I said. Rath agreed. Sam took out his map to study our next AO.

"Look any good?" I asked without even raising my head.

"You've got to be kidding," he said.

But I was already looking at the tape on Rath's M-16. The tape was for camouflage; the M-16 was made out of flat-black plastic, but it still reflected light. I reached into my rucksack and retrieved the light green camouflage makeup that we used on our hands and faces. I grabbed my M-16 and started painting the stock. Sam and Rath watched but said nothing. As I finished painting the M-16, Sam said, "Just what are you doing?"

"Pretty, isn't it?" I replied. "There won't be any reflection from *my* M-16." I'm sure that I was the only soldier in Vietnam with a green M-16. Rath just sat there shaking his head, and rolled his eyes.

The day was *very* boring, fourteen hours of staring out into the jungle, looking for movement. When I couldn't stand the boredom anymore, I decided to dig my foxhole a little deeper and wider to make it more comfortable. Almost immediately I hit a rock. It took me three hours of digging with Rath before we finally heaved the boulder from the hole. Then Rath and I sat by the boulder talking about his mother and brother back in Ohio for another half hour. We talked about a mission Boone and he had been on when they came across a fresh excavation. The team leader decided to investigate it because the VC were known to bury weapons and munitions for later use. They started digging with sticks and knives and almost immediately ran across a skeleton.

"I was grinning from ear to ear when I found that skeleton," Rath said. "We stuck the skull in my ruck and brought it back," he said, still grinning.

"I remember," I said. "I've got a picture of you and Boone profiling (showing off) with it." Later when Richie Wyatt's team killed an NVA with a gold tooth, one of the team members brought back the tooth and put it in a tooth cavity in the skull. The skull, tooth and all, ended up on a shelf at Third Platoon's club. Looked great and was the perfect decor, the first thing anyone saw entering the club.

Nightfall came and this time I would sleep next to the hole, not in it. When morning arrived I was glad to be going out again, at least doing something.

We had gone about eight hundred meters and saw nothing. Sam and I decided to head up a hill to our north. I hated humping up hills, but there was nothing in the valleys. We humped for an hour and a half and had hit the peaks of several small hills and were still climbing when I smelled something. The strange thing about the jungle is its odor. The dampness, the rotting vegetation, and the dirt make up their own special smell. Any other smell such as food, deodorant, body odor, is completely different and stands out. As I sniffed the air I thought the new element smelled familiar but couldn't place the new odor. I called Sam up from about ten meters back, and he could also smell it. We scanned the area and there it was: a fifty-five-gallon drum of powdered CS split open right down the middle. My face was starting to itch just looking at it.

"Let's get the hell out of here," Sam said. I wholeheartedly agreed.

About fifty meters upwind, we called in what we had found. Then we humped the rest of the day seeing no signs of life before heading back to our base. All the teams were in, our perimeter was set, we had our dinner, and were settling down for the night. It was pitch black.

Sam and I were whispering when I heard a dull thump. "Sam, did you hear that?" I asked.

"I sure did," he whispered back. "Sounded like a mortar." That's what it sounded like to me, but I'd wanted him to say it.

We both braced for the sound of the *whoosh* of the shell, and the blast. Nothing. Then another dull thump. Another tense moment of waiting for the shell to drop. Nothing, but the sound seemed to be coming from the sister hill.

"Sergeant Cheek," Sam whispered, "I'm coming in."

"Come on," Sergeant Cheek whispered through the darkness.

Sam turned and said, "I'll be back." He ran to the center of our perimeter.

By this time my heart was beating 240; I was scared because I couldn't see a thing. "I'm coming back," was the next thing I heard, then Sam returned to my position. "Cheek thought the same thing we did." Cheek had called higher-higher to see if anyone was getting hit, and got a negative in response. He thought the gooks didn't know we were around and had set up a tube right next to us. He said we'd send a team to check it out in the morning. It was going to be a long night. First light had broken and I think I had only slept an hour. At least I could see if someone was going to attack our position. At least I would be able to have a target. I was relieved to learn that everyone in our perimeter had heard the noises. Sound is deceiving in the jungle; for all we knew, the source could have been miles away.

The missions were all running the same. Teams went out and set up ambushes on old trails without results. We humped all over the area and saw nothing. Then it was 3-1's turn to guard the base again. The other teams had already left in the direction of their AOs. 3-1 was watching the team head for the mortar tube on our sister hill. They arrived at the top of the hill, found nothing, not even signs of broken brush or overturned leaves. The team continued to search but found nothing.

As I was sitting in my foxhole, now big enough to house me comfortably, just daydreaming, Sam came over and announced that the press was coming out to interview our team. "They want to see how Rangers operate."

"But *this* isn't the way we operate," I said.

"I know," Sam replied, "but they're coming anyway."

At 0900 hours we heard the choppers coming. We figured the correspondent must be very important to warrant a gunship escort. As the Huey touched down, the correspondent got off the chopper. He was wearing standard-issue jungle fatigues with a leg bush hat. Cameras and bags were hanging everywhere. As he approached our perimeter I was disappointed that it wasn't Walter Cronkite, just some leg REMF. The choppers took off and the jungle would soon be quiet again. We watched until the choppers were about a half mile away and getting smaller, then the escort gunship opened up with its M-60 machine guns, the steady red stream of tracers racing to the ground. Sergeant Cheek was on the phone talking to the gunship, asking for a situation report. It turned out the door gunner had seen an elephant and thought he would fire the animal up. The pilot then called back to say, "Be advised the tracers started a small fire."

The reporter was already talking to Sam, asking him about operations and what it was like to work with just six men. When he finished with Sam, he made the rounds talking to every member of the team. His questions were all good ones. He was a leg, a nice enough fellow but we were all snickering. After questions came pictures. First Rath LRPing in a posed position, then me. I posed perfectly, I might add. "Where is the article going to be published?" I asked.

"In *Typhoon* magazine," he replied. "It's a First Field Force magazine published once a month."

That's just great, I thought. Our pictures and story are going to appear in a magazine printed for REMFs. The REMFs would probably memorize the details so they had some war stories to tell when they went back to the World.

By the afternoon the leg correspondent was packing up to go, and the choppers could be heard in the distance. Sergeant Cheek was talking to the lead bird. "Be advised," the pilot said, "you have a full-scale field fire coming up your way." Sergeant Cheek picked up the field glasses and looked in the direction of the fire. Sure enough, the wind in the valley was whipping the fire toward our position. It had gone almost a quarter mile in a matter of hours. Then the correspondent boarded the chopper and was off, back to safety, where other legs guarded his perimeter.

All thoughts were now focused on the fire. Cheek got on the phone and recalled all the teams. The last came in around 1730. As we ate dinner, Cheek instructed us on what to do: the claymores were to stay out; if the fire reached our area, all the grenades were to be thrown, all the grenade-launcher rounds were to be expended; no explosives were to remain in our possession. We couldn't run, because there was nowhere to run, and a platoon-size helicopter exfil at night would have been impossible. As we ate and talked, the smoke began to drift through our position. As it got darker the flames reflected from the trees and sky, and an eerie feeling descended on us. The smoke was now a thick unseen fog, the air heavy. Sergeant Cheek was on the phone telling higher-higher of his decision to ride the fire out. I was glad that I had dug my foxhole deeper, but I also cursed myself for not having dug it a lot deeper. I removed all the important things from my rucksack, I would only keep the essentials: web gear with its magazines, bandolier with all *its* magazines. I would not be without ammunition. I never carried water on my web gear in the field because it interfered with the aluminum-frame rucksack, but this night I attached a pair of quart canteens. In the dark I double-checked the web gear: on the harness I routinely carried a magnesium trip flare so that if the team was wiped out, I could attract the attention of a helicopter crew (a burning magnesium flare could be seen in even the brightest daylight). As my hands searched the other strap I came across my compass taped to it and further down was a CS canister; both had to stay. CS was an excellent way of deterring anyone who might be chasing me if I was running. I always tried to prepare for the worst contacts I could be involved in; I wanted to come out of a nightmare war alive. Then my hands found a taped-on canister of serum albumin; I ripped off the tape and stuck it in my rucksack. I was ready. I double-checked the pockets of my fatigue pants. Fluorescent signal panel, mirror for signaling, strobe light for night signaling, .22 caliber pen flare gun for night signaling, URC-10 emergency radio for signaling only (every plane and helicopter was supposed to monitor this radio beeper). I now was remembering the time Sam and I tried it on a C-130 airplane. No response, no wing wagging, no turning around; I carried it anyway. The last thing I laid next to me was my poncho liner, which if the fire got close, I could spread above me to protect me from the heat and the falling embers. As I turned to set my rucksack behind me and out of the hole, the sky about two hundred feet from the perimeter was alive with fire. The fire was running up the trunks of the trees, burning the loose bark, and then dying out for lack of fuel. The air was solid smoke, and burning embers fell everywhere. Because of the great amount of heat it gave off, the fire was producing its own wind.

Then Sergeant Cheek was yelling, "Get your heads down." No sooner had he finished yelling, when a claymore went off, then another and another and another. The sounds were deafening, the fire was licking at our perimeter, and the trees were starting to ignite. Then the grass and leaves around us were burning. I could hear the sounds of coughing and retching all around the perimeter. And claymores were still going off. Then the fire was inside the perimeter and burning at full force, devouring every rucksack in its path. The next thing, I heard someone yell, "Frag out!" With a thunderous roar, the perimeter turned bright white. Some dumb SOB held on to a willy peter (a white phosphorus grenade) and then got scared. As the flames swept over my area, it became extremely hot but not unbearable. What really hurt was the falling red-hot ashes. I kept patting them out as they fell on my fatigues. I decided not to hide under the poncho liner because I had to see what was going on. My rucksack was still on fire as I glanced around the perimeter. Sergeant Cheek was looking right back at me. "Has your claymore blown yet?" he asked.

"Not yet," I said, "but any minute now." As we were on the south side of the hill, 3–1 was the last to take the brunt of the fire. Then our claymores were exploding and the worst of the fire was gone. Everyone was coughing and gagging; noise discipline had completely disappeared. If the gooks had been in the area, they would have been laughing their heads off.

Morning was upon us now and we could assess the loss. Burnt rucksacks lay everywhere, as did cases of C rations with exploded cans of ham and lima beans. The wood of the D-handle shovels had burnt away. Sergeant Cheek called in the situation report and suggested that we be pulled. It was agreed that we should come out and morale jumped five hundred percent. That night probably cost the government ten thousand dollars in equipment and munitions.

We were ordered to bury the half-burnt equipment and foodstuffs, and my foxhole made an excellent burial ground. As we sat waiting for the choppers to pick us up, we knew we had been lucky; the whole mission had been a fiasco. At least I now had firsthand knowledge about how it felt to be a line company; it sucked.

We had been back in Phan Thiet for two weeks and had pulled a couple of normal missions when Sergeant Cheek walked into our tent and handed us each a copy of *Typhoon* magazine with Rath's camouflage face on the cover. And my name under his picture. (What do you expect from a leg journalist?) The pictures were good, but the article was about the cloverleaf mission, and that was not how we normally worked. We had gone as a platoon not as six-man hunter-killer teams. We laughed at the article and the mission. (Fifteen years later I was watching *The Ten Thousand Day War* documentary, Volume 6, on the video when I saw my picture [at "1329," on my VCR]. There on my television was a picture of me taken on some godforsaken mission in some godforsaken place.)

We stayed in Phan Thiet for a couple of weeks but had no contacts to speak of, so we packed our gear and were on our way to our next AO.

CHAPTER 7

APRIL 1970/PLEIKU
John L. Rotundo

The one thing that will remain forever etched in my mind about Camp Holloway in Pleiku was the red dust that the Chinooks and Hueys kicked up on Charlie Rangers' little tent city right off the chopper pad. Keeping anything clean was impossible due to the frequency of takeoffs and landings.

The first night we had just put up our tents, and as dusk set in the alert warning sounded. We had no shelters, just small depressions in the ground for protection as the mortar rounds dropped in. Our weapons were locked up, so we were completely helpless should the dinks infiltrate the perimeter. We just lay there as the mortars and 122mm rockets slammed into Camp Holloway. Fortunately, the gooks were not aiming for us or they were lousy shots, as the rounds landed far enough away from us to do nothing more than let us know they were out there.

The next day my buddy Don from Cha Rang Valley, who everyone called Eric, myself, and a few others went over to the other side of the compound where the Air Force was billeted. While we were walking around we came across an unoccupied photo laboratory, so we went in to take a look. Inside we found a complete facility to develop, enlarge, or reduce any picture imaginable.

We hustled back to Tent City and gathered up every picture and negative we could find, then brought them to the photo lab. Within the hour Don was reproducing all the photos we had, either from negatives or from the pictures we brought with us. He was even enlarging our pictures to 8×10s to send home. The air force had to have spent a small fortune to put the lab together and we were making good use of it. When we were finished, we went to the PX and bought film so we could take pictures around Camp Holloway. Fotomat had nothing on us then, same-day service and all.

After several days of settling in to our new home, we went out to the field again. All four platoons had teams patrolling, but the area the brass wanted us to check out was devoid of enemy activity. I know Team 3-3 did its part, because Niebert had us playing mountain goat, going up and down mountain after mountain trying to find a trace of the gooks, but like the other teams, we came up empty this time out.

The first day back, the major decided to have us do PT, so early in the morning we were doing push-ups, side-straddle hops, and the like, finishing off the workout with a run, the Airborne way. At first we ran a mile or so around the general area. But after a few days we ran through the leg area, chanting and clapping as we passed their barracks, knowing full well they were trying to get that last hour of sleep and that we would wake them up. One morning we went through the motor pool then capped off the morning run with a jaunt through the officers' latrine. We got some strange looks from the junior officers who were showering and shaving as a company of Rangers ran in one door and out the other.

Since the first time out, we hadn't pulled a mission in over a week and we were all getting antsy, so I decided to get a haircut. A Mohawk. I remember reading about the Airborne in World War II and how men of the 101st had their hair cut into Mohawks just prior to D day. I talked to Niebert about the idea and he was all for it. In fact, not only would Niebert and myself get the Mohawks, but so would Boone and Paxton. Only Josh and Geehold couldn't be talked into it, but hell, what could the army do to us for getting innovative haircuts—send us to Vietnam?

The four of us walked to the barber shop on post and tried to tell the Vietnamese barber how we wanted our hair cut. (How do you say Mohawk in Vietnamese?) After five minutes of Pidgin English and gestures, he smiled as he seemed to catch on. I went first and watched in the mirror as he started on the side of my head. Till he had the sides grazed clean, I kept my hands over the middle of my head so he wouldn't touch the hair there. When he had the sides done, watching closely I let him start on top. When he finished cutting I had him shave the sides to make the mohawk stand out. Then Niebert jumped into the chair. By then it was obvious the barber was enjoying the new hair style. By the time he got to Paxton and Boone he was cranking out them haircuts in *ti-ti* time. We paid him, and as we were looking at ourselves in the mirror, one of Camp Holloway's regulars sat down in the barber chair. He looked at us then at the grinning, expectant barber and the look on his face said it all: "No fuckin' way!"

We walked back to Tent City and created quite a stir, but received no hassles from any senior NCOs or officers. They probably thought we'd grow up one day but that until then hounding us wouldn't do any good.

On our last mission out of Pleiku, Niebert agreed to let me carry "The Gun" (M-60). I went to Scotty, as he was the resident—unauthorized—armorer and knew the weapon well.

"Always make sure you've got plenty of LSO [a lubricant] on the bolt. You want to make sure when you're firing it the oil splashes all over you, then you know it's working, ya know, pal?" Scotty's face was two inches from mine when he finished. I listened intently. Not only was Scotty always at the firing range practicing with different weapons, he had been with a team that got hit just as they were infilled. The hot LZ was a bomb crater and one member of the team was carrying the gun. He raised it to fire and *bang*! one round fired. He pulled back the

charging handle and raised it to fire again. Again just
one round fired. The team was pinned down and Scotty
rolled over to the man with the gun and took it away from
him, pulled out a little wrench he carried with him
("Better to have and not need than need and not have.")
and unscrewed the bolt in front of the gas-cylinder cham-
ber. He took out the cylinder, reinserted it the right way,
screwed the bolt back in, and returned the M-60 to the
amazed Ranger. All this with bullets flying overhead. The
guy raised it to fire and it cranked out rounds on automatic. The gooks broke contact after the gun started firing. I could learn a lot from Scotty, and I wasn't ashamed
to ask.

On this mission, carrying the gun, I chambered a
twenty-five-round teaser belt, all tracers for effect, and
six hundred extra rounds, while each member also carried a hundred rounds, giving us a little over eleven hundred rounds for the gun should we make contact. Six
hundred rounds of M-60 ammo, a dozen LRP rations,
four frags, a claymore mine, eight quarts of water, smoke
grenades, a CS grenade, poncho, and poncho liner made
for one ass-kicking rucksack, not to mention the weight
of the gun, which was supported by a rope (tied to the
barrel on the front end and around the stock on the rear)
that would let it hang from my neck when breaking the
bush. As clumsy as the rig sounds, it didn't affect our
noise discipline on that mission.

With the gun I would walk fourth behind the RTO,
Boone assuming the rear security position. Once again
Niebert led us up and down hills, breaking the bush,
hunting for signs. The vegetation in that AO wasn't so
bad, so we made good time, and the gun and the ruck
hurt the first day and the better part of the second, but
by late afternoon the weight didn't bother me.

We found nothing except a small stream that didn't
have any trails near it. The only excitement came when
Geehold went to put his claymores out for our night halt
and Boone went out with him to cover. We could hear
just a hint of their voices as they came back in. Evidently
Geehold put his claymore out but it was tilted a bit and
Boone was giving him hell about it. Boone just sat there

that evening and glared at Geehold while there still was light.

On the third day, I was ready to take on the entire NVA army all by myself. Unfortunately we came up empty and were pulled the next day. I was the most dejected when we were coming in. I wanted to see what the gun would do in a real contact. Maybe next time—but next time would be in our next AO. Because in the second week of April, once again we were rolling up our tents and loading them on the deuce and a half for our trip to An Khe, where we would be pulling missions within a week.

CHAPTER 8

APRIL—MAY 1970/AN KHE
Don Ericson

After a terrible job of coordinating with the transportation people, the company left Pleiku and arrived in An Khe about five hours later. Transportation was no better in An Khe. Due to a lack of deuce and a halfs, we had to be ferried from the airfield to the company area. Two hours of sitting on the runway in the blazing sun did nothing for morale.

This was the first time our company was in An Khe since I joined the forward element of Charlie Company. Even though An Khe was the rear headquarters, we had never worked or run missions in the area. An Khe was also headquarters for the 4th Infantry Division, the outfit we called the "Funny Fourth." In 1970, the 4th Division was the largest conglomeration of misfits, losers, and heads (drug users) I had ever seen assembled in the army. (I apologize to the men of the 4th who didn't fit this category. However, the men of the 4th that I saw certainly fit the description.)

An Khe was a pleasant break from the sands of Phan Thiet and the red dirt and dust of Camp Holloway in Pleiku. An Khe meant mail immediately, a real mess hall with Vietnamese KPs, real wood-and-metal barracks with concrete floors and army-style *beds* instead of cots.

Price was back from the rear for some reason or another; with his rank he would fill the slot of the ATL and I would drop down to be the slack man. There was no set rule on position in the team. If someone arrived with more rank, he was inserted into a slot and lower ranking Rangers dropped down. Rangers came and went all the time.

We went out for four days and found absolutely nothing; discouraged, we arrived back at camp for four days of relaxing. Four days later we were going out again. Agner came back from the VR and said the area looked good. We would be going out tomorrow; Agner as the team leader, Price as the assistant team leader (Sam had more rank, it being his second tour in Vietnam), Rath as the RTO, Sullivan, Paxton, and myself. Not a bad team. All had good endurance. All had good noise discipline.

Junior Sullivan was our new team member; he stood five foot eight and had a stocky build. His baby face gave away his youth. He was always laughing and had a good sense of humor. He was an all right guy. Though we all had Ranger savvy, the team needed a kill; the morale of the team was good, but a kill was essential to keep us sharp. A body count or even a contact kept everyone on his toes. Without a kill or a contact, a mission was just a walk in the woods. A walk in the woods made men lazy and very careless.

Same routine: rucks on one last time for fit and comfort, then wait for the word to hit the chopper pad. Sergeant Cheek would come by and address us with his usual greeting: "Let's go, girls."

"Coming with us today, Sergeant Cheek?" I would ask, already knowing the answer.

"Fuck you, boy." Sergeant Cheek was a top-notch NCO, always sharing a beer with his men. Even though he was a sergeant first class, an E-7, he never gave us a hard time or hassled us without reason; he was one of us. He even wore pink, heart-shaped glasses. And he also wept when Murphy was killed. He had all the right tools for a leader.

Sergeant Cheek inevitably gave the order to saddle up

and we donned our rucksacks. Mine seemed especially heavy, and as I turned around I saw Paxton had been pulling down on the back, where I couldn't see. He was laughing his head off as I shook my head in disgust. We went out to the waiting truck.

When we arrived at the helipad, the slicks were already running and the air was full of dirt and debris. We settled into the slick, legs hanging out; the other teams were already taking off. Our slick was building up RPMs as it started to shudder and bounce. Once we were airborne, the cool air felt great as I watched the people and buildings grow smaller and smaller.

We gained altitude and my mind drifted off just as it had every other infil I'd been on. Will I make it back? What happens if we hit a hot LZ? What do I do if the dinks shoot the slick down? What if they kill everyone except me? A thousand questions ran through your mind at this time.

I unconsciously lit up another cigarette, then figured that it was my fourth in less than twenty minutes. Scared? Scared shitless of the unknown. On the ground we can more or less control our own destiny but in the air, in this huge loud machine, we're very vulnerable. I see the door gunner giving Sam the one-minute signal. In one minute we could be in the breech of Hell or we could be in for another cakewalk. The slick pitches hard to the left and it feels like I might slide out, but Agner's hand is on my rucksack holding on. I look back and smile and know I had nothing to worry about. The pilot is good, he comes in fast and low the way we all like it, no pussyfooting around. As the slick touches down we're off in a matter of seconds and in the woodline. With the absence of the chopper's thumping blades comes silence, dead silence. I thank God it wasn't a hot LZ. I'm still amazed at how quiet the woods can be. So quiet all you hear is your own breathing.

The camouflage makeup keeps the sweat from evaporating off the face; it itches. You want to rub your face but are afraid that if you do you'll rub off some of the cammy and expose your white skin.

Agner looks at Rath and Rath nods yes; Rath gets a commo check immediately and he hears a Charlie Mike.

Sam signals the team up, and we're off. An Khe is more mountainous than we thought, up one mountain and down another. Even though the team is in good shape we stop more often to avoid breaking noise discipline. Noise discipline is everything for a Ranger team.

Agner is walking point, setting a good pace. I'm walking slack, Price is the ATL next, Rath as the RTO, Paxton, then Sullivan as rear security. I think, What a killing machine. We're ready.

All of a sudden Sam halts the team. Instinctively everyone freezes, each watching his area of responsibility. Sam looks at me and holds up two fingers. I think to myself we're in the shit as I'm smiling, relaying two fingers down the line. Sam motions me forward, and as I reach his side he points to our front. Two NVA are guarding two Montagnard farmers in a cornfield. Good God, I think, there's going to be two less plates at someone's table tonight. Sam whispers to me that we're in a poor position and we'll move over on the left bank and take them out. I disagreed; I was all for taking them out with head shots. But it was Sam's second tour in Vietnam and I respected his experience. (Later I would find out how right he was!)

We pulled back and regrouped to parallel the cornfield. As we were slithering through the bush we came upon a four-foot-wide hard-packed trail. Sam got on the horn to X-ray and advised them of what we had found. X-ray relayed that we should sit tight and observe the trail. It would have been so easy to blow the two NVA away and be exfilled; we could have been sleeping in a nice bed that night getting fucked up on beer, but just then our job was to be reconnaissance.

No sooner had we pulled ten meters off the trail than a little boy and girl about ten years old walked by carrying two huge bunches of bananas. We hadn't even had time to set out our claymores. It was getting dark as the kids passed. To our rear there were farmers being guarded by NVA, and to our left kids bringing in food. The only explanation was that a base camp existed in the area. We were six Rangers against what? Darkness was falling quickly and a reaction force trying to link up with a team at night would be a total disaster. Options now closed:

Sam instructed us to put out our claymores for a defensive perimeter. The claymores went out in a three-hundred-and-sixty-degree perimeter with one man guarding the other who was setting up the claymores. After our claymores and our night defensive position were set, we knew, because of our situation, nobody would sleep that night.

Before a complete darkness fell Price somehow detonated his claymore. Why no one fired his M-16, I'll never know; that's supposed to be the instinctive reaction after a claymore goes off.

When the dust and dirt cleared away, Sam put his finger to his lips as if to say "Shhh." We scanned the area for signs of movement, but saw nothing until Sam said, "Look, there's some motherfucker in the tree watching us."

Now we were the hunted. The NVA were watching us. The only thing I could figure out is that they were guarding something big, something they didn't want us to know about. They didn't know that we'd figured out there was something there. Sam called X-ray to update them on our situation. X-ray relayed the TOC's question, asking us if we wanted gunships. Sam replied, "Negative," but asked that they be ready as he wanted a reaction force to come in at first light. His request was approved as we got ready for a tough night. No sleep, eyes playing tricks, but no actual movement from the NVA, who seemed to be gambling on what we knew. They were going to lose. We were either at the limit of artillery range or just out of it, but Shadow was on call and ready to help us. Shadow is a C-47 with six miniguns, each of which could put a round in every square inch of a football field in about a minute.

Sam called the 0-1 to get a fix on our position. As he held the strobe light up it was like a signal to my brain saying, "This is the last resort." The strobe light is only used in real emergencies to signal our position to our gunships but not to the enemy.

To say the least, it was a long night, but dawn finally arrived. The team was beat, physically drained. We had humped up mountains and gone down valleys the day before, then stayed up all night. As dawn came through

the trees, Sam was on the horn with the commander of
the reaction force from the 101st Airborne, coordinating
our position. Sam turned to us and whispered that the
ships were 1–5 out. We breathed a collective sigh of relief. Sam monitored the reaction force's landing as we
sat waiting for them to come up the trail to our west.
What seemed like hours was in reality minutes until we
finally spotted the point element, Sam made visual contact, and the linkup was set.

Sam, the reaction force commander, and I conferred
about what we had hit. The reaction force would sit tight
until the gunships prepped the area and Sam agreed.
Within minutes the first ship was buzzing overhead. It
was a LOH (light observation helicopter, pronounced
loach) that had a door gunner with an M-60 machine
gun, both suspended by a bungee cord.

Truly an awesome sight. The LOH made its first pass
without drawing any rounds. The second pass drew
automatic-weapons fire. The LOH immediately pulled off
station and the Cobras took over, screeching in with
rockets and miniguns blasting away only to be answered
by Russian .51 caliber machine guns. I looked at Sam,
Sam looked at me; no words spoken. Seeing where the
.51s were coming from, the Cobras came in for a second
run. The pilots of the Cobras had to have had brass balls
flying into the muzzle of a .51. As they screamed in,
rockets blaring, the .51s became silent. Charlie Company, Third Platoon, Team 3–1 hit it big. The NVA were
protecting something there and they weren't about to
leave.

Only after thirteen runs of the Cobras, LOHs, and
Huey gunships did the NVA cease firing. Now it was the
101st's turn. Sam met with the company commander a
last time before his men assaulted the bunker and cave
complex. Sam motioned me forward to their meeting.
When I reached them, Sam did the talking, "The trail
down here is lined with punji sticks four feet deep and
as far as you can see. The captain here wants us to walk
point. What do you think?"

"Sir, fuck you," I said. "Our mission is done. Your
turn!" As I turned to walk away, Sam saluted the com-

mander, smiling all the way. I was proud of Sam that day.

As the reaction force filed by, our little team regrouped in the security of the rocks in which we had spent the night watching. If the NVA had been in position with their .51 they would have shot the reaction force down like ducks. As we watched, I pointed out a black soldier with a boom box to his ear, weapon slung over his shoulder, listening to a Temptations tape. What a way to die. That was our reaction force, people who just didn't give a fuck. People whose leaders didn't care. God, I'm glad I'm with the best; Charlie Rangers is going to keep me alive. In the meantime I was going to celebrate being alive.

We got back to the compound and could relax for four days; I mean really relax. Since teams normally pulled missions all the time—out for four days max unless contact was made, then in for four days—the time spent with those not on your team or even in your platoon was limited. But a stand-down was time to get reacquainted with old friends and make new ones.

When Charlie Company let its hair down and partied, we partied! Every barracks rocked to its own sounds: Creedence Clearwater Revival, Chicago, The Rascals, The Temptations, Herbie Mann's Memphis Underground, just to name a few. And every barracks had its own sounds: half-drunk or half-stoned soldiers telling their personal war stories and bullshitting. Very few told stories of home; that was too personal. That was meant for a one-on-one with a friend. Third Platoon was made up mostly of juicers (drinkers), though we had our share of heads. We all got along well, but the little clique I hung around with liked to booze it up.

The first afternoon we decided to make some Ranger punch. I knew I was in for one long evening. We made a list of what was needed and detailed two-man reconnaissance teams to scrounge up the ingredients. Mine was easy, I was to "search out and capture" the largest cooking pot in the mess hall. As I was leaving the mess hall I yelled back at the cook, "Third Platoon barracks, 2330 hours, be there."

"Ranger," was his response, and I was off. I think he

was more worried about the pot he was responsible for
than he was at missing a party. We arrived back at our
rendezvous point about the same time except for the
Ranger who was assigned to get the marijuana and speed.
We figured he was having a hard time finding someone
to donate theirs. But eventually he showed up, grinning
from ear to ear, eyes glazed over, and chuckling to himself.

"Where've you been?" someone asked.

He giggled out, "Wow, man. I had to try some to see
if it was any good." And he started to giggle again.

As the "Master Chefs" started their magic, I watched
in horror. In went two bottles of Jim Beam, two bottles
of vodka, two bottles of Ron Rico rum (for our Latin
brothers), one can of grapefruit wedges with juice, one
can of peaches with juice, one can of fruit cocktail, two
cans of serum albumin, two vials of speed, and about a
quarter bag of marijuana. Stir well, very well, and add
ice.

Word traveled fast and soon fifty people were watching. The majority loved it, the hard-core drinkers using
the intravenous tubes from the serum albumin cans as
straws, sitting next to the cooking pot and drinking until
they were pushed away by others.

I was on my second glass when the effect hit me. By
then the group that had initiated the punch had been
pushed to the side. We were having our own party on a
nearby bunk in the middle of the barracks. About this
time John L. stood up and said, "I think we should have
a toast." Everyone raised their glasses and John L. hes-
istated for a moment and spoke again. "No, not yet."
We were puzzled as he bent over and started unlacing
one of his jungle boots. "If we're going to toast, we're
going to do it right," he said.

John L. bulled his way to the pot, swaying back and
forth, then dipped his size-ten boot into the punch, filling
it. Ten soldiers backed away from the pot in disgust while
he laughed. Bubbles rose from the boot while the guys
with the intravenous tubes were still getting their share.
The boot was finally full and he pulled it from the pot
and headed back to our private toast. As he arrived back
to us he stood there, his boot leaking all over, and said

in a drunken voice, "Gentlemen, Charlie Company, 75th Airborne Rangers." Then he raised the boot to his mouth, the punch dribbling all over his already badly soiled T-shirt. When the boot reached me, I raised it and said in a loud voice, "Charlie Rangers." I hoped that the alcohol had killed whatever was growing in his boots.

Quite a crowd had gathered around us by then, everyone recoiling as we drank from the boot. But any one of them would have given his left testicle to be in or to be part of a close-knit group like ours. We had a camaraderie known to only a few.

I don't remember much about that first night after the toast, and maybe that's better, but the next day I had a feeling the other Rangers looked at us in a different light.

It was a rough morning; I had a hangover equaled by none. Sam came in and put me on a detail of filling LRP bags with CS. It seemed an easy enough job: We were to fill the bags with CS, then tape them shut. Then the packs would be taped to the claymore mines in an offensive ambush. My assistant and I started filling the bags; it was a breeze. We took off our gas masks and had a cigarette and took our time. After about fifteen minutes my nose started running. We were just finishing up when I started itching—and scratching (first mistake). All of a sudden the whole compound was screaming at us! We were done and it was all I could do to run into the shower, clothes on and all, and get some relief. I stripped off my clothes and stood under the water for at least a half hour laughing about what happened. After another half hour I got out of the shower and threw my clothes away; I knew that CS wouldn't come out of the fabric. I giggled to myself thinking that some gook hootch maid would take them home not knowing what they contained.

On the way back to the barracks I received several catcalls and derogatory remarks about my very naked body.

APRIL–MAY 1970/AN KHE
John L. Rotundo

As the trucks made their way through the huge compound, it was good to look up at Hong Kon Mountain, which dominated the terrain, and see the 173rd and the 1st Cav shoulder patches painted on top of the mountain, which could be seen from just about anywhere in the camp area. An Khe was the rear area for both the 173rd and the 1st Cav during the early years of the war, and they had seen to it they wouldn't be forgotten.

When we arrived in the Ranger area of the compound, we found ourselves sharing barracks with the 4th Division's Rangers, K Company. "Kangaroo Company," we called them because of the Australian bush hats they wore to the field and in the rear. Kangaroo Company was about as sorry as Ranger companies come. It pains me to write about a sister company that way. K Company worked in four-man recon teams whose missions were to snoop and poop, making no contact if at all possible; straight reconnaissance. Even though K Company's Rangers wore the Airborne Ranger scroll, which implied they were Airborne qualified, most were not; those who really were insisted on wearing their silver jump wings to the field! More than once we'd see them getting ready to go out to the woods wearing camouflage fatigues, their faces and hands cammied up in different shades of green, only to see the gleam of silver wings from their bush hats. It doesn't take a mental giant to know those wings reflect sunlight, and the cammy stick and camouflage fatigues won't hide the sun's reflecting off them. Word was that a few of their Rangers had been shot in the head while on mission. No wonder their parent unit was called the Funny Fourth. The fact that K Company was sharing our barracks and mess hall was a constant source of irritation.

The biggest irritant was the fact that K Company had been working around An Khe for some time before we arrived and had not made much contact (no surprise there; *that* wasn't their mission), but they hadn't reported many sightings either. And they had repainted the Ranger scroll near the school, a huge wooden replica of our shoulder patch with a "C" on the left side, "Airborne Ranger" in the middle, and "75" on the right side. The scroll was mounted on two telephone poles at the entrance to the company area. The Fourth's Rangers had painted over the C and in its place had inserted a K. One of our first nights back, some Charlie Rangers went out and repainted the C in its rightful place. The next morning we all felt a bit better when we looked up at the sign.

However, the next night it was repainted with a K.

A day later a loud blast sounded in the middle of the night as someone blew the poles down with C-4 explosive. No more repainting the sign for a while.

Charlie Company had been sent to An Khe to work the area, and we were always a little apprehensive of new terrain. New terrain meant new and changing techniques of handling the lay of the land. Handling different types of bushes and shrubs, thicker or thinner vegetation, mountains, and hills, et cetera. Vietnam was as different in terrain as Illinois is from the Rocky Mountain states. The Rangers had to adapt to many different styles of movement and procedure. Of course, on the other side of the coin, the dinks didn't know about us when we went into a new AO, and it took them time to adjust to us. Advantage Rangers.

As we prepared to pull missions in An Khe, someone from Headquarters Platoon mounted a loudspeaker in the company area so we could monitor contacts. An Khe proved it was a veritable shooting gallery from the first day the teams from Charlie Rangers were inserted. Almost immediately the loudspeakers were blasting away. First a siren sounded, then a voice called, "Attention in the company area, Team 1-1 in contact." Those of us in the rear area awaiting insertion or just milling around between missions cheered loudly.

In a few minutes the loudspeaker gave us an update on the team's contact. "Team 1-1 reports engaging three dinks carrying weapons and rucksacks—gunships working area now," and again we whistled and cheered at the news. Fifteen minutes later the loudspeaker sounded the siren again then delivered another report: "Team 1-1 reports three confirmed kills, two AK-47s and equipment captured. No friendly casualties.'' That set the tone. Not more than fifteen minutes later the loudspeaker's siren went off followed by a report of another contact.

''Attention in the company area, double deuce (team 2–2) in contact.'' Again we shouted and cheered while we awaited the outcome. Meanwhile the legs from Kangaroo Company were avoiding eye contact with us.

''Attention in the company area, double deuce reports two confirmed kills and one probable . . . one AK-47 and one SKS captured along with equipment . . . no friendlies hit.'' From the first day in the woods, we were finding dinks where the 4th said there were none. That had to frustrate the clowns from Kangaroo Company, as they couldn't figure out why we were finding them and they couldn't. (Professionalism maybe?)

Since our team wasn't scheduled to be inserted till the next day, we went over to the mess hall for chow. The conversation was about the other teams' good hunting and how we just hoped they would save some of the dinks for us tomorrow. Coming back from the mess hall after lunch we passed Major Holt, who was just going to eat. As he neared us he seemed to be walking a bit taller than usual, a swagger in his step. We saluted him and, in unison, gave him our own greeting. ''Charlie Ranger, sir.''

He returned our salute with an ''Airborne,'' as he gave us a wink. Obviously the morning was going well for him.

The next day we were up around 0530 and, after breakfast, headed back to our barracks to ready our equipment. I was going to carry the gun again, and I checked and double-checked my rucksack, packed the night before, to be sure I hadn't forgotten anything. A few last adjustments on the rucksack, then the cammy stick on the face and hands, and finally the waiting began for our ride to the helipad. Not long after, we were once again airborne with the rest of the teams being inserted. There was an unbelievable air of confidence in the slick as we waited for our turn to be inserted. As the slick banked and began low-leveling to the LZ, my adrenaline was pumping like mad. I looked at Niebert, who was just starting to stand on the skid, leaning out, waiting for the slick to get close enough to the ground so he could jump off. He was hungry for a kill, as were the rest of us. As the Huey began its hover, Niebert and Josh jumped from the slick's right side. Paxton, the RTO, and I were right behind them, followed by the rest of the team, who exited from the left side. In minutes we were all in the woodline, catching our breath while Paxton made contact with the X-ray. When he gave Niebert the nod, we got up and began to break the bush. We hadn't gone more than two hundred meters when Paxton clicked his fingers just loud enough to get our attention. Another team had made contact, and the X-ray advised all teams to go "ground hog," that is, lay low till the other team was extracted because with only the single 0–1 to coordinate the gunships and the slicks, if more than one team made contact, the support would have to go to the team that needed it more.

We waited for the word to Charlie Mike, and then we moved out, looking, listening, and sniffing. The first day we didn't find any trails or streams. In fact there were no signs of activity in our area. This was frustrating, especially to me, since I had the gun and wanted desperately to see how it would perform. Niebert seemed calm, but you could tell he was getting as anxious as the rest of us. On the third morning we heard M-16s firing in the distance, followed by Paxton's clicking of his fingers. We knew what he was going to say, so Niebert took the team to an area with good cover and concealment and waited for the other team to get extracted. Since we could hear the contact, we knew dinks were in the area for sure.

When the other team was pulled, Niebert changed directions and we headed toward the area of contact, figuring we could get closer to a contact of our own. When we got to the border of our AO, Niebert had us going up one hill and down another, but we just couldn't find any sign. Despite all the dinks in the area, it seemed we had drawn the one dry AO. We humped and humped but came up empty, and on the fourth day we were to be extracted but there was too much ground fog and the birds couldn't get up. So we would wait another day and fume over our predicament. Because of the number of contacts made

the company's first day in the field, none of us had
planned on spending much time in the woods, so we
hadn't packed extra food. There was enough water, but
food was on everyone's mind. We just lay in our positions looking and listening, trying to concentrate but
thinking about food. As we lay there with our minds
going off in different directions we heard the unmistakable rustling of a plastic LRP wrapper: Boone had one
dinner left, and at the sound of his trying to quietly open
it, five pair of hungry eyes were fixed on him and his
precious freeze-dried beef stew.

Boone tried to give us that "You should have packed
an extra like me" look, but the expression on Niebert's
face persuaded him to share it with us. We savored each
bite; it would be the only food that day unless Boone was
hiding another. I made a mental note to pack an extra
LRP ration or two on future missions. I could hear Scotty's voice: "Better to have and not need than need and
not have."

The next morning the fog lifted and we were extracted
with the other teams who had not made any contact. It
was embarrassing to go back to the barracks or the mess
hall and listen to the other teams repeating endlessly the
stories of their contacts. Granted, some team leaders
could be categorized as "runners" (that is, having a reputation of avoiding contacts), but Niebert was definitely
not a runner!

A few days later we were once again to be inserted,
but in the early afternoon, which didn't set too well with
us, because we wouldn't have time to thoroughly check
out the new AO; patrolling the first day would be limited.

As we neared the LZ, the slick began to flare, and then
just hovered about twenty or twenty-five feet off the
ground. We waited for the pilot to go lower but he just
stayed there. The door gunner on the right side motioned
for Josh to jump, but Josh gestured that we had to go
lower. The door gunner said they couldn't, then yelled,
"Go," and Josh yelled back at him, "No." Then the
door gunner told him if we didn't jump the slick would
crash, so Niebert was first to go. I watched him as he hit
the ground, rolled over, and ran right into a small tree
on the LZ, broke the tree with his head, and continued

to the woodline. Josh followed, but before jumping he dropped his weapon butt first, then his rucksack, and went out. I followed Josh's lead and dropped my M-60, butt first, then my rucksack, and instead of jumping I began to climb down the skid. As I got hold of the skid I felt the slick begin to surge upward, so I released my grip and made my first skydive into an LZ. When I hit the ground I executed a jump-school PLF (parachute landing fall), picked up the M-60 and rucksack, and ran to the woodline to join the rest of the team.

We took our tally of walking wounded and it was obvious that medical attention was called for: Niebert had three good-sized dents on his head from running into the tree; Paxton had screwed up his leg and probably would need a cast; Boone had the wind knocked out of him and was having a hard time getting his breath back.

Niebert got on the horn to the 0–1 and called for an extraction chopper since we couldn't continue the mission in the state we were in. Besides that, the amount of time that sorry son-of-a-bitch pilot hovered announced to anybody within a five-hundred-meter radius that they were about to have company. Within a half hour we were told to stand by to pop smoke. As we popped smoke, the slick came over the LZ, flared his nose, and touched down on the same spot the asshole who inserted us said he couldn't land because of "the obstacles."

When we got back to An Khe we went to the hospital. After which we went to the helipad looking for the slick that had inserted us, but we never found his tail number. I don't know what we would have done had we found it, but we *had* to look for it.

A couple of days later while waiting for the rest of the team to recover, I got called to saddle up as part of a reaction force. A team in the Second Platoon was in contact and had requested another team to help. We jumped on the slick just as it warmed up and we were airborne in *ti-ti* time. As we were en route I heard it was the team Scotty was on. I got a sinking feeling in the pit of my stomach.

When we touched down, the team leader had the general coordinates of where we had to go. We heard the gunships finishing their passes. By the sounds, we weren't too far away. We pushed on for a hundred meters then caught sight of the team awaiting us. They knew where we were coming from and were ready to meet us just over the rise of a hill.

The team was in pretty good spirits and began explaining what had happened. There was little cover and the team leader decided to come down the side of the hill toward the woodline that was at the base of the hill. When the team was about halfway down the hill, the dinks opened up, sending them back up the hill. Scotty was carrying the gun, and as the team was being shot at he stopped in his tracks and in perfect John Wayne fashion turned and opened up on the woodline where the fire was coming from. Needless to say the dinks stopped firing; they were keeping their heads down since Scotty had a pretty good idea where they were. As he stopped firing and began ascending the hill himself, the dinks opened fire again. Their bullets were hitting all around him; once again he stopped, turned, and began laying down another base of fire. By now the rest of the team was over the top of the hill and they began firing into the woodline, allowing Scotty to finish his run up the hill. That's when the team called for the reaction force and the gunships since they didn't know how large a force it had engaged.

When we caught up with them, the gunships had finished and we spread out and moved down the hill to the woodline. When we got to the base of the hill we found the trail the dinks had traveled, but didn't find any bodies. One team went one way down the trail while the other went the other way. After a thorough search both came up with negative results and joined up to plot our next course of action. Evidently the team had been spotted by a group of dinks who just happened to be at the right place at the right time and opened up on them. We searched again, just in case, but with the same results. Since the mission had been compromised, the TOC decided to pull both teams. We headed back up the hill and waited for the slicks to come and pick us up.

When we got back to An Khe we were told that the company was going on a stand-down. That meant four days off and I really mean off. Four days of party, party, and more party.

I was a social butterfly, as I hung around not only with the men of the Third Platoon, but of the First and Second as well. My buddy Don Norton, whom I attended the Ranger school with, was assigned to the First Platoon, and we hung around a bit together. Scotty was in the Second Platoon, so I spent a good deal of my time sharing beers with that platoon also.

Every platoon had its share of very good team leaders (those whose actions and field decisions always seemed to be correct) and a favorite story associated with that platoon. In the First Platoon the man to talk about was a team leader named Gary Poppell. Tall and lean, he was from Florida and could be categorized as either extremely brave or extremely crazy. He was a headhunter all the way. Poppell didn't get along with the first sergeant back at An Khe. Conditions didn't improve after Poppell got ahold of the first sergeant's glass eye and hid it for days. On one mission at Phan Thiet he had placed the team on the top of a ridge. It was late afternoon as the team was preparing for its night halt. Below them a company of NVA came by and was beginning to set up for the evening. The team counted between eighty and a hundred NVA. Poppell asked the team what they wanted to do; either call for help or charge the dinks. The team voted to charge, so Poppell got his team on line about ten meters apart and on command began screaming and shooting as they ran into the valley, throwing grenades in front of them. The gooks dropped their weapons and gear and ran. Six men against a company, and the six won.

After securing the area, Poppell called for help and got it. Along with the reaction force came a chopper, which hovered overhead. The team put all the captured equipment into a net suspended beneath the chopper for the ride back to Phan Thiet. Unfortunately the net broke on the way back and all the equipment was scattered all over the countryside. Needless to say Poppell was furious.

Second Platoon could always hang their hat on Team 2-5's contact. It was the contact they talked about most and had become somewhat of a legend among us Rangers. By the time I got to the Rangers all of those on Team 2-5 had since departed, so what we heard was handed down from platoon member to platoon member. Team 2-5 consisted of Harold Williams, known as Ranger Williams, the team leader; Frank Walters as the ATL; John Leppelman, known as Lepp, was the RTO; Hoa was the Kit Carson scout; Gary Frye and Camilo DeJesus, "D.J.," rounded out the team. Their mission was to locate an NVA general who, according to intelligence, was in the area and was guarded by a group of elite NVA guards. Either a platoon or a company. If the general located, the team was to try and snatch him. If they couldn't capture him, they were to kill him and *di-di* out of the area.* The team would be working quite a distance and would be ferried out to an old base where they would be picked up for the remainder of the flight. The Second Platoon's Lieutenant Grimes ("Candy Grimes") would insert the team.

At 0400 hours the team was awakened by the platoon sergeant as quietly as he could without waking the men from the other teams. Team 2-5 headed for the latrine and did their wake-up call and then applied camouflage to their faces and hands. Team 2-5 put its cammy on in war-paint style to look meaner. When that was accomplished they headed for the mess hall for some coffee and a candy bar. Rangers tried not to eat big breakfasts, because that tended to make them feel heavy and move slower than usual. After chow they moved back to the Second Platoon tent, where Frye and Lepp adjusted cammy parachute headbands around their heads. The others wore boonie hats. They then loaded their gear into a small trailer behind the company jeep and piled in. The driver took them to the helipad to catch the slick that would take them on the first leg of their journey. Lepp and Frye had their last cigarette while the others just shot the shit with one another. Hoa sat on his ruck with an unhappy face. He acted as though he didn't want to go on the mission.

Around 0630 they heard the *wop-wop* of the incoming slick. Three of them automatically saddled up and moved to the other side of the pad so that when the slick landed

*After the war, Lepp was told the target of this mission was actually General Giap, but he's never had that confirmed.

three men would enter from each side. As they jumped in, the door gunner counted them, and they gave him the thumbs-up. They flew about forty minutes over uninhabited areas and jungle, then the slick banked steeply down into an old rubber plantation and landed on an unused airstrip made before the Americans entered the war. After 2–5 got off, the slick departed. They hung around the airstrip for a couple of hours while an X-ray team was being inserted. There was nothing at the airstrip but rubber trees, and beyond the rubber trees, jungle. The team faded into the bush and lay low waiting for the second leg of the mission to begin. At 1200 hours Lepp got a call over the horn that another slick was on its way to take them to the LZ. A half hour later the slick touched down and the team was on its way. They flew for another forty-five minutes when Candy directed the Huey to the LZ. The slick banked sharply and came in at almost full RPM. At three feet off the ground they jumped, and in an instant the chopper was gone. Their LZ was an open area with grass about three to four feet high, the trees starting thirty meters to the south. To the north was a straight drop-off. There was no way to go except south, and if it had been a hot LZ their shit would have been weak. As the team entered the woodline, it formed into a defensive perimeter while Lepp checked for commo. After waiting fifteen minutes without moving they heard several AK-47 shots to their south. Ranger Williams crawled to Lepp and asked which direction he thought the shots had come from. Lepp pointed straight down the mountain to the south. Ranger agreed. Lepp got on the horn and advised Candy that they definitely had bad guys in their AO and that they had heard several shots below them. The team waited another half hour and heard more shots down below. They decided to investigate. As they moved through the woods, Williams was on point with Frye walking his slack. Lepp was third with D.J., Hoa, and Walters pulling rear security. It was hot and the team was sweating like porkers on a spit. They moved down the steep mountain very slowly, being sure not to make any noise. All communication was by hand signals. It took several hours for the team to maneuver halfway down the mountain in double canopy. While they were

moving down, the bird dog, which had gone back to refuel, returned, circling several klicks to the north. At that
time it was getting dark and they could hear activity below them although they couldn't see a thing.

They settled down just before nightfall and formed a
tight circle. Fifteen minutes after they were in their night
halt they heard a Vietnamese woman speaking on a PA
system directly below them. According to Hoa, she was
addressing a group of unknown size on the functions of
the new AK-47s they had just received. The team was
tense; they knew they were onto something big. Williams
got on the horn and advised Grimes of what was going
on. The woman finally stopped her lecture at 2000 hours.
Lieutenant Grimes asked the team's opinion of the situation. They debated in whispers whether they should go
down into the valley or leave the area and let higher-
higher send in a company of grunts for a search-and-
destroy. With the exception of Hoa, the team decided to
try to carry out the original mission. They figured where
you found a group with women giving instructions over
a PA system, in the middle of nothing, that's where they
would find their general. Hoa was very negative and kept
saying over and over, "Beaucoup VC, beaucoup VC."

Williams called back to the bird dog and informed him
the team would move down into the valley at first light.
He told Grimes to be on station with the bird dog, as
well as with several Cobra gunships over the north side
of the mountain where they could not be heard. Grimes
rogered his request and departed back to Phan Thiet while
the team settled in for the night.

At 0600 hours the next morning Lepp made contact
with the bird dog. He was in position and had two Cobras
in the air with two more on standby. The team saddled
up and began to move silently down the mountain. Below
them wood was being chopped and they could smell fires.
After a half hour 2–5 reached the bottom of the steep
incline and moved out toward the source of the noise.
After about three hundred meters, Williams froze and
held up his hand to signal—VC! Ten dinks moved from
the team's left to its right, not more than five meters from
where Williams was. They never spotted the team and
continued on their way.

John L. Rotundo

Don Ericson and John L. Rotundo—An Khe, April 1970.

John L. Rotundo

Silencium Mortum

C. Co; 75th. Ranger LRP (Abn) 3rd PLT.

Will Supply, On Demand, The Following;

Murderers
Sadists
Perverts
Mercenaries
Arsonists
Hunter-Killer Teams
Assassins

We Also Specialize In: Counter-Insurgency. Revolutions.
Coups-de-etat, Riots. Street Fights. Bombings. Terror & Arson.
Contact Our Central Office In An Khe. R.V.N. For Special
Contracts.

Dealers Of Death

Co C: 75th Ranger LRP (Abn) 4th Platoon

Ron Novelty Shop

For A Small Remittance We Will Supply

VC/NVA EARS
KNEE CAPS
NOSES
GOLD TEETH
SCALPS
ONE PIECE COMPLETE HEADS
FINGERS

We Also Will Supply Vc/Nva Shitburners And Hoochmaids.
All Items Are Guaranteed Genuine Sorry! Cannot Be Mailed
Thru U.S. Postal System Members Of CCWA   (Crotch
Cannibals World Association)

"THE GRIM REAPER OF DEATH"

2 PLT

C AIRBORNE   RANGER 75

A BEER AND A BODYCOUNT
"SIR !"

SATAN'S PLAYBOYS
"FROM HELL WE RISE"
1st Platoon L.R.P.'s
WE KILL FOR FUN

Charlie Rangers' Death Cards: Upper left, 2nd Platoon;
upper right, 1st Platoon; lower left, 4th Platoon; lower right,
3rd Platoon.

Don Ericson

Cammying up prior to mission—Phan Thiet, July 1970.

John L. Rotundo

Team 3-3's new haircuts. (L to R): Rotundo, Boone, Paxton, and Niebert.

Don Ericson

Team 3-1, Pleiku, March 1970. Standing (L to R): Rath, Ericson, Price and Rassler. Kneeling: Sam Agner.

Don Ericson

POW. Phan Thiet, July 1970. Note the two people in civilian clothing.

John L. Rotundo

Sharkey with one of the victims of the third platoon's two teamer—Cambodia, May 1970.

Rick Harrison

Soon-to-be-dead NVA. Fats was in an ambush position when he put down his M-16, took the picture, then picked up his M-16 and blew him away.

John L. Rotundo

Scotty (Left his cake out in the rain, huh pal?)—An Khe, April 1970.

Don Ericson

Veterans Day at the Vietnam War Memorial. Standing (L to R): Agner, Ericson, Wells, and Rotundo. Kneeling: Case and Fats.

At this point the team knew they were in the middle of a NVA base camp and they proceeded with even more caution. They moved another hundred meters and bunched up behind a large tree. Lepp called Grimes and he made a mental note that the NVA had new khaki pants and shirts and looked in damn good shape, which meant they had just recently come down from the north. Several of the dinks carried axes and the others had AK-47s that looked new. Within ten minutes, three more small groups passed them.

Williams decided to split the team into two three-man teams. He took Hoa and Walters with him as they moved off to recon the area. Within fifteen minutes several more groups passed their position, chattering like magpies.

Williams and his group had moved approximately two hundred meters to the west of the tree when they came to a clearing. In the middle of the clearing, nine NVA officers with documents and maps were standing around several large wooden tables. Hoa said that the highest ranking officer at the table seemed to be a colonel; there was no general at the meeting. At the same moment, Williams, Hoa, and Walters stepped from behind the bush they were concealed into and opened up on them, killing all nine. Williams and Walters moved to the tables and crammed the maps and paperwork into their rucks while Hoa covered them. When the rest of the team heard the gunfire they knew contact had been made, and they started putting down suppressive fire on the direction they saw dinks moving. A few minutes later Williams and his group came out of the trees at a full run and slid into their original position. Lepp got on the horn and called in the contact. Then it got very quiet. The gooks had disappeared.

Williams looked at Lepp and told him he was going to take point and Lepp should walk his slack. They crossed a cleared area that was about fifty to sixty meters wide, then had moved into the clearing for about forty meters when a .30 caliber machine gun opened up on them from their direct front. Williams and Lepp dived out of the way but Frye took a round in his leg. The bullet entered through Frye's left leg pocket where he was carrying a red smoke grenade, and set it off. Frye was thrashing around on the ground yelling, "I'm hit, I'm hit."

The men behind Frye had already hit the dirt and were facing out. Lepp came out of the dirt and moved to within twenty meters of the machine-gun bunker, saw two NVA inside, and fired a magazine into them, killing them both. He was reaching down to throw a frag when Williams yelled, "Lepp, the radio." He ran back to the team's position, and just as he came to a halt near Williams a frag landed between the two of them. Both Rangers rolled into a ball, facing away from the frag, and when it went off they were thrown into the bushes from the blast. Being that they were in the open, they knew they needed to get to cover, so they took off into the direction they had come from as there was a slight incline that might afford them some cover. Lepp led the group with Williams right on his heels. D.J. and Walters were carrying Frye while Hoa covered their rear. They were about halfway to their cover when another frag landed amongst the group.

"Grenade," Lepp yelled as they all tried to melt into the ground. It went off with no further damage to the team. As they made another ten feet two more frags landed and blew everybody down. As they lay there for a moment they heard the *woosh* of an RPG and a terrific explosion. Frye, D.J., and Hoa were all hit with shrapnel in their legs and arms. As Lepp tried to move away, another frag exploded in front of him, shrapnel tearing into his left upper arm, giving him a five-inch wound deep enough to expose the bone. As they tried one more time to get to cover, two Cobra gunships came over, firing rockets and miniguns right through their position. The ground shook as pieces of trees, bushes, and everything else were flying around them. Lepp, Frye, D.J., and Hoa were peppered with fragments; Frye and D.J. had pieces of shrapnel sticking out of their arms. The whole team now dashed for the incline and, after reaching it, all slid into position, facing out. All the team except Lepp had dropped their rucks in the clearing. Lepp couldn't, since he was carrying the radio.

The NVA moved across the clearing and the team threw frags, a willie peter, and fired them up, driving the survivors back. Once again it got quiet and Lieutenant

Grimes informed them that two more gunships were on the way and to hang on. He didn't have to tell them; they were making every possible attempt to do just that. It was hard to believe, but as of yet neither Williams nor Walters were wounded. It had to be some sort of miracle after the hail of bullets and steel they had just run through.

Frye was lying on the ground really hurting, as he, as well as the team, thought that the .30 caliber had got him in the nuts. Lepp radioed Grimes for a Dustoff for Frye as his crotch area was all red and they figured he was going to bleed to death. Williams figured someone should cut his pants open and examine his wound. Walters crawled over and cut open Frye's pants and looked down. All he could see was red.

While the team waited for the next two gunships to come on station, the dinks rushed them two more times. Both assaults were repulsed. Then Grimes radioed the team that two more Cobras were inbound, which would give them a total of four to work the area at the same time. Also there was a Dustoff heading their way to take Frye out.

Team 2-5 responded that there was no place for the slick to land as the area was still hot. The dinks came one more time and were once again driven back. The first rush was with ten men, more in the second, and the third time about thirty dinks charged.

Finally the gunships arrived and worked in the tight circle around the team firing everything they had, and the gooks responded by firing back at the gunships with everything they had. In the meantime the slick hovered over the team and lowered a stretcher basket for Frye to get in. Of course the gooks began shooting at it. The copilot and door gunner were hit and the team could see the slick being riddled by bullets. The pilot couldn't hold on and aborted the pickup. Frye didn't mind. He didn't want to get into the stretcher anyway, figuring he'd be Swiss cheese by the time they got him into the slick.

Then the team got word that one of the Cobras had been hit bad and was going to try to make it home. Grimes informed them that another Dustoff was on its way and would give it a go. The pilots had guts flying into that hell hole.

At that point the dinks' firepower was so intense that Williams just told the gunships to fire over and around their position. Lepp watched as the first gunship came on straight at them. As the minigun bullets came closer and closer to him he said it looked like a pencil line coming at him. When it got to six inches away, he yelled to Williams, ''Call 'em off.'' Williams told them to abort. This went on several times and it did keep the gooks' heads down. But Grimes informed them that another gunship had been hit and one of its crew was wounded; it was heading back. However, more were coming, as well as another Dustoff. The second Dustoff arrived but never got close to their position because of the incoming fire.

At that time they decided to take another look at Frye and determine what could be done. Williams and Walters took another look while the rest of the team kept a lookout. Suddenly Williams said, ''Hell, you're not hit in the balls.''

Frye sat up and said, ''I'm not?'' What had first appeared as blood was nothing more than red dye from the smoke grenade that had gone off in Frye's pocket. Lepp immediately got on the horn to advise Grimes that while Frye was still wounded, it didn't appear critical anymore.

The gunships kept coming in and laying down fire all around the team to keep the gooks from overrunning their position.

Grimes called the team leader to advise them that a reaction force from the Herd was being airlifted to about one klick from their position. It would consist of one platoon of Sky Soldiers, and that was just about the best news they could have asked for.

A half hour later Grimes called to inform them that the platoon was down and making its way to them. When the reaction force was 300 meters away, it came under fire and immediately had three men hit. The Rangers were beginning to feel desperation.

Two gunships were delivered to the reaction force's position to support it while the others stayed to support 2–5.

As the reaction force got closer, the enemy fire got more intense. It took the platoon two hours to link up with the team, running the last fifty meters in a mad dash, and set up a perimeter around the Rangers. The reaction force brought two M-60s and a medic. After the linkup, the medic started to patch people up. The reaction platoon had thirty-one people, and four had already been wounded.

Williams called for Lepp to go out into the clearing with him to retrieve the rucks that they left behind with the maps and documents. But Lepp had been hit and was having his arm looked at, so Walters volunteered. The two of them stood up and walked out of the perimeter. They hadn't gone five feet when a machine gun opened up on them. Lepp and the medic hit the dirt, and when Lepp looked up, Walters was slumped against a tree at the edge of the perimeter. He had taken one round through his chest, and Williams was still outside the perimeter and was down. The gook kept firing but he was countered by two American M-60s. When the 60s opened up, Lepp crawled out and grabbed Williams's boot and dragged him back to the perimeter. At the same time Hoa jumped up and ran to Walters under intense fire and dragged him around behind the tree to cover. The medic immediately moved Walters as it was evident he had a sucking chest wound. Williams had been hit twice in one leg and once in the other. Lepp plugged his wound and gave him encouragement while the medic worked on Walters. Both sides were shooting at each other and the gunships were working out again. Finally, after several minutes of firing, everything got quiet.

Williams was lying on his back and asked Walters if he was okay. He responded that he was and asked Williams how he was doing. Five minutes later Walters's breathing became ragged and his face started turning a gray-white color. He couldn't get enough air. A few minutes passed and Walters died quietly. The medic moved over to Williams, who was lying motionless, and started working on him. Ten minutes later, Williams was going into shock, his eyes started to roll back, and his face became almost white. Lepp yelled at him and he became more alert, but only for a moment. This went on for a few more minutes with both the medic and Lepp working on him. Finally the medic said, "He's gone," and returned to work on Lepp's arm.

The sergeant from the Herd said their present position was lousy and the remainder of 2-5 agreed, especially since it would soon be dark. They grabbed what gear they could, and with the gunships firing up the area they moved out to the northwest, slowly carrying the two dead Rangers and the two wounded who couldn't walk.

The group moved three hundred meters and then found a large depression about fifty feet long and twenty feet wide. From there they formed another perimeter. The gooks could be heard setting up positions around them. As it was getting dark Grimes advised them that he and the gunships were departing the area but Puff (a C-47 armed with miniguns and infrared and low-light sensors) would support them during the night. After the gunships left the gooks probed the perimeter. First they were repulsed with grenades. The second time the gooks came through the grenade shower and the Americans had no choice but to open fire. The gooks returned fire so fiercely that the Americans had to keep their heads down. Lepp got on the horn and advised X-ray that Puff was needed and needed *now*! A short time later Puff arrived on station and began raking the area with its miniguns. None of the Americans slept that night.

First thing in the morning Grimes was back on station in the O-1. Puff pulled out and Grimes informed the team that two companies of ARVNs were on the way. It had gotten very quiet just before dawn, and as they waited for the ARVNs to show, there was no sign that the enemy was still around. The ARVNs were to land about a klick to the west, and the team monitored the insertion. When the first slick arrived, the ARVNs wouldn't get off, so the door gunners began pushing them off. After a few were chucked out, the rest decided that they should jump, too. One of the ARVNs who was thrown out landed on a thin tree stump and was impaled and died.

The sergeant from the Herd said there was a small clearing a few hundred meters to the east and they could get the dead and wounded out. When they arrived they found that the clearing was too small for a slick to touch down but that an LOH could set down. Within minutes an LOH set down and Frye climbed aboard while the remainder of the Americans pulled security. Leppelman got on the second LOH. D.J. was followed by Hoa, and all four were reunited at Phan Thiet along with Major Holt and about twenty other Rangers who helped them with their equipment.

When they got to the hospital they shared the ward with a few pilots and door gunners who had flown in support of them. It was there that they learned that they had been in contact with an NVA battalion. One of the pilots said that from the air it looked like someone had cut the throats of three elephants and had dragged them through the woods, there was that much blood on the ground.

Due to the circumstances they never did get a body count, but a safe estimate would be that a few hundred NVA didn't make roll call the next morning.

Major Holt recommended the following:

Williams—Congressional Medal of Honor, posthumously
Walters—Distinguished Service Cross, posthumously
Leppelman—Silver Star
Frye—Bronze Star with "V"
DeJesus—Bronze Star with "V"
Hoa—Bronze Star with "V"

When the awards came down, the Rangers received the following:

Williams—Distinguished Service Cross, posthumously
Walters—Silver Star, posthumously
Leppelman—Bronze Star with "V"

It seemed that only three Rangers in the history of the Vietnam war were ever awarded the Medal of Honor. While small Special Forces teams that ran similar missions had many Congressional Medal of Honor winners, the Rangers had that one medal withheld from them because the men were enlisted volunteers and no officers ran with the teams. This could not be accepted by the superior officers in the rear area, or apparently by the US government. In addition, all medals had to be approved by rear-echelon types of the 173rd ABN Brigade, to whom Charlie Rangers were attached on temporary duty at the date of the mission. Those officers had little use for the small teams of Rangers that gathered their intelligence and ran other types of missions that are still highly classified, because Charlie Rangers was officially a part of and under the "First Field Force."

In Third Platoon we had Sharkey. He was a Canadian citizen who elected to come south and join the US Army, a twist from all those pussies who fled the United States to avoid military service. Sharkey was medium height and quite muscular. In the rear, he only occasionally had a beer or a cigar. Sharkey had a Kit Carson scout on his team named Hai. A Kit Carson scout was a former VC or NVA who had "rallied" to the side of the South Vietnamese government. The Kit Carsons knew the areas and how to read trails better than any GI could ever hope to. Every platoon had Kit Carsons, and those teams that used them had more contacts than the others. Sharkey and Hai had a special bond between them and it showed in the field as well as in the rear. It seems every time Sharkey took a team out he came back with kills.

The stand-down had begun and I was rapping with Norton and an old friend from the Herd, O'Dougheraty (like O'Donnell, we called him "O.D."), the guy who jumped into the stream after I had fallen in and rescued my helmet.

Norton was a part-time juicer, and having grown up in blue-collar Detroit, O.D. really liked his beer.

We just sat around the barracks rapping when the hard-core juicers began getting loud and somewhat belligerent. Of course O.D. had to put his two cents in and argue with them. Things sounded like they were getting out of hand, so Norton and I left the Third Platoon's barracks and sat on a bunker just outside as he lit up a joint. He took the first drag and inhaled deeply, closed his eyes, and just smiled. "Nice," was all Norton said. He was a man of few words; he let his actions speak. He opened his eyes and passed the joint to me. It had been quite a while since my first and last experience with grass, and I was still a bit apprehensive about it, but I took the joint from him and inhaled it deeply myself.

We passed it around till it was almost gone, myself waiting for a bust at any second but doing it anyway. We sat out there the rest of the night but I didn't indulge anymore as I wasn't used to it and I didn't want to get used to it.

That night I had another sound sleep. The next day for fun I tried something different. All around the barracks of Third Platoon were large anthills which I decided to burn out. Entrance holes were all around, so I began uncrimping M-16 rounds and pouring gunpowder down the holes. I spent a couple of hours doing that then poured some at the entrance of the hole I was concentrating on and took out a pack of matches. Not knowing what to expect I lit the match and touched it to the powder. In a flash it ignited with a *whump*. Smoke began pouring out of the holes scattered around the hillside. I began digging down through the hill and soon came across a bunch of dead ants, all burnt to a crisp. I had had my own little napalm strike there and was really getting into it. There certainly was enough gunpowder around to satisfy my needs. I spent the rest of the day pouring gunpowder down the holes then lighting it and digging up the bodies. Talk about body count.

The next night we were on alert, as sappers broke through the wire and blew up a dozen choppers at the helipad. Cringing as the satchels went off, we heard the muffled explosions. But some Cobra gunships were airborne, and caught the sappers retreating out the wire. What a sight at night as they unleashed their miniguns in the dark. I had watched Stringer work out while I was with the Herd, but that had been off in the distance. This wasn't so far away from us, and their glowing tongue of destruction sweeping back and forth, coupled with the *Bbbbbbrrrrrrraaaaaattttttttt* sound, was something to behold. I was glad not to be on the receiving end.

Two days later we were back in the woods, and once again spent four days following Niebert up and down hills and through the woods, looking but not finding. When we got back in we got the word that we'd be mov-

ing out again. This time Rumor Control had us going to
Cambodia, and word of a possible combat jump by the
Herd.

Talk was heavy among us about transferring to the Herd
so we could make the jump, but Major Holt quickly
squelched that rumor. However, part of the rumor was
correct. We were going back to Pleiku, but this time we'd
be in the compound called Engineer Hill and have a hot
area to explore. An area called Cambodia.

CHAPTER 9

MAY 1970/CAMBODIA
John L. Rotundo

We headed this time to Engineer Hill in Pleiku. This would be our second time in Pleiku. The first time we were there we had lived in tents by the helipad, red dirt and clay everywhere. Every day our cots, tents, and duffel bags, as well as our clothes, would turn red by 0900. This time around was different, as we were to be housed in wood and steel barracks with separate shower rooms. Unbelievable!

Since Charlie Rangers were the eyes and ears of II Corps, we worked as a bastard company. The other Ranger companies worked for a division or brigade and fed the division or brigade intelligence. Of course, the Corps above that division or brigade shared in the information, but Charlie Rangers worked strictly for the Corps, so any intelligence we acquired from the dead gooks went straight to II Corps. But our pay, awards, promotions, and orders came from the Herd, the 173rd Airborne Brigade, so we were really accepted by no one. We were under the direction of II Corps, which called on Charlie Rangers when an area was suspected of having an enemy build-up. Little did we suspect this mission would be the Big One, but President Nixon had indeed ordered the invasion of Cambodia to find the enemy sanctuaries on and across Cambodian border. No longer would the VC or NVA have a haven to hide in. US troops were going to kick ass.

We left An Khe by truck convoy through the infamous Mang Yang Pass, where, in the fifties, hundreds of French soldiers were ambushed in a truck convoy. We were told that Mang Yang Pass was second to only the An Khe Pass for the number of ambushes of convoys. Where the An Khe Pass was east of An Khe, Mang Yang Pass lay to the west. In both areas the Americans took several small beatings but nothing like those the French took. Mang Yang Pass is a road nestled between huge boulders and a steep grade. A picture-book ambush site, one where it is hard to guard against or prevent ambushes. Everyone sighed when we were safely past it. As the trucks rolled westward, I kept thinking to myself that Pleiku is near Kontum and Dak To. The Herd had taken quite a few casualties around Dak To in 1967, when it finally took Hill 875 on Thanksgiving Day. Everything we heard about the area was demoralizing. Pleiku, this time around, was going to be a son of a bitch.

The ride to Pleiku was uneventful, however, and we really got to see the absolute poverty of Vietnam. Beggars everywhere, kids hawking Cokes, whores coming out of the woodwork, houses an American wouldn't let a dog live in.

Not long after we got settled in, the Fourth Platoon was inserted, the first to draw blood and the first to spill blood.

Team 4–4 made contact when they initiated an ambush on the NVA and reported a number of kills. A few minutes passed and the team again reported contact and called for a reaction force, *now*! We watched as another team from Fourth Platoon grabbed its gear and was sped away to the helipad. Myself and a few others walked over to the TOC to find out what was going on. Nobody at the TOC was saying much, but by the look on their faces it was obvious Team 4–4 had run into real trouble.

When we reached the TOC, the team had been in contact for close to an hour. A Ranger team cannot sustain a long contact. Our mission was to kill and get out. As we tried to listen to the X-ray over the TOC's loudspeaker relay, I guessed 4–4 had hit either a platoon- or a company-size element. The team had WIAs but was holding on while gunships were making runs and receiving fire. Then a lieutenant came out of the TOC and shooed us away. As we headed to our barracks we wondered what was out there. Later that afternoon we found out.

Team 4–4 had three friendly KIAs—one of those killed was Kit Carson Scout Hoa, of team 2–5's contact mentioned earlier. That's half of the team. The next day a memorial service was held on behalf of the three dead Rangers, complete with M-16s inverted in blocks; that helped no one. After the service the survivors told us that when 4–4 sprang its ambush on a number of NVA, there was no movement or sound from the kill zone, a sure sign of a good kill. But when the team heard no movement, the team leader, Foster, and another Ranger went out to the kill zone to check bodies. Those two were then ambushed and killed by other NVA who had hastily set up an ambush covering their dead comrades. While trying to retrieve the bodies, two other Rangers were hit and one would die from his wounds. When the reaction force came on the scene, the NVA broke contact and ran, leaving their dead as well as the bodies of the dead Rangers.

As a result of Team 4–4's losses, Major Holt decided that the teams would go to the field carrying powder CS packets taped in front of their claymores. CS differed from tear gas (CN), as tear gas made the eyes water, burned a bit, and generally gave the victim a feeling of discomfort. CS, on the other hand, burned something fierce; your nose, eyes, throat, and lungs as well as your skin. CS also inhibited breathing and you really couldn't catch your breath. And, most of the time, it made you puke. And that was for CS in the canister form, which put out a cloud like a smoke grenade. With CS in the powdered form, the victim had all the same problems, but he carried it with him wherever he went and it continued to have its effects. Major Holt also decided to assign some two-ambush teams. That is, two teams acting as one in the same ambush. Same technique but twice the firepower.

The night before we were to go out, talk was reserved as Second and Third Platoons would each be inserting a two-teamer. Those of us going out hit the sack early, and those teams that weren't going to the woods in the morning kept their partying down to allow us to rest. We appreciated it.

The next morning we got up, went to breakfast, and prepared for the mission. We would go out as a team of twelve chosen from the various teams at Third Platoon. Niebert would be in charge but Sharkey and Agner were going out as well. Once again the rucksacks were fitted and refitted to make sure they were as comfortable as possible.

I was elected to carry one of the radios on the mission, but this time I didn't mind. I was happy to have been selected. Niebert, Sharkey, and Agner checked out all twelve of us going out, and when they were satisfied, the waiting game began because ground fog prevented the choppers from getting up. We just sat around the helipad, thinking our thoughts, and I started to wonder if I was in the right frame of mind to go through this mission. Fuck it, it don't mean nothing, I told myself as I took another drag on my Camel. I looked around at the others with me and then it dawned on me that I would be all right. I was with the best: Niebert, Agner, Sharkey, Giossi,* Ericson, and Hobo, to name just a few. We were all professionals and we had one goal, to avenge Team 4-4.

"Saddle up," Niebert yelled, "we're going in." With that the huge main rotor blades of the Huey began to turn as the engines whined, getting up to the proper RPMs. The slick hovered and rose for a minute before touching back down. Sam and Sharkey's slick did the same and the two other teams staggered to their respective chop-

---

*Although Giossi doesn't come up too often in this book, he was an excellent hunter in the field.

pers, the team members giving each other the thumbs-up or the three-finger war symbol.

"See you all in Cambodia," Sharkey yelled to Niebert.

"Last one on the ground's a leg," Niebert responded. I got in first, as I was carrying the radio and would march third, behind Niebert, who was to walk Hobo's slack; and those two would be sitting in the door. As we lifted off and departed Pleiku, the slicks headed west, low-leveling all the way out. Since Cambodia was only thirty miles or so west of Pleiku the ride wouldn't be that long. As I watched the other slick follow the contours of the countryside and rise and descend with us as we flew over the trees and small hills, the song "Pushin' Too Hard" by the Seeds came into my mind. Over and over the instrumental part went through my mind as I watched the other slicks match our maneuvers over the terrain. I still get goose bumps when I hear the song.

The door gunner leaned over to Niebert and said something. Niebert in turn looked at us and yelled over the sound of the rotors that we were leaving Vietnam, next stop Cambodia! I looked at my watch and saw it was just past 1030. We flew another ten minutes or so when again the door gunner said something to Niebert. Again he looked at us, and this time told us to lock and load; we were going in. I pulled back the charging handle of my M-16 and chambered a round. The Huey banked left and immediately began to flare. I looked between the pilots and saw the LZ directly in front of us, not more than twenty meters away. Niebert was ready to go as Hobo was already standing on the skids, bracing himself with his left hand on the frame, ready to jump as the slick began its hover. I was on my knees, facing out, when the two of them jumped from the door at six feet off the ground. Both slicks unloaded their cargo of bodies in record time as we ran to the woodline following the leader. We formed up and entered the woods for fifty meters, then moved into a defensive perimeter while I made contact with the X-ray and the rest of the team listened for any sounds of the enemy.

"X-ray, X-ray, this is 3–3, Commo check. Over," I whispered into the handset.

"3–3, this is X-ray. I've got you Lumpy Chicken [loud and clear]. How me? Over."

"X-ray, this is 3–3, I've got you same-same. Give me a count. Over."

The X-ray then began to count from one to ten then back down to one again. While he was doing this, I adjusted the volume control on the radio so only I could hear radio traffic while we were humping to our destination.

"X-ray, this is 3–3. Thanks much. Out."

I put the handset on the shoulder harness of my web gear and gave Niebert an affirmative nod. As we lay there, the heat, humidity, and tension of being in Cambodia caught up to us. The chopper ride had been very cooling, but after being on the ground for only a short time I believed Cambodia was the hottest place on earth.

I watched as Niebert, Sam, and Sharkey were silently conferring over the map and pointing in the direction of our travel. After fifteen minutes of listening for sounds, we got to our feet and formed into a file, following Hobo. Slowly and carefully we LRPed through the woods, always replacing branches that we moved so that we moved quietly. As amazed as I had been on my first mission as to how quiet six people could be in the woods, I was doubly impressed at how quiet the twelve of us were as we broke through the brush without even a twig snapping.

After an hour, the humidity was taking its toll, so we broke to quench our thirst. Our cammies were completely soaked with sweat. After ten minutes we again got to our feet and moved out. We repeated the pattern, moving for an hour and resting for ten minutes, until we found our objective, a four-foot-wide hard-packed trail off which we would set up our ambush. We positioned ourselves in a linear ambush with me in the middle behind a slight rise that might afford some protection for the radio. Niebert and two others collected our claymores and daisy-chained them together with det cord. Sam and Giossi were on the left side of the kill zone and would control three claymores. Sharkey and another protected our right side with their claymores. Niebert would control the team from the center. His clacker was connected to the four claymores to our front. I was next to Niebert. The claymores weren't more than ten meters off the trail and we were about twenty meters behind them. As dusk was approaching we took turns eating LRPs, all the time keeping alert for any signal of someone approaching.

Around 1730 or so the radio cracked and I put the handset to my ear and listened. Second Platoon's double team had made contact, ambushing eight or nine NVA with their claymores and taking no incoming fire. I turned the handset over to Niebert, who monitored for the rest of the contact till they were extracted just as darkness had set in. Second Platoon's contact was just a few klicks north of our ambush, so with any luck we should make contact the next day.

As I was getting ready to go to sleep I pulled the poncho liner halfway up my body and looked at Niebert. He was looking out in the direction of the trail, then looked up at me and smiled. He knew tomorrow would bring our turn.

Around 0200 I was awakened for my turn on guard. I took the handset and keyed the mike.

"X-ray, X-ray, this is 3-3. Time check. Over," I whispered into the mike.

"3-3, this is X-ray. It's just after 0200 hours."

It was always comforting to know I would have some company on the radio and that somebody else was awake with me. Just in case.

My mind wandered back home where I wondered what my parents and girlfriend were doing. They wouldn't know I was lying in an ambush somewhere in Cambodia with eleven others just waiting for some unsuspecting dinks to be-bop down the trail so we could blow them away. It was so quiet out there, no sounds of anything anywhere. The others were all asleep and weren't rustling a bit. I looked at the luminous dial on my Seiko. It was already 0210. Time flies when you're having fun. An Khe taught me not to assume contact would come just because the dinks were near; we'd been very close to the other team's contact that one mission and still had gotten no action. I would take it in stride if we didn't make contact: on one hand, that trail was so wide and so hard-packed that surely they were using it every day; on the other hand, Second Platoon's ambush might have signaled them not to walk any trails but rather to beat the bushes looking for us. My mind was so busy rationalizing why we would make contact and then again why we wouldn't that I decided to let it drift off to something else before I went nuts. I spent the rest of my watch trying to concentrate on the sounds of the woods at night, but there were none, so I just kept ready. When 0300 finally came, I woke the next watch, gave him the handset, and went right to sleep. If we made contact, we made contact. If we didn't, we didn't. It would be as simple as that. No sense fretting it, so off to sleep I went.

Around 0600 I woke up to find the rest of the team already awake. Some of them already had their LRPs out and were breakfasting on beef stew or chicken and rice. As I pulled the poncho liner and began to sit up, I felt a stabbing pain in the middle of the back of my neck. I felt back there and found a small lump. Evidently during the night I was stung by a bee, my very first bee sting. I reached over to my rucksack to grab an LRP for breakfast when *boom, boom, boom*, the claymores went off followed by the barking of the M-16s firing on full automatic. I rolled on my back and grabbed the handset from the radio.

"X-ray, X-ray, this is 3-3, 3-3. Contact. Over!" I yelled into the handset.

A *thump* followed by an explosion told me the thumpers were being fired into the kill zone as frags were going off also.

"X-ray, this is 3-3. I repeat; contact, contact! Over." And with that I dropped the handset, rolled back on my stomach, and began firing, remembering to keep my shots as low as possible, as anyone out there would either be dead or hugging the ground. I remembered the firing-range instructor in basic training telling us to keep our shots low because there's always a chance of a ricochet kill, while firing high would just cut up the trees.

I was firing into a slight clearing in front of me and heard Giossi yell from his flank, "I counted nine of them," over the noise of our M-16s and the grenades being launched from the thumper.

"Watch the rear," Sharkey yelled from the other side as we continued to pour rounds into the kill zone.

I rolled over on my back and picked up the handset once again from where I'd dropped it. "X-ray, X-ray, this is 3-3. Did you copy contact? Over."

"3-3, this is X-ray. Roger your contact. What is your sit rep? Over."

"Wait one. Over." I gave the handset to Niebert. He began talking to the X-ray to get the gunships and extraction slicks heading our way. Everything was going by so quickly that reactions took over. By now we were firing single shots into the kill zone. When I called in our contact, X-ray alerted the TOC, which scrambled the gunships, so they were inbound while Niebert was on the horn. I watched as Niebert talked directly to the gunships, describing our position and where he wanted them to concentrate their fire. We could already hear their rotors beating the air to our right.

"Giossi, Sharkey, pop red smoke when I tell you," Niebert yelled. He went back to the handset and said something to the gunships.

"Pop smoke," he yelled; red smoke began drifting up from our flanks.

"Make your first pass with the 60s only," he told the gunships. Within seconds the quad 60s of the lead ship were firing from our right flank to the left as he passed overhead. His wingman followed suit. Niebert stuck his head up and watched as their 7.62s ripped apart the trees and foliage to our direct front. He was watching where the rounds struck as a reference for their next pass, which would be both rockets and guns. Niebert made an adjustment and they came in again firing volleys of both rockets and machine guns, destroying what was once a peaceful piece of jungle. *Sssssssssscccccchhhhhhh-HHHHHH—BOOM! rat-tat-tat-tat-tat!* After their second pass the area became thoroughly quiet and it was then that I heard the first direct benefit of our using powdered CS: moaning coming from the kill zone.

Niebert, Sharkey, Agner, and Giossi went out to the kill zone to check the bodies as I was given the radio to monitor. Quietly and deliberately the four of them moved out while the rest of the team looked for any signs of activity or movement of any kind.

I couldn't see what was going on out there, and the only noise being made was from one or more of our victims as he or they were feeling the wrath of claymore pellets, M-16 rounds, shrapnel, powdered CS, or a combination of all four. The relative quiet was broken by Niebert's laugh as he spotted a couple of wounded NVA trying to hide.

"Ah-ha." *Bang* as he fired his M-16. "Ha-ha." *Bang bang.* "Ha-ha-ha." *Bang bang bang.* The four of them stripped the dead bodies of their weapons and equipment and crawled back to the rest of us. Niebert got on the radio and began calling for the extraction LZ we would be using. After he got the information and passed the word, I spoke to him.

"Jim, I brought my camera and I've just got to get a picture of this." He looked at me, then at Sharkey, who nodded that he would go out to the kill zone with us for the pictures. It wasn't hard to find a body to choose from, they were lying all over the trail and I could see five without even hunting. I gave my camera to Niebert so he could take the picture as Sharkey grabbed one of the dead dinks by the hair and began to smile. I reached down with my left hand and grabbed a lock of hair, but before I could get my face down with the dink's and Sharkey's, Niebert took the picture.

In the meantime the rest of the team was more than just whispering, saying, "Let's get the fuck out of here." Back to the team we crawled, collected our gear, and began to hump to the exfil LZ. It took us over an hour to get there. When we arrived we formed a perimeter while the 0-1 guided the slicks closer to our position. As usual, the command was given to pop smoke, and once more the pilots identified the color. As the slicks began to touch down, we made a mad dash and boarded them.

When we arrived back at Pleiku we all took showers and put on clean fatigues, then headed toward the mess hall for some chow.

The next day we were just hanging around when somebody brought in a copy of a newspaper article which quoted Mayor John Lindsay of New York City saying he felt the real heroes of the young generation weren't those who went into the military service, but those who opposed the war and refused to serve. After passing around the issue I had an idea and drafted a formal letter to Mr. Lindsay.

To: Mr. John Lindsay
    Mayor, New York City

From: Co. C. (Ranger) 75th Inf. (Airborne)
      APO San Francisco 96294

Dear Mr. Lindsay,

GET FUCKED!

Signed,
The men, not the boys, of
Charlie Rangers

I passed the letter around the company, and after collecting over a hundred signatures, sealed it and a copy of the article in an envelope and mailed it to Mr. Lindsay's office in New York City. Whether he received it or not we never found out, since he never responded. Not that we expected him to, but it would have been neat to have that sorry son of a bitch write us back and try to worm himself out of defending what we regarded as cowardice and treason.

I went over to Second Platoon's barracks to get the rundown on their ambush, and talked to Kelly, a short Irishman from New York City, who had signed the letter to Lindsay.

The team had set out the claymores and had just finished eating when one of the team members had had a bad attack of diarrhea as the claymores were going off, so he had just pulled his pants up and rejoined the teams. To hear Kelly tell it, the ride back on the chopper was endless as everybody tried to distance themselves from the smelly Ranger. But the cabin of a Huey is quite small . . . Needless to say, the Ranger threw away his cammies as soon as he got off the chopper.

During mail call I got a letter from a girlfriend along with a newspaper article about four students at Kent State who were shot by Ohio National Guardsmen. She thought it was awful. I felt just the opposite, and wrote back to tell her I wished the Guardsmen had had an M-60 so they could have killed more protesters. They were protesting our going into Cambodia, well fuck them; they were probably the same assholes who would fly the VC flag during a rally. That really infuriated me. They had no idea of what we were doing in Cambodia, or why the invasion was necessary. To those of us in Vietnam it was frustrating, not to say ridiculous and dangerous, that the enemy had a safe place to hide. Nixon removed the restrictions that Johnson had imposed years before, restrictions which, if they had never been imposed, might have shortened the war. But I was not a politician, just a grunt doing his job.

Within a day somebody started walking around showing four fingers on one hand and making a circle with the other.

"What's that?" I asked.

"The score."

"What score?"

"National Guard four, Kent State nothing."

I loved it. We all loved it.

MAY 1970/CAMBODIA
Don Ericson

Agner went on a VR the next afternoon, and when he returned he briefed the team on the next mission. We went to bed early that night but 0530 came awful early, as usual when you're going out to the woods, and even though I had been doing it for quite a while now, there was something about Cambodia that scared me and the majority of us.

As we were en route Agner said that wherever we went in Cambodia we were going to hook and jab with the NVA. It was their domain, their backyard. I agreed.

After the slick low-leveled in, we finally touched down near a creekbed. We hurried off only to be met by an AK-47 firing from the opposite bank. My worst fear had been realized, a hot LZ! The bullets were going high as we hit a bamboo thicket. Agner immediately got on the horn to the 0-1 and called in our contact. While we returned fire, I counted seven NVA moving toward the creekbed. We kept firing as one would try and slip down the bank, and kept them at bay. It was a stalemate as neither side could move. We couldn't run and neither could they.

Agner was on the horn with O.D., who was the Third Platoon leader. "Bird Dog, this is 3-1, we got problems," Agner said in his Florida accent. "Get the fuck back here. Now."

"Roger, 3-1." The 0-1 spotter plane was over us in less than a minute.

"3-1, this is Bird Dog. What's your problem?"

"Bird Dog, I've got seven NVA shooting at us. Is that a problem, sir? Over."

"Roger, 3-1. Do you request guns? Over."

"Affirmative, I say again, affirmative. Do you copy? Over."

"Roger, 3-1. Pop smoke. Over."

As Agner threw the smoke out I thanked God the gunships were still on station. Smoke was identified and the gunships lined up for their runs. The death ships came in, miniguns blazing.

We heard moaning from the other side of the creekbed but we could confirm no kills. On their second pass, the gunships came in with rockets. The first thing I heard was a deafening explosion and one of the team going "Ooohh."

"Check fire! Check fire!" I yelled, but it was too late; the Cobras were coming in fast. *Sssshh—BOOM! Ssshhh—BOOM!* as another round of rockets found their mark. What firepower! The rockets were landing within twenty meters of us. One of the pilots found two dinks climbing the bank on our side and took them out. Agner called them off and silence settled in. Every ear listened for the sound of movement. The only thing we heard was the quiet moans from our team; everyone except me had caught some shrapnel from the gunship's rockets. One knee wound was especially nasty as the blood was flowing freely; but it was not life-threatening. The bleeding was controlled by a basic field dressing.

Agner was busy trying to get us an extraction chopper but was getting negative results. I heard him yell into the handset, "What do you mean you won't get us out?"

O.D. broke radio security and said our company commander was down. Another team (Sharkey's) was in the area and was sent to secure the major and the crew of the slick.

Agner always had a bad taste in his mouth for O.D. putting Major Holt's life over ours. I'm sure O.D. was doing what he was told, but our lives were in the balance.

As Sharkey maneuvered his team over and secured the major and the crew, he came upon a road. Most Rangers in Vietnam hoped to find a high-speed trail to ambush or observe, but this was a *road*. It was six feet wide, and hard-packed, and triple canopy hid it from the air. I would venture to say no Caucasian (except maybe the odd Russian) had ever seen that one. As Sharkey and the major watched the road they saw porters and NVA marching south. Maybe the Cav or another unit was pushing them out. Sharkey counted one hundred and seventy-three when he saw Major Holt tearing off the oak-leaf insignias from his collar. The major knew that if the drinks found an officer with the Rangers, the team wouldn't have a chance. However, the NVA passed without incident and we were pulled without any further casualties.

When we arrived back at Engine Hill I went to my bunk, took out my towel, and took a shower, hoping to calm my nerves. I put on a clean set of cammies and proceeded to get drunk. My nerves were frayed.

* * *

After futile attempts at making contact, we were told that Charlie Rangers would be going to a new AO: Dalat.

CHAPTER 10

JUNE 1970/DALAT
John L. Rotundo

Once again we found ourselves living in tents, but this time we pitched them in an old ammo bunker complex. The city of Dalat was everything that First and Fourth Platoon said it was.

It had a Vietnam's West Point where the ARVN's future officers were training. Rumor had it that Dalat was also an R&R center for the VC and NVA. Not that they walked around in their uniforms or anything like that, but there must have been some unwritten rule or agreement, since there never was any trouble.

We had heard of a place called Ann's House, a combination restaurant, bar, and whorehouse. A number of us went directly to Ann's House while the others were sightseeing, and immediately fell in love with it; it had all the steak, whiskey, and women we could handle. I was with three others from Charlie Rangers who had recently joined the company. McCoy, whom we called Mac, was a second-tour buck sergeant whose first tour had been with Special Forces. He had a line a mile wide and could hold up his end of a good conversation. Short and thin, he had an uncanny way of getting people to do the things he wanted done.

Thorne and J.C. were cherries in the company, having just arrived from Ranger school in An Khe a short while before. Thorne was tall and slender with reddish hair. In the rear he walked around with a constant grin on his face. He was easily accepted by the Third Platoon. J.C. was also tall with curly hair, and always seemed to be just a few pounds overweight although he really wasn't. Army fatigues are just not for the fashion conscious.

The four of us ate our fill of some very good steak (of course, it could as easily have been water buffalo, for all we knew, but it wasn't LRPs, C rations, or regular army chow) and washed it down with whatever we were drinking.

It didn't take long for the girls to visit and try to get us to buy them Saigon Tea or "whiky coke" (whiskey and Coke). Initially we turned them down, since there were plenty of girls to choose from and the day was still young. Eventually we called the girls back over. For Vietnamese bar girls they had class. Mine was a short, slightly chunky girl with big brown eyes that seemed to light up whenever she spoke. Her name was Ann but she wasn't the owner, who was a large Vietnamese. Mac had a cute little thing who seemed to be very horny. Thorne had picked a young kid, which made sense as he didn't look a day over sixteen himself. J.C. had one of the most beautiful girls I had ever seen, Vietnamese or American.

After a couple of hours of joking with them and their teasing us we got down to the business of getting down on them. Should we stay with them for the evening at $20 MCP or should we head back to the KP pickup point and return to the compound and our tents as we had been instructed?

Mac spoke up first. "Gentlemen, we are all Rangers, and in keeping with Ranger tradition, I feel we should stay and reconnoiter the building for signs of VC or NVA activity. By then J.C., Thorne, and I weren't feeling much pain, so we agreed to spend the night. We called Big Ann (the owner) over from behind the bar and informed her of our decision. She told us that the girls didn't get off till 2100, then accepted our money.

We went upstairs, to the room we would share for the evening, and caught a nap. Around 2000 we woke up and went downstairs for another drink before retiring for the evening with our dates. As we sat in the bar area with other GIs an alarm sounded that makes the hair rise on any enlisted man: "MPs coming!"

We looked at Big Ann, who escorted us behind the bar. As we huddled down I noticed only Mac, Thorne, and I were back there. J.C. was still sitting in the bar with his girl. We heard the MPs taking the others out, and waited for one of them to poke his nose behind the bar looking for strays. But they must have been happy with their haul; they left us alone. After the MPs left, the three of us sat in the bar and had another drink to help think things over. For whatever reason, Big Ann decided it wouldn't be a good idea for us to spend the night after all, so she asked us to leave. Normally we might have obliged her, but we had already paid for services not yet rendered.

One of us confronted Big Ann and told her we were going to our rooms, and if we didn't have the girls up there by exactly 2100 hours, we would take her place apart, room by room, board by board, and nail by nail. He was very convincing as he talked in his slow southern drawl and used exaggerated facial expressions to make his point.

Up to our rooms we went, to await the girls and to decide what to do if they didn't show. At exactly 2100 a knock sounded on the door. Had Big Ann gotten the MPs or did she tell the local VC three unarmed Rangers had holed up in one of her rooms? Mac slowly opened the door. Two lovelies were waiting to be invited inside!

There was only one bed in the room, and since I was first on it, it was mine for the night.

The next morning we all met for breakfast and Little Ann (my date) presented me with a little necklace that she said would bring me good luck. I thanked her for it and told her I would cherish it. I hoped it didn't mean we were engaged.

After breakfast we caught the KP truck back to the compound and compared notes. Mac was sore from spending the night on the floor and poor Thorne it seems had a young virgin, or so he said, and spent a very frus-

trating night trying unsuccessfully to get anything. Other
Rangers returned on the truck with us, so we weren't the
only ones playing hooky that night. In fact, when we
arrived back at the compound a good portion of the company was being herded to the briefing room to receive
Article 15s (nonjudicial punishment). Great! I had been
a PFC for thirteen months, had been promoted to SP-4
just a month earlier, and it looked as if I would soon be
a PFC again. While we waited for the major, we decided
that if we were busted we would all put in for transfers
to the Herd. We'd show him. Hell, it sounded good at
the time. We were all caught and we were looking for
something, anything to defend ourselves with. At the appropriate time Major Holt made his appearance and began to rip into us for what we had done. He was quite
upset, but as he spoke I got the impression that he was
more hurt at our disobedience than angry. He had trusted
us and we had let him down, pure and simple. After a
twenty-minute ass-chewing, he told us there would be no
Article 15s this time, but God help us if it happened
again.

I left the briefing room feeling relieved for obvious
reasons, but even more I felt I now belonged to the unit.
I felt I owed the major something more than my last three
and a half months in-country. It was then that I decided
to extend my tour another six months. Not only would I
receive a thirty-day leave that wouldn't count against my
accrued leave time, but I could put off for another six
months my returning to Fort Bragg and all its bullshit. I
talked to Sergeant Cheek and he provided the necessary
forms; I was then set for an additional six months. All I
had to do was write home and explain to my folks that I
had elected to stay in a war zone another six months.

We were all sitting around the tent shooting the shit
when Mac came in. We were adding another team to the
Third Platoon and Mac would be the team leader of Team
3-5. Mac told me I was going to be the ATL! I didn't
know what to say, so I offered him a beer which he proceeded to throw down his throat.

Mac wore the black and gold Ranger tab signifying he
had been through the eight-week Ranger course at Fort

Benning. Normally the only people we saw wearing the tab were officers and a few enlisted men who never went to the field. The conversation somehow got to the difference between us and the "Stateside Rangers," since we LRPs really thought very little of them. Of course, Mac was one of them, and he began his speech about the tough training a guy had to endure to be eligible to wear the black and gold Ranger tab.

"Big and bad, brave and bold. Proud to wear the black and gold," he'd say.

"Black and gold, you're nothing more than a fuckin' bumble bee!" someone shouted. At that we all began to buzz like bees. Every time Mac opened his mouth all you could hear was, "Bzzzzzzzzz."

"Hey, Mac," another shouted above the buzzing, "danger is no stranger to an Airborne Ranger." That got a round of cheers. Mac finally gave up and left the tent amid more buzzing.

A few days later Mac and some of the other team leaders went out on a VR while the rest of us readied our gear for the next day's mission. Mac came back and briefed us on our AO, order of march, et cetera.

After chow we went back to our tents, and with Robert's tape player blaring songs by the Friends of Distinction we all got ready for sleep. "You got me going in circles . . . round and around I go . . . You got me going in circles . . ."

The next morning we awoke at 0530 and had breakfast as usual. As we returned to the tent we cammied up, checked and rechecked our rucksacks and web gear, and finally off to the chopper pad we went. When we arrived at the pad the slicks were already warmed up; all we had to do was hop on.

We were comforted by knowing our old friends of the 192nd Assault Helicopter Company, the Lonesome Polecats from Phan Thiet, were going to be inserting us and providing the air support.

On this mission Hobo was going to walk point and I was going to walk his slack. As the slick neared the LZ, Hobo stood on the skid and I braced myself, half sitting, half leaning out the door, waiting for him to jump. As the slick began its flare and approached the ground, Hobo jumped off and I followed him into the elephant grass. In seconds the entire team was in the woods and had formed a defensive perimeter, listening for the sounds of uninvited company as the slick made two fake infils a couple of klicks away to confuse VC LZ watchers who might be in the area.

After commo was established with the X-ray and we had assured ourselves that the area was secure, we formed a single file and moved out. As I was walking Hobo's slack I noticed how fluid his movements were as he slithered through the bush without a sound. And it really amazed me that I was as quiet as he was. On and on, we walked cautiously, eyes checking to our front and each side as I tried to time my movements so that when Hobo looked to the left I was covering the right and vice versa. Around noon we broke for chow, and since we all had done this before, we automatically formed a defensive perimeter, one man eating at a time while the rest of us kept vigil. It began to rain while we were chowing down. Not a heavy downpour, just a steady drizzle that looked like it would keep up for some time. Mac thought it would be a good idea to move out in it, as we could cover more ground. The rain would mask any noise we might make moving faster. Since we hadn't yet spotted any trails or streams, that sounded like a good idea. We buried our LRP bags and moved out again more quickly, heading up a small hill.

When we got to the top we found that the other side faced a valley, and there was what looked like a sheer drop-off going straight down. The rain was coming down harder by then, and we continued to walk the ridgeline looking and listening. But the rain was an equalizer not only for us but for anybody else in the area.

One minute Hobo was right in front of me and then he was gone. I looked down the cliff and saw him holding to a small tree that jutted from the side of the hill. I motioned for the team to halt, and Mac and I crawled to the edge and looked down at Hobo. In a low whisper I asked him if he was okay.

"Fuck it, man, just fuck it," he whispered back. He looked so funny down there that Mac and I both began to laugh. "Hey, fuck both of you." Hobo said as he pulled himself around the tree. Now he was facing us.

"Throw me your rope and I'll pull myself up." I took the rope from my web gear and threw it down to him. As he grabbed it I pulled it on my end and watched as his feet slipped on the side of the hill while he tried to get his footing. It didn't take long for him to get to the top.

"Are you all right?" Mac asked.

"Yeah, Mac, no sweat." Aside from being covered with mud he looked okay to me, but I asked how he felt.

"You got to remember, back in the World if you fall down, you try to brace yourself so you don't get hurt, and you normally end up hurting something cause you're so tight. Over here you just say fuck it and relax 'cause you know if you get hurt, you're out of the field and maybe back to the World. So just fuck it and let yourself go." I filed that wisdom in the back of my mind for future reference.

The rain continued to fall and we continued to hike through the woods until around 1600, when we broke for chow. Once again we took turns eating, and when we were finished we moved to the night-halt position and put out claymores. A last cigarette before it got dark and we settled in for the night. The rest of the mission was quite uneventful, as that was truly a dead AO. The only thing good to come out of it was the fact this new team seemed to have its act together in the field. Mac had Hobo heading to all the possible locations that the gooks might have been, so I knew Mac wasn't a runner. On the fourth day we were extracted.

When we got back to the rear area I noticed quite a few of the guys were sporting black berets instead of the usual floppy hats. "What's going on?" I asked Kelly from Second Platoon. He looked quite dapper in his.

"We found a place on the other side of the compound that sells them and we just decided to wear them." After I got cleaned up, a bunch of us walked to the Vietnamese tailor shop and bought berets. Within a day the majority of the company was wearing them and none of the officers or senior NCOs said anything to us, so I guess they accepted it.

Since all the teams were in, that night, the major decided to have a barbecue for the company. We fashioned grills out of fifty-five-gallon drums, and cooked steaks, potatoes, and corn. Everybody was hanging around the grill waiting for the chefs to call out the different levels of doneness, rare, medium, and well done. I had my eye on one of the well-done steaks and when I felt it was ready I speared it with my fork and put it on my paper plate. By the time I had stabbed a potato to put it on my plate, some sorry son of a bitch had stolen my perfectly done steak. Luckily there was plenty to go around, and everybody was having a pretty good time. The rains held off while we were cooking and chowing down, and as far as I could see most of the company was present. I guess the major felt the barbecue was one way to keep his Rangers on the base and out of town.

After eating, I drifted from tent to tent and listened to the various music and war stories being told over and over. I saw how well everybody got along and decided I had done the right thing by extending; nowhere else on this earth would I find the kind of closeness I had in Charlie Rangers—certainly not at Bragg.

A couple of days later we went to the field again but made no contact, and in the middle of June we once more pulled up stakes for another move. Back to Phan Thiet. We hadn't been there since March, and higher-higher thought maybe we could catch the dinks half-stepping. We had become skilled at striking tents and could knock one down, fold it, and pack it in *ti-ti* time now. But now as we loaded the deuce-and-a-halfs, we looked back at Dalat with fond memories.

JUNE 1970/DALAT
Don Ericson

Our new orders came down for the company to move to Dalat. The First and Fourth platoons had been in Dalat when I first came to the Rangers months ago and I'd heard all sorts of stories about how great it was there. I suspected they were stretching the truth just a little, because they had gone while the Second and Third Platoons remained in Phan Thiet. I was wrong. Dalat was quite a little village with real Shell gas stations, restaurants, and steam baths. And it was almost clean! Vietnam was such a poor country. To the pampered nineteen-year-old American who always had a nice clean bed, a television, and plenty of food in the refrigerator, 'Nam was a hole. Everywhere I had been in the country, I saw filthy squalor and unbelievable poverty. Homes and hootches were made out of wood, tin, and even cardboard that had been discarded by the rich Americans. Only in the bush could you see the real beauty of the country. There it was clean and fresh. The towns reeked because of poor sanitation facilities and—when GIs were around—burning shit. Whenever the Vietnamese had to relieve themselves they pulled down their pants wherever they were. I think the Americans introduced them to the idea of burning their wastes. Before that they just didn't care, or so it seemed.

We were just setting up our GP mediums (tents that are about 12 feet by 25 feet) when it started raining and turning cooler. The monsoons were on us. Till then we had been used to one-hundred-degree-plus temperatures; suddenly it was dropping to seventy or eighty degrees and we were all freezing. It rained every day and then the thick fog would roll through. Fog that dense would be trouble if a team had a heavy contact and the Cobras and gunship Hueys couldn't support them. Teams had already been inserted to probe the area. After a few weeks, minor kills were coming in but nothing major.

About three weeks after we set up on a rare sunny day, all hell broke loose on the other end of the base's perimeter. Small-arms and automatic-weapon fire could be heard everywhere. The VC were attacking the general's golf course! Hard to believe the United States government put a golf course in a combat zone. We had heard stories of bowling alleys and swimming pools around Saigon but had never seen them. Yet here was a golf course, and the VC were running all over it. And we were to be the reaction force. I could just see it; my parents would be notified that I died on the ninth-hole green defending some asshole general's golf course. No wonder we didn't win the war.

All the general had to do was unleash a Cobra or two and take the gooks out. No such luck—the general was probably a bad golfer who didn't need or couldn't handle "any more roughs."

As John L. said earlier, rumor had it that Dalat was an R&R center for the VC and NVA. Dalat was a wide-open village to American soldiers. The fantastic open-air fish and vegetable markets were something to see. The blackmarket hawkers with their wares had everything from stereos and Seiko watches to everything the American Army issued us. Whores were everywhere. Many of the "ladies" were extremely lovely, partly because they were half French. I had been in-country about seven months by then and had seen only jet-black hair on the Vietnamese. In Dalat the the majority of the ladies had extremely light hair and had almost round eyes.

Our only restriction was that we had to be back at the compound by ten-thirty. Nevertheless, fun was had by all. This was the first time in over seven months that I had actually sat in a real restaurant and ordered a real steak. It was such a treat that I had two steaks. It's unbelievable how much we take for granted whenever the simplest things are denied us.

There was a shortage of team leaders at that time so I was assigned a team, but given no promotion (still a Spec-4!), just added responsibilities. On my first VR, I saw a few good ambush sites but picked my target, a small trail in the southwest corner of our AO, and hoped for the best. After returning I briefed my team and told them it was probably another dead AO and that Charlie company was in Dalat so some general could sleep a little better, knowing a Ranger company was on site to secure his outer perimeter.

Later that day we were all sitting around the tent drinking massive quantities of beer, probably too much for the day before a mission. After a couple of hours of drinking I left the tent to go relieve myself. On the way I encountered a Ranger I knew, stoned on dope. He said something I didn't like, and I grabbed him by the shirt and told him I'd kill him myself if I ever caught him smoking dope in the field. Everyone was staring at us. I was dead serious. All I could remember was Murph and me that time. In the field dope was deadly because it dulled the senses. Later I felt guilty for what I said, but lives rode on my decisions in the field.

I had returned to my tent and pounded down a few beers by the time Sergeant Cheek came in and handed me a piece of paper. As he inhaled a beer. I looked at the paper. It was a citation for the Air Medal.

CITATION

By Direction of the President
The Air Medal is presented to
Specialist Four Donald R. Ericson 342–40–5986
United States Army

Reason: For distinguishing himself by meritorious achievement while participating in sustained aerial flight in support of combat ground forces of the Republic of Vietnam during the period 3 October 1969 to 5 March 1970. During this time he actively participated in more than twenty-five aerial missions over hostile territory in support of counter-insurgency operations. During all these missions he displayed the highest order of air discipline and acted in accordance with the best traditions of the service. By his determination to accomplish his mission in spite of the hazards inherent in repeated aerial flights over hostile territory and by his outstanding degree of professionalism and devotion to duty, he has brought credit upon himself, his organization, and the military service.

As I finished reading I looked at Sergeant Cheek, who was already pounding down another beer and we started laughing. For a Ranger LRRP, the Air Medal was awarded for taking the taxi to and from work. Medals are a joke, and were awarded for nothing more than doing your job.

The next mission was the mission that changed my life forever; for the first time I initiated a massacre. This was the mission that made me years later ask myself, Did I do the right thing by taking lives? Were Cassius Clay and the rest of the conscientious objectors right? They had to live with the easy way out; I had to live with what I did. After considerable self-analysis I know I was right: I loved my country. It sounds corny, but when you are in a situation when all your luxuries are stripped from you, you enjoy them ten times more when you finally get them back. The only regret I have was that the choppers weren't blaring the song ''Born in the USA'' (had it been out) over the loudspeakers after a kill. I was twenty years old, and I was one of the best hunters in the woods.

Everyone was up early, and ready. The adrenaline was already pumping when we were sitting at the chopper pad. The camouflage makeup was on, the rucks packed, the weapons ready. The team comprised myself; Paxton, a short, dumpy guy from Virginia; Barkley, a tall, muscular kid from Texas; and Junior. Due to availability of Rangers, this was to be a four-man mission. I always wanted to try a three-man team, but that was nixed by the company's standard operating procedures. The perfect team would have been Agner, Rath, and myself.

The rains in Dalat were finally starting to subside, but it stayed cloudy or overcast. Anything was better than rain. I could hear the choppers coming in the distance, but I decided to let the team sit instead of saddling up and putting on the heavy rucksacks. Sergeant Cheek would have us up soon enough. And soon enough came a few minutes later, when he gave the thumbs-up signal as they approached. Then we were all up and ready.

The propwash from the rotors was blowing garbage everywhere; dirt, rocks, and anything that wasn't nailed down were whirled in the air. Our team was on the chopper and settled, and when it shook violently and started to rise, I looked over at the other teams waiting their turn to load, gave the universal one-finger gesture, and smiled. I lit a last cigarette. We froze all the way out.

The chopper landed in a near-perfect LZ about ten miles out. We were off and in the woodline within seconds, communications were established, and things were so quiet you could almost hear your heart beat. The noise discipline with this team was excellent. The amazing thing about the woods is that there is absolutely no noise. Once in a while a bird or a monkey was heard, but very rarely.

During one mission, we had elephants in the area but had seen only signs of them. Their feces looked like loaves of bread, and lay everywhere. An elephant makes his own paths and can blaze a trail ten feet wide, leaving everything knocked down in its wake. We had stopped for our night halt, and around nine o'clock we heard crashing noise. For some reason the elephants were on the move about thirty meters off our flank. We were scared: we couldn't see them, and even if we could, I wasn't sure the M-16 would kill them. I doubt it, they are absolutely massive. It was a long night for all of us as they moved on.

The next morning we were to leave around ten o'clock. We were sitting watching the area and the stream when all of a sudden on the other shore we saw the elephants coming down the mountain for water. Firsthand, I saw these beasts knocking down six-inch-diameter trees by just rubbing against them. What an awesome sight.

As we sat listening for movement I studied the map, our line of travel, and our trail objective. I motioned the team up and we were off. I took point, Barkley was my slack man, Paxton was the RTO, and Junior had rear security. Our area was extremely rough going. Its terrain was mountains, hills, and deep valleys. None of the other teams had made a contact of any significance and it looked like ours would be another four-day mission, although I hoped this would be different.

The days crawled: no trails, no streams, no signs of life. Another dead AO. As we made our way to the last night halt, I'm sure everyone on the team was thinking about Dalat and its pleasures. The problem with a dead AO was that we all became lax. Almost sure nobody was around, we got bored and let up.

We arose from our night position, ate, and moved toward the next objective, our exfil landing zone. We were about three hundred meters from our LZ when I came upon a trail. It appeared to be grown over with weeds in some spots, so I didn't get excited. We set up a seven-claymore daisy-chained ambush (one more than usual because for some reason I had decided to carry two clay-mores instead of one) and also set up the rear and flank claymore security and waited. Only two more hours and we'd be heading back to Dalat for showers and cold beer. I looked at the rest of the team and sensed they were a bit down. A dead AO will do that to you.

I was sitting on a log, watching the trail, my M-16 by my side when my heart stopped. Movement to my right! A VC entered my line of sight about twenty meters away. To this day I think he stared me right in the eyes, but I guess my camouflage makeup did the job. The ambush had been set up hastily with good cover to the kill zone only. The rear and flanks had heavy brush but no effective solid cover. The kill zone was about ten meters to my front. The claymores had a back blast of about twenty-five meters. Each claymore had a package of powdered CS taped to it.

The gook was about ten meters from the center of the kill zone when I very quietly and slowly crouched behind the log. The team's eyes were on me but no one said anything. My eyes never left the first VC as three approached the kill zone. The first VC was quickly approaching the end of the kill zone when I depressed the clacker. The earth shook and hell broke loose and centered on the trail. After Cambodia all our Ranger teams carried gas masks, but we'd had no time to put them on. The back blast and the concussion temporarily immobilized the team and the CS left everyone coughing, puking, and eyes watering. Automatic instincts took over and the team was firing three hundred and sixty degrees within seconds. No return fire yet. Good. No movement in the kill zone. Good. No movement up or down the trail. Good. After everyone went through two magazines they started yelling—

"What's happening?"

"What's going on?"

They knew we'd hit something, but they didn't know what. I yelled to Paxton, "Call it in, *now*!"

"What do we have?" Paxton asked.

"Contact, five gooks!" I yelled back.

Paxton grabbed the handset and called it in. "Bird

Dog, this is 3–1. We have contact. Get the guns now! Over.''

"Roger, that," Bird Dog confirmed.

Junior began screaming, "I've got movement. I've got movement.''

"Blow your claymores now," I yelled. As Junior detonated the claymore a sheet of red went up with the blast. The poor fucker I'd let walk through the kill zone must have only been wounded and had probably crawled right next to Junior's camouflaged claymore. By this time Junior was laughing hysterically that he got a kill. I could just imagine that if there were any gooks alive in the kill zone yet, they would have been freaked out by Junior. Time was passing and the guns weren't overhead yet. I wouldn't let the team fire their M-16s, but we were throwing frags in the kill zone.

The choppers were now on station and Paxton was throwing smoke to mark our position. The smoke was identified and the Cobras were coming in hot.

The Cobras were worth every penny the government paid for them, and their pilots were excellent. First run was on the far side of the kill zone knocking down trees, bushes, and everything in its way. The second pass was on our side. I was lying flat on my back when the miniguns opened up, starting down the trail and past the ambush. As the Cobras approached our position, I knew something was wrong—the path of the projectiles was in line with my legs. I screamed, "Check fire! Check fire! Check fire!''

Paxton yelled into the horn and the Cobras stopped just as the bullets were striking the earth about three feet from my boots. I stared at Paxton and he looked back at me. We both knew the guns would have cut my legs off had they continued.

Paxton was on the horn with the bird dog, then he was yelling to me that we had six KIAs in the kill zone and that it was a perfect kill. Good frag layout. And I smiled, thinking to myself we should have been drinking beer two hours ago.

My biggest fear was over—hitting a point element for a company or a battalion; the Cobras took care of that.

Paxton requested Bird Dog stay on station until we stripped the bodies.

"Roger, that." Bird Dog confirmed he would stay.

The Cobras were now off station. I motioned Barkley up to help strip the bodies and he started crawling out. From my position I could see very little of the trail. As I kept crawling I could see the absolute carnage of what I had done. The bodies of the VC were lying everywhere. Bodies still smoking from the direct blast of the claymores. I finally crawled into a position where I could observe all the bodies. One by one I fired a shot into the head of each VC; their grotesque body positions told me they were dead, but Murphy's death had taught me a good lesson. Don't take chances. Every time I shot, the head would rock but didn't bleed: no blood, no blood pressure, no problem. I signaled for Barkley to crawl out and physically strip the bodies.

He shook his head no.

"What do you mean, no?"

He said, "I can't."

I didn't want to argue, because I was scared myself. As I looked back again he was throwing up. As Junior covered me I stripped the bodies myself. As I took their rucksacks off I threw them to Junior, who threw them back to our tiny perimeter. We'd hit this one big. We got two officers with Chinese K-54 pistols, holsters, and web gear, and one AK-47 Soviet model. The more I looked the more I found. In debriefing we found out that among the documents in the four rucksacks were all the names of the VC in the area of Dalat. What a kill! And we had thought that this was a dead AO. I was done in the kill zone. I stripped the bodies naked (the clothing was used to confirm the kills) and crawled back to our perimeter and said, "Let's get the fuck out of here."

"Choppers are 1–5 out," Paxton said.

I instructed the team to fire for effect all the way to the LZ, leaving three magazines in reserve for the LZ. Barkley was in the middle while we were on line with the M-60 blazing away. Anything in our way was ours. The team had a devastating effect on the trees but we were taking no chances. Bird Dog was now informing us that it was such a significant kill contact that they were sending in a company-size reaction force to look for further activity. Because of what the rucksack contained I thought it was a good move.

The choppers touched down as the reaction force was coming in. I briefed the CO of what and where the contact was made and I was out of there. I climbed into the chopper, lit a cigarette and inhaled deeply, breathed a sigh of relief, and finally relaxed. I pulled out my two pistols and tapped the pilot on the shoulder to show him; his eyes went wide. The chopper touched down, and the team headed to the TOC for debriefing.

When we arrived, about twenty people were waiting to shake our hands. It was almost as if we had hit a ninth-inning home run to win the game. We were debriefed by a major who came down from higher-higher. All the brass were really pleased. Patting each other on the back.

I was looking through the black pajamas when I found a VC's wallet. I went through the wallet and found several piaster notes and a family picture. It was a picture of the gook I had just blown away, his wife, and son. God, did *that* hit home. I also found a picture of Ho Chi Minh and a patch that represented his rank, though I had no idea what rank it was.

The reaction force was now calling back with their finds. I had left an M-16 out there, from Junior's kill on the flank (when he blew his claymore). I never did find out who the M-16 belonged to. They also found a Chinese jewel-handled dagger with Chinese characters on it.

It was a good mission. Not one round was fired at my team. Not one person was wounded. It was a good body count. They never knew we were there. Yes, I had several beers that night.

CHAPTER 11

JUNE, JULY, AND AUGUST 1970/
PHAN THIET
John L. Rotundo

I spent the last week in June and the first three weeks in July working with Team 3–5 hunting the gooks in and around Phan Thiet, but except for one sighting where we saw them as we were about to be extracted (when all we could do was fire them up from a distance of over two hundred meters with the thumper and our M-16s while the gunships worked the area over) that was the extent of 3–5's contribution to my time in Phan Thiet. The last week in July I received my orders for extension leave and packed my gear.

I would spend the last few days at An Khe waiting for the flight to Cam Ranh Bay and my thirty-day leave back to the World.

Sharkey was by then an instructor at the Ranger school, so I spent the days watching the new group of Rangers going through the same paces I had gone through some six months ago. In the evenings the guys going through the school asked me what it was really like in the woods. I told them the best thing they could do right now was pay attention to what Sharkey and his staff were telling them because Sharkey had his shit together. I knew Hai and the Third Platoon would miss him in the woods, but he had a wealth of knowledge, and if he could only communicate ten percent of it to his students, they had a better-than-average chance of surviving the rest of their tours.

Just before I left Cam Ranh Bay, Sharkey came to say his good-byes. Before I left he said I would see more shit after I got back than I ever dreamed of. I told him I'd remember that. We shook hands.

Next stop was Fort Lewis, Washington, and the World.

Upon arriving at Fort Lewis, all returnees were treated to a steak dinner with all the trimmings. My group stayed just long enough to eat, get final orders, change into Class A uniforms, and take a bus ride to Seattle-Tacoma Airport for our flights home. It was late Saturday night when I arrived at my parents' house, and I received the traditional welcoming home. Throughout my first tour I wrote to my mother that I would really be looking forward to some strawberry shortcake when I got home. True to form, she fulfilled my wish. I called my girlfriend and told her I was in, and that I would see her and her family the next day, but that night was to be spent with my parents.

I'll never forget that first week home. First of all, everybody I saw asked me what it was like over there, and why did I have to go back? All the people knew about Vietnam was what they saw on television or read in the newspapers.

How do you explain what it's like to LRP through the woods looking for the dinks? How do you explain the feeling of a contact? It was similar to when I got out of jump school and people asked what it was like to jump out of a plane. You can't describe it, you have to experience it. After fumbling with my explanations the first couple of times I just told my friends they would have to try it for themselves. Of course, I had to try and tell my parents why I had elected to extend my tour for another six months. It was tough. I just hoped they would accept my explanation that I felt I had a home with Charlie Rangers.

The rest of my first week I spent at the Federal Building in Cleveland seeing a medic for treatment of the clap, which I'd caught just before leaving An Khe though it didn't show up till I was home. The medic said I not only had a dose of the clap, but as he put it, "a very good case of the clap." (I didn't know a case of the clap could be very *good*.) I received my penicillin and that was that.

The next week I decided to go to Virginia to visit my brother, who was still in the Navy. He took me to the NCO club in Norfolk and we did our share of partying till I started burning when I urinated again. I told my brother of my past condition and, after busting out laughing, he brought me to the Navy Dispensary to see a doctor. I told him what had happened and he asked me if I was doing any drinking. Is the Pope Catholic? Of course I was drinking and would continue to drink. He told me my drinking Jim Beam was actually killing the penicillin, so he gave a prescription for tetracycline. As long as I was going to drink, the tetracycline should take care of my problem.

I returned home and in a short time my girlfriend found the tetracycline. As she had a sister who was a nurse, it didn't take her long to figure out what the pills were for. Oh well, what the hell, some people have no sense of humor.

The last two weeks were spent staying drunk and thinking about the guys back at Phan Thiet, hoping all was well. My mom kept telling me I had a chip on my shoulder. Maybe she was right. I toyed with the idea of returning early but changed my mind time and again. On the one hand I was glad to be home, but on the other hand I had a strong desire to go back. After a brief run-in with the law for a traffic violation, I was set to return.

Upon my arrival at Fort Lewis, I was determined not to pull KP, police calls, and all the other bullshit details I had been assigned when I first went over. That's when I remembered someone telling me to put sergeant E-5 tabs on my collar instead of the SP-4s. The ruse worked and I was roomed with another buck sergeant. We supervised police calls and were generally left alone. After a few days we flew back to Vietnam and I kept remembering Sharkey's words about seeing more shit on your second time around. I wondered how true it was.

We flew to Cam Ranh Bay again. This time I knew the routine and, since I was already assigned to a unit, I was gone the next day. When I arrived at An Khe I checked in and was informed that the company was now working out of Nha Trang, that it was catching the dinks half-stepping on just about every mission, and the slaughter was on.

"How quick can I get to Nha Trang?"

JULY AND AUGUST 1970/PHAN THIET
Don Ericson

Smokey Wells and I had just returned from the beach when Sergeant Cheek entered the tent. He had a beer in his hand and was heading my way. "Got another one?" he asked, already knowing I did. I handed him one, which he immediately started to inhale. Taking a breather from his beer, he said, "You're the new team leader of Team 3-2."

"What's the occasion?"

"Cunningham's getting short, Sharkey will be leaving soon to be an instructor at Ranger school in An Khe, and Agner received an in-company transfer to the rear as a clerk."

"Do I get to keep my original team members?" I was hoping that only the team number had changed.

Cheek started laughing. "You gotta be kidding."

Cheek and I were drinking buddies and I could talk to him as if I were talking to my own brother. This kind of friendship is not common between E-4s and E-7s in the Army. Smiling, I said, "Fuck you."

"All right, you can keep Boone and Paxton, but that's it," he replied immediately. Boone and Paxton were good in the field, and that made a lot of difference to me; much better than taking out four or five FNGs. I would only be stuck with two FNGs.

Cheek and I talked for a few minutes about Agner's transfer. He was to fill a vacancy left by the last clerk. The tension of the field and the sense of loss at Murphy's death, not to mention that Sam was on his second tour of duty, had taken a toll on him. Later, I would understand how much such things could drain you.

I looked Sergeant Cheek straight in the eye and said in a serious voice, "I'll take the team, but only if I can have the number 3-1."

"You've got to be kidding," he replied, reaching for another beer, obviously proud of himself.

It was important to me to have my original team number: I broke my cherry under 3-1; Murphy was killed on 3-1; I made friends with Agner and Rath on 3-1. Then I noticed what hadn't been mentioned—Rath, I wouldn't have Rath anymore! I begged for Rath, but Cheek only laughed. "I gave you all you are going to get, asshole. Oh, by the way, you are now an acting sergeant."

"What do you mean, acting? I have been a Spec-4 for six months; why shouldn't I get paid for being a team leader and the responsibility for four or five other lives."

"It's out of my hands," said Cheek. "Sharkey just made E-5 but got Spec-5, I know it's a joke," he said. "But the 173rd, who we are paid by, keep all the hard rank for themselves and send us the specialist ranks."

God, what a pisser, I thought. We work for the First Field Force but get paid by the Herd. Isn't the Army amazing? Our company travels all over II Corps, gaining almost all its intelligence, and we're treated like bozos. Typical Army politics.

"One more thing before I leave," he said, taking another beer. "We've got a POW and she is going to lead a two-team ambush on her base camp!" Cheek smiled.

"You've got to be kidding!" I shook my head in disgust and disbelief. "You're going to trust a fucking gook defector?"

"Have no choice," he said as he hung his shaking head. "That's the Army. The broad, *chieu hoi*ed about a week ago and they want to get there while the dinks are still there."

"How big is the camp?"

Cheek hesitated. "Company size, could be battalion size. We don't know."

"Wonderful. My first team and we might get sucked into a battalion base camp. Just fucking wonderful."

"Don't get fucking bent out of shape," Cheek said with a smirk. "I'm going with you." I could hardly contain myself. I was rolling with laughter. "This ain't funny," he said. Cheek was as scared as I was.

The mission was just about as far from a Ranger operation as you could get. It was a line company's job, one that required the area to be prepped by artillery, then a sweep by at least a company or two of line soldiers. Definitely not a two-team, twelve-man Ranger mission. Our teams went out on hunter-killer operations and were very effective. Just six men, undetected, could do more damage than a line company. It's the way the whole war should have been fought.

Cheek *was* rattled. He had probably been in the service fifteen years by then and Charlie Rangers had been his first combat station. He did have his act together, but the thought of attacking a base camp with just twelve Rangers and a POW was enough to rattle him. "Wednesday, Sharkey and I will go on a VR to see what we can see. We'll know more then," he said. As Cheek was about to leave, he reached for another beer and said, "Relax, Sergeant, everything will be fine." I don't know if he was trying to settle me down or himself.

I watched him leave the tent, and muttered to myself, "Just fucking great."

When Sharkey and Cheek returned from the VR, I was summoned to the TOC. The area in question was on top of a hill about three hundred meters high with intermingled triple-canopy and single-canopy jungle. Only one trail, hard-packed, could be seen from the air. The POW had stated under interrogation that a bunker complex there housed thirty-five to fifty NVA. Sharkey was grinning because he had the best kill ratio in the company. Cheek was grinning partly because he was scared shitless and partly because he knew I was also. We set a line of travel, primary and secondary LZs, and where the POW would walk. My team would be third in line. Cheek would walk just ahead of us with the POW and four ARVNs, an interpreter, and another three ARVNs. At least I wouldn't have to worry about getting shot in the back. Sharkey's team would take the lead.

My team consisted of Paxton, Boone, Mason, and two FNGs. One was just a young kid; months later I heard that he had crawled out of a team's perimeter on a mission to take a shit without telling anyone he was going. One of his own team members had then taken him for an NVA and opened up on him. The guy wasn't killed, but a round had grazed his face, shearing off both lips. Mason was our new Kit Carson scout who pronounced his name *Masahn*. He was a Montagnard, a non-Vietnamese people who lived in the high lands and whom the Vietnamese detested. Montagnards had good reputations as trackers and for knowing the woods, but that was yet to be proved to us.

Paxton could be counted on in the woods; his nickname was Chumpy Chip. What can I say about Boone? He always had a cup of coffee in his hand. In the wee hours of the morning Boone would shake me. "I wanna talk." And I'd get up and we would talk till the sun came up. Talking about anything and everything. Most of his responses were "Wow, man," "Heavy," or something of that nature.

On one of those occasions, I asked him, "Boone, what do you want out of life?"

"Well, I don't want to be chairman of the board of Standard Oil. However, I do want to be comfortable." I don't know why, but I will never forget those words spoken at three in the morning in some stupid tent pitched on the sand. Boone was one of the best in the field. If his own mother had walked into the kill zone wearing an NVA uniform, he would have blown her away. Boone could be counted on.

I briefed my team on the mission and order of march. I told Paxton and Boone to keep their eyes on the three others. It was going to be a long night before our mission.

Agner came up from An Khe to deliver mail, so we decided to have a farewell party for him because there'd been no time when his orders had come down, and he soon would be going back to the World. Just about everyone from Third Platoon came. It was held at the EM (enlisted men's) club just beyond our tent complex. We all drank too much.

As Sam, Smokey, and I were heading back to Third Platoon's tent, we met an obviously drunk Ranger who wanted to pick a fight with me. After our opening exchange of compliments, he surprised us all by reaching into his camouflage fatigues and pulling out a .32 caliber pistol which he held to my head. I didn't move, I didn't breathe, I just stood there.

"What the fuck are you doing, man?" Smokey said.

The guy grunted. "Get the fuck out of here."

As Smokey was talking to the guy, Sam slowly snuck into our tent, grabbed my M-16, came out and stuck it to the back of the Ranger's head, chambered a round, and let the sound vibrate on his neck. "Go ahead, motherfucker, blow Don's brains out," Sam said. "Pull the trigger and your brains will flow like water." The drunk put the pistol down and Smokey grabbed it. It was over. Later the idiot tried to explain he was drunk, that he was just playing around. Some joke. Thank God for Sam and Smokey. Who knows what would have happened if they hadn't been there with me. Sam and I went through a lot in the field together, but we never experienced anything as tense as that. They were as different as night and day. Or were they?

Then Sam and I said our farewells; he was heading back to An Khe. He knew we were going out to the field, and I'm sure that he felt a twinge of guilt at not going with us, but he had done his duty and done it well.

The team was ready. We left Tent City and headed for the choppers. Sharkey's team was also on its way. Then I spotted Sergeant Cheek coming from the NCO barracks dressed and cammied up. "Come on, old man," I yelled as he labored under the weight of his rucksack. He looked up and gave me an incredibly dirty look. We all wanted to say, "Okay, asshole, now you know how it feels," but we didn't. When we reached the airfield, our POW was being guarded by three ARVNs, an American in civilian clothes, and a Vietnamese in civilian clothes. I was impressed; I don't think even our company commander knew how important this one was.

The choppers were starting their engines and we would soon board. The POW and three ARVNs were wearing camouflage fatigues and they already had camouflage makeup on. They were ready, they knew our operations, they knew our dress. I just hoped that we could count on them when the bullets started to fly.

We were in the choppers. Three slicks, the first with Team 3-1, the second with Team 3-3 and Sergeant Cheek, the ARVNs and the POW in the third. It was a short trip out. My guts were churning.

To my knowledge this was the first time a team of Rangers would assault or be led into an NVA base camp. I did know we were out of our element. Maybe at that time in Phan Thiet the infantry was down just then and LRRPs were the only alternative. The leg company commander at Phan Thiet had been complaining about Charlie Company teams coming back without proof of a contact. I remember one team going out on a mission, making contact, and calling for an exfil. After extensive and ridiculous questioning by superiors, the team was brought in. Before the chopper landed, the team leader had the pilot fly over the base commander's headquarters. Then the team dumped out the naked body of a dead gook. The sudden impact of a dead dink from six hundred feet is not a pretty sight. I think that made a believer out of the commander.

We were nearing our position. The crew chief held up one finger, meaning one minute. The team locked and loaded. We really didn't need the crew chief's signal as we were now at five hundred feet and rapidly descending. The LZ was a big one, enough to handle all three birds in single file, which is how they landed. I can still remember all the noise the choppers made coming in. Talk about announcing your arrival. The three slicks unloaded easily and we were off in seconds.

In our tiny perimeter at the woodline, commo was checked as we sat and listened. The only sound was

that of the 0–1 bird dog in the distance making sure
that we had communications. Since this was a "special" mission, the Cobra gunships were already standing by with their crews on board. The fast movers, the
F-4 Phantom jets, were on call and ready out of Cam
Ranh Bay. It was to be a one-day mission for the Rangers. The coordination of support, air, artillery, and reaction force on this mission were the best since I'd been
in-country.

The stage was set and the Vietnamese princess POW
knew exactly where she was. I looked at Sharkey's position on the woodline, and the POW was pointing toward the hill not more than six hundred meters to our
south. I thought to myself, We're at the gates of Hell!
Sharkey looked at me and smiled with his thumb up.
Oh, fuck, I thought. I turned to my team and gave the
same signal, but I wasn't smiling. Team 3–1 was up and
standing as Sharkey's team was already heading for our
target. Sergeant Cheek was with Sharkey's RTO. The
POW was surrounded by the ARVNs, who were suppos-
edly guarding her. They probably had orders to guard
her from us.

As Sharkey's team moved out, Sergeant Cheek and his
contingent followed, and Team 3–1 brought up rear security.

Ever since Murphy had been killed, I had insisted on
walking point. Even as a team leader, maybe especially
as a team leader. In my opinion, full control of a six-
man element can only be achieved by seeing firsthand
what's happening. Most of our AOs were no larger than
an area of two thousand meters square, the teams having
four days to cover that area. They walked at the ready,
the weapon was aligned with their eyes and ready to fire.
We moved at an agonizingly slow pace so as not to make
noise. Every footstep was thought out. Every vine moved,
held, then replaced so as to avoid rustling noises. Eyes
always moving, brain always straining, ears always listening, we actually became part of the jungle.

Sharkey was moving out as slow or slower than usual.
Usual is an interesting word. Nothing in any of our missions was usual. We knew the NVA were there, and that

was unusual. We knew where our objective was, and that was unusual. We had traveled to within one hundred meters of the base of the hill when Sharkey, Sergeant Cheek, and I discussed the plan of attack; the ARVNs were climbing trees, climbing huge boulders, and looking to our front. All our noise security and discipline were for nothing; the ARVNs were giving away our position. Maybe it was just me, a cherry team leader, feeling scared, but the jungle is so quiet that noise travels forever.

Sharkey and Sergeant Cheek motioned to the ARVNs to get down, they obeyed. Had we not been sitting next to a base camp, I would have shot them down.

We were ready; the POW said we were on the doorstep. I'm sure this was a first for a Ranger tactic: we would walk in single file to a certain point, then go on line. As the teams moved out, we found hard-packed trails everywhere, and almost all led to the top of the hill. The POW was leading us into a big one.

We were still in single file when Sharkey halted the team about halfway up the hill. I was thinking that we had reached the area where we were to go on line when an M-16 opened up on automatic at the front of the column. It was a member of Sharkey's team. At this time every member of the two-team ambush was firing. It was a three-hundred-and-sixty-degree ring of death. CS was thrown and the jungle was being consumed by a fog of gas. By the time we put our masks on, the gas was already in our noses, eyes, and clothes. I put on my mask but I couldn't see worth a damn on the flanks, so I ripped it off, knowing if someone was going to kill me, I would at least be able to die fighting. The firing had ceased and word passed along that Sharkey had just killed two sentries. One had been walking around a makeshift outpost, and one had been lying in a hammock no more than twenty meters away. The two sentries were part of a base camp's early warning system. The POW now refused to go any further. Hai, the scout who had spent almost a year with Sharkey, was also saying he would go no further.

After a short conversation, Cheek and Sharkey decided

to pull back; we'd leave, and the personal effects of the two NVAs could be picked up by a line unit. That was okay by me.

The teams regrouped three hundred meters away and air support was called. We had a clear view of the hill. In less than fifteen minutes the fast movers were on station. Sergeant Cheek was coordinating predetermined targets with the bird dog, who in turn was coordinating with the Phantoms. The Cobras were also on station waiting. Smoke color was identified, and the fast movers were incoming. Sergeant Cheek yelled, ''Get your heads down.'' The jets roared by at treetop level. I raised my head in time to see the bombs falling from the planes. Fire everywhere. An explosion. The ground shook violently; the earth actually moved under my body. The explosion raised huge clouds of smoke and fireballs a hundred feet high. When the Phantoms had expended all their bombs, they came over with their cannons, and the shell casings fell like rain. The sound was like that of a chain saw, and the trees were being smashed into toothpicks. The fast movers were done and the Cobra gunships never got a turn. Higher brass decided to recall the gunships and put in the reaction force. Our job was done. I won't ever forget the awesome power of a single Phantom.

Total body count of our mission was never known by Charlie Company, but I'm sure it was more than two.

We arrived back to the compound and were on standdown again. Smokey Wells and I went down to the beach to relax and swim. It was a pleasant break from lying around in the tents in hundred-degree temperatures. When you live in a tent for months at a time, anything is a break for your nose. We were sitting on the beach drinking beer, smoking cigarettes, and telling each other lies when we saw something wash up on shore. We got up and walked over to find the strangest snake we had ever seen, four feet long and thorns all over it. It resembled a thick green rosebush stem but the thorns were uniformly spaced. And its fangs were at least a half-inch long. It was the first of many that we'd see at the beach. Apparently the Vietnamese fishermen caught the snakes in their nets and clubbed them to death before throwing them into the sea. Then they would float to shore.

One of the great things about Phan Thiet was the availability of fresh fish. Many times the company would have fresh fish, lobster, and crab barbecues.

A new platoon leader joined Third Platoon, his name was Lieutenant Joiner. He seemed like a nice enough guy, a little Stateside for my liking, but what the hell. Though platoon leaders in LRRP units ranked between the higher brass (the company commander and the XO) and the senior NCOs, they filled a slot with no authority: no one listened to them because the majority of them were between the ages of nineteen and twenty-four years, "butter bars" (second lieutenants) fresh from officers candidate school, ROTC, or from West Point. They knew platoon-size tactics, but LRRP teams used six-man teams. They had to learn "our" way of doing things. A "cherry" platoon leader would go out on a few missions to get the feel of what we did, then retire to the rear to fly back seat in a bird dog. The rear seat was to establish the exact location of teams in contact. Actually, I always assumed the pilots did all the work, pointing out to the rear seat where the teams were. But I wasn't there and that's just a guess on my part.

On one mission I called for a fix on my location because of constant marching up and down mountains and valleys. I sat the team down and told Paxton to monitor the bird dog and signal the location with fluorescent panels. Bird Dog came back and verified our position. I wasn't far off from my reckoning, not bad. There was one problem: Bird Dog made the same mistake I did, putting me five hundred meters south of our true position. It almost cost me and my team our lives.

Sharkey was working the area immediately to my south, but according to Bird Dog he was well over one thousand meters to the south. We thanked Bird Dog, saddled up, and paralleled the blue line (stream) until I came upon some Ho Chi Minh sandal tracks in the sand. I halted the team and we sat and watched the creekbed for thirty

minutes. Nothing. We had perfect vision up and down
the creekbed for about one hundred meters to the west
and about fifty meters to the east before the creekbed
wound to the north. I decided to walk parallel to the
creek in the brush, then cross at the bend where I could
see in both directions. As we moved through the brush
we were especially quiet, because we knew the enemy
had been there. The riverbank was steep, straight down,
five feet on both sides. Very little water, a perfect high-
speed trail for gooks on the move. A perfect ambush
site with its steep banks and unlimited vision both
ways.

As I slid down the bank, tracks were everywhere on
both sides of the twenty-foot creekbed. My asshole was
really puckered and I knew we were going to get into
some shit. By the time we were all down the bank and
into the creekbed, we had left a trail of loose dirt and
grass, but it didn't matter. By the time the gooks could
see it, they would be well within the kill zone. And
dead. I had just climbed the other bank and gone five
meters with the rest of the team when my name was
being called. I froze. It should have been one of my
team, but the voice was coming from my flank. I turned
with my M-16 on automatic: Rath's camouflaged face
was staring at me from the brush. My mind must have
gone on automatic because I automatically started yelling, "Don't fire, don't fire." Rath would have already
blown me away if he had not seen my boonie hat, a
regular boonie hat with approximately five hundred one-
inch-by-one-inch pieces of camouflage nylon squares on
it. Everyone had laughed while I was sewing the damn
squares on day after day. I'm sure it was the only one
in 'Nam like it. No one laughed at it now because it
had saved my life. Rath's recognition of my hat saved
my life because he was cool enough to identify his target first. Thanks, Rath!

We left Sharkey's ambush, the same site I was going
to pick. We moved out a hundred meters and took a
break. I must have smoked six cigarettes in a row and
still couldn't settle down. After eight or nine, I started
to relax. The team was quiet as I cursed the bird dog for

giving me the wrong location and almost killing me and
my team. But I ran it over in my mind and finally came
to the conclusion that it was not only the bird dog's fault
but mine as well. A team leader should always know his
location. Always! Talk about guilt feelings. It took me a
long time to get my confidence back.

CHAPTER 12

SEPTEMBER 1970/NHA TRANG
Don Ericson

The time in my tour was getting short. My time in Vietnam, shithole of the world, was nearing its end. I had done my job and done it well. I had a respectable body count and had intercepted quite a bit of valuable intelligence for the brass. I felt good about the job I had done but was looking forward to returning to the civilized world.

I had been in Nha Trang when I first came into the country and had gone to recondo school some seven months ago. I had pulled one mission in Nha Trang and lost some classmates on our field-training exercise. The hills and mountains, the valleys and streams, were as beautiful as they had been all those months before. This time, though, the great scenery was Charlie Company's area of operation and Charlie Company's home. I was getting just a little bit nervous being so short. Thirty more days and they would pull me out of the field. I loved the field, the excitement, the adrenaline-pumping high that you got every time you entered the chopper. I was made for our type of operation but was getting too cocky, too confident. The edge of fear was disappearing; you were either afraid or you were a fool. I think that's why operations ran four days followed by four days off. The mental strain was unbelievable.

I pulled a few missions but no significant kills. A gook here and there, but the contacts were starting to feel insignificant; if we didn't slaughter a platoon or at least a squad of NVA, the contact seemed insignificant. The challenge was gone. My attitude must have been apparent, for Sergeant Carter, the platoon sergeant who replaced Sergeant Cheek, pulled me with twenty days left in-country. I wasn't angered. No longer would I have five other lives in my hands. It was a load I would gladly give up. It's hard to understand your decisions could take the lives of your fellow soldiers and friends. Now I could understand how Sam felt when he left the field. I would now have the dubious honor of being in charge of the platoon EM club.

The platoon EM club was a small section of an unused barracks cordoned off by a plywood wall. It was four walls, a roof, and a floor when I took it over. When I finished with it, it was four walls decorated with captured AK-47s, pith helmets, and various other NVA paraphernalia. The skull that Rath and Boone had brought back from one mission, the skull that housed the NVA gold tooth from another mission was on a shelf at the end of the bar. One wall was completely devoted to *Playboy* pin-ups, which everyone would come by and kiss or give each picture a friendly pat on the rear. It was interesting to meet all the other Rangers from the other platoons who now became regular customers.

I'm sure that I took a lot of business away from the EM club the legs ran on the base. Our beer was cheaper, the club wasn't as far to walk, and I know I was prettier than the gook whores who were waitresses at the leg bar. John had brought back about twenty eight-track tapes on his extension leave, and now after eleven months in-country, I could catch up on the current tunes.

Bartenders lead extremely interesting lives, hearing the problems of everyone else. One day a soldier I didn't know walked in and everyone almost fell on the floor. He had just come back from medical leave after having been shot through the arm. Everyone was patting him on

the back when off came his shirt and he produced the
most disgustingly ugly scar I have ever seen. The bullet
entered about mid-arm above the elbow and exited around
the top of the arm four inches higher. The wound was
healing but looked terrible. Pus was draining out of the
purplish wound and running between the sutures. God,
he kept dabbing it with cotton but it just kept flowing. He
should have been in bed, but he was proud he wasn't,
and probably couldn't have been tied down. We told him
that he was lucky, a couple of inches to the right and he
wouldn't be standing there. He laughed (obviously proud)
and said, ''Ranger.''

Rucker was a Fourth Platoon soldier who came into
the club frequently. He was a very personable fellow who
talked to me for hours at a time. He constantly talked
about his wife and his son and how proud of them he
was. I liked him; however, Smokey told me that Rucker
was a real beat-off—a ''Shake-'n'-Bake'' (a PFC who
goes through NCO school for six weeks and automatically jumps two ranks). Smokey had to go to the field
with him, so I guess he would know, but judging by what
I saw of him he was okay. He was always friendly and
courteous and he had a good sense of humor. Rucker had
been coming in to the club on and off for the better part
of two weeks and I got to know him pretty well.

We were sitting at the bar one night when he said he'd
better go because he had a mission the next morning. So
I cleaned up when everyone left and went to bed.

The next day was boring, as usual. People in and out
all day. Boone always came in early and had a few beers
with me for free. I took good care of my friends; they
were the people I had spent eleven months with; they
never bought a thing. The drinks were always on me, or
should I say Sergeant Carter, a lifter to the bone.

At 1700 the next afternoon, the club opened and I was
ready for business when the door swung open. Smokey
stood there, as white as chalk. ''Rucker's dead,'' he said
in disbelief.

''What?'' I asked, confused.

Smokey sat down and started to explain. ''Rucker's
dead, he was shot through the leg. The team was pinned

down and we couldn't get to him. Christ sake! He bled to death, and we couldn't do a thing.''

"He bled to death! How the hell can you bleed to death from a leg wound?'' Smokey, still in shock, shrugged his shoulders, then shook his head. "Smokey, why didn't he reach down and apply a tourniquet?'' The team must have been half-stepping; that's why I became a bartender.

Smokey began recalling what happened. "We ran into an ambush and the team returned fire but couldn't get the edge. Rucker was on his back and the gook tried a head shot. The bullet ricocheted off the M-16 on his chest; he would have been dead immediately if it hadn't. Rucker rolled over and and was shot in the leg. The fire was so intense he had all he could do to lay flat. He must have passed out and died from loss of blood. We couldn't get to him.'' We sat shaking our heads for a long time.

Rucker was the second friend I had lost over here. Rucker's death didn't hit home quite as hard as Murphy's, but he had been my friend, and I remembered all of the plans that he'd had for the future with his wife and son.

Another frequent visitor to the club was Scotty; a big, strapping dude from Second Platoon who had to be a psycho. He always put his face about an inch from whomever he was talking to and would start talking without moving his lips. He always ended his sentences with, "huh?'' ("Nice day today, huh?'' "Major Hudson's an asshole, huh?'' "Rucker left his cake out in the rain, huh?'') Scotty was one of those Rangers you just agreed with. He knew his stuff in the field, but he wasn't a person to mess with. I would have gone on any mission with him, and I was a very fussy team leader; I didn't take yo-yos into the field.

It was about 1400 hours when word came down that Niebert had been shot. The worst part always was never knowing how bad the wound was. Niebert was an E-6 staff sergeant who was built like an ox. He was about thirty years old and had the attitude of a twenty-one-year-old. He could hump or march your shorts off. He was tough. I had only worked one double-team ambush in Cambodia with him, but he seemed to know what he was doing. Our double-team ambush produced at least five dead NVA. Finally word came down as to what happened to Niebert. He was shot in the crotch (the gook must have had a sense of humor). They had a good body count on the mission and Barcus, one of the team members, was awarded the Silver Star.

Awards are a big farce. I have no problems with awards except for the fact that the army handed out too many of them. They were a morale booster. Like anyone else over there, Rangers were just doing their job.

As I grew shorter, the days dragged on longer. I was bored running the Third Platoon EM club and getting tired of being a bartender, and most of all I was tired of being in 'Nam. I began thinking of the thirty-day leave I would have when I left, but then I had to remember that when my leave was up I would be at Fort Bragg and back with the 82nd. Pitiful duty.

On one particularly monotonous day, Rath and I were shooting the bull, and we pounded down a few beers as we talked. We talked about our first days in-country and all the contacts we had made together. We talked about our original team, with Price as team leader and how he liked to avoid contacts. We remembered Murph and how he died and the fact that we both still missed him. We had been through a lot together. After the reminiscing he got up and left early because he had a mission the next day.

I opened up as usual the next day, and was just sitting at the bar listening to everyone's problems when Rath came in all excited; he had only been out for about three hours. "I got what I wanted," he said. "I got a Russian pistol, look!" The pistol was in excellent shape, still coated with cosmoline (a heavy lubricant).

"What the hell did you hit?" I asked.

"We smacked three gooks crossing a stream on the trail," he replied, grinning from ear to ear.

"Head shot?" I already knew the answer.

"Naturally, is there any other way?" We laughed, and he signaled me over to the end of the bar so he could not be heard. "Look at what else I got," he said. He reached into his pocket and pulled out a roll of piasters that would gag a tiger. "I hit a paymaster; the gook with the pistol was a pay officer," he blurted.

"God damn, Rath, good for you. Better you take it

than some fucking intelligence officer.'' We had a beer together.

My time was finally up. I was going home. The last night I was in Nha Trang the platoon gave me a going-away party. Hell of a time. The topper to the evening was being presented with a wooden plaque, shaped like most plaques. On the top were jump wings, under them were the Vietnamese flag to the left and the American flag to the right, below them to the right was a map of Vietnam showing the cities where I had worked, to the left mounted on a brass rectangle was a silver square that read:

PRESENTED TO
SGT. DON ERICSON
FROM THE OFFICERS
AND MEN OF 3rd PLT
CO. C RANGER 75th INF.
FOR A JOB WELL DONE
AS LEADER OF 3–1 ELEMENT
A PROVEN KILLER AMONG KILLERS

What a fitting end to my stay in that godforsaken place.

I returned home from Vietnam in one piece. It had been a long tour, but I was extremely proud of my duty and my accomplishments. It was hard to dodge the questions that my family and friends asked me about Vietnam, but I knew that they wouldn't understand, so I tried to avoid talking about Vietnam at all.

I felt that I had gone to Vietnam as a young kid and come back as an old man. I saw the killing, the poverty, and the hopelessness of a country that had been at war forever. Thanks to a few junior NCOs and one senior NCO (Sergeant Cheek), I had excellent leadership. In my opinion those NCOs were my edge; they had the field experience, and they were the ones who went into the field with us. Those NCOs felt what I felt. The Third Platoon's leaders, O'Donnell and Joiner during my tour, were just there. Among the officers there were two exceptions, Captain Colvin and Major Holt; they cared about their men and their problems. As for Major Hud-

son, he was a rank seeker; he wanted Charlie Company
to make him a general and admitted it. He tried to run a
Stateside company in a combat zone.

I was home to enjoy my thirty days before reporting to
Fort Bragg to finish my commitment to the army.

SEPTEMBER–OCTOBER 1970/NHA TRANG
John L. Rotundo

For one reason or another I had to stay in An Khe for
a week before I caught a plane to Nha Trang. In that
week I went to Phu Tai, which was the Herd's rear area,
to process my paperwork and to let them know I was
back. While I was there I ran into the sergeant I'd roomed
with at Fort Lewis before coming back. He looked at my
SP-4 tabs on my collar and asked what I'd gotten busted
for. I told him what I had done, and after the initial shock
he broke into a grin and bought me a couple of beers.

When I arrived at Nha Trang the company sent a jeep
to pick me up, and it was just as well that I had the jeep
to myself and the driver because I had brought back
beaucoup junk from the World, including all the Creedence Clearwater tapes I could find and a portable bar for
the Jim Beam I conned the NCOs into buying for me
with their ration cards. As the jeep rolled into the company area, I was met by a lot of familiar faces and saw
quite a few new ones. J.C., Scotty, Kelly, Thorne, and
the others all greeted me, shaking my hands, backslap-
ping, and all that. And every one asked the same question: "What's it like back in the World?"

"It sucks," I told them. "They've got no idea of what's
going on over here." I rehashed some of my Stateside
experience and they brought me up to date on Nha Trang.
The place was beautiful: it had a number-one mess hall,
a super EM club, hot and cold running water, flush toi-
lets, and even Stateside telephone service. All that plus
plenty of dinks out in the woods just waiting to be am-

bushed. The company was staying in real barracks again, and although there were plenty of empty ones, I was told to wait till 1700 hours when the meat market opened up at the main gate.

"What the hell is the meat market?" I asked.

"Just wait and see . . ."

I spent the rest of the afternoon getting my gear squared away, resuming old acquaintances, and meeting some of the new guys. At 1700 it was time to decide whether to go to the EM club or to find out what the meat market was all about. I'd been to EM clubs, so . . .

When I arrived at the main gate half of the company seemed to be there. Two hundred Lambrettas must have been pulling up to the gate to drop off Vietnamese females of every size and shape into what looked like a holding pen as GIs looked them over. One by one they would be paired up, and the girls would accompany their escorts onto the post for a movie, ice cream, or just plain screwing till they had to be picked up later in the evening. The meat market was an interesting sight, and I spent the first hour of the evening just watching. But there would be plenty of opportunity to take part during our stay in Nha Trang, so I went to the EM club.

J.C., Thorne, myself, and a few others made our way to the club, and upon entering I could see why everyone raved about it. It was spacious, clean, and even had Vietnamese waitresses to take our orders and wait on us. On stage a Filipino band trying hard to sound like the Rascals was singing "Good Lovin'." At first I couldn't see any Rangers in the place, but J.C. pointed to the floor in front of the stage, which was crowded with Charlie Rangers who were whooping it up and generally having a great time. I joined in and spent the rest of the evening catching up on what was going on: the company was indeed striking it big, contacts on almost every mission. The dinks hadn't caught on to us and were losing people left and right while we hadn't lost anybody. In fact the only casualty was Niebert, who was recovering from a groin wound received in a contact the first of the month. In fact one of his team members, a fellow named Greg Barcus, would receive the Silver Star for his actions. Barcus was a tall, thin guy from northern Illinois. He not

only carried the gun in the woods, but he humped twelve
hundred rounds for it by himself, along with all the other
equipment we carried. Barcus relayed the story to us.

The team was comprised of seven. Six Rangers and a
Kit Carson scout. As they left the LZ they came across
a well-used trail. Barcus was walking fourth. Niebert decided to walk the trail for a bit and see what happened.
They weren't on the trail long when one of Barcus's legs
plunged into a punji pit, the other remaining on solid
ground. After Barcus extracted himself, the Kit Carson
scout turned pale because he suddenly remembered digging the pit a few years earlier. Undaunted, Niebert kept
on the trail. They hadn't gone far when they picked up
the scent of nearby cooking. After crossing a small stream
that lay ahead of them, they carefully made their way
across and found themselves in the middle of a way station, complete with two hootches and bowls of rice cooking. While checking out the area, the team dined on the
gooks' rice breakfast before following the trail into the
woods. After an hour of humping, Niebert decided to
return to the way station and set up an ambush. He set
up two Rangers with claymores to guard the trail they
had just come back down. One Ranger was placed on the
one flank and the scout was watching the other. Niebert
and Rassler positioned themselves across the other end
of the trail with Barcus opposite them, hidden in the tall
grass. After a short wait they had movement, not from
the trail but from the bush on the other side of the stream.
As the gooks walked into view, Niebert tried to blow the
claymores, but they wouldn't go off, so he and Rassler
opened up with M-16s. Barcus couldn't see much but
opened up with the gun. After two minutes of firing up
the area and not receiving any return fire, Niebert yelled
to check fire.

Slowly Niebert and Rassler went out to the kill zone
to check the bodies. Barcus couldn't see anything and
told Niebert so. Niebert told Barcus to cover him from
the other side of the trail and to stay behind them. As
Niebert and Rassler entered the kill zone, Barcus saw
flashes from his left and right, and the ground was kicking up around all three of them. Niebert and Rassler went
down, and as they did Barcus lifted the gun and began

blasting the woods from left to right. During the firing, Niebert and Rassler made it back to the team, leaving Barcus, standing all alone, shredding the woods to his front and sides. When the other two were relatively safe they yelled for him to come on back also. The rear security blew their claymores and the team moved closer together to form a defensive perimeter. The RTO called in the contact and requested a reaction force. The team maintained its fire and finally the reaction force came on the scene. The gooks broke contact and left the area, only to be spotted by the choppers, who caught some of them in the open and worked them over pretty well. The team had opened up on the point element of a company and lived to tell about it. Niebert's injury was limited to a bullet that had grazed his inner thigh. It could have been much worse. As they examined him, the Rangers saw that two bullets had actually hit his zipper and been deflected. Later Niebert cut the legs off the pants and framed them. Talk about luck.

We continued to talk about what was going on since I left. Major Holt had left the company and been replaced by Major Hudson, a short, chunky lifer who announced to the company that "he wanted to make general and we [the company] would help him." That got a good laugh, as did the "surprise dope bust" called for while the company was still in Phan Thiet. Some of the Rangers caught wind of it and were prepared. Besides hiding their dope where it couldn't be found, the Rangers sprinkled black pepper around their belongings. As the MPs came into the tents, their dogs sniffed around then began sneezing and backing away. As the dogs backed away the MPs tried to push them forward. The more the MPs pushed, the more the dogs sneezed and backed away. Then the Rangers began to criticize the MPs for mistreating their dogs. The scene was repeated in tent after tent.

A Sergeant Carter—everyone called him "Pop Carter"—had replaced Sergeant Cheek as platoon sergeant. Medium height and rather skinny, he had a long face with cheeks that were sucked in, and had a hard look about him. Pop Carter was from the deep south and had lifer stamped all over him. We didn't like him much. In fact Thorne had already planted a frag under his pillow

one night. He first unscrewed the firing assembly, pulled
the pin, and dropped the assembly, setting off the blasting cap. Then he screwed it back together, replaced the
spoon but not the pin, and laid it under Carter's pillow.
When Carter went into his tent to crash for the evening,
he screamed when he moved the pillow and the frag's
spoon released. Way to go, Thorney.

Also, my buddy Don Ericson was living the life of a
REMF because Pop Carter had put him in charge of the
Third Platoon's club. Talk about giving the fox the keys
to the henhouse. I think he remained in a state of controlled inebriation for the balance of his tour. I gave Don
all the tapes I had brought back so that he could play
them at the club. I was rewarded by not having to pay
for many beers when I visited.

The next afternoon we were sitting around when a
group of Rangers ran out of the barracks with their web
gear and jumped into a waiting truck. A team from the
Third Platoon was in contact and had requested a reaction force. O.D. was going to take the team in, and J.C.
was carrying the radio. I ran to the truck and pulled J.C.
off, grabbed his rucksack, web gear, and weapon, and
told him I was going. Normally he would have fought me
for it, but I must have caught him by surprise; he relin-
quished his equipment. I told O.D. I'd walk his slack
and he agreed. It had been a while since I had been in
the field and I wanted to get back something fierce. We
lifted off and headed for the contact area with my heart
beating faster and faster. I hadn't felt so much excitement
in a long time and I ate up every minute of it, feeling the
wind at my face as the trees rushed below us. We orbited
the contact area as the gunship worked out below us.
What a sight. O.D. was on the horn with the bird dog,
getting instructions on the LZ we would use. He saw
it, the slick banked sharply, dropped altitude, and began its
low-level run. O.D. was now standing in the skid on the
right of the slick and I was once again half sitting, half
leaning right behind him. As the slick neared the ground,
O.D. jumped off with me right behind him, followed by
the rest of the team. As we hit the woodline we ran into
a trail that would lead us to the team in contact. Like the
majority of the Rangers, I didn't like walking trails, but

we had to make good time to help the other team. O.D. took the point and I assumed my position as his slack man; the rest of the team was on its toes as we moved down the trail. O.D. stopped us as we neared a bend in the trail, obviously a good spot for an ambush, and pulled a frag from his web gear. He looked at me and the bend in the trail. I nodded that I understood as he pulled the pin, released the spoon, and threw it into the bushes of the trail. *Boom!* The frag went off and we waited. No movement, good. We got up and proceeded down the trail to link up with the team in contact. It took us close to an hour to finally get in sight of them as we spread out to form a larger perimeter.

"Where are they?" O.D. asked the team leader, a Shake-'n'-Bake E-5 who just recently had joined the company.

"Over there." He pointed to a woodline a hundred meters away. We were sitting at the edge of another woodline, a ravine in front of us. Evidently the TL had elected to have the team walk across a log that bridged the ravine, instead of finding an alternate route. When the point man was halfway across, the dinks opened up on them. After the team returned fire they called in the contact and requested a reaction force. Talk about over-reacting: the team was probably spotted by a lone VC who just happened to be there, fired a magazine, and *di-di*'d. O.D. looked at me and shook his head. In the meantime I was trying to look at the Shake-'n'-Bake's left shoulder patch for a subdued "bumble bee" (Stateside Ranger) patch. We scouted the area but found no one. So we called for an exfil bird and headed back to Nha Trang.

Two days later I was going to the field with Team 3–5. This would be my first real mission in nearly two months, excluding the reaction force. Since he was an E-5, Mac would be the team leader and I would walk point as well as being the ATL. I hoped Hobo had taught me enough.

As the slick began to circle before dropping altitude I was sitting in the door looking for the LZ in the distance. It seemed that the slick was half turned as I was staring at the ground when looking straight ahead. I remembered the guys telling me you couldn't fall out because centrifugal force kept you in place, but I had some serious

doubts, especially since I had nothing to hold on to just
in case they were wrong. We circled until finally the pilot
dropped altitude and I knew we were inbound. My heart
was racing as Mac told us to lock and load. I grabbed
the doorframe and stretched my legs out to touch the skid
for the rest of the ride in. I didn't have the time to think
about what to do; I just let my training and instincts take
over as the forward movement of the Huey ceased and it
began to hover over what looked like a giant rock jutting
out from the mountain. This was our LZ and it meant
the entire team would have to un-ass from the right side
of the slick, since the left side was a sheer drop. We
exited in record time. I ran to the woodline with the team
right behind me. We inserted ourselves about fifty meters
into the woods and set up our perimeter. I realized I had
forgotten how quiet the woods could be as we lay there
looking and listening while the RTO covered his mouth
to the handset and made sure we had commo with X-ray.

We had been there for fifteen minutes when Mac motioned us up. It was strange walking point, knowing that
Mac had confidence that I could handle it, while I prayed
I wouldn't miss something and get the team in a bind.
Slowly we wove through the bush, moving steadily uphill
to the top of the mountain. The vegetation was sparse,
so we made good time, but it still took us an hour to
reach the top. Once there, the team fanned out once again
into a defensive perimeter. I pulled out my canteen and
drank a couple of good-sized gulps of water, followed by
a cigarette, as Mac and I plotted our next direction. We
dropped our rucksacks with the team and inched forward
to check out the area we would be traveling. We hadn't
gone too far when we spotted a well-used trail. It was
about three feet wide and hard-packed. We crawled closer
and examined it for signs of footprints, as they can say
a lot about who is using it, how much equipment they're
carrying, and their speed. Deeply embedded footprints
mean troops are carrying a lot of equipment; footprints that have the toes deeply embedded mean they're
moving quickly. We couldn't see any footprints, but a
trail that wide with hardly any vegetation growing on it
meant the trail was used quite frequently. We returned to
the team, and Mac and I discussed our next move. I

wanted to parallel the trail, find a suitable ambush location, and ambush the fuckers when they came walking
down it. After all, we had Barcus on the team with his
gun and he had proved he could use it. Mac wanted us
to walk the trail and see where it led.

"Bullshit," I whispered to him. "I ain't walking no
fucking trail." It would be too easy for us to get ambushed, which was not our job.

"Take it easy," Mac replied. "We'll just take it for a
short time and see if it breaks off anywhere." Hell, Mac
must know what he's doing, I told myself, he's a second-
tour vet and his first was with the Special Forces. But
under my breath I gave him a *buzz*. We saddled up and
began our journey down the trail. I checked to the left
and then to the right before each step. Mac was right
behind me walking my slack as we moved very slowly
down the trail, our eyes searching both sides, looking for
the slightest movement that would give away an ambush.
Most point men kept their M-16 on rock-'n'-roll (automatic) but I didn't trust myself, so I kept slight pressure
on the trigger with my right index finger while my thumb
stayed on the selector switch. I had practiced this at the
range many times and I could move the selector switch
while squeezing off rounds in a split second.

After we moved maybe a hundred meters down the
trail, I spotted a tree to the right with what looked like
three horizontal cuts in the trunk. I froze, crouched, and
motioned Mac up to take a look. He crept up next to me
as I pointed out what I saw. He looked at it, whispered
that it didn't mean anything and that we should keep going. I moved out again, searching even more intently
while I sniffed the air for any smell of them.

After another thirty meters or so, I spotted another tree
with the same horizontal marks. Again I halted and motioned Mac to come up and take a look-see. He moved
up, looked at the tree, told me not to worry and to keep
moving along the trail. I should have told him no, but I
trusted his Green Beenie experience. I continued down
the trail. Not more than ten meters later I was plunging,
feet first, into a punji pit. I waited for pain to shoot
through my legs but felt none. I looked down and saw
that I had landed between punji sticks which surrounded

my jungle boots. The pit was only chest high so I wasn't
hurt, just pissed at Mac for not heeding the warning signs
we had come across. I got myself out with no problem,
and *off* the trail we went. From now on, we would parallel the trail, but first we would take a break because
ahead the trail seemed to enter a clearing, and Mac and
I wanted to plan our next course of action. Thirty meters
or so off the trail was a huge boulder with some trees
around it, and we decided to take our break behind it. I
sat down, lit up a cigarette, and took a long relaxing puff,
trying to unwind. I was still angry with Mac. Now it's
true we had no standard operating procedure about what
to do if we came across dink warning signs—generally
we didn't even know what they meant—but I felt then,
and still do, that Mac should have paid more attention to
them and taken us off that trail.

It didn't take long to figure out what to do next, because we heard voices coming from the trail we had left
not five minutes before. Dinks! They were chattering up
a storm, probably wondering who or what had fallen into
the punji pit. The boulder offered us excellent cover but
we couldn't see a thing. Barcus wanted to peek over the
rock but Mac shook his head no.

We listened as the voices came closer then began to
fade. We gave them a five-minute head start, then moved
out to the trail. There was no doubt that we would try to
find out where the dinks were headed. As I hit the trail
I looked down both sides for signs of company. There
were none, so I began to walk in the same direction the
dinks took. The area ahead looked as if it had been de-
foliated, as the trees had no foliage to speak of and the
trail entered a large dirt clearing.

We stayed close together until we hit the clearing, then
began increasing intervals to fifteen or twenty meters.
Slowly I crept into the clearing, my eyes straining for
signs of the enemy while I listened for any sound. I was
thirty meters into the clearing when my ears detected
voices. I froze into a crouch and looked to my right where
I thought I heard the voices. Mac looked to the right but
all he could see was the ridgeline overlooking the valley.
He looked back at me and gestured no, he didn't hear
anything. I concluded that I must have imagined the

sounds, so I straightened up and continued walking through the open area. Not more than ten meters farther, Mac clicked his fingers quietly. I stopped and looked at him. Now he was pointing to his ears. We both stood in a crouch, turning our heads to pick up sounds, but again found nothing.

For the third time we began down the trail. I heard something again. Voices. I looked back at Mac. He heard them, too! He motioned the team down where they were as he and I squatted, took off our rucksacks, and began moving toward the voices. As we neared the edge of the ridge we began to low-crawl. Sure enough they were talking, but how many of them were there? At the edge we found ourselves on a large rock that hung over the ridgeline. The dinks were right below us, with an excellent view of the valley. But how were we going to get at them without making any noise? I was lying on the right side of the rock with Mac on the left. We could try to crawl down our sides and get the jump on them, but the slightest noise would alert them.

Mac looked at me with a puzzled expression on his face. He started to crawl to the edge of the rock but stopped and rolled back to his former position. He had noticed a large crevice in the rock. He motioned to the frags on his web gear and then to the crevice. I nodded to him that I understood as I laid down my M-16 and took an M-26 grenade from the ammo pouch it was strapped to. Then we low-crawled to the crevice. Mac and I peeked down. I could see the ground about ten feet below me and the crevice was wide enough to fit our frags. We each held a frag in our right hand with our left index finger in the pin. Mac nodded to me to pull my pin as he pulled his. Grenades in our right hands, Mac nodded to me once again as we released the spoons and dropped the frags down the crevice together. As soon as we released them, we rolled to our respective sides of the rock, picked up our M-16s, and covered any attempt to get away. The fuse of an M-26 is supposed to be four and a half seconds long, and in that time we assumed our positions. The frags went off simultaneously. I motioned for Barcus to come up with the gun and to cover as Mac and I went down to check the bodies. But Mac motioned me to stay on top; he would go down. He slowly inched his way down till he was no longer in sight.

"Got two of them," Mac yelled from below.

"Any weapons?" I yelled.

"I'm looking but I don't see anything." *Bang-bang*, Mac's M-16 cracked as he put a bullet into each head to be sure. "Call X-ray and advise them we have two confirmed kills and get a bird out here to exfil us," Mac yelled as he finished policing the kill area. I relayed the information to the RTO, who told us the bird was on its way.

Mac surfaced and came around his corner grinning. Within minutes the bird dog was on the horn to advise us the slick was inbound and we should stand by to pop smoke. We would use the overhang as our LZ. In two minutes we popped smoke and were on our way back to Nha Trang. Except for the punji pit, we'd gotten away quick and clean, the way most teams were finding Nha Trang.

When we got back we took showers, put on clean sets of cammies, and went to the debriefing. There we told the major and the operations officer, a Lieutenant Rob ertson, what happened and what we found. Lieutenant Robertson was a formei platoon leader of one of the platoons, and we lost nothing when Captain Colvin left, as Robertson was one of those officers who looks out for the enlisted man's welfare, just as Major Holt and Captain Colvin had. All the men liked Robby.

When we were through, we went to the EM club to celebrate. A few days earlier Niebert and a few other Rangers had been sitting in the club in the afternoon and had ordered some steaks. One of them, Sergeant Lewis, who was a quiet black from Chicago, asked the waitress to take his steak back to the kitchen because it wasn't done well enough. Somehow the REMFs got all upset about it and began causing a commotion. Niebert, who was still recovering from his wounds, Rassler, Lewis, and four others turned the tables over and called out the entire club. The REMFs had backed away to the wall as the seven Rangers challenged them.

This day Team 3-5 sat together reliving the mission

through round after round of drinks as the Nha Trang REMFs kept to themselves. Later on that evening, the band began to play and the Rangers took their normal positions, on the floor or in front of the stage or in the first row of tables. I was sitting at a front-row table with Norton from First Platoon, the same Norton I'd gone through the school with. We were listening to the music and getting into the band with the rest of the troops. Then, having been turned down by the cocktail waitresses, some of the Rangers began to dance with one another.

"Fuckin' Rangers think you're hot shit," a voice called from behind us. Norton and I turned around: one of the REMFs was feeling his liquid courage.

"You talking to me?" Norton asked.

"You're one of 'em, aren't ya?"

Norton pointed to the door. "Let's go." He got up and headed out the side door, the REMF following behind him. It wasn't even close; Norton's fists found his face, beating him to a bloody pulp. Norton left him lying there. "Chump son of a bitch," was all Norton said as we walked back into the club to continue partying.

A couple of days later a Ranger got into a fight with a Vietnamese QC (their MPs) on post. Unfortunately the Ranger broke his fist while tattooing the Vietnamese's face and had to have a cast put on it. The local QC commander wanted the Ranger punished but didn't know who he was. So we had to stand formation while the Vietnamese commander and his beat-up QC examined us to find the guilty man. As the QCs pulled up, Major Hudson ordered the men of the company to unbutton one button on their fatigue jackets and insert their right hands into the opening. Obviously angry, the QCs departed the area and we all broke into laughter. The major's stock had gone up two points.

In the meantime Pop Carter called for me and told me I was now the team leader of Team 3–5. Not too shabby for a guy who spent thirteen months as a PFC before becoming a SP-4 (only four months earlier). The Army is all right!

The day before we were to be infilled, I went up with a couple of team leaders and "Patches," a lieutenant

who would be infilling us from the 0-1. Patches came by
his nickname for calling to the attention of anyone who
would listen that he was Airborne qualified, Ranger qualified, been to Pathfinder school, et cetera. And he would
always point to the patch that signified his qualifications.
He had lifer written all over him, a two-mission commando. *Buzzzzz.*

Each team leader had maps highlighting his AO, and
as we approached an AO, the team leader would orient
his map and begin looking for prominent terrain features.
About the time the Huey was over the AO, the team leader
would begin looking for an LZ to his liking, either close
to a blue line (stream) or near a valley, since the gooks
needed water like the rest of us and a blue line in a
valley, hidden by vegetation, could be a location they'd
pick for a base camp or a way station. If you were lucky
you might spot a trail and want to be inserted close
enough by. After flying over the AO, the Huey would
continue for a mile or so, then turn around and fly over
it for a second look. This was done so as not to alert
anybody on the ground that company was coming. On
the second pass the team leader would double-check his
map against the terrain, mark the primary and secondary
LZs, and make sure the inserting lieutenant had the same
information. Even with all the coordinating, a team would
occasionally be inserted into the wrong LZ.

After all the team leaders had finished their VRs, the
slick returned to Nha Trang for coordination between
the 0-1 and the slick pilots. I picked out a small LZ at
the base of a small hill. I could see blue lines, so I proposed our route of march would take us up the hill, we
would move west for a hundred meters or so, which
would take us to another field somewhat larger than our
LZ. From there we would check out the valley and head
up another hill. If any dinks were around I wanted to
make sure we found them.

Upon returning I briefed the team on our AO, showing
them our insertion LZ, and our route of march along with
our order of march. Hobo had transferred to another team
as team leader, so I would walk point.

The next morning we got our gear on. As team leader
I had to check everybody to make sure the team had the

proper equipment: twenty magazines per man, minimum, a claymore that worked (that is, no one had taken
out the C-4 to heat his LRPs), four frags, smoke and CS
grenades, poncho, poncho liner, gas mask, and enough
food and water to last at least four days. Even though
most teams were making contact and coming in early, I
remembered An Khe and how hungry we'd been on the
fifth day. Scotty's words of wisdom kept coming back to
me: "Better to have and not need than need and not
have." When I was sure everybody was okay, we headed
for the trucks. By midmorning we were airborne and
headed for the LZ. I hoped I hadn't forgotten anything,
but it was too late to fix even if I had.

As we neared the LZ, the door gunner looked at me
and said we were a minute out. As he readied his M-60,
I yelled for the team to lock and load. We each chambered a round into our M-16s except Toro, my ATL, who
carried an M-14 with a sniper scope. As the slick began
its low-level run to the LZ, my heart was racing again.
God, this was exciting!
The slick began to flare and we readied ourselves. Just
before it touched down we un-assed and headed into the
woods. But our progress came to a quick halt because
we ran into incredibly thick vegetation, something you
can't see from 1500 feet on the VR. The AO was undoubtedly a training area for wait-a-minute vines, and
they were living up to their name. As quietly as we could,
we moved into the woodline and spent the next fifteen
minutes listening to the sounds, or lack of sounds, of the
woods while the RTO made contact with the X-ray. We
moved out at an excruciatingly slow pace due to the vegetation. I had been in thick vegetation before but nothing
so bad. And it was so thick we couldn't see more than
ten meters in any direction.
After an hour I called for a break; the humping, the
vegetation, and the heat were beginning to take their toll.
We just sat, drained. I was so tired I didn't even feel like
a cigarette. We hadn't been sitting more than five minutes when, from our left, we heard voices coming our
way. Instinctively we moved into prone position, weapons silently going from safe to semi or auto. Whoever

was coming obviously didn't know we were around or they wouldn't have been making so much noise. Closer and closer the voices came till they were right in front of us and slightly above. For the second time in two missions since my return I was watching them half-step so we could blow them away, and for the second time the team position was obstructed by Mother Nature. First that huge boulder and then vegetation. As the voices passed I guessed they were walking the trail just ahead. After they passed, we gave them five minutes then moved out.

We continued our climb, and after twenty-five meters or so we ran across the trail they used at the top of our hill. It was surrounded by thick vegetation on both sides. I poked my head through the opening and checked both sides of the trail. There were no signs of the dinks in either direction by then, but the trail looked well used and I knew they'd be back. After my last mission I was determined not to walk trails, but because of the thick vegetation we had no choice. Besides, all I wanted was to find a suitable ambush site as soon as possible and set up. Concealment was all around but no cover, so down the trail we went. As the trail wound to the left I thought I saw an opening. I halted the team while Toro and I went ahead to check As we crouched forward we saw that the trail forked at the top of the hill. We crept closer till we were at the fork and we sat down to observe as both trails wound down the hill. To the right was a field, obviously the larger field I had seen on the VR. To the left the trail seemed to reenter the woods. We moved back to tell the team what we had found. I whispered to the RTO to advise X-ray. I decided to follow the trail to the right side of the hill, paralleling the trail and finding out what was down there.

From the top of the hill to the bottom was only fifty feet and it wasn't steep, so we made good time. Upon arriving at the base of the hill we did find a cornfield, and right in the middle was what appeared to be a fifty-five-gallon drum. We set up, two men facing the trail as it circled the woodline we were sitting in. The trail was just far enough into the woods that it couldn't be seen from the air, but I should have seen the drum sitting in the middle of the field. The field was maybe a hundred meters long by seventy meters wide, with a damn fifty-five-gallon drum sitting right in the middle of it.

Toro and I went to check it out, and as we crept closer to the drum I kept asking myself why someone would put it where it could be seen from the air, not to mention from all points of the woodline surrounding the field? Was it booby-trapped or was it bait for a nosy GI? As we got up to it I examined it as best I could, looking for wires. Finding nothing I slowly lifted the lid, and there before me were fifty-five gallons of corn. A fifty-five-gallon drum of corn would feed more than just a couple of people. We replaced the lid and moved back to tell the team of our find. One of the team hadn't been feeling well and thought he'd be sick.

"Can you hold on? We'll probably be making contact in *ti-ti* time."

He shook his head no. I could see he had the shakes, and his face was covered with sweat. Maybe he was scared, but, hell, weren't we all? Maybe it was malaria.

We were onto something. I called the X-ray and reported the corn, then requested a slick to pull the sick man from the field. After giving our position (in code) I was told a slick would be in shortly to pick him up. Instead of popping smoke—which would compromise our position even more than a landing slick—I advised we would use our signal mirror to guide the slick in. We waited at the base of the hill for fifteen minutes before we heard the rotors beating the air. Bird Dog was also in visual range, and I sighted in on the signal mirror with one hand while talking into the handset with the other.

"Bird Dog, this is 3-5, at your ten o'clock, about four hundred meters. Over."

"Roger, 3-5, I have visual. Get your man ready, slick will be inbound in two mikes. Over."

"Roger, Bird Dog. Advise slick obstruction we discussed. We'll be standing by. 3-5 out." With that we all braced ourselves, as the inbound slick would surely announce company in the area. We heard the Huey coming. I hoped the 0-1 had relayed the previous transmission about the drum so that the slick wouldn't mess up his tail rotor. The Huey came over the trees, and as he began to touch down I ran out to the LZ with my sick man. He jumped aboard as the slick turned around. It gained altitude and in an instant was gone.

As we moved back up the trail to set up our ambush, silence again ruled the field. The problem was, where to set up the team? I wanted to be able to see both trails, and due to the lack of cover I decided to place two members of the team facing the trail that we had followed down and safely hide the RTO in the brush just off the trail. I would conceal myself in the brush in the middle of the trail junction so I could observe both trails. Toro was to the left, covering the trail to the left. If contact was made on the trail to our rear we would use the cornfield as our extraction LZ.

After everybody was in position I sat down in the middle of the trail junction and waited. To pull off an ambush successfully the team must remain absolutely still. No noise. No movement. No smoking. No nothing. You just sit and wait . . . and wait . . . and wait. Sitting in the intersection of two trails might not have been the smartest thing to do, but I was counting on surprise. The few small bushes did offer a bit of concealment. I hoped. I had thought of ambushing the trail near the cornfield, but that might have meant missing someone using the other trail. Also, I didn't want to be in an ambush with a trail above and behind me.

I scanned the trail to the left and then to the right. I was leaning forward a little, M-16 across my lap, right hand on the pistol grip and my left hand on the hand guard. To my left, Toro was in almost the same position. At a time like that each man's thoughts are his own. I worried about the dinks: Would they come up the right trail or the left? Would they come down the trail to our rear? How many would show? Would they show? Steady now, John L., I told myself as my right index finger touched the trigger, just to make sure it was there if I needed it. On and on we waited, sitting in the heat as the midafternoon sun's heat beat down on us. Suddenly, to my left, there was movement. The adrenaline began to flow. My hand tightened around the M-16 and very slowly I began to move it up to my face to sight it.

I hissed to Toro to make sure he saw that I was looking

at something downhill. I couldn't take my eyes off the dink: he was walking in our direction on the trail to the left, half-stepping, rifle over his shoulder, the way the dinks carried it when they thought they were safe. Out of the corner of my eye I could see Toro sighting in his M-14 and giving me a slight nod to signal that he was ready. I took my eyes off the dink for just long enough to see if anybody else was with him. He was alone. As I again picked up the dink in my sights, Toro's M-14 cracked and a puff of smoke flew off the left side of the dink's chest; he spun around twice, and dropped to the ground. I yelled for the RTO to call in a contact as Toro and I fired up the area. We each fired off a couple of magazines, just in case the dink hadn't been alone. As we let up, an ominous quiet descended on the area. We watched for movement. The RTO yelled to me that the contact had been called in and the birds would be on their way.

ETA was fifteen mikes, so I decided to go down the hill to check out the kill zone. I passed the word to watch the trail; Toro would cover me as well as keeping an eye on the trail to the right. At the bottom of the hill, I found a hootch just off the trail. I froze for a minute as I scanned the area. As I moved closer to the hootch, I saw an SKS (a semiautomatic rifle) lying just off the trail. I followed the trail into the woods, looking for an opening the wounded dink could have crawled into. Then the RTO yelled down that the birds were on station.

I ran back up the hill and grabbed the handset to co-ordinate the gunships and the slick. After describing our position, I instructed the gunships to make a pass that would sweep the area just off the trail we had ambushed. I threw a red smoke grenade down the hill to mark the target and waited for the gunships to do their damage.

On our right we heard the ships open up with quad-60s. After each made a pass, I checked out the area once again. I was about two-thirds of the way down the hill when I heard a chopper coming in from the right side. He passed overhead, but when his wingman flew over, the door gunner on the left side opened up with his own '60. Bullets and tracers were dancing not more than ten feet ahead of me as I ran back up the hill.

"Check fire, Check fire," I yelled as I turned around, and *bang*! I ran right into a low-hanging tree branch. The gunships began to circle with orders not to fire unless we called for it as Toro and I now went down the hill to look for the body. Once again we followed the trail until we found an opening in the bush about thirty meters from the hootch and saw him lying there in a puddle of blood. The M-14 round had struck him just above the heart, and although it hadn't killed him instantly, he was just as dead now. I fired a round into his head just to be sure, and as we were leaving the area I threw a willie peter grenade into the hootch and yelled for the team to meet us at the field that we would use for an LZ. As we got to the field I put another willie-peter into the fifty-five-gallon drum of corn followed by a CS grenade. Bon appétit.

Two missions since coming back, two contacts, and confirmed kills on both. So far so good. The entire company was having the same luck as we were and morale was soaring. Each night we partied at the EM club or tried our luck at the meat market. One night the manager of the club bought us drinks for the better part of the night to keep us from dancing with one another. During the band breaks we would all sing "our song," the one we learned at the school and sang as often as possible.

We are Rangers, raiders of the night,
We're dirty sons of bitches who would rather fuck
    than fight,
Oh, heidy, deity, Christ Almighty who the hell are
    we
Shit, fuck, cock suck,
75th Infantry

On one occasion, a Ranger who was annoyed at the club for some reason decided to CS it. He had a small bag of the powdered CS and was going to blow it into the air-conditioning system. Unfortunately he blew it into the exhaust fan, and the CS blew back on him. He came back to the company area to find some sympathy, but all he found was a barracks full of belly laughs.

* * *

After insertion on the next mission, we moved up to a ridgeline, arriving just before dusk, then set up for the night. As we were chowing down, it began to rain and the rain persisted throughout the night. Around 1900 hours we were all still awake trying to keep comfortable with only our poncho liners for warmth and ponchos to keep us dry, when down in the valley about one hundred and fifty meters below we could hear the clanging of pots and pans. It was too dark to move down to surprise the dinks, so I decided to call in some artillery. I had never worked artillery before, so I thought that night would be as good as any to get some practice. Having called in our position to the X-ray previously, I had a good fix on where we were. I would adjust from one of the three preregistered DTs (defensive targets) and the first shot should hit in the valley below us, and from there I could adjust in either direction. After giving the information to the X-ray, I waited for them to relay the information.

"Shot over," the X-ray announced.

"Shot out," I replied, signifying I rogered his transmission and would wait for the crash.

"Splash over," X-ray said as the round should have hit about then.

A few seconds passed before we heard the very distant *crump* as the round hit. "Splash out," I said into the handset, signifying that we heard the round hit. But I couldn't tell where, so I asked the rest of the team if anybody had a fix on the impact. All I got were blank stares and heads shaking back and forth.

"All right, guys, keep your ears peeled and look for the flash," I whispered. "X-ray, this is 3–5. Drop fifty on the next one. Over."

"3–5, understand drop fifty. Wait one. Over." X-ray then relayed the information to the guns. "3–5, this is X-ray. Shot over."

"X-ray, this is 3–5. Shot out." I turned to the team. "On its way." We strained our eyes and ears hoping to get a glimpse of the impact flash or at least figure out where it was hitting by the sound.

"3–5, this is X-ray. Splash over."

Again came a very distant *crump* as the round impacted, but no flash. "X-ray, this is 3–5. Splash out." I looked at the rest of the team and once again the response was negative. "X-ray, this is 3–5. Drop one hundred and left one hundred." I figured a hundred meters one way or another wouldn't matter, since by the distant sound of the impact we were a couple hundred meters off anyhow.

"3–5, this is X-ray. Roger drop one hundred and left one hundred. Wait one. Over." Below us the clanging of the pots and pans continued. The dinks must have thought the artillery fire was just a few H&I (harassment and interdiction) rounds fired at another area.

"3–5, this is X-ray. Shot over."

"X-ray, this is 3–5. Shot out." A hundred meters closer probably wouldn't hurt us, but it would give us a pretty good fix. From there I could make one final adjustment before telling the red-legs to fire for effect.

"3–5, this is X-ray. Splash over." Once again from the distance, not sounding a bit closer, came the familiar *crump*.

"X-ray, this is 3–5. Splash out." I looked at the rest of the team, but again no member of the team had seen the flash or gotten a good audio fix. Maybe, the three hills surrounding the valley below us were concealing the flash and distorting the sound. Good fortune was still with us, as our friends below were still making noise.

"X-ray, this is 3–5. Drop two hundred and left two hundred. Over."

"Roger, 3–5. Understand drop two hundred and left two hundred. Wait one. Over."

The guys at the fire base must have thought a real yo-yo was calling in adjustments, now three hundred and fifty meters from the first request.

"3–5, this is X-ray. Shot over."

Two hundred meters closer *should* put this round where we could see the flash or at least get a firm audible fix on it. *Crump! Closer! That* one hit in the valley below us, but I couldn't tell where; the hills muffled the explosion. "X-ray, this is 3–5. Splash out." I could drop in fifty-meter increments until I had a positive fix or leave well enough alone. "X-ray, this is 3–5. Have red-leg give us a volley of three, same-same. Over."

"Roger, 3–5. Three rounds same-same. Wait one. Over."

Since nobody on the team could get a fix on the rounds, and as far as I could tell they weren't getting any closer or farther away, I might as well give them something to make up for it.

"3-5, this is X-ray. Shot over."

"X-ray, this is 3-5. Shot out." I advised the team that three rounds were on the way, and if nothing else we might as well get some practice.

"3-5, this is X-ray. Splash over."

Crump, crump, crump! Three rounds went off in the valley somewhere below us. "X-ray, this 3-5. Advise red-leg noise has ceased. Tell them good shooting," I lied. They were still down there clanging and talking as they were before I started playing with artillery. I was thoroughly frustrated, a team leader who couldn't call in artillery right. I wanted to grab my M-16 and sneak down on them to correct for my ineptness, but decided not to press our luck. Morning would come soon enough, and we would get an early start down the hill to attack the dinks before they broke camp. The rest of the night we sat in the rain, monitoring the radio. We were miserable. The only thing that kept us alert was the fact that a number of dinks were sharing the same conditions not more than two hundred meters below us.

The next morning we were ready to go by just after 0600 hours. We moved to our left for about a hundred meters before descending, so as not to come right down on top of the dinks without getting an idea of how many there were and how they were set up. Also, since it had rained all night, our footing wouldn't be good and I didn't want to announce our arrival by crashing down the hill. We did our share of slipping and sliding but our noise discipline remained pretty good. I was impressed by the way the team handled itself. When we reached the base of the hill, we swung right. We should have been close within minutes. I was sniffing the air for the aroma that told you they were close. I remembered Team 2-5's entering an NVA base camp without being detected and opening up on the dinks before coming under fire themselves. I didn't want *this* team leader getting killed, but the idea of secretly entering an NVA base camp intrigued me, as well as most other Rangers, who looked at finding a base camp as hitting a grand slam.

We LRPed on through the woods, each step deliberate, as we should just about be on them at any moment. I looked up the hill to estimate where we had been last evening, since the voices had been right below us, but no feature stood out, so we had only our instincts to guide us.

Something was wrong. After a while I felt we had gone a lot more than the hundred meters since hitting the base of the hill. Could we have passed through their camp and missed it? I sat the team down as Toro, my ATL, and I quietly discussed our next move. I decided to go another hundred meters. If we didn't find anything, we would circle and approach the area from another direction.

We sat for a break to gather our strength and courage, then got back up and continued our search. After a hundred meters and not so much as a hint of a dink, we moved to our left for fifty meters and back in the direction we had just come from. When we reached where they should have been, we spread out on line to cover more ground. But we came up with the same results, nothing! No trails, no footprints, no campsite. It was beginning to look like a very small group had visited the valley then moved out sometime during the night. The rain had covered their sounds and their tracks and we came up completely empty.

I was really frustrated. Maybe I *should* have taken the team down at night and tried to catch them by surprise. But night contacts in unfamiliar territory are dangerous and stupid if you don't have a grasp of the situation. I tried to rationalize that I had done the right thing by waiting for the morning, but to be close to a contact and come away empty-handed was really annoying. We spent the rest of the mission checking out the surrounding hills but found nothing. The morning of the fourth day we were exfilled. It was a very quiet chopper ride back to Nha Trang.

The news at Nha Trang did nothing to lift our spirits. We were doing an excellent job in the field killing gooks, but our behavior in the rear, especially at the EM club, left a lot to be desired by higher-higher, who didn't appreciate our lifestyle. As a result the generals had requested our departure from Nha Trang. We were being kicked out, not by the dinks but by the lifer REMFs whose rear-area expectations we obviously didn't fulfill. It seemed Nha Trang was a nice place to visit but not to stay if you wanted to fight a war. It was again time to pack our gear and move out, back to Phan Thiet, and familiar hunting grounds. That meant pitching tents again and filling sandbags. There were few contacts out of Phan Thiet this time. My only memories of that visit are of being issued a brand-new M-16. The first time I took it to the range it jammed. I wanted the old one back because it had new parts I had installed over the course of the year, but the brass wanted us to have new equipment. Such is progress.

In November we pulled up stakes and went up the coast about a hundred miles to our new home, Tuy Hoa.

CHAPTER 13

NOVEMBER 1970—JANUARY 1971/
TUY HOA
John L. Rotundo

I'll never forget my first impression of Tuy Hoa. It was November 1970, and with the monsoon season upon us, the gray clouds hung low over the horizon, giving the impression of impending doom. Since Tuy Hoa was right off the coast of the South China Sea, it could get quite cold at night. It reminded me of November back home in Cleveland off Lake Erie, with the waves crashing in under the gray gloomy skies. The only thing missing was the snow. To this day when the weather gets overcast and there's a chill in the air, my mind automatically puts me back in Tuy Hoa.

When we arrived at our new home, we found ourselves sharing the area with a company of ROKs (Korean infantry). Every morning we woke up and watched them in their tiger fatigue pants beating the hell out of each other while they practiced *Tae Kwando*. For the most part we kept to ourselves and they did likewise. They smiled at us when we passed them, and on occasion they would invite us to partake in their early morning rituals, but we declined their offer. Some of us had studied karate in the States, but these guys practiced every day and would undoubtedly have beat the hell out of us.

After a few days of settling in, Charlie Rangers was ready to begin pulling missions. Team 3–5 was to be the stay-behind team: if a team made contact and got some kills, 3–5 would be inserted in the exfil chopper to set an ambush around the bodies when the original team departed the area. Major Hudson also implemented a new policy whereby no team would receive credit for a kill unless they brought back the clothes from the dead. No longer would a captured weapon prove a kill. It was too easy to take in an SKS or an AK-47 strapped to your rucksack and say you just took it from the kill zone. Hudson also thought it would be a good idea for the ROKs to learn about our operation, so he assigned ROKs to certain teams. Two ROKs were assigned to Team 3–5 to learn firsthand how we operated.

We were cammied up and hanging around the company area, waiting, when a team in Fourth Platoon made contact and had two kills. We put on our gear and raced to the helipad, arriving as the slick was already warmed up. As the Huey circled outside the AO before our approach, Team 3–5 lay down to make the slick look empty, just in case dink LZ watchers were on-site. At the same time, the team on the ground would make a lot of noise and pop smoke grenades to let people close-by know somebody was in the area. After we touched down, the other team pointed out the two dead dinks. We gave each other the thumbs-up sign, and in an instant they were gone and we were running into the woods for cover.

I had Toro as my ATL, the two ROKs, the RTO, and a new team member, a young black from South Carolina named Cravis Taybron. C. T. had been with the company for a couple of months. He was said to be good in the woods. With two ROKs on the team I knew I needed all the help I could get. We waited for a few minutes to get adjusted to the area, then moved into the woodline, circling the area of the previous contact, ending up on a slight rise overlooking a trail. I set the team in a linear ambush as Toro and I went out to check the bodies, which

should have been right in front of us according to the
team leader's direction.

The trail was perhaps a hundred meters from the woodline, and in a matter of minutes we found the bodies.
The first dink's brains were sticking out from the side of
his head; now I knew why the brain is referred to as gray
matter. I wondered what would happen if the skull was
hit with a blunt object and the brain wasn't there to absorb the impact. With the butt of my M-16 I smacked the
dink's head. The skull cracked like the head of a plastic
doll. That was so neat that I gave him one more. As I
looked down on the now grotesque face, I thought it
would be neat to reach down and grab the brain to show
the guys back at the compound, but on second thought I
decided not to.

What would ever possess me to do something like that
to a corpse? God only knows. I felt no remorse for the
gook. He was dead and I was alive, that's the way it
was.*

Toro and I went back to the rest of the team, and tried
to explain to the ROKs what we were doing. They nodded as I whispered in Pidgin English and used hand gestures to say that we were going to wait for others to come
and bury the two dead gooks (I didn't use that word).
The ROKs nodded and smiled in agreement. I hoped they
understood that we had to remain completely quiet while
we waited. They must have; for the next hour they didn't
move a muscle.

From my left, the subdued snap of fingers alerted us.
I looked at C. T., who was on the left flank. He showed
two fingers. We slowly drew up our M-16s and waited
for them to come in front of us. They were just be-
bopping along the trail as I waited for them to come
abreast of the team, which would put them just about at
the bodies we were ambushing. I sighted in on the lead
dink. Procedure called for the flank man on the side they

---

*What tragedy may be found in this scene comes from the fact the dink
was dead. But legal participation in war gives the soldier the right of life
or death over strangers—and I had exercised it legally. If you don't like
the result, don't send kids to war with guns.

were coming from to wait till the dink point man was even with the other flank before opening fire.

C. T. opened fire first and then we were all firing. Both of them dropped and vanished into the elephant grass that surrounded the trail. There was an old dead tree twenty meters on the other side of the trail, so Toro and I changed magazines and raced toward that. As we circled to the right I could hear someone yelling in Vietnamese. The voice was coming from the direction of the tree, so when we got to within thirty meters of the tree I took out a baseball grenade and pulled the pin. The baseball grenade was something relatively new. Unlike the old pear-shaped M-26 grenade, the baseball was round so you could throw it like a baseball. Inside, instead of having a coil of shrapnel, the baseball had hundreds of ball bearings, like a claymore mine. I had four and a half seconds left after I released the spoon; I was going to try for an airburst over the tree. I released the spoon and counted "one thousand one, one thousand two," then hurled the grenade toward the tree. It rose and then began its descent as I counted to myself, "one thousand three, one thousand four, one thou—" *Boom!* It went off exactly where I wanted, and I looked at Toro with a smug expression on my face. John Wayne had nothing on me!

After the smoke cleared we heard screams coming from near the tree again, which surprised me as I thought no one could have survived the grenade. As we crouched and moved toward the tree through the elephant grass, I saw the two dinks cowering by the trunk. Somehow the frag had gone off right above them but neither seemed to have been hurt. So much for modern technology. As we crept closer, I saw that a woman was doing the yelling. Behind her, practically hidden, was a man wearing a white pith helmet. Toro and I kept our guns trained on them as I raised my left finger to my lips to signal her to be quiet, but she kept yelling. *"Dung noi!"* I shouted to her to shut up, but to no avail; she continued to yell. Something wasn't right; she wasn't looking at us while she was yelling. It was as if she were yelling at someone else out there, but I couldn't understand what she was screaming. I raised my left hand and motioned her to come to me. *"Lai day!"* I shouted at the same time. I still had my rifle pointed at her now and I sighted in on her. *"Dung noi!"* I yelled a last time, but got the same results.

"Fuck it." I looked at Toro, who just shrugged his shoulders. I was aiming at her mouth as that was the center of attention, and gently took up the slack in the trigger until there was no more, and just squeezed.

Bang! The first round caught her just above the mouth and tore the upper lip away as her head jerked to the side. *Bang!* The second round went into her cheek and made a perfect round hole going in. Two more rounds just to make sure, and then I moved my rifle to take care of the one wearing the white pith helmet and trying to hide in the dead tree. *Bang-bang!* Two rounds made their way through the helmet into his skull. My drill instructor in basic training would have been proud of the tight shot group; the bullet holes touched. Toro and I began to strip the bodies to confirm the kills. I took the white pith helmet from the dead dink and put it on my head, in place of my boonie hat.

As soon as we had initiated contact, the RTO called it in to X-ray, who reported it to our TOC, which in turn, had the exfil slick and gunships inbound to our location. As we were finishing, a gunship roared overhead and we waved to him to signal all was okay. Right after he passed overhead the RTO yelled from the woodline that the gunship had spotted two people, one of them wearing a white helmet.

"Jesus Christ, get on the horn and tell them that's us down here!" I screamed.

"Roger." I immediately took off the helmet.

We arrived back at the camp and dropped off our gear along with the clothes we took from the dead. Pop Carter told us seven NVA were spotted heading our way by another team when we made contact. The woman was trying to signal to somebody, and those seven were probably the somebodies. A while later Carter told us that from the papers found in their clothes, the two we killed were a VC burial detail. This stay-behind worked.

After we got cleaned we went to the EM club to celebrate and found the Tuy Hoa EM club to be almost as nice as the one on Nha Trang. Plenty of beer and booze along with a Filipino band for entertainment. But in Tuy Hoa the black-power movement was really big, and the blacks would go through five-minute "dap" gyrations. We didn't give that much thought until a group sat down in front of us in the club and started up.

"Sit down," someone finally yelled to the blacks as they were "slap-slapping and dap-dapping."

"Who said that?" one of the dappers asked, scowling in our direction.

We turned around. Thorne was grinning. "I did."

"Yeah, sit down," Sweat said. He was sitting next to Thorne.

There were about a dozen of them and about twenty of us. It was a stare-down as we just looked at one another, waiting for the other to make the first move.

"Fuckin' rabbits," one of them called as they grabbed their black-power walking sticks and swaggered out of the club.

The next night was more of the same. The blacks went through their dap only to be followed by Thorne and Sweat doing their own version, which ended with them giving each other the finger, and laughing about it.

"Fuckin' rabbits," would come from one side of the club to be followed by "Fuckin' crows" from the other. It was only a matter of time before the anger would become violent. In the meantime we continued to pull missions while they continued to pull "Green Line" duty. Most of the missions we pulled in Tuy Hoa were frustrating, as it seemed every time we were inserted we had to "go groundhog," i.e., "stay out of sight, don't move or make contact, since we can't get the slicks up to support you because of the rain and fog."

On one of those missions I had an opportunity to work with Rath, or, as he called himself, "the wrath of Rath." Tall and lean with his blond hair and mustache Rath resembled a young Donald Sutherland, but in his heart was a good killer. When he went to the field, his team normally made contact, not with claymores, but with rifle ambushes. Rath was an excellent shot and always hit them in the head. But that time out we spent four days in the field unable to make contact because of the weather and ended up talking about foods and fine wines. Rath was from Columbus, Ohio, and had obviously spent a good deal of time at restaurants in that area. By the time we were ready to exfil, he was laying out seven-course dinners, down to which type of bread we would eat. Even though I had never tasted some of the food Rath was describing, my mouth watered for four days and I had a hard time devouring my LRP rations while wondering what lobster might taste like.

Just before Christmas 1970, we were granted a three-day in-country pass to wherever we wanted to go. Some of the guys elected to go back to Dalat. Others wanted to go to An Khe. Rath, a couple of others, and I elected to go back to Nha Trang. Since we had been kicked out two months earlier we thought we should go incognito. So we put on OD fatigues without patches and wore basic-training baseball hats. However, we did keep our Airborne wings on our hats. Some habits are hard to break.

We thumbed a ride to Nha Trang and spent three fantastic days and nights. I took advantage of the MARS telephone service and called home to wish everyone a Merry Christmas and tell them I was fine.

The meat market was active and we each tried a different girl each night. After the girls left we went to the EM club to talk.

Nha Trang held very good memories, for we had all made contacts there in September and part of October. The gooks never did catch on to our presence or the type of operations we ran; each contact caught them half-stepping, and we blew them away before they knew we were there. Too bad the lifers had to screw it up.

On the third day of our leave, we made it back to Tuy Hoa, finding it just as we had left it, gray skies with steady drizzle. Because of the holidays a cease-fire had been declared, so we weren't pulling missions.

After Christmas the teams that went out didn't make contact, which was frustrating. We spent our nights at the EM club drinking, probably not a great idea as the conflict was growing between the blacks and the Rangers. On New Year's Eve of 1970, it blew up as seven Rangers and twenty blacks got into it. A few cuts and bruises were all the Rangers received. We referred to them as the Magnificent Seven. The next day I formed up thirty of us, we donned our black berets and took the Third Platoon flag as a guidon, and marched in formation to the EM club. Every time our left feet hit the ground, we shouted, "Kill." When we got to the EM club we planted the flag by the door and waited. That night none of the troublemakers showed up, so we sat and drank in peace. In fact, Rick Jason from the TV show *Combat*, made an appearance at the club that evening. He sat and talked to us for a while. Schumaker, we called him Shu-shu, a team leader in Third Platoon confiscated Jason's lighter. As he left he waved to everybody and we all waved back. Shu-shu grinned and told everyone he had an "official Rick Jason lighter."

The next night we were sitting around the club when the blacks entered in groups, all carrying black-power sticks, and dapping one another while we all went through our version. That went on for most of the night and the words gradually became more than heated between us until tables were cleared away as we faced one another. The band stopped playing and ran off the stage while the NCO who ran the club tried to break up what was about to happen. He only succeeded in getting the blacks to leave first. We all knew they would be waiting for us outside and I noticed Kelly was doing something to his pants. He was one of the Magnificent Seven and he showed me what he had going for him. His belt was a "drive-on rag" (an oversize green handkerchief) tied in a slipknot. On one of his belt loops he carried a Master lock. He tied one end of his drive-on rag around the lock and grabbed a hold of the other, and began swinging it over his head. He had used that on New Year's Eve and broke a few heads with it. I had nothing quite as good as that, so I just grabbed the glass that I was drinking from and put it into my right thigh pocket for future use. I didn't know what I would do with it, but at least I had something. As we filed out, sure enough the blacks were waiting for us, having formed a circle that started at the door and looped around the corner of the building. Our only way out was to fight. The Rangers were facing the brunt of them, but I noticed we had our back to quite a few as well.

"Rear guard!" I yelled as a few Rangers turned around

to protect the others. In an instant fists, feet, sticks, and clubs were winging through the air. The war was on and you could hear the contact as bones and glass were breaking behind us. I was trying to cover the rear when from out of nowhere I felt a blow to my neck just above the breast bone.

I heard someone say "Let's get him, blood," as I was reeling from the impact. I looked up. Two blacks with walking sticks were coming toward me. Instinctively I pivoted my left foot, leaned my body away from them, and shot out my right foot in a side kick, aimed for the solar plexus of the bigger of the two. I made contact. He doubled over and I straightened to take a swing at his buddy, but all I hit was air as he ducked under my fist. I lunged past, and as I turned around he was helping his "brother" away. I turned to face the rest of the action.

Pockets of fighting were everywhere. Right in front of me passed one black looking for a target for his stick, so I reached into my thigh pocket and pulled out my glass. I snuck up behind him and hit him on top of the head. The glass shattered on his head, and I moved back to admire my handiwork. He fell like a sack of potatoes and I moved on, thoroughly enjoying myself. Then I looked down at my right hand and the blood that covered it.

I must have caught him good. I thought to myself as I reached Kelly, who I figured was waiting for another victim. "Hey, Kelly, I got one," I yelled to him as I showed him my hand. "Look at this, I got him good."

Kelly took one look at my hand and started laughing. "That's your blood, not his!"

I looked down. Sure enough, I was bleeding from my hand! "Fuck it, let's get some more." Together we went after some more. Some of the Rangers were shooting pen flares at the group they were facing. By then somebody had gone to the NCO club and our NCOs were joining in. Some of them were black, but that night they were all Rangers. Some of the dappers were calling our black NCOs Uncle Toms, but our Rangers called back, "Fuck you, nigger."

The battle had become a standoff, a few of them and a few of us lying on the ground trying to recover, but most everybody was now standing facing the others. Suddenly someone shouted "Frag!" The Rangers hit the ground, crawling on hand and knees. There was a flash and a *boom*! right between the two groups. I got up and examined myself for wounds but found nothing. Since the device went off not more than fifteen feet from me and I wasn't hit, it must have been a concussion grenade. Of course, given my recent experience, it could have been a baseball grenade. Whoever threw it got the desired results; both sides quickly cleared the area.

We made it back to the company area to get our weapons, only to find that they had been locked up in the conex—a corrugated steel container—and Major Hudson wouldn't release them. Those who needed first aid were put into trucks and sent to the hospital, the drivers ordered to "run them sons of bitches over" if they started any shit. I went to the hospital to have my hand looked at. It only required stitches, but a few of the men were in a lot of pain. During the fight a very well built Ranger named Vince DiMaio went down and was being pounded by four blacks with their sticks and feet. He was trying to shield himself but kept getting hit. Finally he reached up, grabbed something, and pulled as hard as he could. One of the blacks let out a horrible screech—Vince had pulled the poor guy's scrotum away. He let out such a scream that his buddies backed away, enabling DiMaio to get away. Thorne looked to be the worst of the Rangers. His head had been knocked open in a few places and for the next two weeks he wore a huge bandage that looked like a turban around the company area. The wounds must have hurt him something fierce, but the guy was always smiling. Word had it that five of "them" required evacuation to Japan or to the World for medical attention; we had a few Rangers with broken bones and slashes that would keep them out of the field for a while, but nobody requiring hospitalization.

We continued to pull missions as the war wound down though with fewer teams. With the weather continuing as it had, that meant fewer teams had to go groundhog.

The second week in January 1971, I took my R&R to Bangkok, Thailand. Even though Thailand and Vietnam were both in Southeast Asia I found the people of Thailand much nicer than the Vietnamese. But R&R in Bangkok followed the usual routine: the first day a dozen girls were brought to pick from. After picking the week's escort, the time was yours to do with as you wanted. The usual routine was screw first. Get something to eat and screw again. Do some sightseeing and screw again. Maybe a movie and, of course, screw again. I'll admit I had a good time on R&R. Not only for the obvious reasons, but another guy from the company was there at the same time, a tall Texan from Dallas, with black hair and one of the fullest mustaches I'd ever seen. His name was E.C. McLaughlin: no first or middle name, just the initials E and C. He fit the mold of most Texans, always talking and bragging about his state, but E.C. was liked by everyone. He had a wild sense of humor and would get totally smashed while on stand-down. On one mission his team sprang an ambush, and when one dink tried to run away, E.C. ran after him with a frag in one hand and M-16 in the other, yelling at the dink as he chased him down the trail. We partied together on R&R and returned to Tuy Hoa the following week.

After arriving from Bangkok I started drinking early the next afternoon and was talking with the other guys in the Third Platoon barracks when we heard the call, "Fire!" Evidently someone had dropped a cigarette in a trash can in the barracks next door and soon flames were licking at the roof. I ran into our barracks and grabbed a bag of marshmallows from the bunk of a guy who had just bought them for his hot cocoa. As I made my way to the burning barracks, Staff Sergeant Lincoln, the new Second Platoon sergeant, was trying to direct the fire fighting. He stared at me for a good ten seconds, looked at the obviously lost barracks, looked at me again, broke into a grin, then a laugh, and reached into the bag. "Anybody got a stick?" he yelled as the two of us stood there roasting marshmallows in the fire until it was finally out.

Lincoln was a wizard with ropes. He could tie just about any kind of knot, and when we had to equip a chopper for rappelling or emergency extraction he was the one called on. He was one squared-away NCO who earned the Second Platoon's undivided loyalty, along with that of a few others, myself included.

One of the last missions we pulled found Team 3–5 on X-ray security and, as usual, after the first day the clouds rolled in and all teams were told to go groundhog. We were on top of an incredibly steep hill and I thought it might be a good time to play mortarman. I grabbed the thump gun, and as fast as I could I fired rounds up and out one after the other and listened for the sound in the valley below. *Crump-crump-crump-crump.* After that we took turns pulling pins on frags, releasing the spoons and counting to two before tossing them into the valley to watch them explode. The remainder of the time on top of the mountain we spent doing our best to protect ourselves from the wind and rain. It was too wet and cold to write letters, so we just shared the misery.

On the third day a call came in from one of the Fourth Platoon's teams. They were in contact and had a friendly WIA; the gooks had come right up on them and there had been no way to avoid contact. As we were on top of the mountain, the team was the nearest to us; normally we would have been afforded a great view. But because of the weather, we couldn't see a thing except low clouds. We monitored the radio and listened to the play-by-play as the team held its own but remained in contact. Somewhere in the distance we could hear the 0–1 flying over the team's area as the bird dog attempted to guide the slick in through the fog and rain. The X-ray was out of the conversation and the 0–1 was in direct communication with the team, the company TOC, and the slick on another frequency. We heard the team tell the 0–1 that the wounded Ranger was now a KIA. That sucked!

Somehow the slick extracted the team. When they were in the air we heard the 0–1 tell the TOC that a door gunner said he counted at least fifty dead dinks near the contact area. Some had been killed by the team and the others by the door gunners.

When we got back to camp the next day everybody was angry because with most of the teams being in the field, Major Hudson had taken the opportunity to have all our dogs destroyed. He said it was because of a rabies scare but that was nonsense. His stock, which had soared in

Nha Trang when he called the formation with our hands in our shirts, was now worthless.

The other news was that the company was again being moved. This time back down the coast to Phan Thiet.

CHAPTER 14

JANUARY–FEBRUARY 1971/PHAN THIET
John L. Rotundo

It was the third time the company had worked out of Phan Thiet, and for the third time we pitched our tents in a different location, this time closer to the EM club, but that's all we were close to. In the evenings we'd build a bonfire and bring whatever we were drinking and just sit around swapping lies. It was on one of these evening sessions that my future after the army was molded. Dutch, a second-tour vet, made a remark about paratroopers making the best salesmen. Like everyone else I was Airborne all the way, but I found that a bit hard to take. "Why the hell would you say that?"

"When was the last time you bought something from a salesman—well, not so much the product, but bought the salesman?"

"I'm not sure I follow you."

"Look. You go out to buy something and you shop around. Suppose you find the same product for the same price? Who would you buy it from?"

"I don't know," I said. "Probably the guy with the best line."

"Best line of shit! You're right. The salesman who does

249

the best job convincing you that you should buy it from
him. With words and phrases he creates a picture in your
mind of what the product will do for you or how you'll
look in it or whatever. The point is, he uses your mind
to create the image he is talking about.''

''Yeah, I guess so,'' I mumbled. ''But what does that
have to do with paratroopers making the best salesmen?''

''Did you ever listen to a jump story?''

He caught me completely by surprise. I tried to think
back to Fort Bragg and how after we made a jump everybody would stand around swapping stories. Rarely did
anyone say he had stood up, hooked his static line, and
jumped, counted to four, and the chute opened up and
he rode it to the ground. No way! Guys would describe
in the most precise details, using hand gestures and joking about something or another to tell their own story.
That would be followed by someone else's trying to top
the last story. As I was thinking about this I laughed to
myself about Dutch's analogy. He was right. Every time
somebody was telling a jump story I put myself into their
shoes and pictured myself in their situation, doing the
same thing. ''Ya know, Dutch, you're right,'' was all I
could say.

We sat talking for another hour with the tape player
cranking out the Rascals' *Time Peace* album, and then
one by one we hit the sack. I was going on a VR the next
day and didn't want to be too hung over, so I went to
crash in the hootch that Rath and I shared. He was already out in the field so he wouldn't mind my snoring.

The next morning after breakfast, myself and two other
team leaders met at the helipad for the VR. One of the
guys was carrying a radio and said that Rath's team had
made contact and had six confirmed kills. About that
time Major Hudson came strutting by with one of the
lieutenants and heard the news. The major took the pipe
out of his mouth and exclaimed that ''those claymores
do a damn-damn,'' while the lieutenant agreed. Hell,
anybody who knew Rath knew he never used claymores
for his ambushes. He preferred a rifle ambush; claymores
were used only for defensive measures when he took a
team to the field. Nothing like knowing your people, sir.

The next day we had to wait for the slicks at the helipad

because they were already inserting teams and 3-5 wouldn't be going in till the early afternoon. After the pilots had their ships refueled, we boarded and took off to our LZ. Our cherry on that mission was nervous but trying not to show it. I remembered my first mission many months earlier and the way I'd felt: scared and excited at the same time. I told him not to worry and just to remember what he'd been taught in school. We circled while the gunships caught up to us after covering for another infil, then the slick dropped and began making its low-level run to the LZ. There is still nothing in the world like the feeling of low-leveling, going along at a hundred knots or so while playing tag with the ground and the trees.

"One minute," the door gunner yelled to me over the rotors' noise.

I nodded to him, then to the team. "Lock and load. We're going in."

As soon as the slick began to slow down I put my feet down on the skids to ride in the last thirty seconds. Ahead and just over the trees I spotted the LZ and braced myself. As we cleared the trees, the slick dropped down, and when it was about three feet from the ground I jumped and headed for the woodline, followed by the rest of the team. As soon as I hit the trees I was looking at a beautiful, hard-packed trail that went into the woods right in front of me, and from where I was standing, continued into the woods to my right. I jumped over the trail to avoid leaving prints, then turned to my slack man, C.T., making sure he did likewise. We were right at the trail and it didn't take long to figure out where we would set up an ambush—a slight rise about fifty meters off the trail which offered excellent cover and concealment. The kill zone was actually a clearing in the middle of the woods. From where we set up we had an unobstructed view. Fort Benning couldn't have designed a better site for an ambush. I moved the team halfway up the little hill we would be perched on, then spread them out in a linear ambush. From our position we could observe the kill zone and a good fifty meters of the trail to either side. I had a cherry sitting next to me as I was describing the benefits of the site and what we were attempting to do when my eyes caught movement to the right side of the trail. Gooks!

"Pssst," I whispered to C.T., who was on my left flank. He nodded and was already bringing his rifle to bear on them. I looked around to the rest of the team and they all were doing the same, so I brought my M-16 up and sighted in on the point man. There were three of them, the point man carrying an SKS over his shoulder while talking to the other two—women carrying packs. We let them approach until they were directly in front of us. I whispered to the cherry to just watch what happened as I picked up the slack in the trigger and squeezed off the first round. With my shot as cue, the rest of the team opened up and we sprayed the area while the RTO called the contact to the X-ray. We each followed with another magazine, trying to make out the bodies through the smoke. After my second magazine I ordered the team to check fire so we could get a fix on the bodies. I turned to the cherry and asked him what he saw.

"I saw the first tracer hit the point man in the head and then just a steady stream going into him and the second one," he said.

Everything had happened so quickly that we still had our rucksacks on when we went to the kill zone. As we got closer to the trail I saw two bodies, the point man and a woman, right on the trail. They must have been killed instantly since there were no signs they had tried to crawl away. Lying near the point man was his SKS, mine now, a souvenir to take home. As we crouched on top of the bodies, I put the muzzle to the point man's head near the temple and fired a magazine on rock 'n' roll. His head vibrated with the impact of the rounds and his brains spurted out the other side of his head. I followed with the woman and did the same thing to her. Meanwhile, C.T. was busy looking for a sign of the other woman. I joined him in the search, looking for a blood trail or any other kind of sign that she might have cut through the bush along the trail. Near the kill zone was a depression with a large tree stump in the middle of it. C.T. and I each tossed a frag in there. After the explosion we went down to check it out. Unfortunately we came up empty-handed, so we decided to strip the bodies we had and get out.

C.T. stripped the woman while I started to strip the man. I had his pants and sandals, but he was wearing a shirt with buttoned sleeves and I was having a hard time getting it off. I ripped open his shirt and got off one sleeve but had trouble with the other. C.T. had finished with his and saw I was having a hard time. "Here, use this." He handed me a machete from his rucksack. I took a swing and severed the hand from its arm in one motion. When I pulled the rest of the shirt off I noticed that the corpse wasn't bleeding from the wrist the way one would see in the movies. We collected the clothes, weapon, and both packs. Since their friends would no doubt be by soon to find them, why not give them something to look at? The man was already on his back, so I grabbed the woman's lifeless body and pulled it over to his, placing them in the 69 position. I left a platoon card where it couldn't be missed so that Charlie would know who had done it, then raced back to the team.

"Slick's standing by," the RTO said. "0-1 said to use the same LZ."

"Okay, let's move it." We retraced our steps to the waiting LZ. When we neared the edge of the woods the RTO whispered to pop smoke. I let the cherry throw the smoke and the 0-1 identified it. Within a minute the slick was flaring over the trees and we ran to it and boarded. As the slick rose it didn't turn around, but rather flew over the area of the woods we had just left. I was sitting in the door again looking out at nothing in particular when a rifle barked in my right ear. The cherry was emptying his magazine out the door. Then the door gunner on my left opened up with his M-60.

"Gooks!" the cherry yelled. "Down there." He continued firing along with the door gunner. I looked down but couldn't see a thing. As we gained altitude and they ceased firing, the door gunner said he had spotted seven NVA running for cover as we were about to pass over them. They were headed for our contact area. They had not been too far away from us. Gulp!

When we were en route to Phan Thiet I decided to celebrate and do a little profiling. When we were almost back to the compound I took out a red smoke grenade from my harness and began untying my boot laces. When they were almost completely untied I attached one end of them to the neck of the smoke grenade. I pulled the pin and dropped the grenade out the door. As it was still attached to my boot, it hung a few feet below the slick and we trailed red smoke as we entered the compound, signifying a kill.

After debriefing I went back to our hootch, saw our little hootch maid walking out, and asked her how much for boom-boom (a screw). I gave her a 500-piaster note and got my satisfaction, cammy stick still on and all. It was just something I had always wanted to do.

I didn't really care about anything except killing gooks. When I was home on extension leave my mother kept saying that I seemed to have a chip on my shoulder about something. She was right: as far as I was concerned the World sucked. For those thirty days I did enjoy being home with my family and friends, but down deep inside I missed the war and the camaraderie that existed between Rangers, something the people back home could never understand. How could they understand the raw power we felt by killing? Granted it was war, but there was something gamelike in our operations: going undetected into Charlie's backyard, finding his avenues of travel, putting him in the sights, pulling the trigger or blowing claymores. In an instant he and his friends were dead. That plus the fact we got out before his comrades could take their revenge made us feel almost invincible. That's *power*! And we had it.

Some evenings while we sat around the bonfire we discussed life and death. One question that almost always came up was why we had volunteered for LRP duty. That there was a war going on and we were saving America from Communist aggression just didn't wash. The truth of the matter was, we volunteered because of the adventure and excitement we were looking for. We were all Airborne, but we were looking for something more than just jumping from an airplane. War fit the bill, but "Vietnamization" was taking over and there wasn't much war left by the time we had come along. Besides, we didn't want to be lost in some line outfit where you made contact only if Charlie wanted to engage. No, we wanted to be part of the action where *we* picked the time and place, so we chose the Rangers. Some say we had a death wish, but those aren't the right words for our motivation. Putting our lives on the line as often as we did taught us to appreciate life. Even though at nineteen and twenty years old we wouldn't understand it for a while, we knew the things we did now would mold our lives in the future, as would the personal satisfaction we got out of being associated with the best America had. Maybe that's why we got into so many fights in the rear. People mistook our unit pride for arrogance. We were cocky, but we were good, too, and we knew it. And the gooks knew it, that's why we each had a price on our head.

The next day we got some mail and I got a Dear John letter I had been expecting for quite some time. I hadn't written to her much since returning and was relieved that it was over.

A couple of days later Team 3–5 was to pull stay-behind duty, and once again Rath's team made contact and had some kills. This time a staff sergeant named Cheshire was to be the team leader, and I was to be the ATL and walk point. Cheshire was a tall, thin individual from the south. A second-tour vet, he had spent his first tour with the First Air Cavalry. He generally handled administrative duties within the platoon, so I didn't know how he was in the field. We were inserted after the contact but didn't meet Rath for directions to the bodies because we were being directed by the 0–1. According to his directions, the bodies were about three hundred meters from the insertion LZ, and we were going to circle the area to set up our ambush.

The terrain proved quite difficult to navigate in as we found ourselves getting turned around constantly, seemingly going away from the contact area half the time. The briars and bushes were so thick it was virtually impossible to walk through. Cheshire decided to move us uphill to navigate around the brush, coming back down when we were abreast of the contact area. The woods on the hill proved no more open than the area below, but I was doing my best to slither through the brush without making any noise. We were silent but very slow. Since the contact had been in the afternoon, and we had already humped for almost two hours, stopping only briefly to catch our breath and to check our position, Cheshire decided to stay on the hill for our night halt.

We set out the claymores and chowed down, one at a time, ending just as the sun was going down. Then we pulled our poncho liners over us, keeping one man on guard at a time, and crashed for the evening. That night, during one of my watches, I started thinking about extending again. My tour would be up 20 April and I didn't really cherish the idea of duty at Fort Bragg. From what the guys who had already rotated wrote back, Fayetteville was now topless in the bars, but it would take more than that to make Bragg bearable. I loved riding in the slicks, so I thought I might want to try my hand at being a door gunner. I'd lose jump pay but would make it up in flight pay. I decided to give it some more thought later on. Just then I was concerned about finding the bodies before Charlie found them and buried them.

The next morning we ate, pulled in our claymores, repacked our rucks, and headed out, circling the area again. We hadn't gone more than a couple of hundred meters when I spotted something in the distance. The team got down as C.T. and I dropped our rucks and moved forward to investigate. As we crept closer I made out a hootch on stilts. C.T. and I spread out and moved in from both sides. I came in away from the door and ended up under the hootch while C.T. covered me. The hootch was too small to house anyone, so I took a deep breath, glanced at C.T., and jumped in front of the door, pointing my M-16 in the doorway. Inside was a large burlap container of rice that about took up the entire hootch.

C.T. and I went back to the team and reported our find to Cheshire. We were almost abreast of the contact area, so Cheshire told us to dump the rice on the ground then move down to ambush the bodies. Carefully I checked for signs of a booby trap in the hootch, then pulled out the bag. We took it into the woods then dumped the rice on the ground, trying to grind it in the dirt. When we were done, we moved down the hill to the contact area.

We arrived at the contact site but found no signs of the bodies at all—no blood, no footprints! Nothing! We swept the area but found nothing. There wasn't even a trail. It didn't make sense. We spent the rest of the day looking for a trail, a stream, anything. We found nothing.

The next day was spent going up and down the surrounding hills. Again we came up empty. We stayed in the valley for that night's halt since the extraction LZ was only a hundred and fifty meters away.

The next morning we awoke and took our time eating and getting ready to move out, since our estimated pickup wouldn't be till later on in the morning. About 0800 we broke camp, policed our area, burying our LRP bags and trying to make the place look as uninhabited as possible. We moved from the base of the hill into the valley, about fifty meters from the woodline although we were still in the brush. I found a slight clearing where the team would wait for exfil orders. We just lay around waiting, occasionally whispering to one another, but for the most part just taking it easy, when a twig snapped in front of me. We froze. I moved my M-16 to point it in the direction the noise came from while moving the selector switch to SEMI. *Crack* went another twig, closer this time. Once again the adrenaline began to pump. Whatever or whoever was out there was getting awfully close. I tried to control my breathing. In an instant a head broke through the brush not more than twenty meters from where I was lying. The head looked to his left, away from me, and as he turned to look in my direction I opened fire. The rest of the team opened up when they heard my first shot, and sprayed the area with M-16 rounds, the thumper going to work blasting the area where he had come from. After I had fired one magazine and was in the process of changing it, I heard Cheshire yell, "Frag out!" as he threw out a baseball grenade. I watched its flight from Cheshire's hand as it went up and out, hit an overhanging branch, and came dropping straight down in front of us.

"Frag in!" I screamed. We ceased fire and hugged the earth. *Crump!* It went off in front of us but none of us was hit. After my past experience with baseball grenades that really made me a believer in the old M-26.

"No more frags, Cheshire," I yelled as dirt continued to fall on us. We again began firing in the area.

"Check fire," Cheshire shouted. Again the eerie silence descended on an area that just seconds before had been filled with the barking of M-16s and the explosions of the thumper's 40mm grenades. We lay there for a minute trying to pick up sounds from the area in front of us, but there were none. I looked at Cheshire, who nodded to me and then to the kill zone.

I looked at C.T. and whispered, "Let's go." Slowly and carefully we moved out from our position to the area the gook had been in, and without going very far I spotted the body. He must have been hit by my first round since he was lying right where he had broken through the bush. C.T. and I moved up to him and I put two rounds into his head just to make sure. As we stripped the body, I took the SKS from alongside the body and gave it to C.T. for his souvenir. After stripping the body, we returned to the team to move out to the LZ, but the LZ was in the direction that the gook had come from. The RTO called in the contact and the 0-1 was already in the air by the time C.T. and I returned from the kill zone.

We had an idea where the LZ was, but with the thickness of the brush it would be easy to get off track. We moved out slowly with me on point, but after a half hour of quietly trying to break the brush and going what I thought was perhaps fifty meters, I was losing my temper. Cheshire called the 0-1 and had him fly over our area. When he was in sight, Cheshire used his signal mirror so the 0-1 could get a fix on us and how far we had to go to the LZ.

"Angle a little to your left and it's about fifty meters ahead," Cheshire whispered to me. I nodded that I understood and again began moving out.

The sun was now beating down on us. We were all soaked with sweat and were becoming irritable, but we pushed on. After I figured we had gone the fifty meters I looked at Cheshire and whispered to him, "How much farther?"

He looked up ahead and guessed we should be there, but figured maybe another twenty meters or so . . . With the vegetation as thick as it was, we could have been five meters away and wouldn't have known it. For the third time we restarted and by then I really wasn't very concerned about our noise discipline. I started bulling my way through the vines and brush, clearing a path for the others and making it easier on myself, but Cheshire didn't like that, so we halted, and he asked me if I wanted to walk slack and let C.T. take the point. I motioned for C.T. to take the point. C.T.'s slender frame made good time through the bushes and I had a chance to cool down as I followed him, staying right on his tail just in case.

We had gone about twenty meters when we made out an opening ahead. C.T. gave me a wink and we both knew it was the LZ. I relayed the information to Cheshire, who called the 0–1 and advised him we were there. We were told to stand by to pop smoke as the slick was circling close enough for us to pick up the sound of his rotors.

On the way back to Phan Thiet, I once again took out a red smoke grenade and, as we were approaching the compound, popped the smoke and let it dangle from my boot. After the first time I did that, some of the other teams picked up on the ritual and hardly a day passed that a slick didn't come home trailing red smoke.

Toward the end of January we were again given some allocations for rank, and I and a number of other SP-4s had to go before a board for an oral exam to earn our sergeant stripes. One after another we pretended we really cared about the army, then answered all the questions the officers asked us. I was surprised at how easy some of the questions were. I only hoped they wouldn't ask me to adjust artillery fire by sound, at night. I left feeling confident, since the only question that gave me any trouble was on judging how many miles a road on a map from point A to point B was. I was close enough, but one squirrelly little West Point lieutenant had to point out exactly how many miles the distance was to the tenth. "Yes, sir, you're absolutely right about that." (Asshole!)

I had spent thirteen months as a PFC and had been a SP-4 for almost eight months. If I made sergeant E-5, that just meant more money in my pocket. And I was to DEROS (rotate) in just three months, unless I ex-

tended again, and Fort Bragg would be a bit more bearable as an NCO. The promotion eventually came through
on 28 January.

The next time out I had the team once again, and we
humped the woods for two days before finding a trail. By
the looks of it, it hadn't been used in some time, but it
was the only game in town so I decided to set up an
ambush. This time I wanted to make sure that if we made
contact nobody would get away, so I set up the team
fifteen meters off the trail. We didn't have much cover—
only one tree of any size, and I put the RTO behind it—
but there were enough plants and bushes to conceal us.
I figured if Rath could pull off rifle ambushes close in so
could I. We sat for a couple of hours before I decided to
pull back, thinking that if we searched the area we might
find signs of activity. I was wrong. It proved to be a dead
AO, but we covered most of it and could report in all
honesty that there were no gooks around that area. We
were pulled.

The following night after chow, we were sitting around
the bonfire talking. We had done that almost every night
while in Phan Thiet and every other place we worked
where we lived in tents, and it was something we all
looked forward to. I had my bottle of Jim Beam and a
couple of cans of Coke, so I was set for the evening. As
usual, a nearby tent had an eight-track tape player going
so we would call out requests. Creedence Clearwater Revival and the Rascals were my favorites and I had brought
back plenty of tapes from the World for us to listen to.
Conversations always centered around the war or how
fucked up the World was. We'd talk about our past missions, what we thought we did right, and what we would
do if we could do it over again, no bragging, just self-
analysis and self-criticism that we could share with one
another. Dutch was in his usual position as moderator
and emcee.

"If you told people that we could just sit around here
like we're doing and that's all we need to be comfortable,
they'd think we were crazy back in the World. Back there,
everyone's trying to get to the top of the corporation or
to keep up with his neighbor; they never stop to appre-

ciate what they have. When you guys get home, ask your buddies what's important to them. They'll say their jobs or their cars. Everything is material to them since they're judged by their peers on how much they've got or how they look. With us it's different. We're trying to do our job and come back in one piece. No one's trying to stab his buddy in the back for a promotion, because tomorrow he may have to count on his buddy for real, not in some stupid corporate chess game.''

Dutch was on a roll that night, so we let him keep talking. "But you'll all change, too. You'll leave here and go back on the block and blend in with society and sooner or later these little things we're doing, like just sitting around, will seem so stupid that you'll forget how much it meant to you. Some of you will make it back in society and live happily ever after. Others will find it hard to cope and will probably come back into the Army. Others won't be able to handle the lack of excitement and will either go into a nut house or kill themselves. Remember, to survive war you've got to become war.''

He looked around at all of us in the light of the fire. "How many of you ever gave any thought to what it means to kill someone?" That question hit home with me as I've always wondered if one really *did* carry blood on his hands.

He had our attention as he continued. "How many of you ever thought you could do the things you're doing now?" He was getting at our having volunteered to push ourselves to the limit.

"Yeah, this fuckin' army is all right!" J.C. chimed in.

"Hey, I'm no lifer," Dutch continued, "but you'll all have to admit the army gave you a chance to play out your fantasies, right?"

I thought back to the gook's head I smashed in in Tuy Hoa and the gook whose brains I blew out on the trail when we hit the three of them. It was something I'm sure I never dreamed I'd ever do until now. Had we, as Dutch suggested, become war? I don't think so. People might think we were all psycho, but put in this environment a nineteen- or twenty-year-old could legally experience something he would never be able to experience again.

We were all deep in our thoughts when we heard the unmistakable *ploop* of a thump gun. We looked in the direction it came from. A Ranger stood there with an M-79 in his hands. "Fuckin' legs," was all he said. He turned to look at us. "Don't worry, it's only CS."

He walked away. We looked in the direction he had fired. Sure enough, it was the enlisted men's club. A cloud rose from the door and guys were running out and falling down. The son of a bitch had put the gas round right into it. We continued our conversation, and as the fire was dying out we all went to our tents to hit the sack.

I was fast asleep later that night when I heard someone screaming "Gas!" I jumped out of the cot and groped for my mask, but I couldn't find it in the dark so I ran outside. Right into a cloud of CS. I remembered hearing that if you were caught without your mask you should hit the deck and try to burrow your face into the ground so you can breathe. I fell down and tried to dig a hole in the sand, which was really easy, the only trouble was I was getting the full effects of the gas and was trying to breathe. With every inhalation I brought the gas into my lungs and gagged it out, eyes burning and skin on fire. I felt like puking. The only consolation was I knew it wouldn't last forever. As the cloud passed overhead and I got to my feet I looked in the direction of the EM club. "Fucking legs" got their revenge.

Two days later we were inserted again. We moved through sparse vegetation checking out the AO and coming up empty. On the third day we were moving through the woods rather briskly but maintaining silence. Around 1700 I stopped the team for chow. As we were starting to heat the water for our LRPs and coffee, I sniffed the air because my nose sensed something . . . Gooks! That unmistakable aroma was coming from our north. I grabbed my M-16, snapped my fingers to get the others' attention, pointed to my nose, then pointed in the direction of the smell. The rest of the team readied their weapons. C.T. and I crawled in the direction of the smell. After we passed the team's perimeter by fifty meters or so, we heard voices. C.T. and I froze while we looked at one another. The voices were still quite a bit away so we inched up, alert to any sound or movement. As we moved forward we came to a small stream. The voices were coming from just the other side.

Night was coming on. Should I bring the rest of the team up and run into who knows what? Or should I go back and take a look in the morning? C.T. and I moved back to the team while I called X-ray. X-ray relayed the information to the TOC, who advised us to pull back and investigate first thing in the morning. (I had forgotten the war was by then an 8:00 to 5:00 job, no overtime for some units.) I moved the team back another one hundred meters and we set out the claymores. None of us got much sleep that night.

In the morning we policed the area, pulled in the claymores, advised X-ray, and started out. When we got to the stream I stopped the team. C.T. and I would go over first, the rest of the team covering. The stream was only fifteen meters wide and a foot deep or so. Slowly C.T. and I moved out, each intently inspecting the other side for signs of movement. When he and I were across we motioned the next two to follow as we covered from our side while the remaining two covered from the other. As the next two made it over I signaled for the final two to cross. When the team had crossed we spread out to reconnoiter. Through the bushes I saw an opening just ahead. As I inched forward I began to make out what looked like a hut. When I got closer I saw it was indeed not one hut, but three. I crouched on the fringe of the woodline looking at a small village. Three grass huts and a pen for pigs and chickens off to the side. I scanned back and forth but saw no signs of life. They had been there not twelve hours ago, but they'd gone. If it had been a regular village, women and children would have been around. I saw no one. Or perhaps it was some kind of trap. Had they detected us last night and understood that we'd be dropping by in the morning? I moved and told the team what I saw. We spread out to surround the village—as well as six men could surround it—then moved in, eyes and ears perked as never before. When I popped into the open, the rest of the team covered me while I advanced to the first hut. I circled around it till I came to the opening. Steady now, I told myself as I took a deep breath and jumped to the opening, M-16 poised to blow apart anything that moved. Nothing. I poked my head in and scanned the inside. Empty. I moved to the second hut, circled around till I got to the opening, and did the same thing. Same results. Likewise the third hut.

I left two members of the team to cover a trail that went from the village to the west while the rest of us looked for signs of recent activity. We saw where they'd cooked their meals the previous night but saw nothing else. No signs of footprints, human or animal. I told the others not to disturb anything just in case the gooks came back. I decided to parallel the trail heading west. We'd follow it till we found a suitable ambush site, then set up. We hadn't moved more than sixty meters when I found something that would fit the bill: few trees for cover, enough concealment, and a decent view of the trail. I set up a linear ambush and we began our vigil. I got on the horn with X-ray to advise them of our status. After two hours I decided to pull out of the ambush and continue parallel to the trail. We followed it for a couple of hundred meters, until we came to a clearing. About halfway through, we heard a rifle shot. It was too far off to have any effect; it was either a signal or a sniper with bad aim. I had an idea and kept the team moving till we got back inside the woods. The team formed a perimeter while I grabbed the handset from the RTO's web gear.

"X-ray, this is 3–5. Over."

"3–5, this is X-ray. Go ahead. Over."

"X-ray, is Bird Dog up yet?"

"3–5, wait one. Over." After a minute X-ray came back on the line. "3–5, this is X-ray. Be advised Bird Dog is in the air and will be in contact with you direct. Over."

"Roger, X-ray. Thanks much. 3–5 out." I then continued, "Bird Dog, this is 3–5, do you copy? Over."

"Roger, 3–5. This is Bird Dog. What have you got? Over."

"Bird Dog, we just left what appears to be either a very small village or a possible way station used just last night. About two mikes ago we heard a shot, either a signal or a sniper. Was wondering if you could come over low and draw some fire so we could get a better fix? Over." There was a pause.

"3-5, this is Bird Dog. Say again. Over."

"Roger, Bird Dog. I'm requesting a low fly-over to draw some fire so we could get a better fix. Over."

"Negative on that, 3-5. Suggest you Charlie Mike with what you have. Bird Dog out."

Some people have no sense of humor.

We moved out, paralleling the trail, and set up another ambush a few hundred meters down the trail. When nothing materialized we pulled back and set up for the evening. Our exfil LZ wasn't too far away and we were to be one of the first teams exfilled in the morning. I considered going back to the tiny village, but decided against it for now. I was going to request bringing the team back to the same AO in the future.

When we got back, I explained in the debriefing what we had found. I was then told to get the team ready, as we were to go in with another team from Fourth Platoon as reinforcements.

The following day we lifted and landed at the same LZ at which we'd been picked up the day before. The two teams acted as one as we made our way through the woods to the outskirts of the little village. Once again we surrounded the area; the other team leader and I went in to check it out. We came up empty in the huts and searched the immediate area for bunkers. The village had to be a way station for the VC and it had been effectively hidden from the air so as not to be seen.

Those of us with lighters ignited the thatch that made up the hootches, watching as they were engulfed in flames. As the huts burned, rounds hidden in them began to cook off. We watched from a distance as all three huts blazed before leaving the area. I was a bit dejected at not having made contact, but rationalized that I had done the right thing by not exposing the team to a night contact when we didn't know the area or how many dinks there were. The VC would be pissed, having their little way station burnt to the ground, but they would build a new one there or somewhere else. I wished I had a Kit Carson scout with me on that mission to listen to the conversation the evening we heard them. A scout could have known just by looking at the way station how many visited at a given time, how often it was used, which direction they were coming from, and which direction they were going to, et cetera. As we boarded the slick to return to Phan Thiet I could only take consolation in the fact that nobody had been hurt. We'd make contact next time I told myself.

We pulled a few more missions from Phan Thiet before packing away our tents in February and returning to An Khe.

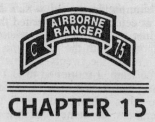

CHAPTER 15

FEBRUARY–MARCH 1971/AN KHE
John L. Rotundo

The company had been growing the past couple of months; the war was winding down but more young paratroopers wanted to see it up close before it was over. We were constantly taking cherries out to the field and breaking them in with contacts. For the most part they performed well.

Our new home in An Khe was far from the old company area that had been left to the ARVNs, who promptly took everything they could from our old barracks and transported it to town to fix up their houses.

Team 3–5's first mission in An Khe once again put us right on top of a high-speed trail that I hadn't seen from the air on the VR. As the slick touched down, I ran to the woodline and damn near stepped right on the trail, stopping at the last second. This one paralleled a fifteen-meter-wide stream then crossed it. Since the trail was packed so hard I guessed it was used quite frequently.

After we made radio contact with the X-ray, I set up a four-man ambush on a hill overlooking the trail; C.T. and I sat just off the junction of trail and stream, facing the trail where it turned into the stream. We sat and waited for a while, then I looked at C.T.'s and my position. I had a bad feeling about what I had just done; we were taking too much of a chance where we were, so I decided we should rejoin the rest of the team. Slowly we moved in a crouch the twenty-five meters that separated us from the team. I motioned to C.T. to set up on the left flank, and had started to move myself to the middle of the team when I looked up at Ti-Ti, one of the newer team members, so named because of his height. Ti-ti is Vietnamese for little. He was squatting, weapon up and aiming just over my shoulder. It dawned on me he was aiming at something right behind me. My heart was now racing as I froze then slowly turned. In the water, not more than thirty meters from us, two gooks were washing. I dared not move a muscle for fear of making noise, and it was very uncomfortable as I was half standing, half crouching with my upper body partially turned. The team hadn't opened fire because I wasn't in position. The two gooks continued to wash up and were chattering back and forth. Finally they finished up and continued on their way on the other side of the stream. Neither one carried a weapon but I was convinced we would have another chance later.

After they left, I got into position in the middle of the team. I also passed the word if we had another opportunity like that, the team was to shoot first and worry about me not being in position later.

Meanwhile, I called X-ray to report the sighting. We waited for the balance of the day but nobody else showed up, so around 1700, I moved the team a hundred meters away from the trail and we set out our claymores for the night. Since we hadn't humped any that day and had good prospects of a contact, I felt we would have no problem staying alert that night.

The next morning we awoke, ate, policed the area, and moved back to the previous day's ambush site. Once again we sat and waited, not daring to move. Eyes and ears straining to pick up the slightest noise of movement, anything that would signal we had company coming.

We waited as the early morning gave way to midmorning; it wouldn't be long before the heat would affect our alertness. Then, from our right, we heard the crunching of feet on the path. M-16s lifted and pointed in the direction of the sounds. Two dinks walking into view on the trail. Something was different with those two, they weren't half-stepping; they were carrying their weapons at the ready. Even though they walked at a brisk pace, it was obvious they were looking for somebody. For the first time I actually looked at the face of the point man. He had a determined look on his face. On the other contacts where I had time to watch the dinks, they carried their weapons over their shoulders and talked to one another with no concerns apparent. This one was different; the point man was busy looking at both sides of the trail as he and his buddy came down it. We had our weapons sighted in, so it was only a matter of time before the dinks turned to cross the stream or spotted one of us.

I took up aim on the point man and let my reactions take over. It was kind of funny that at a time like that I remembered the word BRASS from the rifle range in basic training: Breathe, Relax, Aim, take up the Slack, and Squeeze. I found myself taking a deep breath and slowly letting it out as I aimed and felt my trigger finger take up the slack in the trigger. Any second they would hit the stream, and sure enough into the water they went, barely slowing down. I waited until both of them were in the water and squeezed the trigger. *Bang! Bang! Bang!* As I was firing on semi just as fast as I could pull the trigger, the rest of the team opened up, spraying the area just as fast as they could pull their triggers. Both dinks went down as they hit the other side of the stream. I yelled for the RTO to call in our contact and told the team to spray our area, just in case. C.T. was busy putting rounds into the trail they had just come down.

After we each had fired two magazines, I called check fire so we could listen for signs of life from the other side of the stream. Once again we went from controlled pandemonium to the eerie silence that almost always follows a contact. C.T. and I waited for the smoke to clear, as well as our ears, and made our way across the stream to check out the kill zone. As we crossed the stream and hit the other side I saw the rifle the point man had been carrying. It was an M-1 carbine. I motioned to C.T. and he nodded an acknowledgment; now we had to find the body that had been carrying the carbine. Then we were looking for them in the elephant grass that just yesterday had been our LZ. I had gone in the direction of the trail for about fifteen feet when I spotted a leg sticking out of the grass. I moved closer till I could see the whole body and immediately put two rounds into his head, just to make sure. C.T. was still looking for the other one.

As I stripped the body I decided to try out my Vietnamese linguistics: *"Um di dac oi, do mammy muc gnay."* Which was translated as "Go to hell, you stupid mother fucker." As I was yelling, our cherry shouted from the other side of the stream, "Sarge, I hear them yelling."

"That ain't them! It's me, so don't shoot," I yelled back. When I finished I joined C.T. in hunting for the other body. We scouted the area for a good five minutes with no results. It was as if he had just vanished into thin air. Well, we had one and his weapon to our credit and none of us was hurt, so I considered it a success. As C.T. and I rejoined the team, the RTO told me the slicks were inbound. We collected our gear and crossed the stream to the LZ to wait for the extraction chopper.

As the slick touched down and we boarded, I began to shake. Something had been very different that time out: maybe because for the first time they had been looking for me, something I had never been exposed to before; maybe it was that determined look on the point man's face that I had never seen on a Vietnamese before; maybe it was the fact that once again we had been extremely lucky, from finding the trail so quickly, to setting up the ambush and again making a clean getaway. The more I thought, the worse I shook. If C.T. and I had been spotted when we moved the ambush position yesterday, we could have been ambushed as easily as the dinks. I thought of how many chances I had taken in the past and how lucky I had been. The rest of the team was joking around in the chopper but my mind was on other things. For the first time I was truly scared! Not apprehensive or nervous, but thoroughly scared!

As we were riding back to the camp, I watched a truck convoy moving. Looking closer I saw tracers leaping from the rocks into the convoy. It looked like the convoy was taking a beating. We must have been flying over the An Khe Pass. I could imagine the door gunner telling us at any minute that we were being sent in to help break up the ambush. The thought of that sent further shivers through my body. I had had enough. I wanted out!

We were approaching the compound and I let somebody else tie the smoke grenade to his boot laces. As far as I was concerned, the game was over. Maybe that was what Sharkey had been talking about as I was going on extension leave six months ago.

After debriefing I went to my bunk and just lay there thinking. Since coming to the Rangers I had pulled forty-two missions including four X-rays. Total time in-country was sixteen months, the first three with the Herd, and I was to DEROS in sixty days unless I took another extension to become a door gunner. I had made sergeant on the 28th of January while in Phan Thiet, and the more I thought, the more I wanted to get out of the field, out of Vietnam, and out of the army. First, to get me out of the field in one piece. I went over to Pop Carter's hootch to tell him I wanted out, and needless to say, he was less than receptive. Pop Carter thought no gooks were left in South Vietnam; he had been over with the Herd in '66 and '67 and, according to him, the 173rd had wiped them all out. He refused to pull me out of the field, saying he was sending me back, not only to the field but to the same AO we had just left.

"Pop," I pleaded, "I can't take the team back there, I've got the shakes. I'm scared."

"Probably too much Jim Beam."

"Bullshit. There's something about that AO I don't like, and I refuse to take a team back in there."

"All right, you don't have to take a team there, you'll go along with another team since you are familiar with it."

I could see I wasn't going to win the argument, so I reluctantly agreed to go in as ATL on E.C. McLaughlin's team. Things had changed since I first came to the Rangers. When Major Holt had been the CO, if someone ever had that certain "feeling" about a mission or an area, he could elect to stay behind; somebody else would be assigned in his place. Of course, if somebody had "feel-

ings'' too often, he would have been kicked out of the
company. But Major Holt believed in his people and understood that if somebody really felt his number was up,
he wouldn't be as effective in the field. The men admired
and respected Major Holt and Captain Colvin because
they cared for their people.

On the other hand, Major Hudson seemed to be caught
up in his power. In the mornings Hudson even had us do
PT; I could have understood the necessity of PT if Charlie Rangers was an REMF company whose troops had to
shoot rubber bands at one another to justify combat pay,
but we busted our butts in the woods for the company.
One of Hudson's favorite exercises was for us to ''duck
walk'' around the company area. He'd stand there *watching*, of course, arms folded across his chest, while we
were *doing* it and more than once I could sense his arrogance as he watched.

The next day I went in with McLaughlin's team to the
old AO. Besides McLaughlin, who would be the team
leader, there was myself as the ATL, Vince DiMaio (of
Tuy Hoa riot fame), Harry Fritz as the RTO, and a guy
named Rich Harrison, whom everyone referred to as Fats.
I don't know where he got his nickname, but it didn't
matter. Fats created his own legend within the company
for a picture he took. The team was sitting in an ambush
when a gook started walking in their direction. Fats put
down his M-16 and, in its place, sighted in on his Penn
EE camera. As the gook got closer he took the picture,
put down his camera, picked up his M-16, and blew him
away.

Our mission was to be pure recon, so we had brought
a pair of binoculars with us to monitor activity on the
trail. As stupid as it sounds, we used the same LZ. Of
course we had no trouble finding the trail. I was walking
slack as we hit the woodline, went through the stream,
and began to parallel the trail. We humped for maybe a
hundred and fifty meters when the trail went to a small
woodline on either side of the stream. The wooded area
we were in suddenly ended and we were looking at a
large clearing. We could follow the trail into woodline
so narrow that we would have had to walk the trail, or
we could set up our recon at the edge of a clearing. The

clearing was the side of a hill that had all the trees cut down to just stump. There were a lot of large rocks near the top, so we decided to set up where we could still observe the trail, although we would be over a hundred meters away and the trail disappeared into the woodline.

We pulled our night halt at that position and put out claymores. The next morning we woke up, and around 0800 Fats, myself, and DiMaio relieved the two who were observing the trail. As the three of us watched, I was just about to give the binoculars to Fats when an AK-47 opened up on automatic. I was sitting next to a tree and Fats when it happened. We watched as the bullets ripped a line between us. I rolled left and Fats rolled right; the gook missed, but not by much. We returned fire but couldn't see who was firing at us or where he or they were. The incoming bullets just missed DiMaio also, and in the excitement he fell backward and landed on the hot shell casings being ejected from our weapons. Whoever it was knew exactly where we were. Damn but I was getting too short for this! We fired up the area but couldn't tell if we hit anything. Evidently we were spotted by either a trail watcher or an LZ watcher. Whichever, he earned his pay that day. We called for an extraction bird and used the clearing on the side of the hill as our LZ, jumping over the stumps to get aboard.

When we returned I got a bit of good news. The army was giving "drops" to a lot of guys in-country. With Vietnamization taking over and the withdrawal of US troops, if an individual had five months or less left in service the army would let him go and drop the last five months. They were also rotating guys earlier than their regular return date. When I extended, my new DEROS was to be 20 April but with my drop it was changed to 28 March. I had been short before, but now, 27 February, I was three weeks shorter. Not to mention that when the gook opened up with his AK, I forgot about being scared and let my reactions take over. Now I wasn't shaking any more and had another talk with Pop Carter. I would have gone back to the field but he decided to make me the Third Platoon's supply sergeant, which meant I had the keys to the conex that housed our weapons and equipment when the teams weren't in the field.

That night we all celebrated my good fortune and partied, ending up at the bonfire again, just talking with one another and enjoying the brotherhood that we all felt for one another, the kind that Dutch said the people back in the World would never understand. I was going to be a REMF again, but at least I had accomplished what I wanted to do back in July of 1969, to see war firsthand, to experience it in all its horror and glory. We talked about what the war meant to all of us, how we felt about it before coming to Vietnam and what we felt now that we had been a part of it. I remember saying, "You know, one thing I'll never forget is that contact differs so much from what I thought it would be like. The feeling I have before a contact. Sitting off a trail waiting for the gooks to come down it, and even when I hear them coming, I'm still somewhat surprised when I actually see them. It's almost like a dream, you know?"

"There it is," J.C. said. "I get the same feeling. But I'll tell you what, I never feel sorry for the cocksuckers." We all laughed, knowing . . . Charlie would blow us away if he had the chance; he did with many of our line companies.

"I'll tell you what," said Dutch, "the reason a lot of us are alive today is because of the type of unit we're in. People think we're crazy to do the stuff we do, but what they don't realize is that it's our size that gives us our strength. Look at how many GIs get fucked up every day with booby traps or are caught in an ambush. Because of their unit's size, they think they're safe and Charlie won't mess with them. But a simple thing like a booby trap not only messes up the GI who set it off but the entire column has to stop while he gets med-evaced. And after, the rest of the squad or platoon isn't thinking so much of Charlie, they're more concerned with not being the next victim of a booby trap. Charlie is messing with their mind, and it works."

I had to agree with Dutch. We were alive because of the unit we were in. Sure we had some duds and a few runners, but for the most part we did our job in a professional manner, like most Ranger companies. I was proud to have had the opportunity to serve with Charlie Rangers. It was an experience we'd all remember.

When it got late, I left the few who were still sitting around the fire, sipping beer or bourbon, and I headed for my bunk. At Phan Thiet, Kelly, J.C., and I decided to sleep in body bags at night. They kept the bugs and evening chill out, but unlike a sleeping bag, which had a zipper on the inside, the body bag's zipper was on the outside. It wasn't designed to deal with bodies that wanted out. However, hardly a night passed without some smart-ass zipping my bag all the way up so that I'd need help getting out in the morning.

The next day there was nothing to do, so I meandered over to the TOC to see what was going on. It was 28 February. Exactly one month earlier I'd made sergeant and exactly a month later I would be on the Freedom Bird back to the World. At the TOC I met up with Second Platoon's Sergeant Lincoln. He had a fantastic sense of humor and could laugh at about anything. On one mission the team was in contact and had to get extracted with a rope ladder, all the time Charlie was shooting at them. Lincoln hooked himself to the ladder with his snap-link, then smiled at the gooks shooting at them and gave them the "peace" sign, yelling at the rest of the team on the rope that "this is a heavy experience."

We were just hanging around when the X-ray called in a contact. "Hot damn! Get some," I said as I patted Lincoln on his back. We were trying to visualize what was going on since we couldn't hear much and presumed a team had initiated a contact. X-ray came back on the speaker and announced that the team had a friendly WIA whose initials were Kilo Tango. It was Schumaker's team and Kilo Tango would be K.T., Kevin Thorne. Shit, old Thorney got himself a Purple Heart coming. Lincoln and I joked about the extent of Thorne's wound.

X-ray came back on the speaker ". . . is X-ray. Team advises that WIA is now KIA." There was a pause. "I spell Kilo, Echo, Victor, India, November . . . Tango, Hotel, Oscar . . ." He continued to spell the name, but I never heard him finish. It was like a sucker punch to the solar plexus, the kind that leaves you numb and nothing more. Thorne of all people, the guy behind the bar in Dalat with McCoy and me when the MPs came. Thorne, the guy who fragged Pop Carter with the dummy grenade. Thorne, who had walked around the compound at Tuy Hoa with his head in a huge bandage after the riot. Other guys had died, but I didn't know them that well. But Thorne was one of *us*, one of us who felt we led a charmed life. Now for the second time in days I realized just how mortal we really are.

I slowly walked back to my cot and sat down, staring at nothing in particular and caring about nothing. The tent was empty as I grabbed my bottle of Jim Beam and began to drink it straight. I just sat and drank out of my bottle and thought about Thorne, the carefree, happy-go-lucky guy who was always good for a laugh. I kept seeing his face and I wanted to cry but couldn't. Under my breath I began cursing the war, the army, the lifers. I cursed everybody and everything associated with the military. The more I drank the louder my cursing became until I was in a rage. I wanted to hit somebody and the TOC seemed like a good place to start. First I'd deck the major and then work my way down to the lieutenants. I finished the bottle and staggered out into the daylight, aimed myself in the general direction of the TOC, and began walking. For every step I took forward I took two backward, occasionally stumbling and falling on my face. I was hammered to the max. Finally Staff Sergeant Lincoln came over and helped me back to my cot.

That night when I awoke and cleared my head, I learned what had happened. The team had been just breaking its night-halt position, and as the men were putting on their rucksacks, Thorne stood up to adjust his. A Tiger Team (two LZ watchers) opened up with an AK-47. One round hit Thorne in the back and exited through his heart. He never had a chance, but we were consoled that he suffered no pain.

After Thorne's memorial service I asked Pop Carter if I could go out just once more before DEROSing.

"What about the shakes you had?"

"No sweat, Pop. They're gone."

"Cheshire's got the team now. I'll run it by him. If he says it's okay, then it's okay with me."

"Thanks, Pop." I was looking forward to the field again.

A couple of days later we were again at the helipad,

packed up and ready to be inserted. Captain Robertson would be inserting the teams this day. We all felt a certain sense of confidence when Robby inserted the teams. We knew we would hit the right LZ with him in the air.

The 0–1 wasn't available, so Robby would be using our slick as his C&C (command and control) ship. He got in first and pulled down the seat to sit on, something the teams didn't do because with all the gear the men couldn't sit comfortably on them. We preferred just to sit on the floor and stretch our legs. Cheshire was 3–5's team leader, and I was to be the ATL, walking point. I was sitting in the door as we circled the AO while Robby controlled the insertion slicks. The ship descended and picked up speed as we raced to the LZ. The door gunner on my side looked at Cheshire and showed his index finger, signaling we were one minute away. I leaned back and made a final adjustment to my rucksack.

"Lock and load," Cheshire yelled in his southern drawl.

The slick began to slow, and I climbed down to stand on the skid just as the Huey began to flare. Just before touching down I glanced back at Robby, who was busy talking to the pilot. He happened to glance up at that time, and as our eyes met I sensed a mutual affection of sorts. His expression seemed to say "Keep your head down and be careful." I nodded to him and turned as the grass of the LZ came up to kiss the skids.

At three feet off the ground I leaped away and ran to the cover of the woodline with the rest of the team in pursuit. Just as I hit the woodline I froze. Once again I was staring at a very well used high-speed trail. I quickly looked in both directions, then jumped over it. When we were all across it, we moved about fifty meters into the woods and up a very gentle slope. From there we had cover and concealment, but we couldn't see the trail because we were too far back and there were too many bushes. We sat motionless, giving our ears a chance to recover from the rotor blast of the slick and to become accustomed to our silent new environment. The only sound was the barely discernible voice of the RTO as he tried to reach X-ray, speaking in a very quiet whisper. I looked over to the RTO and the expression on his face told me he wasn't having any luck. Cheshire told him to try and raise Robby in the C&C ship, as he would be on our net. The RTO called once. After a pause he repeated his call and again he got no results. While this was going on we were in a circular perimeter, each of us lying on the ground facing out as we'd done countless times before, when off to our right we heard voices coming down the trail we had just crossed. The gooks were really talking up a storm, and since we couldn't see them we could only figure there were two, maybe more, but we couldn't tell. As their voices came closer we braced ourselves since we didn't know where the trail led to. As their voices came abreast of us, one of them yelled something in Vietnamese.

To our surprise, he was answered by a voice behind us. We had them in front of us and behind us, size and equipment unknown, and to make matters worse, we had no commo. If we made contact we couldn't call in the gunships or an extraction slick. As I lay there I tried to figure which direction the trail went. The worst possible scenario had the trail making a sharp left turn twenty meters from where we jumped over it and continuing on right in front of us. Here we were, not on the ground five minutes, gooks to our front, gooks to our rear, no commo, and my heart beating so loud they could pick up the vibration in An Khe.

Once again I remembered Sharkey's comment when I was getting ready to go home on extension leave. How right he was! With my left hand I slowly moved the selector switch from SAFE through SEMI to AUTO, something I never did on a mission; I always had had reasonable good luck firing in controlled single shots. But now, not knowing what lay ahead for us, I figured we would need all the firepower at our disposal. I hoped we still had surprise on our side. We lay there waiting for the inevitable. The voices continued till they moved to our left and finally were gone. We stayed where we were, since we still had no commo and were still unnoticed. Maybe Little Ann's good luck charm from Dalat was paying off after all. I could only hope.

After an hour we made contact with the X-ray and we all breathed a bit easier. Cheshire crawled to me and whispered that I should take someone to recon the area to our rear. I looked at C.T. and motioned to the rear. We took off our rucksacks and crawled away from the trail in the direction the other voices had come from. We hadn't gone fifty meters when we came upon a field. We immediately backed up into the woodline and began to circle. As we moved along the perimeter, we found a hootch elevated on stilts. We both got up into a crouch and moved for a look-see up close. In my imagination some gook had us in the sights of his AK-47 and at the appropriate moment he would open up and blow us away. Well, we had come this far, so we might as well go all the way. We made our way to the base of the hootch.

C.T. covered me as I raised myself up for a look inside. Rice! And by the looks of it, quite a bit more than was needed for some poor Vietnamese farmer to feed his family. We *di-di*'d the area and made our way back to the team, where I told Cheshire what we had found, and discussed our next move. Should we move closer to the trail and set up an ambush, or should we continue to snoop around the AO and see what else we could find? Cheshire decided we would stay where we were till morning, then play it by ear.

He got on the horn and reported what we had heard and found already. The rest of the afternoon we lay there and kept our eyes and ears opened for activity. Around 1700 we put out claymores, one by one, and put the clackers all together, just in case. When the claymores were out, we took turns eating LRP dinners. Because of our predicament there could be no heating of water; I had cold chicken and rice. Thank God for hot sauce.

We started watch at 1800 and it took me quite a while before I finally got to sleep. We hadn't humped at all and the events of the afternoon kept going through my mind. Finally I closed my eyes and fell asleep. Then my arm was being nudged and I awoke to find C.T. handing me the handset.

"You awake?" he asked.

I shook the cobwebs from my head and took the handset. "Anything happening?"

"Naw, man, just the re-up lizards and fuck-you birds."

I took hold of the handset and whispered into it, "X-ray, X-ray, this is 3–5. Time check. Over."

"3–5, this is X-ray. Be advised it's 2300. Do you know who your reenlistment counselor is?"

I chuckled. The sky was clear, and even in the middle of the woods I could make out the outline of a large tree to our rear. I pulled my poncho liner around me, then listened to the sounds of the night. "Re-up, re-up," said the lizard. As usual it was answered by a bird whose call was, "Fuck you, fuck you." First I looked in the direction of the trail and listened, then to our rear, trying to pick up any noise of movement, but so far all was quiet. I looked down at the luminous dial of my Seiko and saw it was going on 2330. I was fully awake and really wanted a cigarette, but common sense told me not to do anything stupid, so I just thought of how good the first one would be in the morning. Not only would that first one taste good but it was my last mission. Within a couple of weeks I would be on the Freedom Bird back to the World. First another steak dinner for the returning heroes at Fort Lewis, then back home for thirty days till I had to report to Fort Bragg. I had had second thoughts about extending for another six months as a door gunner. The army was giving me a three-week drop on my tour and I really thought I had used up my luck these last six months. I wasn't going to push it.

Crack! A twig snapped somewhere to our rear. I froze for an instant as the sound registered. I turned my head in the direction it came from and tried to see through the darkness, but found nothing. Being careful not to make any noise, I slowly moved from my sitting position to a crouch, then to a prone position, reaching for the clacker that was connected to the claymore facing the rear. As I was looking in the direction of the noise to our rear, my right hand felt for the clacker till it made contact. I brought it closer and laid it in front of me. Then I reached over to my web gear and found my ammo pouches. On both sides I carried frags. I unbuckled the strap on an ammo pouch and picked up a frag, putting that next to the claymore clacker.

Crunch! The sound of a dried leaf being stepped on, from the same direction as the twig but much closer. My heart was going a mile a minute, and I was sure anybody out there could hear it. My mind was also racing, what to do? Throw a frag? Blow the claymore? Shit, how the hell did I get myself into this mess anyway? Should I wake the team or handle it myself? Of course I might just be imagining those sounds. I strained my ears and eyes, trying desperately to see something, some kind of movement, anything!

Another *crunch*, this time very close. Whoever it was was taking his time so as not to make too much noise. In the darkness one thing was for sure, I wasn't going to give our position away with a muzzle flash, so I never touched my M-16. The noise was coming closer as my eyes strained to see through the darkness. I wished I could wake up and find out it was only a bad dream, but such was not the case that night. Whatever was going to happen was going to happen, as I resigned myself to waiting to take more of them than they did of us.

The next crunching sound was damn near on top of me, but I still couldn't see anything. If they were that close, the claymores wouldn't really help, although the back blast might screw them up.

Movement! Directly to my front, but what the hell was it? I strained my eyes for all they were worth till I could make out the outline . . . of a wild chicken. Finally I picked up a clump of dirt and threw it. The bird scurried away. I took a very deep breath and let it out slowly, trying to calm my nerves. "Short," I whispered to myself.

The next morning we collected our claymores and chowed down on cold LRPs. When I finished, I crawled over to Cheshire and asked him what we were doing.

"We were awful darn lucky yesterday, coming in undetected and having them come up on us so quick. If we move out, we might get compromised, although I would like to know what's around here. If we set up an ambush on the trail, we have a good chance of a contact, and we can use the same LZ we came in on yesterday."

He had no argument from me, so when we finished eating we moved closer to the trail, but not too close. I motioned to Cheshire that I wanted to set up a bit closer than we were, but he insisted we stay where we were since a few small trees offered us some cover. The RTO called X-ray, making sure we had commo and advising them that we were setting up our ambush. The waiting began.

I was positioned on our right flank with C.T. on the left; Cheshire and two others were facing the trail while the RTO covered the rear. Fifty or so meters to our front lay the trail and ten meters beyond the trail was the LZ. It was 0700 when we got into position, and we had been waiting for a few hours when I looked at my watch. It was going to be 0900 and the coolness of the morning was giving way to midmorning heat and humidity. The stillness was broken by voices coming from our right. I raised my M-16 and aimed it in the direction of the voices. It always seems so unreal to be looking through the bushes when, out of nowhere, somebody appears in the flesh.

I watched as two of them half-stepped down the trail, chattering, unaware of our presence. As they came closer, I saw both were carrying large boxes or crates on their backs, but I didn't see any weapons. As they passed in front of me I snuck a quick peek where they'd come from to be sure nobody was following them. They had just passed my position and I figured they would be abreast of C.T., so again I touched the trigger to pick up the slack, aimed at the number-two man, and squeezed the trigger. C.T. opened up at the same time. The rest of the team opened up, and over the barking of the M-16s I heard the RTO yelling into the radio, "X-ray, X-ray, this is 3–5. Contact. Contact. Over."

As C.T. and I opened up, both dinks dropped, but since we were so far away I couldn't see what was happening down on the ground. I hadn't finished firing my first magazine when Cheshire threw a canister of CS into the kill zone. And don't you know, it began drifting toward us as soon as it went off. We all had to cease firing, drop our weapons, and put on the gas masks before we could resume firing. As I cleared my mask and picked up my M-16, one of the dinks jumped up and ran back down the trail in the direction he had just come from. I tried to sight in on him but that was difficult through the lenses of a gas mask, so I stood up to get off my shots.

"John L., you're half-stepping," C.T. yelled.

I dropped down, remembering how many of our company were killed doing something as stupid as I had just done. Standing during a contact!

We continued to fire up the area while the RTO talked to the bird dog who was in the air and diverted to our location.

"Keep your eyes posted to the rear," I yelled to the RTO to make sure we weren't to have unexpected company. I still remembered yesterday's voices.

As the CS cleared, C.T. and I took off our masks and moved out to the kill zone. As soon as we neared the trail we spotted the two crates lying on the ground, surrounded by pools of blood. I moved down the trail in the direction the dinks had come from while C.T. checked the kill zone looking for the other one. I walked the trail for a good twenty meters, looking at both sides of it for an opening that the dink might have crawled into. All I saw was blood on the trail. I didn't want to go too much farther, so I sprayed the area with a magazine, hoping for a hit if he was lying nearby, then I went back to join C.T.

When I got to the crates lying on the trail I saw C.T. coming back from the other end of the trail. He too had followed heavy blood trails but come up empty-handed. We each grabbed a crate and dragged it to the team's position. Then we decided to open the crates. One had B-40 rounds, the other new RPG rounds (both were anti-tank rounds that were also used against helicopters and troops). Nice haul, 3-5! Now all we had to do was get out of there in one piece with our booty intact. After yesterday's experience, I was sure the gooks would be coming back.

Cheshire was busy studying our catch when the 0-1 asked if we wanted air support. "Hell, yes," I said into the handset. Robby was back in the air as the 0-1, and that in itself gave me a feeling of security.

"3-5, I'm turning you over to the guns now, tell them what you want and where you want it. His call sign is Gunslinger."

"Roger, Bird Dog. Thanks much. Gunslinger, this is 3-5. Do you copy? Over."

"Rrrrroger, 3-5. This is Gunslinger. Got a pair of snakes standing by . . . aaahhhhhhh, where do you want us? Over."

I looked out at the LZ we dropped in on a day earlier. It was surrounded by woods on all sides. I figured if the gooks planned a surprise, they would be in the woods on either side of the LZ and maybe to our immediate rear, where the field and the hootch were. "Gunslinger, this is 3-5. We're just to the sierra of our lima zula from yesterday. I'd like you to work the woodline to our echo and whiskey, and if possible to our immediate sierra. Over."

"Uuuuuuhhhhrrrrroger, 3-5. Mark your position. Over."

I looked at Cheshire. "Throw a smoke out." I figured he already had the range.

"Smoke out," I said as I saw the red plume drifting our way.

"Rrrrrroger, 3-5. Identify red smoke."

As yet I couldn't see them, but I could hear their rotors; they weren't too far away. As the smoke drifted our way and up to the sky I could see a Cobra gunship coming directly at us through the break in the smoke. My experience with Cobras had been brief, but the sight of them storming down at you is awesome. My eyes must have doubled in size as I saw the lead come angling in right at us. I grabbed the handset and screamed into it, "Gunslinger, Gunslinger, this is 3-5. We're at the smoke! I repeat, we're at the smoke!"

"Rrrrrrrroger, 3-5. Understand. Keep your heads down, boys. We're coming in hot."

I knew I was going to die right there, killed by friendly fire. What a bummer. I was just about to duck my head when the first Cobra kicked his tail to one side and let loose with a volley of rockets into the woods to our left. *Woosh! Woosh! Woosh!* as the rockets left the tubes on his pods under his little wing stubs. At the same time his 40mm grenade launcher and minigun cut loose from the chin turret, raking the woodline to our right side. *Bbbrrrrrraaaaaattttttt . . . Chunk-chunk-chunk,* followed by the sounds of explosives hitting the ground. *Whump! Whump! Whump!* His aim was perfect.

The ground on both sides of the woodline erupted as his ordnance struck the ground, walking a beautiful pattern on either side of us and continuing as he passed overhead, firing all the way.

Shrapnel and branches of trees flew overhead as he was working close, awfully damn close, but—considering the unknown—just close enough.

I joined the team, hugging the ground as he passed overhead, and when I looked up I saw his partner bearing down and letting go with smoke-bringing ordnance on the same spot the first Cobra had worked over.

Bbbbbrrrrrraaaaaattttt . . . Chunk, chunk, chunk, whoosh, whoosh, whoosh, wump, wump, wump. I wanted to stand and cheer, my heart was pounding with pride. As the second Cobra passed overhead, I looked up through the fading red smoke to see a Huey flaring as it approached the LZ.

"Let's get the fuck out of here," I yelled at the team as Cheshire and I grabbed one crate and C.T. and another grabbed the other. We raced to the LZ, getting there just as the slick touched down. Cheshire and I threw our crate on board, following right behind it. C.T. and his partner followed with theirs then crawled in, followed by the remaining two Rangers.

I was already at the door on the other side of the slick breathing a sigh of relief. I noticed the slick wasn't moving. I looked through the doorway of the Huey to count the team, and sure enough, we were all there. I shot a look at the pilot and copilot. They were both staring at our haul.

"Get us the hell out of here," I yelled. With that the slick rose, turned a one-eighty, and gained altitude. We hauled ass out of the AO.

During the ride back to the compound I did an awful lot of reflecting on past missions. I had been lucky. Maybe too lucky for one man's lifetime. Thirty seconds here or there might have meant my living or dying, and I lived. How many other guys hadn't been so lucky? I pulled a Camel from my fatigues and lit up, inhaled a deep drag, then let it out slowly . . . I was truly finished. I had seen war firsthand. I wasn't just an observer but a participant. I had killed and felt the excitement of killing.

I had shot and been shot at. I had hunted and been hunted. I had hated and been hated. I had experienced damn near every emotion known to man and I was alive to talk about it, from the high of a contact to the mourning of a fallen comrade. Deep inside I knew I had challenged myself and had passed my own test. No matter what the World threw at me from now on, I knew I could cope with it. In the movie *Grand Prix*, one of the drivers explains why he races despite the danger. "The closer you are to death, the more you appreciate life." I couldn't have said it any better.

CHAPTER 16

NOVEMBER 1970–SEPTEMBER 1971/ FORT BRAGG
Don Ericson

My thirty-day leave was up and I had thoroughly enjoyed myself staying inebriated the majority of the time. Now, however, I was on my way to Fort Bragg, North Carolina, and more police calls.

I was assigned to the Third Brigade of the 82nd Airborne Division. I really wasn't looking forward to playing games with the 82nd; I had played for keeps in Vietnam.

After months of boring duty and several thousand police calls, a familiar face appeared at the 82nd. Rotundo had returned from Vietnam, and in one piece; standing next to him was another Ranger from Third Platoon, John Case. They were assigned to my sister company and were housed in the barracks next to mine.

My stay there was uneventful until the 82nd was to report to Washington, D.C., to quell any trouble during the peace demonstrations of 1971. We stayed at RFK Stadium and practiced riot control, but we were never called upon for our services. I really don't know what we could have done, because our weapons weren't even loaded,

and couldn't be. We were bused back to Fort Bragg after
five days of being on standby for the National Guard.

Within a month, word came down that our battalion
would pull training duty at West Point. That was about
the best duty I had ever pulled. Like the Ranger operations in 'Nam, I worked four days and was off for four
days. We were stationed at Camp Natural Bridge outside
West Point. Camp Natural Bridge reminded me of Wis-
consin. Our camp was situated on a large beautiful lake
with plenty of bass to catch; the army even supplied
boats. I enjoyed fishing, so the duty was terrific.

I was assigned to be the instructor for the fundamentals
of bayonet fighting. The class consisted of new cadets
and they were mine for two months. I led the class from
a platform eight feet above the ground while my assistant
walked around and gave instruction to individuals having
a hard time. I showed no mercy. I dropped the whole
group if one man screwed up. When one did, I screamed,
"If *one* man lets you down in 'Nam, you will all suffer.
Get used to it," I would bellow. "You are going to be
the leaders and you'd better make the *right* fucking decisions."

Before each class, cadets all at attention, I would walk
around and go nose to nose with a cadet. "Are you having fun, asshole?" I would scream.

"Yes, Sergeant," the cadet would answer.

"I can't hear you." I was still nose to nose with him.
The cadet would shout, "Yes, Sergeant."

"Get down and give me twenty, asshole." Generals
and colonels walked around my classes all the time; they
never said anything. They never tried to intimidate me.
The class was forever staring at my 75th Airborne Ranger
scroll, jump wings, and CIB (combat infantry badge).
Most of all they were in awe of my crudeness.

Every day before class started I would drop the whole
class for twenty push-ups, yelling at them, "I wanna
hear: one-Airborne, two-Airborne, three-Airborne, and
so on. And you'd better get louder with every 'Airborne'!"

A stream running behind my platform came in handy
one day when the temperature climbed to the high nine-
ties. I had the class doing drills when two cadets passed

out. I could have sent a runner across the PT field to summon the ambulance on call, but I decided otherwise. "You two assholes, over there! Pick up those men and carry them to the creek. *Now*, assholes!"

The cadets dropped their weapons and immediately obeyed. That was the response I wanted, teamwork, take care of your brother. The general's mouth dropped but still he said nothing. After I had five cadets in the creek, I eased up. The medics were called after the first drop, and they agreed that my remedy for heat prostration was correct.

Army photographers were taking pictures of my now dwindling class, of my assistant, and of me. My CO, Captain Schockley, was grinning; he knew I was making him look good. Class was over. The men hated me, and that I thought was good. They were learning teamwork. I had instructed the cadets to yell "Airborne" every time they ran to their next class. That day, every time their left feet hit the ground, I heard "Airborne" louder than ever. They were angry. Or, perhaps, they were motivated.

On my return to Fort Bragg from West Point, the 82nd was put on alert to go to the Middle East. The 82nd was never called, so we stayed put; awaiting more police calls.

Sam Agner returned from Vietnam and was also assigned to Fort Bragg. Sam had gotten married on his thirty-day leave when he returned to the States. He and his new bride moved into a mobile home in Fayetteville. I spent many days and nights over there just shooting the bull and reminiscing about old times.

Then my time in the army was up and I was heading home. Good-bye Bragg, good-bye police calls, and good-bye lifers!

MARCH 1971–JUNE 1972/FORT BRAGG
John L. Rotundo

I sat the remainder of my tour in 'Nam playing platoon supply sergeant, opening up the conex so the teams could store their weapons when they returned from the field, and just living the life of Riley. I tried to stay drunk most of the time and had quite a bit of success doing that. The teams were hitting contacts in An Khe, but a lot of them were initiated by the VC Tiger Teams.

Fats got hit in the stomach on one mission. He thought he had spotted someone the evening before, but the team leader thought he was seeing things. The next morning they were in their LZ but didn't use the first one they came upon. Instead they continued toward one further away and then doubled back to set up an ambush. The gooks Fats spotted the night before must have gotten reinforcements; when the team spotted them, over a half dozen were half-stepping up the trail since they thought they wouldn't hit the team for a couple hundred meters. Just as the team was about to spring its ambush, it was spotted, and the Tiger Team point man opened up with his AK. Fats said he watched the bullets chew up a line directly toward him but couldn't move. The last round hit him in the side of the stomach. The team opened fire—J.C. was carrying the gun. He hit the point man, sending him against a tree, and kept on firing, cutting the gook into two. Toro rolled over and applied a first aid dressing to Fats during the contact, then rolled back to continue firing.

At the end of March 1971, I flew down to Cam Ranh Bay to await the Freedom Bird that would take me home. On the 28th I boarded the 707 and, along with the two hundred or so others, tried to sleep on the long flight that arrived in Seattle. From Seattle to Fort Lewis for my second steak dinner, a few more forms to fill out, and onward to Cleveland by way of Chicago. I spent a thirty-day leave at home just catching up on the current fads (micro-miniskirts were the rage then) and bought my first car, a 1971 Mustang. I would need wheels to get around Fort Bragg.

At the end of April, I loaded up my car, named Rat in honor of my dog in Vietnam, and drove to Fort Bragg. First stop was the 82nd Replacement detachment to fill out forms, and finally I was assigned to my new home, Charlie Company, 1/508th Infantry, Third Brigade, 82nd Airborne Division. As I made my way to the company commander's room my eyes popped out of my head: J.C. was assigned to the same company. After we got settled in, we toured the area. The Third Brigade was made up of the 1/508 as well as the 1/505 and 2/505. The 1/508 was like a reunion of Charlie Rangers, for not only were J.C. and I assigned, but Don Ericson was in Alpha Company, and little Kelly from the second platoon was in Bravo, along with a few others. Fats's wound would heal, and he would find himself assigned to Charlie Company in the same platoon as J.C. and myself.

In May there was talk about 100,000 to 150,000 peace demonstrators converging on Washington, D.C., and we were put on alert for riot duty. What did we know? The word came down and we loaded onto buses and were driven to D.C. When we arrived we were billeted at Robert F. Kennedy Stadium, where we practiced keeping protesters away. We learned the inverted-V formation where we're supposed to push the demonstrators back with a bayonet attached to an M-16. I, along with some of the others, remembered a picture of some National Guardsmen having flowers being put in their barrels. Every time the formation moved forward we were supposed to yell, "Back!" but as we were practicing we began to yell, "Kill, kill."

The poor lieutenant almost had a heart attack. "You can't yell that, imagine what the media would do if they heard it?"

"Fuck 'em, sir," came a voice from the formation.

We never were pressed into service, and after a few days we went back to Bragg to pull police calls and drink beer in Fayetteville.

In June we were told we'd be going to West Point for the summer to help train cadets. Everyone who had been there before said it was the best duty to pull. Our company was to instruct ambush and survival, and in July we

once again boarded buses, this time to Camp Natural
Bridge, West Point, New York.

Our training of cadets began on a Sunday night with
an E-7 telling them what they should expect during the
next two weeks. He had a large snake draped around his
shoulders as he was talking, and toward the end of his
talk he shouted, ''Rangers,'' bit the head off the snake,
spit it out, and threw the remains into the audience. Some
of the cadets began throwing up while others looked on
in awe.

On Monday the cadets observed a platoon attacking a
suspected village, watching as the platoon checked out
the grass huts. Of course, one of the members of the
platoon was not paying attention and he got ''killed''
when a booby trap went off in the house he was checking
out. At night we took a group out to navigate through
the woods to our ambush location and sit and wait till
the enemy walked into our kill zone.

The rest of the week was spent on survival in the woods
and on Saturday we made plans to attack the enemy base.
I took a group through the woods, keeping as quiet as
could be, and ended up not more than fifty meters from
the enemy camp as we watched and listened to them
making plans. After an hour we slowly made our way
back to our own lines and let them tell their troops what
they had seen. Needless to say they were extremely impressed by how quiet we were in the woods. I told the
group I had taken that it was one thing to be able to do
that, but as future leaders they would also have to be able
to teach their troops what they knew. It just might save
lives someday.

We left West Point at the end of August and returned
to Fort Bragg to continue doing what we did best, going
to Fayetteville to drink beer.

In November I was told I had been chosen to work with
the Air Force in New Jersey to help train navigators in
hitting drop zones correctly. For two months my job was
to make a jump on Monday, Tuesday, and Wednesday,
and be off the rest of the week. Talk about getting over.
While we were at West Point I had met a girl who lived
outside New York City, so on weekends I would drive up
and visit her. And we were using steerable parachutes all

the time we were there, which made it so much easier to land. Life had been good to me.

In late December I returned to Fort Bragg and finished my time in the army there. Two months before getting out, I enrolled in a program called Project Transition, a program in which the army went to great lengths to train soldiers in a civilian occupation. I chose the Firestone Office and Credit Management course since the counselor told me that an office and credit manager would start at a higher salary than a salesman would. Besides, I knew I could sell.

June thirtieth finally rolled around, and I made my way back to Cleveland, Ohio, to begin a new career. I took the month of July off to get accustomed to civilian life and received a call from an insurance company to interview for a job. I drove to their office and talked to the manager, an ex-paratrooper with the 82nd Airborne. The rest of the interview was conducted across the street drinking beer while swapping jump stories. I figured to start in early August, then Firestone called to set up an interview. The last Saturday in July, I drove to the district office and had my interview. When it came time to sit down with the district manager I thought I'd soon be selling insurance, so I really was relaxed. When the district manager asked me what I did in the army and I told him about the Rangers, his eyes almost dropped out of their sockets. He had been in the army but never got to Vietnam; we spent the morning with me talking and him listening. Finally he talked, convincing me to give Firestone a chance.

EPILOGUE

It was a chilly evening in late September. Don was sitting on the couch watching the tube when the phone rang. His wife, Susan, answered because the phone was rarely for Don. "It's for you," she said, smirking.

"Hello?" Don said.

"Don?"

"Yes," he said.

"You'll never guess who this is."

"You're probably right. Who the hell is this?"

"John Rotundo."

"I'll be God-damned. How the hell are you?"

"Fine, fine."

"I haven't heard from you in years. I thought that you got a divorce because you stopped sending Christmas cards a few years back. How did you get my number?"

"Firestone transferred me to Illinois and we moved to Naperville this summer. My daughter was looking through some boxes that we had in the basement when she came across one of the letters you wrote to me while you were at Bragg. The letter had a return address of Algonquin so I thought that I'd take a chance and call information. There were two Ericsons in Algonquin; Mildred and Larry. I took a chance with Larry. Larry answered the phone and I told him that this was John Rotundo, and that I was looking for a Don Ericson. He said, 'My brother Don talks about you all the time.' So he gave me your number and here I am.''

John and his wife Louisa, and their children came to Sycamore for an evening where John and Don were re-united after seventeen years.

John hadn't changed much, maybe a little grayer and a little heavier, but that was to be expected. As always, Don had that grin on his face.

John and Don talked to the wee hours of the morning. It was through this initial meeting that they could now share experiences that they had kept bottled up for seventeen years. Experiences that were shared between two fellow Rangers and that only a fellow Ranger could relate to, or even believe.

That night John and Don rekindled a feeling of broth-erhood and a friendship born in a war zone, cultivated in battle—the friendship that lasts forever.

The reunion would finally bring them to taking a trip to Washington, D.C., to see the Vietnam Memorial.

AFTERWORD

FINAL THOUGHTS
John Rotundo

The Vietnam War was not fought like any other war America had ever been involved in. It was not a war fought by taking ground from the enemy and advancing toward a known objective and, ultimately, victory. Rather it was a war waged by politicians who involved this country in a no-win situation they created for their own reasons.

We did not lose the war in Vietnam. We just weren't allowed to win it. Far too many restrictions were placed on the military. The NVA or VC could strike targets of their choice in the South and then retreat to the North. But the US troops were not allowed to pursue the enemy. Why? Would the Allies have defeated Germany if we weren't allowed to chase them but instead, hold our advances to their borders? Of course not.

Too many targets in the North were never bombed or invaded.

It wasn't until President Nixon ordered the assault into Cambodia, the full scale bombing of Hanoi, and the mining of Haiphong Harbor in December of 1972 that the communists decided to get serious about signing the peace accords.

In the US, troops were being continually trained to fight a conventional war, but the only war being fought was a guerilla war in the jungles of Vietnam. The only "formal" guerilla training was at the new arrivals' unit replacement training which lasted about a week.

Some say Vietnam was an immoral war. Is any war moral? The Civil War? World War I? World War II? No! War is the epitome of man's inhumanity toward man.

If the country is ever to be involved in another limited war, America's manpower must be used more effectively. The country which requests our assistance must make the commitment to carry the burden and fight their own war.

I for one am not opposed to using our troops, but only if they're used properly and not wasted. The armed forces of this country are going to have to take a good, honest look at the strengths and weaknesses of their commands. Vietnam proved there is a need for highly trained and motivated "elite" troops to perform special missions. Some high ranking officers feel there is no need for the "elite" troops in the military. These officers are longing for mediocrity in the service. Maybe it is because they're so mediocre themselves they can't stand the fact that every man marches to the beat of a different drum.

Some people are themselves highly motivated. They want to be the best at what they do and surround themselves with those who feel the same way. Much like the REMF officers who put one another in for various medals for valor when they themselves never experienced combat in its most pure and basic form, man against man.

The Army Rangers and Special Forces, the Marine Force Recon, and the Navy Seals fit the bill as "elite" forces. Each group has its own strengths and weaknesses. Each is trained to perform specific tasks and each should be left to do such. The Special Forces are skilled in training others to build and also destroy. Let them teach the people of requesting countries to farm and fight.

Let the Rangers, Force Recon, and Seals do the reconnaissance and pull the small unit ambushes. When the enemy is found, send in the host countries' troops to fin-

ish the enemy off. If our infantry divisions are needed,
use them. But only if their mission is clearly defined with
no restrictions.

In Vietnam, morale among some infantry units was
low, especially during the late '60s and early '70s. The
war wasn't popular, and a good portion of line units was
made up of draftees who didn't want to be a part of any
war. Consequently, some units' performance suffered due
to a lack of self-discipline. I'm not knocking them—they
didn't want to be in Vietnam and felt the cards were
stacked against them in combat.

There were some draftees who had the foresight to
make the most of their predicament and volunteered to
fill the ranks of the elite. Consequently they found out
their chances of survival increased and rose to the occasion and performed admirably. The Rangers weren't su-
permen; rather they were average nineteen and twenty
year olds who challenged themselves to perform these
superhuman deeds.

I was proud to have had the opportunity to be selected
and to have served my country as a member of Charlie
Rangers. I have no regrets.

FINAL THOUGHTS
Don Ericson

The process of writing this book for the last two years
has been, to say the least, an interesting one. I've un-
covered feelings deep within myself that I never dreamed
existed. Human feelings of a forgotten brotherhood which
at one time, many years ago and ten thousand miles away,
existed between Rangers whose lives depended on one
another.

A reaquaintance with John Rotundo rekindled some of
those feelings which subsequently brought together many
other Rangers at the Wall—the Vietnam Veterans Memorial—in Washington, D.C. in September 1986. Writing this book was the direct result of that reunion.

That reunion was the first time I'd seen many of my fellow Rangers in seventeen years. The closeness still existed; it was as if it were yesterday, back in Vietnam, pulling leeches off our faces, and humping up and down countless mountains and ridge lines. We were a lot older, but it was as if we were young again, ready to go back and try and regain the adventure and excitement of being twenty years old. That feeling was with us all. We had taken a part in history. We had felt every emotion known to man; the laughing, the crying, the living and dying. Vietnam was our generation's war. Right or wrong, it took place, and I was one of its pawns.

I saw life at its worst; the killing, the poverty, the absolute hopelessness of the peasants who had no control whatsoever over their lives. They were and still are in a desperate situation, each living from day to day.

No money in the world could buy the education I received through those experiences. I was twenty years old, spoiled rotten, and didn't want for anything. It was inconceivable to me seeing the almost prehistoric poverty-ridden lifestyle of the Vietnamese people let alone knowing that some of them were out there just waiting to kill me.

I have no regrets about my tour in Vietnam. I served with the finest unit of professional soldiers in the United States Army. The pride of Charlie Company 75th Infantry (Airborne Rangers) is unbelievable, at times I suppose almost arrogant. I am sitting here writing this book today because, very simply, the NVA never knew we were there, or almost never. And being part of Charlie Rangers is what kept me alive.

Charlie Rangers had a saying about the killing: "Fuck 'em, kill them all, let God sort them out. It don't mean nothing." To this day I feel that God will decide who was right and who was wrong, and they will be dealt with.

For those Vietnam veterans who hold their experiences and feelings deep within themselves and have found it hard to convey them to others, an experience I had with my wife at the dedication of the Illinois Vietnam Memorial might help.

My wife is the editor of the Sycamore (Illinois) Republican News and after returning from the dedication wrote this:

A TIME FOR SHARING

The dedication of the Vietnam Memorial in Springfield, Illinois, on May 7 was an experience I shall never forget. I attended as a member of the press and also as a wife of a Vietnam veteran.

I recently typed my husband's manuscript of this book on his experiences in Vietnam and even after four hundred or so pages, I still didn't completely understand the deep feelings that Vietnam veterans have for those experiences.

At the lighting of the eternal flame ceremony as the Huey helicopters passed overhead, I truly understood these feelings. At that moment I felt a part of Don—a part that I had never felt before. I finally felt let in; finally allowed to enter this very special part of his life, that in fifteen years had been closed to me. It was like he was saying, "Come in, I'm finally home."

As the Hueys came over the tree tops, the veterans, already aware that the helicopters were on their way from the thumping sound in the distance, felt time turn back. At that precise moment each veteran was in some godforsaken place waiting for the Huey to get them out.

There was not a dry eye in sight.

When the Hueys were overhead, cheers from the crowd echoed throughout the cemetery. The pride felt at that moment was overwhelming; pride for each vet's unit as well as for their country—to have finally come home, recognized and accepted by their families, their friends, their state, and their country.

I do not think that I have ever in my life experienced such an emotional weekend. And to my husband, I thank you.

APPENDIX

THE MEN OF CHARLIE COMPANY, 75th INFANTRY

The following is a list of members who served with Charlie Rangers. It was compiled by various members who looked through their orders, pictures from the past or just plain memory.* In some instances first names were forgotten so only the last name is listed.

Aberle, Louis R.
Acox, William
Adams, Herbert
Adams, Ralph B.
Adams, Robert J. jr.
Agner, Sam
Aguilar, Shorty
Aiken, Chauncy
Allison, Ervin
Almond, Roberto
Altop, Ray
Ambrose, Michael
Anderson, Dave
Anderson, Michael
Anderson, Robert B.
Anderson, Robert D.
Anderson, Roger B.
Anderson, Roger L.
Andrews, Eugene S.

Antongiori, Angel A.
Appling, Stony
Armstrong, Thomas
Arnold, Jack
Arrington, Red
Austin, Johnnie
Avilla, Al

Baca, Arturo
Badmilk,
Bai, Do Van
Bailey, Richard C.
Baker, Haymar M.
Baker, Jeffry
Barcus, Greg
Barker, Fred
Barkley,
Bauer,
Bean, Sgt.

*This listing is, for obvious reasons, incomplete, and the authors apologize to those men whose names are not listed. Any former members of Charlie Rangers who are reading this, please contact the authors by writing care of the publisher (c/o Owen Lock, Ballantine Books, 201 East 50 Street, New York, NY 10022), including a return address, so that this list may be updated.

Bechtold, David S.
Beer, John A.
Behr, Henry
Behr, John A.
Bellomy, Alton
Benitez, Juan R.
Benniman, Joe
Benton, Darryl
Beverley, Robert G. jr.
Beyer, Darslin L.
Billy, Terry
Bisantz, Allen (Buzz)
Blackwood, Gary T.
Bloniarz, Richard P.
Bohrer, Raymond
Bolton, Worth
Boone, Bennie
Boone, Richard
Borkowski,
Bourne, Charles D.
Brandis, John
Brandon, Bennie
Brennan, Thomas
Bright, Cyfes
Brinker, Ronald V.
Brinson, Otis
Brinthaught, Joseph A.
Brocato, Sylvester
Brokaw, James
Brown, Dave
Brown, James
Brown, John
Buccille, Richard
Buchanan, Nicky
Bunting, William R.
Burdette, Hilburn
Busby, Jimmie

Caldwell, Ulyses
Calvin, Curtis B.
Campbell, Edward P.
Campbell, Leslie
Caplinger, Randy
Capp, Morton
Carcon, Joseph
Carmack, Craig L.
Carpenter, Stephen L.
Carr, Alfred
Carreras, Francisco
Carter, Bobby E. (Pop)
Carter, Henderson
Case, John (J.C.)
Castro, Angel
Cathy, Ben
Causey, Ronald D.
Causey, Ronald R.
Chambers, Roger A.
Cheek, Joseph
Cheshire, Robert
Church, Richard A.
Cipri, Joseph
Ciprio,

Claiborne, James A.
Clanton, James J.
Clark, Rod
Clarke, Larry
Clay, James E. jr.
Clements, Stephen S.
Coates, David
Cochran, Jack (Corky)
Coles, Michael
Colgan, Galen
Colton, Willie (Blue)
Colvin, Capt.
Comstock, David (Tatar)
Connelly, Andrew
Cook, Ronald
Coomb, Stephen
Coonrod, Gary G.
Copeland,
Coronado,
Coroni, Leonidas
Cowles, Glen
Cox, James
Craig, Joseph
Crowe, Harold H.
Culeford, Robert
Cumming, Gary
Cunningham, Micky
Cunningham, Thomas
Cupp, Don
Curtis, Charles E.
Custer, William

Daniels, Sylvester W.
Daukus, Mike
Davis, Calvin
Davis, John H.
Davis, Paul
Day, Louis N.
De Vault, Lee
DeJesus, Camilo
Dela-Cruz,
Deleon, Jose
Demerest,
Dennis, Wayne B. (Swamp Man)
DiMayo, Vincent
Dischinger, Robert (Dish)
Dolby, David (Mad Dog)
Donald, Timothy P.
Donelson, Michael J.
Dotson, Larry
Dove, Robert
Dumas, James E.
Dunagan, James (Jimbo)
Dunkleberger, Herman

Edens, Fred
Edner, Lt.
Edward, Scott
Elsea, Harold
Ensign, Thomas
Ensor, Thomas (Lurch)
Erickson, Eugene

Ericson, Don (Eric)
Evangilista, George
  (George of the Jungle)
Evans, Joseph
Everly, John J.

Farmer, David
Fattizzi, Vincent
Fayetteville, Sgt.
Fenton, SFC
Fleming, John
Flemming, James
Flock, Lynn V.
Flores, Jamie
Flynn, Kerry A.
Ford, Sgt.
Foster, Gary
Foster, Tommy
Foster, Tony
Fowler, Marvin
Fowler, Tatum
Francis, Martin (Doc)
Freeman, Gleen
Fritz, Harry
Frye, Gary
Frye, Vincent
Fussner, Andrew F.

Gaines, Virgil L.
Galena, (Huck)
Galvin, Arnold P.
Garcia, Luis J.
Garcia, Roel
Garcia, Ted
Gardner, Franck
Garnecia, Gerardo L.
Garrison, Larry J.
Gartic, Milton
Gaus, Richard
Gayton, Carlos
Gazard, Richard
Geehold, Wallace
Geisler, Brad
Giossi, William
Gipson, Leonard O.
Godfrey, James
Gold, Eric S.
Golden, Chester
Gonzales, (Pancho)
Gove, Steven P. (Doc)
Green, James
Green, Willie E.
Griffin, Daniel
Griffith, Ben
Grimes, Rich (Candy)
Grinnell, Joseph
Guerra, Mario (Doc)
Guin, Harold
Guthrie, Richard

Hai,
Hall, Jamie L.

Hallowell,
Halquist, Ernest (Swede)
Halverson, Gilbert M.
Hamilton, Ellis
Hamilton, Teddy
Hamlin, Lt.
Haney, Mack
Hanneman, Richard A.
Hanson, Conrad
Harrington, Phillip
Harrison, Hubert
Harrison, Richard (Fats)
Hart, (Pappy)
Hauk, Robert
Haynes,
Helphilstine, Charles
Henderson, Lathaniel
Henderson, Robert C.
Hensley, Larry
Henton, Stephen L.
Hightower, Steven H.
Hinson, Steven B.
Hinton, Charlie (The Cat)
Hoa,
Hogan, George
Hoggard, Oliver (Hobo)
Holmes, Josh
Holt, Bill V.
Hom, Tak
Honneonan, Richard
Hopkins, Stephen J.
Houston, Richard
Howell, Roger D.
Hudson, Maj.
Hunter, Roger W.
Hutchinson, George
Hyett, Ron
Hynes, Loren J.

Jackson, Terry
Jason, Rick (Combat)
Jenkins, Butch (B.J.)
Jenkins, William
Jensen, Ernie (Gabby)
Joe, Johnnie
Johnson, Anthony R.
Johnson, Donald G. jr.
Johnson, Douglas (D.J.)
Johnson, Henry
Johnson, James
Johnson, Larry M.
Johnson, Richard P.
Johnson, William
Johnston, Larry M.
Joiner, Joel
Jones, Thomas B.
Jordan, Fowler
Jordan, Paul
Juiab, Charles J.
Julks, Charles J.

Karow, Phillip

Keefer, Kevin
Kelly, Martin
Kessler, James (Jimmy Slick)
King, Larry D.
King, Robert
Kiscaden, Michael
Kithcart, Larry W.
Klino, (Kilo)
Kochy, Bruce
Kociniski, Chris
Kolfar, Frank
Krantz, Mike
Krause, Robert
Kuamoo, Calvin (Savage)
Kuebler, Paul M. jr.
Kuhns, David G.
Kyle, Ron, (Rick)

LaBarge, John
Ladd, Boy
Ladeaux, Robert
Lake, James
Lane, David
Lang, Keith
Lavighetti, Vince
Lazarov, Lazar (Mad Russian)
Ledford, Chuck
Lemieux, Earl
Leppelman, John (Lepp)
Lesley, Ron
Levendowski, Daniel J.
Lewis, (Lou)
Lewis, Randolph P.
Lewis, Reco
Lewis, William
Lincoln, Sgt.
Lizenby, Albert
Loisel, James
London, Otis, W.
Lopes, Raymond
Louera, Chico
Loving, Herbert
Lowry, James L.
Ludwick, Rick
Lumonyon, Terry
Lund, Vernon
Lyons, Thomas C. jr.

Macras,
MaGee, William C.
Maher, Patrick J.
Malone, Dandridge M.
Malone, Robert L.
Manning, Sgt.
Manopulos, John T. (Greek)
Mantooth, Steve (Manfred)
Marchionda, Mike
Marcum, William (Homer)
Maropulos, Theodore J.
Marr, Barry F.
Marsh, Steven W.
Martin, Clinton L. jr.

Martin, Scotty (Doc)
Maynard, Julius
McCabe, Roy
McCaslin, Lt.
McCoy, Robert
McDaniel, Robert E.
McDaniel, Sidney
McDermott, Eugene
McDonald, Mike
McDonaldson,
McDougald, James
McFarland, James E.
McGitty, Kenny
McKnight, Kenneth L.
McLaughlin, E.C.
McLean,
McNamara, Thomas (Mac)
Mendivil, Arnold (Mendy)
Menting, Hilary
Mete, David J.
Miller, Joe E.
Miller, Mark A.
Mills, Randy
Minatt, John C.
Mironda, Emilio
Mitchell, Thomas E.
Monahan, Thomas
Moore, Frank O.
Moran, Walter (C.B.)
Moree, Gene
Morgan, Dan
Morgan, James R.
Mulkey, Bryson
Mundy, Harvey L.
Muntz, Gary T.
Murillo, Richard A.
Murphy, Stephen
Murphy, William
Murrey, Kenneth jr.
Murvin, Clinton

Najera, Joe (Hell's Angel)
Nania, Frank (Boston)
Napier, Edward jr.
Nasau, Feleti
Nazario, Edwin
Nedbalski, Michael A.
Needles, Loren S.
Newman, Al
Niebert, James
Norgard, James
Norsworthy, Garry
Norton, Don
Noszek, Lajos
Nutter, Wallace (Bo)

O'Brien, Lt.
O'Donnell, Brian
O'Dougherty, Thomas (O.D.)
O'Malley, Joseph P.
O'Neel, (Big O)
Odum,

Ogden, James R.
Otero, Carmelo
Otstott, Ron
Oweal, Gary

Paredes, Lawrence R.
Parker,
Parker, John D.
Parker, Joseph E.
Parr, Keith M.
Parson, J.W.
Paxton, Charles (Chip)
Paynter, Michael T.
Peace, Michael E.
Peck, Lester S.
Pelzer, Herbie
Peni, Alan (Uncle)
Penman, Timothy
Perez-Marante, Miguel
Perkhiser, James (Perk)
Peters, (Rockman)
Peterson, William C. (Pete)
Pezza, Lawrence jr.
Philabaum, George
Pierce, Pat (Pop)
Pierce, Ulis A.
Pietrzyk, Kenneth (Polack)
Pietrzyk, Ken
Pietsch, Raymond E.
Polak, John
Poppell, Gary
Posner, Harry C.
Price, Michael
Probst, Steve

Quinata, Tony (Grizzly)
Quintona, Leroy V.

Rapp, Larry
Rasler, Robert
Rath, Richard
Rayber, Joseph
Reece, Keith
Reilley, Dennis P.
Resch, Ralph E.
Reyes, Richard
Rhodes, Francis (Double Deuce)
Rice, Jerry
Riddle, Roger
Rigali, Tony
Rigo, Joseph (Jo-Jo)
Rinnel,
Rios,
Riotutan, Tedtr
Riotutar, Theodore S.
Rivera, Rafael
Rivera, Tony
Rivera-Diaz, Jose
Roberts, Eddie L.
Roberts, James (Feet)
Roberts, Roger L.
Robertson, Darryl (Robby)

Robinson, Charles A.
Robinson, Lloyd
Rocha, Florencio
Rodriguez, Samuel (Mama-san)
Rodriguez-Roble, Jesus
Roguski,
Rork, Jon
Rose, Edward L.
Rosenberry, Lt.
Rosensweig, Ross M. (Jew)
Ross, Rosenberg
Rotundo, John L.
Rubenstein, Mike
   (Shortround)
Rucker, John
Ruggiero, Anthony R.
Russel, Tim
Russo, Robert T.
Rutherford, Robert (Rocky)

Salanas, Ray
Samuelson, C.W.
Sanchez, John J.
Sands, Jerry (Leg)
Sarmienta, Javier (Sam)
Sarver, George L.
Sausey, Ronald R.
Schenkel, James
Schmauch, Gordon B.
Schmidt, Heinrich
Schofield, (Cowboy)
Scofi, Arthur L.
Scott, Allistar (Scotty)
Scott, Leonard (Patches)
Seabaugh, Ron
Sehorn, Talbert
Seits, William F.
Sellers, Bruce
Sepulveda, Carlos
Shaffer, Robert
Shankle, Jerry
Sharkey, Thomas
Shatzer, Berry G.
Sherman, Rex
Shinaberry, David
Simpson, David S.
Skouby, Ernest
Smith, George D.
Smith, James T.
Smith, Michael V.
Snavley, Dennis
Snead, Jimmy
Sneed, Sam
Snider, Jim (Jungle Jim)
Snook, Lynn
Somerville, A.D.
Spearman, Gordon (Gordy)
Spears, Richard
Sperti, Ralph
Squires, Billy
St. Louis, Eugene
Standley, Robert D.

Stansberry, Gregory
Steen, Foster
Stein, Robert O.
Stein, Robert G.
Steinke, Lester D.
Steinke, Lester G.
Stinger, Joseph A.
Stock, Walter D.
Stone, Gerry
Stonebreaker, J.W.
Strawn, Dennis
Stuart, Gary D.
Sullivan, (Junior)
Sweat, Tony
Sweatt, Charles R.
Sweeny, Joseph

Tadina, Patrick
Talag, Alexander E.
Tankersley, Milton J.
Taylor, James
Terwilliger, Jessie
Tetranault, Sgt. ("T")
Tetroff, Sgt.
Teybron, Cravis (C.T.)
Theofile, Daniel
Theofile, George
Thomas, David T.
Thomas, Walter R.
Thompkins, Joseph J.
Thompson, Arren B.
Thompson, Gary
Thompson, John A.
Thompson, Ron
Thorne, Kevin (Thorney)
Tolliver, Edmund
Toro, Edward
Trask, Mark
Trel, Warner
Tuka, Thomas

Unkow, Sgt.
Uribe, Edward

Valez, Jose R.
Van Utrick, Henry
Varble, William L.
Varetan, Bruce
Vaughn, Roger
Villerreal, Piquinto
Voyles, James (Ranger Voyles)

Walsh, Joseph J. jr.
Walters, Frank
Walthall, Michael
Ward, David E. (Dew)
Warner, Michael
Warner, Scott
Washington, Kenneth
Weatherford, Jeff
Weaver, Tom
Weeks, Gerald L.

Welch, Joey
Wells, Gil (Smokie)
Wertz, Steven V. (Fragit)
West, Gary
White, Frederick
White, John
White, Patrick
Whorche, Rich
Wiley, Herbert D.
Wilkenson, Bill
Wilkes, Booth
Wilkes, George
Wilkes, Kenneth
Wilkin, John
Williams, (Deuce)
Williams, Harold (Ranger)
Williams, Oliver (Papa-san)
Williams, Steve
   (Combat Commo)
Williams, William F.
Wilson, Jimmy
Windom, William
Wirtz, John A. jr.
Wiseheart, John W.
Wolff, Pete
Wong, Thomas
Woodbury, Paul
Woodley, Arther jr.
Woodley, Paul
Woods,
Woodson, Steve
Wooton, Bill (Wild Bill)
Workman, Thomas D.
Wyatt, Darnell
Wyatt, Gary
Wyatt, Richard

Young, Charles
Young, Donald R.
Young, Robert

Zalenski, Zygmunt F. jr.

ABOUT THE AUTHORS

Don Ericson served in Vietnam from 1969 to 1970 with the 173rd Airborne Brigade and C Company, 75th Infantry (Airborne Rangers). He lives in Illinois with his wife Susan and their children, Robyn, Amy, and Tim. He currently operates his own construction contracting business.

John L. Rotundo served in Vietnam from 1969 to 1971 with the 173rd Airborne Brigade and C Company, 75th Infantry (Airborne Rangers). He lives in Illinois with his wife Louisa and their three children, Karen, Rocco, and Laurie. He is an assistant zone manager for the Firestone Tire & Rubber Company.